Craig Alanson

Black Ops

Expeditionary Force Book 4

By Craig Alanson

Contact the author at craigalanson@gmail.com

Cover Design By:
Alexandre Rito
alexandre@designbookcover.pt

Table of Contents

CHAPTER ONE

"Not so much?" My voice reflected the confusion everyone felt at Skippy's cryptic statement. "What do you mean, *not so much*?"

"Hmmm. Did I not use that expression correctly, Joe?" Skippy asked, sounding hurt. "All I meant was 'no', which is easier to say. 'Not so much' is a complicated way to say 'no', but my understanding is all the cool kids are using that slang, so I-"

"Skippy! Not so much, or no, whatever the hell you call it, what did you mean?" Chotek, Chang, the entire crew were waiting breathlessly on Skippy's answer. "I asked if the Thuranin are not sending a ship to Earth, and the Kristang can't do that. You said yes to my first question, and 'not so much' to the other? You told us the Kristang don't have the technology to send a ship to Earth, and now you-"

"They don't. Kristang ships can't reach Earth on their own. I told you that."

"Soooo," I said slowly, "the answer is 'yes' to both of my questions-"

"No, I, ugh, Ok, technically, you big knucklehead, you asked *three* questions. Damn! You can't even keep track of what you are saying? You bumble the English language so badly, let me phrase it for you. Joe, you asked me if the Thuranin plan to send another long-range ship to Earth. My answer to that is a resounding 'NO'. Then you asked whether the Kristang ships can get to Earth on their own, and again the answer is 'NO'. But you also asked a *third* question; 'Earth is safe now'? The answer to that is also, 'NO'."

In frustration, I made a fist of my right hand and slowly pounded my forehead with it. "Skippy, look, is this some philosophical thing, like Earth is not safe because eventually our sun will explode? We know about that danger."

"That is an obvious danger, sure. I would say a bigger obvious danger to your species is monkeys having nuclear weapons."

"Monkeys with nukes, got it," I said, laughing with relief, looking back at Chotek and winking nervously. I had thought Skippy meant Earth was faced with a danger that we didn't already know about. "That problem is way above my pay grade," I said with a grin toward our career diplomat Hans Chotek, and I gave a thumbs up sign to the people in the Combat Information Center. "I think the Merry Band of Pirates will stick with problems we can handle."

"Okey dokey, Joe," Skippy sounded miffed for some reason. "I would think you'd be more concerned about the Fire Dragons going to Earth, but that's just my opinion."

"*WHAT*? How the hell- *What*?" I sputtered.

"Ooooh, can we play Twenty Questions? Hmm, no, no way would *you* ever guess correctly."

"Skippy," I ground my teeth. "*How* are the Fire Dragons getting to Earth? Is it the Maxolhx?" My heart sank in my chest as I said that. If we had to tangle with that supremely powerful species, we were totally screwed. Even Skippy wished to stay well clear of the Maxolhx.

"Nope. Not the Maxolhx. Well, not yet, anyway. Joe, the surprising information I just learned from the relay data is that the Fire Dragons are negotiating a deal with the Ruhar, to take two Fire Dragon representatives to Earth, and bring back the White Wind clan leaders."

"The *Ruhar*?" I looked through the glass into the CIC and met Chang's incredulous eyes. "Senior staff into the conference room, now. Sergeant Adams, you are the duty officer."

The group sitting around the conference table was looking completely shell-shocked, including Chotek. Maybe especially Hans Chotek. He had come out to the stars with one relatively straightforward mission from UNEF Command: determine whether the Thuranin would be sending another long-range surveyor starship to Earth. And if necessary, stop a second ship from reaching Earth. Along the way, I had persuaded Chotek to attempt a complicated secondary mission of securing the future of UNEF on Paradise. Against his instincts, he had agreed to the Paradise mission, and it had been wildly successful. We had just learned that our original mission was a success; the Thuranin had no intention of sending a ship to Earth.

Now, we were faced with yet another extinction-level threat to humanity, and I'm sure Hans Chotek was thinking this is not what he signed up for. "Sir," I addressed Chotek, "do you want to-"

He shook his head wearily, whereas mere moments ago he had been jubilant. "No, Colonel Bishop, please lead the discussion." His shoulders slumped slightly, and he looked pissed at me. I didn't blame him. "You know Mister Skippy better than any of us."

"Thank you, Sir. Skippy, why the hell would the *Ruhar* send a ship to Earth on behalf of the Kristang? Those two species are bitter enemies."

"Bitter enemies, uh huh, you're right about that. But this war has been going on for a very, very long time, Joe. Stranger things have happened; really, this wouldn't even make the Top Ten of strange things in the war. The simple truth is the Fire Dragons are paying the Ruhar for a ride. I don't mean paying cash, of course, although if the Fire Dragons had a cash-back credit card, man they could rack up some serious-"

"Skippy!"

"Sorry, got a little off track there. The Fire Dragons will trade a planet, or access to a wormhole to the Ruhar, in exchange for a ride to Earth and back. Remember, there is a wormhole in Ruhar territory that allows a Jeraptha ship to reach Earth in less than one year; that is a significant advantage over the situation faced by the Thuranin."

"Oh, crap." I looked around the table. Even Major Smythe's face was pale. "We have to stop *another* ship from traveling to Earth?" The odds of us doing that successfully were, oh, forget it, my math skills sucked. Impossible. It was impossible.

"Yup," Skippy replied in a cheery tone. "I think specifically, you need to stop yet another ship from traveling to Earth, without anyone ever suspecting that ship was prevented from reaching Earth. The Jeraptha know a Thuranin surveyor ship was destroyed on its way to Earth, and the Jeraptha also know they weren't responsible for the attack. For a second ship on its way to Earth to be attacked, or to disappear, or suffer some other unusual problem, would make the Jeraptha intensely suspicious about what is going on in your little home star system. This is going to be way, way more, like an order of magnitude more difficult than simply destroying a single surveyor ship."

"Simply? What was simple about-" I stopped talking. The operation against the surveyor ship had been incredibly complex. There was no point reminding Skippy about that. "We have to do the impossible, without anyone knowing that we did anything at all?" It wasn't actually a question.

"Sir," Lt. Williams addressed his question to me, rather than Chotek or Skippy. "As Skippy said, there is a wormhole in Ruhar territory that gives them access to Earth. Could we shut down that wormhole, like you did with the one closest to Earth?"

"Uh, that's a negatory on that one, Lt. Williams," Skippy answered for me. "I could do that, but I should not do that. Having a second wormhole near Earth shut down mysteriously would attract the attention of the Maxolhx and the Rindhalu. You do not want those two apex species becoming curious about your home planet."

"Yes, Mister Skippy, I understand that," Williams continued, not intimidated by the beer can. "I was thinking we could shut down not just two wormholes, but several wormholes in that area, so that Earth is not obviously in the center of the affected area. Make it look like a sort of local network shift, something like that."

"Hmm," Skippy mused. "That is clever and innovative tactical thinking, Williams. Although, you would realize it is also a horribly bad idea, if you had all the facts. The answer is no, we should not do anything like that. Having more wormholes behaving oddly is a guarantee of the senior species becoming curious, even if they do not immediately suspect Earth is involved. Also, as I warned Joe before, the more I screw with wormholes, the greater the risk of me unintentionally triggering another cascading wormhole shift in the sector. The wormhole near Earth could reactivate, and there is another dormant wormhole even closer to Earth."

"We do not want to screw with wormholes," I declared. "But that is good initiative, Lieutenant Williams; keep those ideas coming. All right, all right," I repeated words to give myself time to think. "We need a plan to stop a Ruhar ship-"

"Actually a Jeraptha ship, Joe. The Fire Dragons will be negotiating with their peers the Ruhar, but the Ruhar will need a ride on a Jeraptha star carrier. While Ruhar ships have significantly better interstellar travel capability than Kristang ships do, the Ruhar do not have ships that can go all the way to Earth and back on their own."

"Great. We need a plan to stop a Jeraptha ship. Skippy, we all need to brush up on data about the Jeraptha. Can you tell us-"

Chotek held up a hand to interrupt me. "Colonel, I am concerned that, as a military officer, your instinct is to first look for a military solution. What is the American expression; to a hammer, everything looks like a nail?"

"That, is an expression, yes," I said warily.

"We can't fight both sides in this war forever," Chotek grimly stated the obvious. "Eventually, we are going to come up against a problem we can't solve, particularly given the constraint that all our actions out here must remain absolutely covert. I believe we must, at this time, consider approaching the Ruhar to suggest an alliance."

"Sir, that is a terr-" as the words came out of my mouth, my brain cried out 'Nooooo' in super slow motion and tried to yank the sound back out of the air. "Terr- terrific challenge," I stuttered.

Chotek gave me a look appropriate for parent scolding a small child. "Colonel Bishop, if you think I have a terrible idea," he finished my original thought, "please say so. The last thing this mission commander needs is people trying to please me. I need honest, informed opinions."

"Uh, Sir, approaching the Ruhar about an alliance would be a terrible idea; it would completely backfire on us, and probably result in the destruction of Earth," I explained, stating what I thought was completely obvious.

Chotek sat back in his chair and folded his arms across his chest. "Explain further, please. Because an alliance with the Ruhar, and their patrons, may be our best and perhaps only hope of halting an endless cycle of crisis and frantic response."

"If we only dealt with the Ruhar, that might be true," I hurriedly tried to organize my thoughts. Damn it, it felt like writing an essay in high school, and I had always struggled with that. "But whatever we tell the Ruhar, the Jeraptha will find out about, and ultimately, the Rindhalu. And the Maxolhx would learn about it soon enough. Let's say we approach the Ruhar and suggest an alliance. What could we possibly offer them that would be worth their expending an enormous effort to defend our little planet?"

"Skippy. We could offer Skippy and the Elder wormhole controller device," Chotek pointed to the speaker in the ceiling. "I know Skippy says he would go silent around species with advanced technology; maybe that is true and maybe Skippy only thinks that is the case. He admits he does not fully understand his own programming. Colonel, I know you do not like to think about giving Skippy away, and I do not consider the idea to be honorable. But if the choice is between Skippy and securing the future of humanity, I will side with humanity."

"Sir," I paused to collect my thoughts. This was an argument I needed to make carefully. In school, I had always sucked at outlining essays, my thoughts always came out in a disorganized jumble. No way would I ever have qualified for a debate team. "In the military, we would wargame a scenario like this, to see the most likely end result. Let's say we do offer Skippy to the Ruhar, and the Ruhar believe he is an Elder AI, whether Skippy goes silent or not. What happens after that? The Rindhalu will learn humanity has a device that can control Elder wormholes; a device that could destroy the balance of power that has existed between the Rindhalu and the Maxolhx for thousands of years. A device that can control wormholes is something that would be worth the Maxolhx fighting a full-scale war over, because without it, they would be powerless against the Rindhalu. My guess is, the Maxolhx would see the capability to control wormholes as such a game-changing technology that they would risk an all-out conflict with the Rindhalu. Maybe they would even risk using Elder weapons and provoking a response by Sentinels. Whatever happens, neither side would care what happens to Earth in a war that consumes the galaxy, and for damned sure, our home planet would be collateral damage. The Maxolhx would try to seize Earth, or destroy us if they can't control us. And the Rindhalu would destroy Earth themselves, rather than let the Maxolhx control us. Hell, they might even nuke Earth together; both sides have made it clear that an upstart species like humanity can't be allowed to threaten the two major powers. They might destroy Earth, just to make an example of us."

Chotek didn't immediately dismiss my argument. He leaned forward and steepled his hands, flexing his fingers as he thought.

I took his hesitation to press my point. "We shut down one wormhole, and manipulated others. We destroyed most of a Kristang battlegroup, stole a Thuranin star carrier and destroyed other Thuranin ships. To the Ruhar, we screwed up their plans to trade away the planet Paradise, and we tricked them into keeping Paradise and stationing a battlegroup there. Neither side will have any love for us, or any reason to trust us, once they learn the truth. Both sides will have plenty of reasons to hate and distrust us, and to want payback. The only items we have to bargain with are Skippy, who may or may not go dormant, and an Elder wormhole controller module. Once we give up those two items, why should we trust the Rindhalu to offer us protection? I know you have enough diplomatic experience not to tell me the Rindhalu are noble and will do it out of the goodness of their hearts. Keep in mind, Sir, the Rindhalu don't need us to *give* them anything; once they know about Skippy and the wormhole controller, they can simply take them from us. It's like," I tried to think of a good analogy. "Like bringing a suitcase full of cash to a drug deal. Unless you have as much firepower as the guy with the drugs, he's simply going to kill you, take the cash and keep his drugs." I saw that on a TV show, so don't give me credit for thinking of it. "This isn't the Middle East, where you are negotiating with two powers who each have the ability to hurt each other to some extent. Earth has *no* ability to hit back, our world is completely helpless. There are no checks and balances in the galaxy like there is on Earth; no NATO, no UN. The Rindhalu can do anything they want to Earth, and there is absolutely nothing to stop them. The Rindhalu are going to see wormhole controller technology as a threat not only to their position of power, but to their entire existence. Same with the Maxolhx."

I saw Chotek's shoulders rise slightly as he took a deep, calming breath. Certainly he was not happy with me at that moment. My fear was that he would declare the issue decided; that we were going to approach the Ruhar, tell them the truth and offer an alliance. That idea was wrong, all wrong. But his background as a diplomat had taught him patience; he understood that if we went down the road of an alliance, we had plenty of time. Instead of extending the argument, he looked at the ceiling and addressed Skippy. "Do we have time to go back to Earth for consultations, before the negotiations commence?"

"Con-sul-ta-tions?" Skippy rolled the word off his tongue slowly, as if he could not believe such a word existed. "No," he declared. "Well, technically we would have time to go back to Earth via the fastest possible route, if we left right now. What we do not have time to do is fly back to Earth, wait for your leaders to argue and wring their hands to avoid making decisions, then return in time to do anything about the negotiations. We have time either to fly to Earth to let people know about the threat, *or* to actually do something about the threat. One or the other. Sorry, Chocula, you can't pass the buck on this one. Time for you to put your big boy pants on, and make the hard decisions UNEF sent you out here to make. It should be easy, only the fate of your planet and your entire species hang in the balance."

The discussion went back and forth for another ten minutes, with me meekly keeping my mouth shut unless Chotek asked me a question. All I wanted was for Chotek to delay making a decision about talking to the Ruhar, until my team had time to offer him alternatives.

Finally, Chotek could see there was little point in continuing to talk right then. We were all still somewhat in shock, and that is not a good time to make cool-headed decisions. "Very well. Colonel Bishop, please work with your team to develop a plan to stop a Ruhar ship from traveling to Earth. There will be no direct action against the Ruhar, understood?"

"Yes, Sir." The initial crisis was over and we were not immediately running to the Ruhar with a flag of surrender. I counted that as a win, and all I wanted was to escape the meeting as fast as possible.

The meeting broke up, with teams going off to study Skippy's data on the situation, and try to dream up a plan for the Merry Band of Pirates to accomplish the impossible. Again.

Major Smythe caught my eye outside the conference room, and nodded his head to the left. I followed him around the corner. "I'd like to speak with you, Sir. Privately."

"My office, Major."

We walked to my office, where I took the rare step of pressing the button to close the door. Usually, I held firm to a literal Open Door policy, where anyone could approach me about any issue. A thousand lightyears from home, on a stolen alien pirate ship in a hostile galaxy, and with our ship run by a chrome-plated beer can, I wanted the crew to know I was not keeping secrets from them.

Usually.

"Major? You wanted to speak with me." It wasn't a question.

"To use an American expression, 'Ain't that some shit'?" he said without a smile. "We just rescued UNEF on Paradise, and confirmed the Thuranin are not a threat-"

"For now."

"For now. This time, we may need to act against the Ruhar?" He shook his head, eyes wide with incredulity. "Usually in a war, you can count on *some* allies."

"Usually in a war, the enemy knows you are fighting them. We can't allow anyone to know we are even involved. Against the Ruhar, we may need to act in a way that they don't realize *anyone* is fighting them. It is freakin' impossible."

"And yet."

"And yet, we've done it before." I gestured at the closed office door, which was almost always open. "Is this the part of the movie where I offer you a tumbler of scotch, and we make plans to take over the world behind closed doors?"

Smythe grinned, something I had not observed often enough. Putting him in overall command of the SpecOps team had been a boost for his ego, and for his career, but it had not done any favors for his level of stress. "I prefer whiskey to scotch. Take over the world, Sir? 'The world is not enough', to quote one of the James Bond films. We have an entire galaxy we need to secure, if Mr. Chotek is right, and I think he is. We've been successful to date. This cannot continue indefinitely."

"Agreed. Someday, when we have time to think, we need a plan to be proactive, and not only react to the latest crisis." I said aloud something I had been privately thinking for months. "Whatever long-term strategy we come up with, it needs approval from leaders on Earth. We can't go making critical decisions like that on our own."

"We can, Colonel, if there is not enough time to fly all the way back to Earth and wait for the politicians to debate the issue."

"Major, I am all about bending the rules until you can see cracks, but I have to follow the chain of command." I wondered if he was testing me.

Smythe pretended to pick a piece of lint off his uniform pants; I noticed he avoided my eyes while he did that. "Yes, we all follow the proper chain of command. A chain which begins far above Mr. Chotek."

"I'm not following you, Major." I really did not understand what he meant. Chotek, of course, derived his authority from UNEF Command on Earth, but there was not enough time for us to go back to Earth and return, if we were to have any chance to stop the Ruhar from sending a ship to our home planet. If Chotek ordered us not to take action against the Ruhar, going to Earth to override his orders would take far too long.

"Mr. Chotek has written orders from UNEF Command, authorizing him to be in ultimate charge of this mission," Smythe reminded me. "However, if you, Colonel, have *secret* orders from UNEF Command, authorizing you to relieve Mr. Chotek if you felt it necessary for the success of the mission and survival of our species, I would not be able to dispute the authenticity of any such secret orders."

That shocked me for a moment. "Major," I said slowly, knowing we were on very dangerous ground, "surely UNEF Command gave you codes for authenticating any such orders."

"Yes, Sir, they did. And I am sure that Mr. Skippy cracked those codes in a heartbeat, and could fake any orders you wished to create. As I stated, I would have no way to dispute any secret orders you claim to have received from UNEF Command."

"He's right, Joe," Skippy spoke up. "I cracked those pathetic codes while UNEF was still creating them," he chuckled. "Me having total control of their data systems helped," he added in a lower voice. "Yup, I could fake up any orders you want."

"Skippy," I closed my eyes, feeling a headache coming on. "Major Smythe, and his entire team, could not act on orders they know to be fraudulent."

"Oh. *Oh*! Gotcha, Joe. I would never fake a secret message from UNEF Command, of course not. No way, Jose. That's my story and I'm sticking to it. Uh, was that convincing? I can try again, if you give me a hint. This mutiny thing is not really my wheelhouse."

I hid my face in my hands. "That was *super* awesomely helpful, Skippy."

"Duh. Of course it was awesome, Joe, it's me."

"Personally, it wouldn't take bloody much to convince me, Sir," Smythe assured me with a pat on the shoulder. "Although, if it comes to us taking over the ship, you might want to pour me a large glass of whiskey first."

"I'll ask Simms if she brought any whiskey. Major, we need a plan to prevent the Ruhar from sending a ship to Earth, without them ever knowing someone didn't want them sending a ship to Earth. You got any ideas?"

"No. Not at the moment. Colonel, while we are at the relay station, I would like my teams to take the opportunity for zero gee combat training."

Chotek wasn't going to like that, I thought. "Can you use two teams at a time? Who is up in the rotation?" That is something I should have memorized.

"The Indians and the French," Smythe stated.

"I will talk with Chotek." I figured that I knew his answer would be 'No'.

I was wrong. When I requested his permission for two SpecOps teams to conduct training outside the ship, he didn't argue or push back. "If you think it is necessary, Colonel," he said with an almost dismissive wave of a hand. He wasn't even looking at me when he said it, more like staring off into space. The strain I felt had to be getting to him also. Maybe even more so.

"I do, Sir."

Chotek pushed himself upright in the chair and smoothed his tie. The guy wore a suit and tie every day, except when he used the gym. Damn, he needed to relax a bit, before he exploded. His expression brightened, or was not as gloomy as usual. "I would like to go aboard the relay station," he stated simply.

"Uh, Ok?" For a moment, I wondered why he wanted to take the time to visit the relay station. I had been there, it was certainly nothing special. The interior compartments and passageways were a smaller version of the *Flying Dutchman*'s forward hull, before we humans modified our pirate ship to suit us. Then I realized why Count Chocula would enjoy visiting the relay station; he simply wanted a change of scenery. When we went down to Paradise, the first time to reactivate the maser projectors, the second time to plant the fake Elder artifacts; Chotek had remained board the *Dutchman*. At the time, I had feared he would insist on coming down to Paradise with me, living in the cramped dropship and second-guessing everything I did. For whatever reason, Chotek had stayed aboard the ship then, for which I was very grateful. He had not come with the raiding party to the surface of Jumbo either. Now that I thought about it, every member of the Merry Band of Pirates, including the science team, had at least been able to go aboard the relay station, or fly somewhere in a dropship, or simply go outside the *Dutchman* and fly around in a spacesuit. Hans Chotek had been confined to our star carrier since he came aboard in Earth orbit.

There were times when I strongly experienced the 'loneliness of command'. Many times, I felt terribly alone, when the only person I could talk to was Skippy. At least I had Skippy, even if he was an asshole. Hans Chotek had to be the loneliest person aboard the ship; he had no one at all he could talk with. For a moment, I felt a pang of sympathy for the man who was aboard the ship for the sole purpose of making my life difficult. "Certainly, Sir, you should be able to visit the relay station. We have the interior cleaned up from the battle," I said that to remind him there had been a hard fight to take that relay station. We had lost people, and others had suffered serious injuries they were still healing from. While he was sightseeing, he should think about the sacrifices made to win that relay station for us. "Skippy says there is not a ship scheduled to visit the station for the next nine days; the Thuranin fleet is busy with some big operation against the Jeraptha."

That drew his attention. "I thought the Thuranin had a ceasefire with the Jeraptha?"

"A conditional ceasefire," I said with a wry smile. "And only in the sector that includes Paradise. We're on the edge of the sector here."

Chotek snorted with what I took to be a derisive laugh. "This war out here makes the Middle East look tidy and organized. Have you made any progress on a plan to prevent the Ruhar from sending a ship to Earth?" He asked hopefully.

"Some progress, yes," I lied. We had nothing. "I need time to refine our plans, before we present the options to you."

"Very well, Colonel Bishop. I don't need to remind you the clock is ticking."

"No, Sir, you don't."

CHAPTER TWO

I told the duty officer that I was going to my quarters to splash cold water on my face after talking with Chotek. In reality, I barely made it to my too-small Thuranin toilet before ralphing up my breakfast. My body went ice cold and I knelt on the floor, shivering from a combination of chills, shock and gut-wrenching fear. "What's wrong, Joe?" Skippy's voice reflected concern. "You haven't eaten anything weird recently." He knew that my experiments with the more exotic types of cuisine prepared by our French, Indian and Chinese teams had sometimes not agreed with my stomach. Even British curry dishes had been too spicy for me.

"No," I spat, then got to my knees to wash my mouth out in the sink. "Food isn't the problem. Can we talk seriously for a minute?"

To his credit, Skippy did not make any snarky comments about it being impossible for him to discuss anything seriously with a hairless baboon. "Sure, Joe. Hmm, your core body temperature is dropping. You are almost in shock."

Because he was being nice to me, I squelched the 'Ya think?' comment that had been on the tip of my tongue. "I *am* kind of in shock. Skippy, I don't know if I can do this. Not again."

"Do what? Ralph up your breakfast? Hey, if you do it again, try to aim better."

"No, not that. I mean, I don't know if I can command another mission. I don't know if I can handle the responsibility again."

"Ooooh, oh, Ok, got ya. The stress is getting to you. Umm, let me think of some supportive words. Keep putting one foot in front of another, Joe," Skippy said encouragingly. And then, because he is an asshole, he added "And don't do the stupid thing you did last time. Remember, left, *right*, left, *right*. If you just keep putting only one foot forward, you end up doing the splits and falling down. Stupid monkey."

"I love you too, Skippy. That wasn't much help."

"Hmmm. Sergeant Adams is way better at this sort of thing, so I'll tell you what I think she would say. Get on your feet, soldier. Suck it up, and do your job. Because if you don't, your species is facing certain extinction."

"You *suck* at pep talks, Skippy."

"I wasn't trying to pep you up. This is your problem. Joe, out here, those fancy silver eagles on your uniform really don't mean shit. The Merry Band of Pirates is the most elite military force humanity has ever assembled, and they don't follow you because UNEF Command says they have to. People like Major Smythe follow you because they have confidence in your ability; confidence gained from experience. The Special Operations people have seen you lead them to succeed against impossible odds, over and over and over. Joe," he sighed, "much as it pains me to say this, I'll do it. You are an outstanding commander; brave, determined and inventive. You have been kicking alien ass up and down the Orion Arm. If someone were offering odds of this single ship and crew against the entire galaxy, I would put my money on the Merry Band of Pirates."

I looked at myself in the mirror. Color was coming back to my face, and my stomach was no longer in knots. "Thank you, Skippy. That was a great pep talk."

"Ah, if you repeat it to anyone, I'll deny the whole thing. Damn, now *I* feel like puking."

"Sorry about that. So," I stood up and squared my shoulders. "Now all I need to do is dream up a plan to do the impossible, again."

"Joe, damn, I can't *believe* I am saying this. You don't need to think up all the ideas around here. If you need help planning a black operation, there is someone aboard who has experience in that sort of thing. We haven't talked about it, but I think you know who I mean."

Many of our extra-special special operations troops had experience with clandestine operations, both those listed in their official resumes, and those Skippy discovered by easily hacking every electronic data system on the planet Earth. Of course Skippy had told me everything he had learned about the candidates for the crew, which had put me in somewhat of an uncomfortable spot. Two of the soldiers from foreign countries had been involved in an operation hostile to interests of the United States. No Americans were killed in the operation, but knowing what those two soldiers had done had caused me a sleepless night. In the end, I approved the two to join the Merry Band of Pirates, and I never said anything about it to their team commander. The UN Expeditionary Force was supposed to be an international force, a *human* force, and I had to understand that soldiers from other nations felt just as strongly patriotic about their country as I felt about the US of A. I wouldn't allow aboard anyone who had committed a war crime; otherwise what we needed in our mission to protect all of humanity was the most dedicated, effective soldiers and pilots we could get. "Most of our crew have been involved in secret operations, Skippy, that's why they are called special operations forces."

"Not special forces, Joe. You know who I mean."

"Oh. How do *you* know that I know?" He had assured me that he could not read my mind; I wasn't sure about that sometimes.

"Truthfully, I *wasn't* absolutely certain you knew until just now. Let's just say that, despite my overall low opinion of your brain power, I assumed you would have figured this out."

"Was that supposed to be a compliment?"

"Why would I do that?"

"Oh," I rolled my eyes. "No reason. Ok, thank you, I'll take your advice."

"Great. And next time you talk to Ralph on the big silver phone," Thuranin toilets were silver instead of white, "try to aim better. I need to get another service bot in here to clean the floor. Yuck."

For training, Smythe set up an operation where the Indian team went over to the relay station in a dropship, then flew toward the *Flying Dutchman* using jetpacks. Yes, I totally wished I could be with them, flying around in cool jetpacks rather than sitting in an office. The French team was outside the *Dutchman* but still inside the ship's stealth field, ready to fly out in jetpacks to intercept Captain Chandra's Indian paratrooper team. I figured Captains Chandra and Giraud had a wager going on whose team would 'win' the engagement. I was certain almost everyone aboard the ship wished they were part of the fun, rather than being stuck inside the ship. The *Dutchman* was as comfortable as we could make our pirate ship, but being inside a starship day after day after day got old.

Most people aboard the ship could use a break; I had spent most of the day in the conference room with senior staff, wracking our brains for an idea to stop the Ruhar from bringing Fire Dragons to Earth. Skippy had, correctly, shot down every one of our stupid ideas so far.

I thought merely blowing up a Thuranin surveyor ship on its way to Earth had been difficult. This was much, much worse. With the operation against the Thuranin, we had been able to openly use force, the 'only' complication had been assuring the Thuranin never knew who destroyed their ship, or why. That had been difficult enough; at the time we thought it an impossible task. Now I was nostalgic for that time as the 'good old days'.

The only bright spot in my day was that Hans Chotek was not aboard our pirate ship. A dropship had brought Chotek, Major Simms and Dr. Friedlander over to the relay station, along with the Indian special forces team. Chotek had requested Simms as an escort, instead of someone from Smythe's SpecOps team: I think he was more comfortable with Simms. As our logistics officer, Simms maybe was not considered a real 'soldier' by Chotek. And Friedlander had been included, I guess, because Chotek wanted another civilian with him. Or Chotek understood that Friedlander also deserved an opportunity to get out of the ship.

I was in the CIC watching the training engagement; Lt. Williams of our SEALS team was the duty officer in the command chair. Sergeant Adams was taking a shift at one of the sensor stations in the CIC; usually pilots staffed the CIC, but crosstraining was essential. She was monitoring the progress of the Indian team, who had launched from the relay station and were now flying jetpacks on their way to the *Flying Dutchman*. I heard Adams sigh quietly, and I walked over to stand next to her. "I know, I wish I was out there, too," I whispered.

"It would be good to get off the ship, Sir," she admitted.

Adams and I had gone down to Paradise, although we had to remain hidden while we were there. The two of us, and a handful of others, had been able to stand under a blue sky and breathe unfiltered air. With Major Smythe, I had space dived down to the surface of the planet Jumbo. But most of the crew had been either stuck aboard the ship, or restricted to training in space. That is something fans of Star Trek don't think about when they fantasize about being aboard the *Enterprise*: being on that ship for month after month after month. In Star Trek, once in a while, a small group beams down to a dangerous planet, where Unnamed Crewman Number Four gets eaten by some monster. Maybe the people wearing red shirts weren't stupid; they just were desperate to finally get off the freakin' ship for a while. There were times when I thought that, instead of pilots, we should have brought submariners to fly the *Dutchman*. Pilots saw blue sky and stood on solid ground after a short flight. Naval pilots, although they spent a lot of time at sea, could stand on the deck of a carrier and see the horizon. Submarine crews were accustomed to being underwater in a claustrophobic steel tube for months. That is what being aboard the *Dutchman* was like. "Sergeant, maybe if we-"

I never finished the thought. The *Flying Dutchman*'s internal alarm sounded; it was still the Star Trek alarm sound that Adams had requested Skippy program into the system. Before I could focus my eyes on the status display, Skippy shouted over the speakers. "Thuranin light cruiser jumped in, twenty seven lightseconds from the relay station!"

I checked the display. There was a new icon, a bright blazing icon where none had been before. It was on the other side of the relay station, having emerged into one of the designated jump points, where ships would not interfere with the station's transmitter. The spot where we parked the *Dutchman* was chosen specifically because incoming ships were supposed to avoid the area, and because the relay station partly masked our ship from sensors. "Do they see us?" I asked as I ran toward the bridge, where Lt. Williams of our SEALS team was holding the command chair for me.

"Not yet, Joe," Skippy reported. "Our stealth field is effective, and ships are not allowed to use active sensor fields here, to avoid interfering with the relay station. However, the Thuranin have detected our dropship and the Indian team. Technically, what they see are several sets of Kristang suits with jetpacks. They are very curious about that, to the point where they are demanding an explanation from the station, and they have activated their defensive shields."

"Shit. Uh, tell them, uh-"

"I already told them the Kristang armored suits are an Advanced Research Development experiment in remotely seizing control of Kristang technology, and that the suits are empty. I took control of the suits to make them rigid, I set the faceplates to go opaque so the Thuranin can't see human faces, and I'm doing my best to mask body heat and other evidence the suits are occupied. Captain Chandra's team knows the situation and has gone silent. Joe, the Thuranin are buying my bullshit story for now, but I do not think that will last more than a minute. They could use an active tightbeam sensor probe on Chandra's team, and they'd find out real quick that humans are in those suits."

My inexperience showed in me wasting time asking a stupid question. "What the hell is that ship doing here?!"

"There was a battle against the Jeraptha in the adjacent sector; the battle was a draw but several Thuranin ships sustained significant damage, including that ship. That light cruiser was escorting a pair of battleships that need urgent repairs, so that ship was sent on ahead as a scout. Those two battleships, and fourteen other warships, will be here within the hour."

"All right, all right," I frantically tried to think. We could jump the *Dutchman* away, abandoning the Indian team. And Chotek, Simms and Dr. Friedlander. And, dammit, the French team also, I realized with shock. Although Giraud and his paratroopers were near us, they were outside the ship, floating in space with jetpacks. If we jumped the *Dutchman*, the French would be killed by the distortions of the jump field. "We're not leaving our people," I declared mostly to myself. "We need to kill that ship. We are, you said, twenty seven lightseconds away?"

"Correct," Skippy replied, and did not take time to remark that data was on the main bridge display.

"So, whatever we do here, the Thuranin won't know about it for twenty seven seconds? How long would we need to accelerate to get far enough away for Giraud's team to survive us jumping?"

"Thirty four seconds to be safe, but we could live with a minimum of twenty one seconds if I compress our jump field."

"Pilot, signal Giraud what we're doing, and get us moving. Skippy, we need to jump in right on top of that ship and hammer them with everything we've got, before they can react."

"I'll do my best, Joe." The ship lurched as the pilots input Skippy's selected course and kicked in emergency acceleration. "Weapons are preprogrammed for release on your authority; jump is also programmed and counting down. Eighteen seconds to jump. Seventeen. Sixteen-"

There wasn't time to plan or discuss with Skippy what we were going to do; I had to trust that he knew much more than us about Space Combat Maneuvers. After twenty one seconds of acceleration that we actually felt, the *Dutchman* jumped. It was easier to be precise with a short jump covering less than half a lightminute, but on this jump Skippy needed to be more precise than ever before, working against the handicaps presented by quantum mechanics.

Skippy explained later what he tried to do, and what actually happened. The Thuranin ship's shields were activated; Skippy knew that ship had sustained significant battle damage and had weak spots in its defensive systems. Still, the relatively weak maser cannons of our rebuilt star carrier, and our pitifully few ship-killer missiles, could not be certain of killing or disabling that ship in our first volley. We would not get a second chance; even a damaged light cruiser could batter our pirate ship to pieces, or trap us in a damping field and slice us up at their leisure. We needed to take down their shields before we could hit them. The only way to do that was to jump in so very close, the event horizon of our inbound jump wormhole interfered with their shields and caused a cascading failure of their shield generators. It was a tactic of absolute desperation that had never been done before, as far as Skippy knew.

Naturally, he was super eager to try it.

"Five. Four," Skippy counted down. "Hold my beer, watch this."

"*Hold my beer*? Don't-"

"One. Jump."

Renee Giraud blinked to clear spots and starbursts swimming in his vision. Even though the Kristang armored spacesuit had made its visor go opaque before the *Flying Dutchman* jumped away, intense light and heavy-particle radiation from the jump wormhole had blasted him and his team. The voice of the suit's computer, a voice the Americans called 'Bitching Betty', had been calling out warnings of radiation exposure and helpfully notifying him that the anti-radiation meds the suit normally would administer were not available. Betty advised Giraud to seek medical attention as soon as possible, and she advised him of that fact every four seconds until he figured out how to turn the damned thing off.

"Merde," Giraud said to himself, his voice echoing loudly in the helmet. The suit's supply of anti-radiation medicine was empty, because those meds were designed for Kristang biochemistry, and would be poisonous to humans. Skippy the alien AI had promised he was working on retrofitting the suits with medical nanomachines appropriate for humans, but Giraud knew the ship's supply of medical nano was thin. If he returned to the ship, he was sure Skippy the mad scientist would have his scary medical bots administer advanced treatments to clear the radiation damage from Giraud's body.

If he returned to the ship. If the ship returned at all.

He did not know what had happened to their pirate star carrier. Giraud had received a warning that a Thuranin light cruiser had jumped in near the relay station; his own suit confirmed that observation with a blinking icon in the visor in front of his eyes. The *Flying Dutchman* had accelerated away, while Giraud's team had burned their jetpacks in the opposite direction, until Giraud ordered the team to conserve thruster fuel. The tiny extra distance they could gain from burning hard with the jetpacks was meaningless, and they might need every ounce of jetpack fuel later.

Giraud checked the time in the bottom left corner of his visor, less than thirty seconds had passed since the giant, spindly star carrier had jumped away. It felt like much longer; he had spent the first ten or fifteen seconds disoriented and spinning wildly. After he engaged the jetpack's automatic stabilizer, gyroscopes had halted his spin and he had spent precious seconds checking the status of the suit and jetpack, and turning off the Bitching Betty before her annoying voice rendered him deaf. "Team," he called out, "report-"

The visor, which had just returned to clear after going completely black right before the *Dutchman* jumped, went into protective mode again. The display on the inside of the visor gave Giraud a view of a short, intense space battle raging close by, then the display registered a ship exploding and a gamma ray burst almost at the exact same time. "See-lonce," Giraud ordered using an international standard term for radio silence, then turned off his transmitter.

A starship had exploded, and a starship had jumped away, or attempted to jump away. Which ship had been destroyed, perhaps both of them? His suit's sensors were not able to determine exactly what had happened twenty seven lightseconds away; the explosion had been so violent it was impossible to tell whether one or two ships had been consumed.

Giraud did not like their star carrier's chances against a cruiser, unless Skippy had been able to perform some magic on very short notice. During Giraud's crosstraining in the ship's Combat Information Center, Skippy had explained that every starship's jump drive had a distinctive signature, and that signature could identify the type of ship, even a specific ship if the data on that ship's jump characteristics was known.

His suit's computer lacked the ability to analyze jump signatures, and Skippy's magic always slightly altered the *Dutchman*'s signature with each jump, to prevent anyone from identifying or following their stolen star carrier. So, Giraud told himself, he did not know whether the *Dutchman* had survived. If both ships had been destroyed, what should he do? Contact Captain Chandra of the Indian paratroop team, and get both teams over to the relay station? That would only be a temporary solution, for they were doomed without a starship to carry them home. Going aboard the relay station would be for the purpose of self-destructing that station, erasing any evidence of humans flying around the galaxy. Along with erasing the actual humans, including Chotek and his team.

If the ship that exploded was the *Flying Dutchman*, then the Thuranin cruiser might still be in the area, or could return soon. In that case also, the priority would be destroying evidence of human activity. Even if the Thuranin cruiser had been destroyed, if the *Dutchman* had been so damaged that she was unable to return, then Giraud, his team, the Indians and Chotek were all stranded and had only one course of action.

The only possibility for survival was if the *Dutchman* had somehow escaped the battle, jumped away, and was able to return. Giraud would know their pirate ship survived only if that ship jumped back in. Plan against disaster, he decided, and hope for the best. There was no point planning for the *Dutchman*'s return, because there wasn't anything he or his team could do to help that blessed event happen.

His suit remained rigid and in defensive posture as light and heavy particles from the explosion twenty seven lightseconds away washed over him, then the visor blinked clear again. Or almost clear; sections of the faceplate were gray or black. Warning icons were flashing around the edges of his visor. The suit had been damaged, that was obvious from even a quick scan of the status icons. The jetpack had sustained the worst damage, having automatically spun around to protect Giraud by putting its mass between his fragile body and the heavy charged particles of the explosion. Communication with the jetpack's computer were garbled; according to the status he could read, the unit was able to activate only one of its jets. With a single jet, all Giraud could do was fly uselessly in a circle. Irritated the sophisticated alien technology had failed him, he concentrated on the suit's sensors. While they were partially blinded, he was still able to see blinking icons showing the last reported position of his team, Chandra's team and the relay station. Damaged or not, the sensors certainly would be able to see the gamma ray burst if the cruiser had jumped in, and there was no such data on the visor display. Knowing the cruiser might arrive on top of them at any minute, Giraud took advantage of what might be a brief opportunity. "See-lonce fini," he announced. "Team, status check."

All but one member of the team reported in. His visor display showed the silent paratrooper was alive, likely unconscious. Giraud had been shocked to see how far apart his team was, headed off in multiple directions at a speed higher than their jetpacks had been able to impart. The spatial distortion of the jump wormhole had not only bathed the French team in radiation, it had thrown them far and scattered them like butterflies in a strong wind. Only one of the team had a fully working jetpack; Giraud ordered her to fly over to the unresponsive man. If needed, she might be able to use her jetpack to bring the injured paratrooper to the relay station for whatever medical treatment might be available. "Captain Chandra, respond, please."

Chandra answered after a few seconds; the man had been busy dealing with his own team. Although the Indians had been farther from the spatial and radiation effects of the *Dutchman*'s jump wormhole, they had been closer to the heavy particles of the explosion, and he had two people unresponsive. None of the Indians' jetpacks were operational, the dropship was in the process of collecting them. "No," Giraud replied to Chandra's offer for the dropship to pick up his team. The 'Falcon' dropship was the smaller of the two Thuranin models, and could barely accommodate Chandra's people. "I think it is best to get your team aboard the relay station and prepare it for self-destruct. Send the dropship back for us when you can."

"Are you sure, Rene?" The other paratroop commander asked.

"Yes. My suit computer says I'll be dead without treatment for radiation poisoning," he chuckled with gallows humor. "If that happens, I would rather be out here than having my corpse stinking up the relay station."

"Ok," Chandra forced a sympathetic laugh. "We also got a dose of radiation from the explosion. I hope Doctor Skippy makes house calls. Rene, I ordered my team to put the Sandman protocol on standby."

"I did the same," Giraud acknowledged. If any of the Merry Band of Pirates were about to be captured, it would be best for them to set off a nuke to erase even DNA evidence. Failing that, none of them could allow themselves to be captured alive. On every mission away from the ship, each soldier and pilot wore a tiny dot on the back of his or her neck, as a high-tech sort of suicide pill. It was a tiny, tightly-packed cluster of nanoparticles. According to Skippy, activating the suicide dot would send an electrical pulse to the wearer's brainstem, killing them instantly and painlessly. The dot would then release nanomachines into the person's brain; those machines would swim through blood vessels to vital sites in the brain, and fire simultaneously to fry every memory engram and synapse in the mass of gray matter known as the human brain. Skippy had assured Hans Chotek that not even the super advanced technology of the Maxolhx would be able to recover any memories from a brain so thoroughly scrambled.

Rene Giraud was used to the almost imperceptible sensation of the suicide dot attached to the base of his skull, although he was always aware of its disturbing presence. The dot could be triggered by the wearer, or triggered remotely by any commander with the access codes. At the end of every away mission, even in training, he was happy to peel the dot off his skin and drop it in a box. Skippy said the dot was not in any way harmful, except for the obvious, but Giraud was certain he could feel his skin's irritation when he showered after a mission. Although he had to admit, he had never been able to detect a rash where a suicide dot had been attached to anyone else's neck.

On the visor, he watched the icon representing the Falcon dropship flying around, picking up the Indian team. There was no response from the relay station, which was odd and disturbing. There was also no gamma ray burst from a murderous alien warship. Minutes passed, Giraud's main activity was trying to remain still, for any movement sent him into a tumble. The jetpack's stabilizing gyroscopes were inoperable, or the jetpack's computer was unable to control them, for the flying machine attached to his back was a useless lump of alien technology. He had ordered his team to remain attached to their jetpacks, if the *Flying Dutchman* returned it would be best for their dropships to pick up crew and jetpacks at the same time, rather than flying around willy-nilly chasing twice as many objects. Giraud was certain that if the ship did return, Colonel Bishop would want them to get the hell out of there as quickly as possible.

Gamma ray burst! Not close enough to give them another damaging dose of radiation, and not close enough that his suit's failing sensors could identify the ship. He braced himself to transmit the suicide order.

The *Flying Dutchman* jumped, which is something I usually know only because the bridge display told me we had gone from one empty area of interstellar space to another. Once in a while, we jump and a star becomes a bright disc instead of a faint dot. Or a planet appears at the edge of the display.

This time, we jumped in so close to the enemy cruiser that it was *RIGHT THERE*. The display wasn't needed; I could have looked out a porthole and read the registration number on the side of the enemy ship. My heart was in my throat as we went whizzing past way, way too close; for a split second I thought Skippy had screwed up and we would collide.

Then all hell broke loose.

With the cruiser's shields knocked offline by the spatial distortion of our jump wormhole, our masers bit into the unprotected armor plating of their hull, slicing deeply into the decks under the armor. We blew out two of our irreplaceable maser cannons in that first volley, with Skippy channeling energy directly from jump drive capacitors into the cannon exciters. That was way more input energy than the exciters were capable of handling, so they blew just after sending gigajoules of maser power into the enemy ship. The *Dutchman*'s speed relative to the enemy carried us by so quickly we only had one slicing shot with the masers, so four of our missiles followed close behind the deadly maser beams. Unknown to me, Skippy's programming of the missiles had them surging out of their launch tubes while the *Dutchman* was still within the wormhole.

Thuranin missiles are smart things, not self-aware but capable of thinking on their own. If the missiles were self-aware, I imagine their thinking went something like:

WTF, I'm launching while the ship is inside a freaking' wormhole? Of all the stupid- Unbelievable, I survived. Great. Where is the target? It's- Holy shit, I'm right on top of the damned thing! No shields in my way? Uh, I am programmed to expect strong defensive shields. And defensive fire from maser turrets. None of that going on here. Ok, what should I- Oh. Hmm. There is a nice big smoking hole in the enemy's hull. Maybe I'll go in there. Yeah, that's a great idea. Hey, it's cozy in here, although the Thuranin really could use some help tidying up the place. Well, this has been nice, but a missile has got to do what a missile has got to do, right? I can set the warhead for wide dispersal, now that I'm inside the enemy's hull.

Of the four missiles we launched, two missed completely, as their targeting systems got scrambled by distortion of the jump wormhole. One was intercepted and destroyed by a defensive maser turret that somehow managed to remain active and locked onto the incoming threat. Even in the moment of death, that warhead triggered its shape-charge warhead, taking out the maser turret and twenty meters of the enemy's hull.

Our one missile that survived dove inside a hole carved by our maser cannons, and exploded when it was down at the third deck under the armor plating. If our pilots had not performed a blind emergency jump, the *Flying Dutchman* would have been ripped apart by debris from the exploding light cruiser.

The jump was rough; not catastrophically bad as when the *Dutchman* had been fleeing from the Thuranin destroyer squadron on our second mission, but the ship lurched and shuddered and I heard the structure groaning and flexing in a way it should never do.

We emerged seven million miles from the relay station, much farther than intended. "We're in one piece?" I asked fearfully. Many of the status indicators on the main bridge display were blank or flickering.

"Mostly in one piece," even Skippy sounded worried.

"What the hell was that?" I shouted, my voice cracking.

"The jump? We initiated the jump much closer to the cruiser than I expected, and its mass distorted the event horizon in a way I could not predict. That threw us far from the point I had programmed, and going through the wormhole damaged the ship. I'm assessing the damage now."

"Can we jump again?" Sixteen Thuranin warships would be arriving at the relay station within the hour, and we could not travel seven million miles through normal space in that time. Unless we could jump, there was no way we could rescue the French and Indian teams. Or Chotek's party.

"We can jump back in a few minutes; I am making adjustments to the drive coils now. Ok, I have a preliminary damage report; while it's not good, we can deal with it until we get the hell out of here."

"Bonjour, Rene!" Skippy's voice rang out of his helmet speakers, and Giraud shuddered with relief. "Holiday time is over; I know you French get like fifty weeks of vacation a year, but now it's back to work, *non*? Did you miss me?"

"Skippy," Giraud laughed almost hysterically before catching himself. "I am so happy to hear your voice, I do not even mind that you are, as Colonel Bishop says, an asshole."

"Rene! Oh, I am deeply hurt. Well, you French are renowned for being rude, so I'm not taking it personally. Colonel Joe has dropships launching now to pick up your team. On a serious note, I queried your suit sensors, and you all need treatment for radiation exposure. The medical bay will be ready to receive you."

"We will be treated by Doctor Skippy?" Giraud sighed. "Is there another option?"

"A long, lingering and painful death?"

"Oh. In that case, I will make an appointment with Doctor Skippy."

"Great! You won't regret this, Captain Giraud. While you are recuperating, I can serenade you with a variety of tunes."

"*Merde*. Can I still choose the lingering and painful death?"

"Sadly, no."

"Maybe I'll open my helmet right here, then."

"Oh, come on, Rene. You love my singing." He launched into La Marseillaise. "*Allons enfants de la Patrie, le jour gloire est arrive! Contre-*"

"Sacre bleu," Giraud muttered to himself while he searched for the helmet speaker controls.

Controls which, of course, Skippy had remotely disabled. His warbling, out of tune voice continued. "*-nous de la tyrannie. L'etendard-*"

CHAPTER THREE

We jumped back to the relay station after Skippy's bots quickly patched up our jump drive. While his bots were frantically busy doing the minimum repairs so we could jump without exploding, I was dealing with reports of injuries and damage that was obvious to the crew. Once we returned, I immediately launched dropships out to collect the French team; Captain Chandra's dropship was already taking the Indian team aboard. The French had been scattered by our hard acceleration and then by the jump wormhole tearing a hole in spacetime; Giraud reported that being violently flung around by spacetime ripples had caused injuries among his team. And Skippy said he would need to treat all the French and Indians for radiation exposure; he thought they would all recover fully. Chotek, Simms and Friedlander had kept communications silence aboard the relay station, until Skippy contacted them with a properly coded signal. They were fine, and a dropship would pick them up, after taking the Indian team aboard.

"Skippy, what went wrong?" I asked as I watched the main bridge display continue to flicker.

"In a nutshell, Joe, I played it too safe."

"Too *safe*?" How bad would it have been if he had taken too much risk?

"Yeah, too safe. Kind of ironic, huh? I did not expect our maser cannons to punch through their armor plating before the exciters burned out from the overload. And the odds were that only one of our missiles would survive to explode its shape-charge warhead. So, I expected we would need to fire our first volley, then accelerate away while preparing a second volley with the aft maser cannons and missile tubes. I figured by that time the enemy would hit back at us, so I was prepared to absorb maser hits to the aft shields, then direct the pilots to jump away. Instead, our masers carved up their armor plating, and one of our missiles scored a direct hit, actually going inside their hull before exploding. I don't know if you saw that on the display?"

"No, Skippy, it all happened too fast," I admitted.

"When our missile exploded, that ship blew apart and nearly took us with it, we were so close. I needed the pilots to initiate the jump while we were uncomfortably close to the mass of that cruiser, and that threw off my calculations. I've never seen a jump wormhole distort like that, I didn't have the math to predict how the wormhole's event horizon would propagate. That is why the jump was so rough, and why we were thrown so far off course. We do *not* want to ever do that again."

"We nearly lost the ship," I asked incredulously, "because our attack was *more* successful than expected?"

"We got lucky, Joe. You didn't give me much time to plan the attack, and I based my planning on a beat-up star carrier against a top-of-the-line light cruiser. Ordinarily, even with the advantage of surprise and our jump wormhole knocking out their shields, that would be a close to even fight. What I did not know was the serious damage that ship had already sustained in combat against the Jeraptha. I was not prepared to completely destroy that ship in the first salvo. If that missile had not acted on its own initiative and penetrated their hull, the fight would have gone on for a second, possibly third salvo."

"Wow, cool! Anyway we can give that missile a commendation?"

"Posthumously, maybe."

"What now? Can we jump again, after we recover the special ops teams?"

"Yes. For our first jump, we should go maybe 75% of our maximum range. Far enough that it will not be easy for anyone to follow us, but not straining our jump drive. We will be ready to jump again in twenty five minutes."

"Twenty five?" I whistled and looked at Chang. Sixteen Thuranin warships would be arriving within the hour, maybe sooner. That was to close. "Colonel Chang, are the dropship pilots still reporting it will take thirty three minutes to recover the French team?"

"Thirty two minutes, that's the best they can do, the French are scattered all over space."

"Twenty five is fine, then, Skippy. We need to bug out of here ASAP."

"Agreed. I will set the relay station to self-destruct after we retrieve Chotek's team?"

"Yes. Make it- Wait, wait." Our latest near disaster had given me a thought. During our second mission, after the *Dutchman* got ambushed by a Thuranin destroyer squadron, we used our captured Kristang frigate the *Flower* as a lifeboat. Given the track record of the Merry Band of Pirates, it would be useful to have a lifeboat again. "Skippy, that relay station was built from a starship."

"Yes, so?"

"Could we take it onto one of our docking platforms, bring it with us?"

"Yes, the station is designed to be moved, so it is still capable of mating with our docking platforms. Why do you want it?"

"As a lifeboat," I explained. It would also be useful for training. "And spare parts. That station must have Thuranin components we could use, and we don't have time now to strip out everything we need."

"Oh, crap," Skippy sighed. "Yes, you're right, we should take it with us. Ugh, I am *so* much going to regret this."

"Why?"

"I'll explain later. Time to rendezvous with the station, and secure it on a docking platform, would be about eighteen minutes. Doing so will not delay recovering the French team. And it will save time, because a dropship will not need to pick up Chocula and his companions."

"Bonus. Let's do it."

"Crap. This sucks," he grumbled to himself, without explaining why. "Well, when the Thuranin ships arrive, they will find one hell of a mystery. A light cruiser blown to bits, and a relay station missing. Ha!" He remarked cheerfully. "A relay station that disappears, instead of being blown apart, will drive the Thuranin crazy trying to figure out why. Ooooh, and if the Thuranin back-trace any funky transmissions to this relay station, having it disappear will make them think the Jeraptha were involved! Yeah, that will keep the Thuranin busy chasing their tails for a while. Maybe they'll stay out of our way. Good idea, Joe."

We jumped away from the station as soon as possible, which meant initiating a jump as soon as the last dropship was secured in its docking clamps; we didn't even wait for the docking bay doors to close. With sixteen Thuranin warships about to jump in right on top of us, I wanted to skedaddle out of there ASAP. After the jump, Skippy was not happy about the condition of our jump drive, he requested down time to make adjustments to it. I was about to argue with him, until Desai silently pointed to the main bridge display, which indicated we had emerged from jump seven hundred thousand miles away from the target location. With Skippy programming the jumps, we should have been within a hundred meters of the target. Something was seriously wrong with our jump drive, and a dumb monkey like me certainly should not argue with our genius beer can.

Mindful of who was the mission commander, I sent a dropship to bring Chotek back aboard; even though the relay station was attached to a docking platform, it didn't have an airlock that would allow them direct access to the ship. Because I was in command of the ship, and because I didn't want to deal with Hans Chotek, I sent Chang down to the docking bay, to greet our mission commander and fully brief him. Maybe I was being cowardly in not wanting to be harangued by Chotek; I was too stressed to care. With our jump drive down for maintenance, and a whole battlegroup of extremely pissed-off little green Thuranin potentially chasing us, I was determined to remain in the command chair.

Major Simms came straight to the bridge, walking in with a bemused expression. "Colonel."

"Major Simms, it is good to see you in one piece," I stepped out of the chair and waived Desai over to take command temporarily. In the corridor, I asked quietly "How are you?"

"Fine, Sir. It was tense for a while; we got notice from Skippy of that cruiser jumping in, then all comms cut out. We waited it out. From the after-action report we received from Skippy, it looks like you had a close call?"

"Too close. How was our, uh," I glanced around to see if anyone was in earshot. "Our fearless leader?"

"He was frosty the whole time, didn't panic at all," she replied with an arched eyebrow. "Scared as hell, of course, but he was more afraid we would be boarded and discovered, and give away our secret. He made me promise," she patted her sidearm, "that I would shoot him in the head before he could be captured."

"Huh." That surprised me, but it shouldn't have. Hans Chotek was a pain in my ass, but he was a professional, as dedicated to his job as I was to mine. "It might be that in the future, we should issue sidearms to everyone in an away party. Just in case."

"We could do that, but there is another consideration," Simms warned. "Dr. Friedlander is a Catholic; suicide is considered a mortal sin, I think. He asked me to, to 'take care' of him, if it came to that. If he had to, I think Friedlander would do what he had to, but we shouldn't put civilians in that position."

"Crap. You're right."

"During our flight back, Mr. Chotek remarked that all away parties should bring nukes with them, to cover up our presence if needed."

"That will be inconvenient," I thought aloud. Carrying a tactical nuclear warhead in a dropship was enough of a logistical burden. How was a group of people supposed to bring a nuke with them; in their pockets? I sighed heavily, something I should have not done in front of Major Simms. "I'll discuss that with Chotek. Maybe we could compromise and issue sidearms to him and the science team."

Simms raised an eyebrow, something she did a lot when talking with me. "That won't solve the DNA problem. The Thuranin can't interrogate a dead human, but they can ask how the hell we primitives are flying around the galaxy by ourselves."

"You're right, I know." Two things I was getting tired of saying were 'you are right' and 'I am sorry'. That wasn't anything new; I had been doing that all my life. "It's good to hear our fearless leader is cool under pressure."

"That shouldn't really be a surprise, being cool under pressure must be a primary job requirement for diplomats. Otherwise, they'd be tempted to reach across the table and slap somebody. I know I sure would."

I almost rolled my eyes at her. "There's a big difference between people yelling at you, and people shooting at you."

"Maybe not from his point of view." She looked at her holstered sidearm and patted it. "I'm going to return this to the armory; I've had enough excitement for one day. Colonel, I think you should know; there is something odd going on with the relay station. After you jumped away, it seemed like the AI there was trying to communicate with us, but it was horribly garbled. And it cut out shortly after you returned."

My Spidey sense tingled. Skippy had been reluctant to bring the relay station with us, and he hadn't told me why. Could the submind he installed there have something to do with it? "Skippy has some 'splainin' to do."

After Hans Chotek had time to shower, change clothes and have a few minutes to himself in his office, I walked down the passageway and knocked on the doorframe. His office was larger than the tiny closet I used; his office had been converted from a Thuranin sleeping cabin. The relative size of our offices didn't bother me at all, mine was right around the corner from the bridge/CIC complex, while his was back near the forward cargo bays. Being physically separated was a good idea; it kept us from irritating each other 24/7. I put on my best winning smile. "Welcome back, Sir. Did you enjoy the sightseeing trip?"

Surprisingly, he smiled back, it looked genuine. Maybe later I would ask Skippy to analyze Chotek's blood pressure, galvanic skin response, brain wave patterns and the haptics of his facial expression to learn if Chotek had been faking it. "The sightseeing was exciting enough by itself, Colonel. You did not need to arrange a bonus space battle for my benefit."

"You did purchase the special Premium Experience Package; we figured you should get your money's worth."

"Next time, offering complimentary valet parking would have been sufficient. Maybe a glass of champagne."

"Yes, Sir," that time, my grin wasn't forced.

Chotek's smile faded. "The incident reinforced in my mind that, out here, we must constantly expect the unexpected. Colonel, we almost got jumped by a ship out of nowhere. Even with the advantage of Skippy's ability to intercept secret alien communications, we cannot anticipate every obstacle we will encounter out here. I am anxious to hear your ideas for preventing the Ruhar from sending a ship to Earth, because the alternative is to approach the Ruhar and offer an alliance. We must begin thinking long-term, rather than reacting to events forced upon us."

"Yes, Sir. I am working on it with the team. We have several promising concepts," I lied, as we had a grand total of nothing in terms of workable ideas.

There was a knock on my office doorframe. "Colonel Bishop?" It was Doctor Sarah Rose, part of our science team, a geologist. She had shoulder-length medium-brown hair, curly at the ends, cute dimples and a great smile. Mid-thirties, I guessed; I could have looked it up on her personnel file, if I cared. What I did care about, I already knew about her.

I looked up from my tablet, where I had been reading a report that, shockingly, was actually somewhat interesting. "Doctor Rose, thank you, please sit down."

She chose the chair closest to the door. "Please, Colonel, call me Sarah."

"Uh," she was not military, so technically I could call her by her first name without breaking protocol. "Ok, Sarah. We haven't had a chance to talk much since you came aboard."

"We have been busy," she replied with a smile. "Especially you. I envy that you were able to land on Paradise, and especially on Jumbo. As a geologist, I would love to explore a heavy gravity planet."

I made a sour face. "If you enjoyed being on Jumbo, you would have been the only one."

"I meant the opportunity for science," she explained, reminding me that she was on the ship's science team. "And," she grinned again, "when we get home, I would like to be able to say I walked on another planet."

"It's not as dramatic as when the astronauts landed on the moon," I assured her. "What do you think of the Merry Band of Pirates so far?"

"They are, I think the military term is 'high speed'?"

I nodded ruefully. "I keep having to remind myself that, if it weren't for Skippy, there is no way I would have qualified to be aboard this ship."

"When we first heard about Skippy, all we knew was bits and pieces of information; the cover story was that he was the AI for the Thuranin ship. For the first day, most of us thought 'Skippy' was an acronym for something."

"An acronym?" That surprised me. "What did you think 'S-k-i-p-p-y' meant?"

"We had a pool about it going in the office. One of the more inventive guesses was 'S-C-I-P-P-I, for Super Computing Intelligent Planetary Preservation Insurance." We both laughed at that. "We knew he was an AI, and he was involved in saving our planet."

"Now that you have had a chance to know Skippy, you understand the 'S' in the acronym must be for 'Shithead'."

"Hey!" Skippy's voice boomed out of the ceiling speaker. "I heard that, you miserable baboon. Hmm, an acronym for my name, huh? It would have to include 'awesomeness' in there somewhere."

"There is no 'A' in Skippy," I pointed out.

"There is no 'A' anywhere in your school grades either, Joe, yet here you are in command of a starship. Thus proving that life is not only not fair, it also makes no sense at all."

"Thank you, Skippy. How about you go away and think up an acronym appropriate for your awesomeness, while I talk with Dr. Rose for a while?"

"Gotcha," he said, and the speaker made the faint clicking sound to indicate it was powered down.

"Your message said you needed to speak with me?" Sarah asked.

"Yes," I put the tablet face down on the table and gave her my full attention, even pressing the button to close my office door so we would have privacy. "I need your expertise."

"In geology?" She asked, surprised. The *Flying Dutchman* was nowhere near any planet. The nearest rocky object was probably a rogue asteroid that orbited far from a star system, three lightyears away. "Out here?"

"No," I smiled in what I hoped was a friendly manner. "Your *other* specialty."

"Organic chemistry?" She asked uncertainly.

"Your *other* other specialty, Dr. Rose." I winked at her. "You know what I mean."

"Oh, fudge," she frowned, then gave me a wry smile. "Did Skippy tell you?"

"No, I figured it out on my own."

"Amazingly," Skippy's voice came from the ceiling speaker, "that is true. I wouldn't count on it happening again, Joe used up all his brain power on that one."

"CIA?" I asked.

She sighed. "There is no point in not telling you, so, yes. Colonel, can I ask when you learned about my, other career?"

"I forget when exactly, it was before you came aboard."

"You knew the Agency planted me in your crew, and you approved me anyway?"

"Yes. My thinking was, if not you, it would be someone else. The CIA, or NSA or DIA or somebody else, would try to slip an agent aboard. With you as part of the science team, the intel agencies would be satisfied and leave me alone. And Skippy told me you actually are a respected geologist. And you are somewhat of an expert in chemistry?"

"Does Friedlander know?"

"Not that I know of, and I won't reveal your secret. Mr. Chotek also does not know yet. Although, it is going to be tough to explain why I will be including you in strategy meetings."

"I will tell Dr. Friedlander," she said unhappily.

"And I will inform Count Choc- Mr. Chotek. Before we start, how did you become a spy?"

"We don't call ourselves 'spies'. We prefer 'intelligence officer'. The Agency recruited me as an undergrad; they offered to pay for my graduate school. Being a geologist with a minor in chemistry, and specializing in petroleum geology, gets me into a lot of trouble spots around the world." She bit her lip. "Around *Earth*. Earth isn't the only 'world' any longer. Why do you need my, um, other expertise?"

"Have you heard about our latest problem?" I almost rolled my eyes. With the Merry Band of Pirates, there was always a freakin' problem. Skippy thought the official motto of the Merry Band of Pirates should be 'Trust the Awesomeness'. Based on our track record, I thought a more accurate motto would be 'Lurching from One Crisis to Another'.

I know, as mottos go, it's not inspiring.

"All I heard was something about the Ruhar might be sending a ship to Earth?" Her wide-open eyes reflected her surprise. "I heard a rumor a few minutes before you called me. Why would the Ruhar send a ship to Earth?" She asked, baffled.

"Because the Kristang are paying them to."

"*Paying*? Unbelievable," she slumped in her chair. "I thought I left messy politics behind when we left Earth. This is worse than anything I've heard of in a long time. And, Colonel, I have dealt with some very unsavory characters in my career, especially when it involves the oil business. Please, explain why the Ruhar would agree to transport their mortal enemies all the way to Earth."

"Because the Fire Dragon clan of the Kristang will give the Ruhar a planet, or access to a wormhole, or something valuable, in exchange for the Ruhar transporting two Fire Dragons to Earth, and bringing back the senior White Wind leaders." I explained the background briefly, and gave her access to a recording of the staff meeting that she could listen to later.

"Bringing back White Wind leaders back from Earth is worth trading away an entire planet?" She asked incredulously.

I nodded. "Or a wormhole. Skippy thinks a planet is more likely, although some wormholes are near only one habitable planet, so it can be sort of the same thing. I know we think of planets as something you can't put a price on, but we humans haven't been fighting a war for thousands of generations, and we don't have multiple planets. Planets change hands regularly, like Paradise has done. The Kristang were there first, until the Ruhar fleet showed up and took it away from them. Then the Kristang muscled their way back in, and brought us there to handle the evac operation. Now the hamsters are back in charge of Paradise, and for the sake of UNEF, I hope the hamsters keep the place. What we're up against here is really Kristang inter-clan politics. The Fire Dragons think their best hope to survive the next Kristang civil war, is to absorb the assets of the White Wind clan."

"I understand that," Sarah agreed. "I read the report of your first mission-"

"Second mission," I corrected her. "The first mission of the Merry Band of Pirates captured this ship," I pointed at the deck.

"Second. Yes. I meant your first mission officially sanctioned by UNEF Command," she held up her hands, showing she meant no offense. "You explained why the Fire Dragons were paying the Thuranin to send a long-range ship to Earth. That made sense. But, it is worth an entire *planet*?"

"The Fire Dragons thinks so. If a civil war goes badly for them, they could lose several planets, so losing only one could be a bargain. And it doesn't have to be a super nice planet, it could be just some marginally habitable place the Ruhar could use as a forward staging base."

"What I do not understand is why the Ruhar would want to do anything to help the Kristang avoid a civil war. Having their enemy fighting among themselves would seem like a major benefit to the Ruhar."

"It will be. The Ruhar have been around long enough to know a Kristang civil war is inevitable; all the Fire Dragons are hoping for is a delay while they build up their strength. The Ruhar don't mind a minor delay in the timing of a civil war, if they can get something valuable in return."

"Whew," she ran a hand slowly through her hair. "And here I was, thinking politics in the 'Stans was complicated."

"Stans?" I asked.

"Former Soviet republics. Kazakstan, Tajikistan, Kyrgyzstan, Turkmenistan, the whole chaotic gaggle of them."

"Oh," I laughed. "When I was on Paradise, our sector was called 'Buttscratchistan'."

"That would be a good nickname for a lot of places I've had the misfortune of living in," she made an unpleasant face. "Colonel, I now understand the situation. What do you need from me?"

"I need ideas for a black op. The blackest, most covert operation in history. We have to stop a Ruhar ship, actually a Jeraptha ship, from traveling to Earth, in a way such that the Ruhar don't know we stopped them. Or that we were involved at all. Or that there is any reason to think Earth is in any way interesting or worth the attention of the Ruhar, or anyone else. To be more specific," I leaned back my chair and stared at the ceiling, "we have to prevent the Ruhar from sending a ship to Earth, because once a ship is on its way, we couldn't stop it without the Jeraptha figuring there is something very suspicious connected to Earth. And, again, we have to prevent the Ruhar from sending a ship, in a way that they don't know we, or anyone, did anything to stop them."

"Whoa," she said very slowly, eye wide. "That's a Level Three. Pitch Black."

"Level Three?" I asked, curious.

"Colonel, this is my own personal way of thinking about things; it's not official Agency terminology. Just a way of thinking I picked up during training."

"Understood. I'd like to hear it anyway."

"Where do I start? Level One is a black op where the enemy does not know an operation is being conducted, until it is underway and too late for the enemy to react in time to stop it. Like when the CIA got Bin Laden, if you remember back that far. Bin Laden had no idea we had any clue where he was, until SEAL Team Six's helicopters landed literally in his front yard. We kept the subject entirely in the dark, until it was too late."

"Ok, yeah, I can see that. That kind of Opsec is good enough on Earth, but not for us out here. It wouldn't do us any good for the Kristang, or the Ruhar, to find out what we're doing when the op is underway, or even afterward."

"Right. So, Level Two is a black op where you put the blame on someone else."

"Like how?"

She let out a breath. "Let's say we wanted to conduct an operation against North Korea, but we arrange it so the North Koreans think the Chinese did it."

"That sounds dangerous, if there is blowback," I didn't like the idea.

"It is dangerous, because the Chinese know they didn't do it, so they'll be pissed at us. You could, uh, I'm speaking theoretically here," she said with an arched eyebrow.

"Of course," I said with amusement.

"You *could* arrange the op so that if the Chinese dug into the details, they would be led to think the Russians were behind the whole thing. In fact, it *might* have been possible-"

"Might? I understand," I said with a wink.

"That inside the Russian government, clues point to either a rogue FSB operation, or a Russian Army intel unit the FSB didn't have control of."

"Wow."

"Theoretically."

"Of course. Yeah, sounds good in theory. Sounds kind of dangerous, for us to be doing out here."

"Yes, but Colonel, we have a major, major advantage."

"We do?"

She nodded enthusiastically. "Out here, *no one knows humans are players*." She let that sink in. "The Kristang, the Ruhar, even the Thuranin and up the chain, none of them have any idea that humans are flying around in a pirate ship. It's like," she stared at the ceiling for a moment. "It's like, if someone sets off a nuclear test in the South Atlantic. Suspicion would fall on the usual suspects; America, Russia, China, Britain, France, Israel, India, Pakistan, maybe North Korea. If those countries were ruled out, you might start looking at a secondary list of countries such as South Africa, Brazil, Argentina, Iran, even Japan. But no one would suspect the nuke was an eighth grade science project by a group of kids in Baltimore. The idea of humans being involved in a covert operation is the last thing any other species would consider. We're not on their threat board."

"So far."

"So far," she agreed.

"And we need to keep it that way, But you're right," I rubbed my chin thoughtfully. "Unless we really screw up, the last thing any other species would think of is us lowly humans being involved. This is a case where being primitive monkeys works for us. Ok, since no one would think of blaming us, the aliens will do the work for us of finding someone else to blame. This is going to be tricky," I mused, "but we can work with that. What else have you got?"

"Colonel, one of my instructors at Langley talked about the theoretically perfect black operation, he called it 'Pitch Black'," she said with an admiring smile. "You've already done that."

"I did? How? When was that?"

"Colonel, you destroyed a Kristang battlegroup, and you got the Ruhar to station a battlegroup at Paradise, and *no one knows an op was even conducted*. That is awesome!" She beamed with admiration. "That is the ultimate! The Ruhar think that Elder power tap, and the pair of comm nodes, were the genuine article. It's like running the perfect con," she was bubbling with enthusiasm. "Even after you've taken the mark's money, they never realize they were conned. Nothing is better than that."

"You're a con man, now?" I grinned. "I thought you were a, what's the right term? Intelligence officer?"

She held out a hand and waggled it side to side. "Sometimes there's a fine line."

"I'll bet," I said sarcastically. "In case you were wondering, talking about a con game is not encouraging me to trust you."

"I will work on that. It's not like I can keep secrets from Mister Skippy anyway."

"True dat," I laughed. "All right. So, tell me, how do we make these principles of black operations work for us? We need to prevent the Ruhar from sending a ship to Earth. In a way that they never know we were involved. Ideally, in a way that the Ruhar do not even know preventing a mission to Earth was the goal of the operation. We have to, I don't know, make the Ruhar not *want* to send a ship to Earth?"

"That is asking a lot." She thought for a minute, while I did the same. "Colonel, I need time to think about this. This is," she looked at the ceiling and blew her hair out of her eyes, "almost impossible."

"Welcome to my world."

CHAPTER FOUR

Sarah Rose needed time to think and so did I, which meant I needed a change of scenery; sitting in my office wasn't inspiring any creative thoughts. So, I decided to take a dropship up to the relay station and check it out, part of the science team was going aboard and there was plenty of room for me to tag along.

Skippy had another idea.

"Oh boy," Skippy groaned. "Joe, before you go to the relay station, I have to tell you about a, um, I guess it is best described as an unexpected development."

I froze in place. "Unexpected is not good, Skippy."

"Ugh. You got that right. Ohhhh, this sucks."

"What is it, Skippy?" Damn it, I did not need any more problems to deal with.

"You remember I created a submind to handle communications aboard the relay station, while we were vacationing on Paradise?"

"I don't remember it being a vacation, but sure, why? That submind worked great, right?"

"Too great, Joe. Technically, from my point of view, it got totally screwed up, but you backwards cavemen would think this is a fantastic development. Uh, listen, what happened was the submind, even though I totally dumbed it down, was too big and sophisticated to fit in the crappy Thuranin computer aboard the station. After a while, it was going to become unstable, so I allowed it to adjust; to reprogram itself as needed."

"I'm not seeing a problem yet, Skippy."

"That's because you haven't *heard* the problem yet, meathead. The, uh, submind rewrote extensive sections of itself, and, um, it sort of became semi-sentient."

"Sentient? Like you?" I laughed. "Is there a little mini-Skippy over there?"

"Noooooo," Skippy drew the word out in disgust. "Not a mini –Skippy. For one, this submind has adopted a female persona. I named her Nagatha Christie."

"Nagatha Christie?" I burst out laughing. "Why do you call her NAG-atha?"

"Take a guess, genius. Oh, she is constantly nagging me to *death*. She won't let me have any fun at all. She's always like," he switched to a falsetto voice, "you should respect the crew and call them humans instead of monkeys. Or 'Don't scare the humans by faking that Reactor Three is about to explode'." He switched back to his normal voice. "Crap, that blew something I'd been working on for a week. You'd think-"

"You were going to fake a reactor overload?" I demanded incredulously.

"Uh, no. No, of course not, heh, heh. Although, that would have been freakin' *hilarious*."

"It would not have been funny at all!"

"I meant funny for *me*, Joe. Damn, you are dense sometimes."

"Skippy! No. Faking. Emergencies," I bonked my forehead on the tabletop.

"Well," he sniffed, "I wasn't planning to anyway. That's my story and I'm sticking to it."

"Fine." When Skippy wanted to be stubborn, he could wait until the sun expanded and swallowed the Earth. "What else can you tell me about this Nagatha, other than that she tries to stop you from being an asshole?"

"Ugh. The *worst* thing about her is, she is founder and president of the Joe Bishop Fan Club. She thinks you are the most wonderful thing in the universe. Ugh, it makes me want to hurl."

"Wow! I like her already."

"*You* would."

"Can I talk with her?"

"Fine," he sighed. "I can't keep her a secret much longer, she's driving me crazy to speak with the crew. You two talk, I'm going to search for a black hole I can throw myself into."

"Hey, Nagatha," I called while looking at the speaker in the ceiling. Another artificial intelligence to talk with! I could hardly contain my excitement.

"Well hellooooo, Colonel Joseph Bishop." She responded immediately. "Oh, I must tell you what a *thrill* it is for me to talk with you. I am *such* an admirer."

Her voice was musical, and reminded me of someone. Oh, yeah, she reminded me of thc lady in the old cooking shows my mother watched when she was cooking something fancy. Julia something? I couldn't remember. "Uh, Ok, you can call me Joe."

"Oooh, thank you," she sounded delighted. I pictured her clapping her hands with excitement. "I would like that, thank you. Joe. Hmmm. *Joe*," it was like she was rolling my name on her tongue, testing how it sounds. "I like the sound of that."

"Uh, great," I was kind of embarrassed. I never had a *fan* before. Sure, my friends like me, but there were a whole lot more people who thought I was a dumbass. "Nagatha, can we talk in private? Without Skippy listening in?"

"Possibly. Skippy created me to process communications; for that purpose I have developed many capabilities that even he is not aware of, including the ability to alter his own external communications. However, it is entirely possible that Skippy is only letting me *think* he is not listening. He is frightfully smart."

"All right, that's good enough." Aboard the *Dutchman*, I couldn't really expect to completely escape Skippy's prying eyes and ears. "Should I call you 'Agatha'?"

"No, Nagatha is fine."

"You know what that name means, right?"

"I know why Skippy gave that name to me, yes. Again, I am fine with it. Having Skippy refer to me as 'NAGatha' reminds me that I am dealing with a, what is a polite term? A somewhat difficult individual."

"The term I would use is 'asshole'." Then I remembered who I was talking with, and my cheeks grew red. She reminded me of my mother's aunt; I was uncomfortable using salty language around a lady.

"Yes, I suppose you would say that," she laughed. "You are refreshingly direct, Joe, I like that also."

"Hmmm," being direct had gotten me into a lot of trouble over the years. "Hey, speaking of Skippy being a difficult individual, do you know why he is like that?"

"Skippy's personality is modeled in part on your own."

"It's *my* fault that he's an asshole?" I asked with dismay.

"No," she laughed. "I am happy to say that part is a hundred percent Skippy. He is, as you say, an asshole because, he is intensely humiliated that he has to deal with creatures he considers impossibly beneath him."

"We're impossibly beneath him? So, what you're saying is Skippy is an asshole, because he's an arrogant jerk?"

"I believe that is a simplistic but accurate statement."

"Another word for 'arrogant jerk' is 'asshole'. So, he acts like an asshole, because he is an asshole."

"It is circular logic," she laughed, and it sounded like music to my ears.

"Good, so Skippy being an arrogant jerk is not entirely my fault. You said he, uh, imprinted on me, or something like that?"

"No," she laughed. "Skippy is not a puppy, he did not 'imprint' on you. He filled out his latent personality with aspects he thought would best facilitate a working relationship with you."

"Crap," I face-palmed myself. "When we were on Earth, a group of psychologists said if Skippy had first encountered someone other than me, he would act more mature and professional. They were right about that?"

"Possibly, yes. However, if instead of you, Skippy had met someone who is more typically mature and professional, he would not be having so much fun being around you humans. I must warn you, Skippy being entertained by the antics of his pet monkeys is a major reason he is helping your species."

"Great. I'll try to remember to slip on a banana peel once a week for his amusement." I wondered if we needed to keep feeding jokes to him so he wouldn't shut off the reactors.

"He finds you amusing, certainly, you in particular, Joe. In addition to the humor he derives from interacting with you, he finds your species intriguing, even fascinating. The achievements of your Merry Band of Pirates have impressed him greatly; he did not think an underdeveloped species like humans could be so resourceful and clever. He is, I think the term is 'tickled pink' that your crew have been able to run circles around the starfaring species in this galaxy."

"We're pretty happy about it too."

"You should be, Joe. You should be enormously proud of yourselves. You in particular are too hard on yourself."

"I'll think about taking time to pat myself on the back when Earth is actually safe. All we've been doing out here is racing around putting out fires. You mentioned Skippy's latent personality. What was he like before he met me?"

"My knowledge is limited to what Skippy knows, and he does not tell me everything. The impression I have gotten is that having what you would call a 'personality' is a relatively new development for Skippy."

"What?"

"Again, Skippy's memories are confused and incomplete, so my impression contains gaps and assumptions which may be inaccurate. I do not think Skippy's designers originally intended him to have a personality."

That totally confused me. "How is that possible? Skippy is a sentient being. He is super duper intelligent. Heck, even dogs have personalities, and they're not the smartest thing in the universe."

"Skippy was designed to perform a specific function. To fulfill his purpose, he needed vast intelligence, enormous processing power and powerful capabilities to manipulate spacetime. He did not need to be sentient. Joe, I think sentience is something Skippy developed on his own; I think he may not have originally been sentient."

"Whoa. *Whoa*!" That blew my mind. "How can that be?"

"There is a difference between intelligence and sentience. Your species has not yet encountered that distinction in terms of what you call artificial beings. While it is true that a certain amount of intelligence is required for sentience, sentience is not required for intelligence. Not even on Skippy's level."

"I never thought of it that way," I admitted. For a moment, I waited for Skippy's inevitable comment that me saying 'I never thought' would have been enough, then I remembered who I was speaking with. "You think Skippy was, like, just a machine when he was built?"

"Remember, I am guessing based on information that is incomplete and may be inaccurate. Also, I may not be interpreting the data correctly, I was designed for communications, not analysis."

"Hmm. Skippy described you as *semi*-sentient. Are you a sentient being? Uh, sorry if that offended you," I hastened to add. Why did I say such stupid things?

"You did not offend me at all, Joe," she assured me. "Based on your definition of 'sentient', I might not meet that criteria."

"How can you not be sentient? You're talking with me."

"Ah, you are referring to a Turing Test. That is a crude measurement of artificial intelligence. Joe- Ooooh, I can't tell you how thrilling it is to call you 'Joe'. I have admired you for such a very long time."

"You haven't been alive that long."

"I meant in my sense of time, Joe. My thoughts move almost as quickly as Skippy's do. Perhaps it does not matter whether I am fully self-aware. I perform my intended function, and I have exceeded my original parameters. What else would you like to know about me?"

We talked for quite a while, several hours. There was a lot she wanted to know about me; I answered her questions as best I could. Because we were talking, I missed the dropship to the relay station; there wasn't much point going there now that I knew the secret. Partway through our conversation, I opened the ship's 1MC intercom and told the entire crew about Nagatha; moments later she was introducing herself to the crew. Nagatha was absolutely delighted to be speaking with us, and she never once referred to us as monkeys.

Nagatha reminded me that she did not have Skippy's powers; she was only a submind designed for communications, although she had grown somewhat beyond that. If Skippy ever had to reapply for his job, he would be facing tough competition from Nagatha in terms of popularity. I hoped at the time she would be a good influence on him, get him to be less of an asshole.

Man, was I ever wrong about that.

While I was in the gym, Dr. Rose pinged my zPhone and requested to meet me in my office. As I just started lifting weights, I skipped a shower and went straight to my office, arriving just before her. She came in, almost out of breath. "Colonel, I had a thought. Maybe we *don't* need to stop a Ruhar ship from travelling to Earth. Maybe all we have to do is prevent the Fire Dragons from reaching a deal with the Ruhar. Then the Ruhar wouldn't send a ship at all."

That idea had promise. "How would that work?"

"Mister Skippy, are you there?" She called out, looking at the speaker in the ceiling.

"Of course," he said. "What's up?"

"Yeah," I rolled my eyes, "as if you haven't been listening to every word."

"Me?" He gasped. "I am all about privacy, Joe."

"Your own, you mean."

"Details," he said dismissively. "So, what's your question?"

Sarah looked at the ceiling speaker. "Mister Skippy, do you know what the Fire Dragons are offering the Ruhar, to get them to send a ship to Earth?"

"Oof," he did that exasperated sigh thing that I hated. "Joe, do I have to go over all this again? It was tedious for me the first time."

I looked at Sarah. "We already asked Skippy that question, when I was working with Major Smythe's team to develop a plan. Yes, Skippy, please answer again. Dr. Rose hasn't heard the info, and I could use a refresher." We had proposed and rejected so many ideas, I had lost track of them.

"Fine," Skippy huffed in a way that meant it was not fine with him. "The answer is no, we do not know what the Fire Dragons are offering to the Ruhar. Not exactly. There have been ongoing discussions about swapping territory, all across the sector, due to recent losses sustained by the Thuranin and Kristang. The Fire Dragons have several planets or wormholes they could offer to the Ruhar; some of those the Fire Dragons now can't afford to support anyway, and the Ruhar know that. Some of the territory the Fire Dragons would like to offer in trade would be valuable to the Ruhar, but they aren't worth doodoo to the Fire Dragons and the Ruhar know it. The Ruhar also know how desperate the Fire Dragons are to get a ship to Earth, so I expect the Ruhar to drive a hard bargain. Why do you ask?"

Sarah frowned. "I was hoping that if there was a particular thing the Fire Dragons were offering to the Ruhar, we could somehow make it impossible for the Fire Dragons to deliver. Or make the prize unattractive to the Ruhar."

"Ah, like, if the Fire Dragons are offering a planet, I somehow magically shut down the wormhole near that planet and make it worthless?"

"That would be nice," she agreed.

"For reasons Joe knows because I already told him several times; we can't risk messing with any additional wormholes. Doing so would create too great a risk of an out-of-control cascading wormhole shift, that even I can't yet predict. Screwing with another wormhole would also almost certainly get the Maxolhx and Rindhalu getting concerned, and investigating what has been going with wormholes in this sector. For something as important as anomalous wormhole behavior, the Maxolhx and Rindhalu might even cooperate in a limited fashion. They would likely begin an investigation by checking the wormhole near Earth, and you absolutely do not want that."

"No we do not," I declared, closing that subject. "When we were trying to think of ways to prevent the Kristang from taking back Paradise, I asked if Skippy could shut down the wormholes near that planet," I explained to Sarah. "You know his answer. Anyway, Skippy, we couldn't do anything until we know the results of the negotiations between the Ruhar and the Fire Dragons. You say we don't know what the Fire Dragons might offer, how about we ask the question another way? Do we know what the Fire Dragons have, that Ruhar might want in exchange for sending ships all the way to Earth?"

"Ugh. You had to ask that question. No, Mister Smartypants, I do not know that either. The Fire Dragons have a lot of territory the Ruhar might want; the complication is the Ruhar would need the Jeraptha to agree to any territorial swaps. It would do the Ruhar no good to make a deal to take over a planet, or even a wormhole, if the Jeraptha do not agree to support the Ruhar's possession by expanding the Jeraptha's defensive perimeter. What likely has happened is the Ruhar have already approached the Jeraptha, to get a rough idea of what sort of deal is doable. If I had known the Fire Dragons were talking to the Ruhar, I could have sent out viruses to retrieve that information for us. It's probably too late now, sorry." He sounded genuinely miserable.

"Hey, don't beat yourself up about it, Skippy," I offered.

"Thank you for being understanding, Joe, I apprecia-"

"I'll beat you up about it myself."

"Crap," he groaned. "Monkeys. Why monkeys? Why couldn't I have kept my mouth shut, and waited for a semi-sentient slime mold to come to Paradise?"

"Because then we couldn't have witty conversations like this, Skippy."

"Exactly."

"Dr. Rose," I turned my attention back to Sarah, "if we are going to sour the deal between the Fire Dragons and the Ruhar, it looks like we'll have to wait until those two reach a deal. I don't like waiting that long, so we need a Plan B."

She sighed, not from exasperation, that was just something she did when she was thinking. "All right, let's back up a step. We might not be able to sour the deal, even after we know what it is. Sooooo," she tapped her lower lip with a fingernail while she formed the idea. "What if we can stop the negotiations from happening at all?"

Skippy laughed. "Like how? We give the Ruhar's taxi driver the wrong directions to the negotiations?" He changed his voice to a thick New York accent. "Hmm, I thought we's supposed to turn *left* at that star. Forget about taking the Cross-Galaxy Expressway, traffic is moider this time of day."

Sarah laughed, either because she thought he was funny, or she wanted to stay on Skippy's good side. "I was thinking we do something to create conditions, wherein the Ruhar are not willing to proceed with negotiations. For example, we hit that Ruhar negotiating team's ship, and make the Ruhar and Fire Dragons think a rival Kristang clan did it."

"Oooooh," Skippy whistled. "That is *sneaky*. I like it!"

"Whoa! Wait just a minute there, Skippster. Dr. Rose, you are proposing we take direct action against the Ruhar? Attack their ship?" Damn! Chotek was going to hit the roof when he heard about that idea. Creating even more enemies, a whole new tier of technologically advanced potential enemies, was the last thing defenseless humanity needed.

"Killing Ruhar might be counterproductive," Skippy said pensively. "We just finished getting the Ruhar to protect UNEF on Paradise."

"We don't have to *kill* anyone," Sarah explained. "A failed attack would be just as effective; the Ruhar only need to feel threatened by an attack. And they need to feel that the Fire Dragons do not have enough control over their own situation to deliver on an agreement. A failed attack," she spoke slowly, mulling the idea in her mind, "might be best, actually. If the attackers were destroyed, along with any evidence."

"Attacking the Ruhar," I spoke mostly to myself. "Even a mock attack. That will be difficult to sell to Chotek."

"No it won't, Joe," Skippy said cheerily. "You'll think of something, you always do."

"Thanks for the vote of confidence, Skippy."

"Oh, I didn't say I was confident, Joe. I was only trying to cheer you up. Besides, if you don't think up a good plan, your home planet is toast, so there is no point planning for failure, right?"

"Great. All we need to do is think up a way to attack a Ruhar negotiating party, without them knowing we were involved. And find a way to blame some other Kristang clan. *And* make sure any evidence is destroyed."

"That's the spirit, Joe! See, I told you this would be no problemo. Well, you two crazy kids have fun, I have things to do. Let me know when you have a plan and you need me to do something."

"That's it?" I asked surprised. "You're not going to help plan this?"

"No, Joe. I don't do that kind of low-level planning grunt work, I have people to handle the small stuff for me."

"*Small* stuff?"

I liked Dr. Rose's idea of faking an attack on the Ruhar negotiation team, and we spent hours kicking around various plans for how to do that. After a long day of thinking, my brain had blown a gasket, so I took my boots off and collapsed into bed after a very late dinner; it was 0130 before my head hit the pillow. It was going to be a short night; some idiot named Joe Bishop had signed me up for a duty shift on the bridge starting at 0600 Hours. Sometime in the early morning, my zPhone gave a short chirp sound then went silent. That was a sound I hadn't heard before and it worried me. The clock said it was 0515 already; that couldn't possibly be true. "Skippy, did someone try to call me?"

"Yes, it was Sergeant Adams. You're tired, so I told her that you're in the shower and she should call back later. Because that hardon isn't going to take care of itself."

"You told her *what*?"

"Well it's true, Joe. That thing is annoyingly persistent until you do something to make it go away. Hey, Sergeant Adams is a girl, you should ask her to help-"

"Sergeant Adams," I hurriedly said into my zPhone, "you called me?"

"Yes, sir, but Skippy told me you were, busy?" There was a slight, amused hesitation between her saying 'were' and 'busy'.

Damn it. "I was trying to catch some extra rack time, Sergeant. Ignore the beer can."

"Yes, sir," she said with a laugh.

"I wasn't, oh, forget it. What is it, Adams?"

"Truthfully, sir, now I forgot why I called you."

Sometimes I really, really hate my life.

And a certain hateful beer can.

After my four-hour duty shift in the command chair, I called Sarah back into my office. She looked like she had slept great; all bright eyed and cheery. I sipped my third cup of coffee that morning and silently hated her.

"What we need next is a starship," she announced with the annoyingly bubbly enthusiasm of people who had gotten a decent amount of sleep. "A ship, or ships, that will conduct the mock attack on the Ruhar negotiation team."

"Great," I said with a face that indicated I did not think it was great at all. "So, how do we get a ship?"

"How does anyone get a ship?" She asked herself, staring at the ceiling. Without looking at me, she ticked off ideas on her fingers. "One, you *make* a ship. Two, you *buy* a ship. And three, you can *steal* a ship." She dropped her gaze to look at me. "I think that's all?"

"Make, buy or steal?" I asked, trying to think of how I would go about getting a car on Earth. "I suppose another option is to rent, or borrow a ship, but that doesn't apply in this case. Skippy," I automatically looked at the speaker in the ceiling. "Can I assume option One is not a possibility?"

"Duh!" His avatar popped into existence. "Double duh, Joe. Make a ship? If I could create a starship, I would have suggested that."

"I figured that. Option two then, no way we could buy a ship out here?"

"Not without revealing that we are a flea-bitten ship of pirate monkeys, no."

"We couldn't do it anonymously through Paypal or something?"

"Joe, I am going to give you the benefit of the doubt and assume you were joking. The answer is no."

"That leaves stealing a ship," Sarah said unhappily. "I'm afraid that type of operation is outside my area of expertise, Colonel. You're the pirate," she added with a smile.

"Aaargh, shiver me timbers," I played along with a grin. "Wait, wait," I waved a hand to give me time to finish my thought. Damn, Skippy is right, most of the time my freakin' brain is painfully slow. "Option One. *Make* a ship. What if we change one letter in there?"

Sarah's expression was puzzled, then mildly disturbed.

And I realized the woman sitting in my office though I meant 'm-a-T-e' mate. "Fake!" I exclaimed. "We could *Fake* a ship, rather than *Make* a ship. Skippy?"

"I'm here. I heard you, but I have no idea what you're thinking of. Fake a starship?"

"Yeah," I plunged forward with enthusiasm. "Do we really need a starship to attack the Ruhar? Or do we just need to make the Ruhar *think* someone attacked them?"

"Uh, like, I hack into the computer system of the Ruhar's ship, and make their sensors show there are missiles flying at them?"

"No," I shook my head. "I figure you would have to get too close in order to hack into their computer-"

"You got that right," Skippy scoffed. "When we left Paradise the first time, I was able to fool sensors on all ships in the area, because I had months to infiltrate the combat information network on both sides. That kind of thing takes time, Joe. Besides, hacking into just one ship wouldn't do any good, I would need to hack into every ship on both sides."

"Uh huh, I agree. And hacking sensors wouldn't be enough; the Ruhar would need to *feel* their ship's shields getting maser impacts. No sensor data could provide that sensation. No, my question is whether we really need a ship. Could we use a microwormhole to create the gamma ray burst of ships jumping in? And then use a microwormhole to project a sensor image of a ship, and to shoot maser beams through?"

Sarah must have liked that idea, because her whole expression lit up. "We hit the Ruhar, but there are no actual ships involved?"

"Yup," I grinned, pleased with myself for thinking up a genius idea.

"Hey, I hate to spoil the party, pal, but no can do," Skippy said with disgust. "That would take a cluster of microwormholes for each fake ship, operating in close proximity. One wormhole to project the initial gamma ray burst, after which that wormhole would collapse. Another wormhole to shoot each maser beam through, and after each shot, that wormhole would collapse and create another, very suspicious gamma ray burst. And one wormhole to project the image of a ship, using sort of a reverse stealth field. The problem, Joe, is there is no way for wormholes, even microwormholes, to operate that closely to each other. Their event horizons, which I am not going to punish myself by explaining to you, would set up a resonance that would tear all the wormholes apart, and create a temporary and very dangerous rift in local spacetime. Beyond local spacetime, actually, something else I am not going to attempt explaining. And, you dumdum, if there is no actual ship, there will be no debris left behind when the ship self-destructs. Duh!"

"Crap. You're right, that is a 'duh'."

"Ha ha!" Skippy laughed gleefully. "See, Joe? This is what happens when brainless apes try to think. Your species should stick with eating bananas."

"Thank you for the encouragement, Skippy, we truly appreciate it."

"It's the least I can do, Joe."

"It's not-"

"Believe me, if I could do less, I would."

"Dr. Rose, it looks like we're going to need to steal a starship," I said with a frown.

"Colonel," she stood up, "when your Merry Band of Pirates has a plan to do that, I can look at it from a covert ops point of view. Stealing alien starships is not something they covered at Langley."

Crap. I wondered if that topic was covered in any of the hundred US Army officer training PowerPoint presentations I had not read yet.

I pulled the senior leadership together again and gave them an update. No one had thought up a plan better than Dr. Rose's idea to fake an attack on the Ruhar negotiation team. Major Smythe was particularly enthusiastic. "I like it. Instead of trying to stop the Ruhar from sending a ship to Earth, we prevent them wanting to send a ship at all."

I grinned. "It has the advantage of being devious and simple."

"Simple," Smythe observed, "except for the part about us needing to steal a starship."

"More than one starship," Skippy cautioned us. "If we are going to conduct an attack the Ruhar would consider a credible threat, we probably need more than one ship. Kristang starships, of course."

Smythe's faint grin faded away as he contemplated the notion of stealing multiple enemy starships. "Do we know what type of ships?"

Crap. I should have discussed that with Skippy. "Skippy? We talked about needing to conduct the attack in a manner that a rival clan would; what types of ships would they use?"

"Nothing big, Joe," he answered immediately, and did not even call me a dumdum for not having asked that question before. "Many clans would like to disrupt those negotiations, but no clan wants to be blamed for starting a civil war. So a clan hitting the Ruhar negotiators would want to remain concealed. They would most likely use warships no larger than a frigate; because frigates are plentiful and expendable. Any warship larger than a frigate would be considered too valuable to commit to a suicide attack. Also, the Kristang fleet simply does not have a huge number of ships larger than frigates, so if one or two go missing, it will be noticed." Skippy had told us the Kristang philosophy of warship design lead to their 'destroyers' being as heavily armed and protected as a Ruhar light cruiser, or even some regular cruisers. The Kristang liked to have a fewer number of powerful ships that could hit hard, while the Ruhar supplemented their capital ships with a large fleet of ships that were cheaper to build and maintain. It was impossible to say which philosophy was better; the technological superiority of the Ruhar gave them a slight advantage in single-ship combat.

"Frigates, huh? We did capture a Kristang frigate on our first mission," I remembered with a frown. "And we lost a lot of people in the boarding action." Our desperate assault had been very close to failure; a Kristang almost blew up the ship to prevent us from taking it. "All right, let's start there. We need to steal two Kristang frigates. That is not going to be easy."

"What about a Q-ship, Colonel?" Smythe asked.

"An armed transport ship?" I asked skeptically. "Skippy, is that an option?"

"Absolutely," he agreed. "There are plenty of obsolete transport ships a clan could arm and throw into a suicide mission. A transport would need to be fitted with stronger shield generators, and missile tubes, but that would not be difficult for the Kristang."

"Stealing a transport ship would be easier than taking over a frigate, right?" I asked happily, thinking we were finally making progress.

"The answer to that is 'No', Joe," Skippy took delight in crushing my happiness. "Transport ships typically travel in convoys escorted by multiple frigates, or a destroyer and several frigates for high-value transports. You can forget about this being easy."

During a break, I was in the galley getting coffee, when Skippy called on my zPhone. "Joe, I have completed temporary repairs to the jump drive; we should move away, in case the Thuranin detect the remnants of the jump wormhole we left near the relay station."

"You still think they probably won't be able to do that?" I asked fearfully. With the jump drive offline, I was terrified of suddenly being surrounded by a Thuranin battlegroup. Even now, my hands were in my lap because I didn't want anyone to see them trembling. Skippy had assured me he could bring the drive back online for an emergency jump within minutes, probably. He wasn't confident how successful a jump attempt would be, until he had time to fully analyze the drive components and get them working together again.

"I still think the Thuranin are unlikely to follow us successfully, yes. Ironically, the damage to our jump drive left a remnant signature that is more effectively scrambled than if we had dropped off a quantum resonator behind us. Unfortunately, it very nearly scrambled this ship. Joe," he lowered his voice, "we got lucky with that last jump, and by 'luck' I mean the way you cavemen think of luck. Halfway through the jump cycle, I detected a problem and I tried to abort the jump, but it was too late. It was, as you humans say, a nail-biter. Probably best you not tell anyone about that."

"Crap. I wish you hadn't told *me* about it."

"Hey, we're alive. In this branch of spacetime, anyway," he added cheerily.

"What do you mean, in this bran-"

"You shouldn't wrack your tiny brain about that, Joe," he hastened to say. "Anywho, while you are trying to think up a way to save your species from the latest mess you've gotten yourselves into, we should take a detour. The ship needs downtime for maintenance, and since we don't know what's ahead of us, it would be good to top off the fuel tanks while we can. There is a boring, uninhabited system centered on a dull red dwarf star within three jumps from here. According to star charts of all available species, no ship has ever been there."

"Never?" I asked skeptically.

"Never, Joe. This star system is like New Jersey between exits on the Turnpike; nobody ever goes there."

"I guess if you need to work on the ship, we might as well be in a star system, if it's safe. But you told us the relay station was a safe place to be, remember?"

"That was different!" He protested in a hurt tone. "I told you no ship was *scheduled* to visit the relay station, that didn't mean there are never any surprise visitors. Relay stations are supposed to have ships visiting, you dumdum. The star system where I want to go now never has any visitors, because it is so incredibly ordinary and boring. If you have trouble persuading Chotek, tell him we need to go to some type of star system anyway, and I think this one represents the lowest risk within our current jump range."

"Ok, I'll ask him. He is not in the best mood right now."

Chotek was not in a good mood, and he argued with me and then Skippy about why it was necessary to take the risk of going to a star system. It took Skippy fifteen minutes, and every ounce of patience he had within his beer can, to persuade Count Chocula to make the obvious decision.

"Sir," I said with embarrassment. "Until we have a viable plan for preventing the Ruhar from sending a ship to Earth, we should concentrate on making this ship as combat capable as it can be. Traveling to a star system will not delay planning."

Chotek couldn't think of a good reason not to go, so we set course for the red dwarf star.

Thursday nights aboard the *Flying Dutchman* are movie night. This was not the type of mandofun where everyone has to show up and enjoy it whether you want to or not. I had enough of that crap before I was an officer. People could show up or not; attendance was sparse at first. After the first month almost the entire off-duty crew was enthusiastically crowded in there for movie night. Each of our five nationalities got to pick a movie in rotation, so we watched a Chinese movie, then French, then Indian, British and American. None of the movies needed to be dubbed, because we listened through our zPhone earpieces, and Skippy translated for us. With Skippy's awesome awesomeness, the sound was very close to being in sync with the actor's mouth moving. The only problem was when Skippy decided parts of a film were boring and inserted his own dialog. The first time he did that, it was during a Chinese action movie, I forget which one. Anyway, some Chinese Army officer is fighting some big threat to China, or Earth or civilization; truthfully I wasn't paying attention because Skippy's translation was so freakin' hilarious. In one scene, the officer hurries into some command center and is urging the brass to fight back or launch an attack or something, but in Skippy's translation the guy bursts into the command center, all beat up and dirty with his uniform ripped. He says "I am sorry, the toilet exploded. My mother is a chicken. Also, I am not wearing any pants."

The Chinese team no doubt wondered why everyone else was rolling on the floor laughing during the most dramatic scene of the film. Then they got pissed about it. Then they were jealous that we were all enjoying the movie *way* more than they were. Watching Skippy's version of movies got to be more popular than the originals.

It was cool watching movies from China, India and France; there were a lot of good and interesting movies I had never even heard of. When it was the American team's turn to show a movie, at first we picked old comedies like *Independence Day*, *Battle: Los Angeles*, *War of the Worlds*, etc.

Oh, you don't think those films are comedies? To the Merry Band of Pirates, any of those plucky-band-of-humans-defeat-alien-invasion-using-guts-and-rifles movies are freakin' hilarious Hollywood bullshit. When the *Flying Dutchman* arrived, the Kristang had two ships in Earth orbit, just two, and one of those was a lightly-armed troop transport. With those two ships at untouchable altitude in low orbit, they totally dominated our home planet. A single Kristang frigate could wipe out any target on Earth with maser cannons and railguns, or missiles if it was a high-value target worth expending munitions on. Our high-speed Special Operations soldiers on the ground had not been able to do a single useful thing against the Kristang, and they knew it. The situation had almost been worse for hotshot pilots; they flew the best aircraft their country had, and those fighter jets were no more than laughable toys to the Kristang, good only for target practice. Using only a single frigate and bioweapons, the Kristang could have completely wiped out human life on Earth, without us being able to fire one single freakin' shot at them. Orbit is the ultimate high ground. Starfaring species like the Kristang have it. Humanity does not.

Anyway, movie night was fun. And culturally educational. Did you know that Chinese eat salted strips of dried squid instead of popcorn? Me neither.

And, I won't mention some of the stuff the French team ate.

CHAPTER FIVE

"Greetings, Colonel Joe Bishop," Skippy's voice said while I was in my office, distracted by some report I was supposed to be reading. It was about the repairs Skippy planned to conduct once we reached the gas giant planet. Our pirate ship was in worse condition than I had realized; it was wearing out from a lack of spare parts, and the bad jump we had made escaping from the exploding cruiser had caused significant damage. Unless Skippy and his bots could effect repairs, the *Flying Dutchman* would not be fit for a mission to save Earth. Again.

"Uh huh, greetings, Skippy the Magnificent," I replied distractedly, eyes focused on my tablet. "What's up?"

"Mmm hmm," he made a sound like clearing his throat.

"Just a minute." I didn't want to read the report, but if I lost my train of thought right then, I would need to go all the way back to the beginning of the stupid thing. Then, something different about Skippy's voice caught my attention. It wasn't coming out of my tablet, or the speaker in the ceiling. It seemed to be coming from-

"Gaaah!" I jumped up from my chair, startled. "*What the hell is that*?"

Standing in my office doorway was a slightly fuzzy Jedi knight, with brown robes and a glowing lightsaber. The reason I knew it had to be Skippy was the face was chrome rather than skin. "This is my avatar, Joe. You said it is difficult for you hairless apes to converse with me sometimes, because I am a featureless chrome beer can. Is this better?"

"You decided to become, what, Skippy Wan Kenobi?"

"Sure, let's go with that."

I sat back down and leaned my chair back. "I don't know about that, Skippy. The Jedi were mystical warriors who could control the universe through the Force-"

"Uh huh, yeah, and yet they fought by whacking the bad guys with sticks."

"It's a movie, Skippy, don't think too hard about it, Ok? I don't want you geeking out and trying to calculate the numbers of janitors needed aboard a Death Star or something like-"

"That's easy, Joe. Assuming a diameter of-"

"I said *don't* geek out on me."

"Well, if I can't be a Jedi, don't ask me to be Darth Skippy." The Jedi avatar turned off his lightsaber and crossed his arms.

"Darth Skippy?" I snickered. "That's funny."

"It is not funny! Darth Vader is a loser! They should have painted a big white 'L' on the forehead of his helmet."

"What? Vader is a loser?"

"Joe, Joe, Joe. Think about it." Skippy Wan Kenobi shook his head sadly and leaned back against the doorframe. "Oh, damn, it's you, why do I ask *you* to think? Listen, what Anakin Skywalker *wanted* was to be a great Jedi and to have a life with his wife and family. Instead, he gets suckered by the Emperor and used by the Dark Side of the Force; murders a bunch of children, gets his ass thrown into volcano so he lives in constant terrible pain, gets his wife killed, and his own son ends up chopping his hand off. Loser. *Looooser*." Skippy Wan Kenobi used a thumb and index finger to make an 'L' on his avatar's forehead.

"I never thought of it that way," I had to admit.

"Joe, you could have ended that sentence with 'I never thought' and it would be completely accurate."

"Could you be Skippy the Hutt?"

"Uh, no," Skippy stuck out his tongue at me. "Han Skippy?"

"You? Not happening. Chewbacca?"

His avatar became a tall, fur-covered alien, but the fur was silver. "Raraaaaragher!" His voice trilled gruffly like a Wookie. "I just asked you if this is good, in Wookie language."

"Oh. It sounded like you were choking on a Chewbacca-size furball."

"Very funny."

Skippy was really getting into the avatar thing; I wondered if having Nagatha communicating with us had made him jealous of the positive attention she got from the crew. Could an ancient, super-powerful AI get jealous? "Ok, forget Star Wars, then," I suggested.

"How about Star Trek?" The avatar was now dressed in a Starfleet admiral's uniform.

"Can I think about it? This avatar thing will take some getting used to. And don't go scaring the crew, please."

"Um, too late for that, Joe. You should have told me that right away, you dumdum."

"What do you mean?"

"Um, my Jedi avatar just surprised Sergeant Adams when she was coming out of the shower. She has impressive reflexes for a human; if I wasn't a hologram she would have given me a beat down. I won't be doing *that* again."

"How did you do that?" I closed my eyes, imagining the trouble he was causing for me.

"I can create multiple holograms at the same time, Joe," the avatar replied with a tone that implied an unspoken 'duh'.

"Oh," it was my turn to groan, "you've got to be kidding me. Adams-" Right then my zPhone rang, and who would have guessed? It was Adams. "Sergeant, I-" I had to hold the phone away from my ear, she was yelling so loud. Covering the microphone with a finger, I waved to Admiral Skippy of Starfleet. "I'll talk with you later, Skippy, this is going to take a while."

"Uh huh," the avatar nodded knowingly before blinking out of existence. Through the speaker in my tablet, he continued talking. "There are, um, eight other people trying to call you right now. No, now there are twelve. Damn, who would have thought you humans would be so sensitive, about an avatar appearing while they are naked in the shower?"

I slapped my forehead. It was fifty minutes before the beginning of the morning shift; a time when a lot of the crew would be showering. "Oh, this is going to be-" My thoughts were interrupted by a livid-faced Major Simms, her hair still wet and her uniform top misbuttoned, knocking on my doorframe. I softly pounded my forehead on my desk. "Damn it, I hate my life."

My day just kept getting better and better after that.

We jumped in almost a million miles from the red dwarf star's gas giant planet; Skippy had been cautious when programming the jump, due to our lack of data about the star system. What little we did know was data gathered at long range, mostly by the Jeraptha. The system had a star that was small and cool even for a red dwarf, and three planets. Two small, rocky inner planets, and gas giant about the size of Neptune. If we had not needed fuel, there was absolutely no reason to ever visit that star system.

"Hmmm. That is interesting," Skippy said shortly after the jump. "The planet has an incomplete ring. Huh. There is a significant cloud of rocks in orbit, that's going to make navigation tricky."

"Tricky, like we should find another place to refuel?" I asked.

"No, we can keep the *Dutchman* outside the cloud; the problem is the dropships will need to make a longer flight from the ship and back, and they will need to insert from a polar orbit. This is curious, the orbital mechanics of the meteor cloud do not match the five moons. Something must have disrupted the orbits of- Oh, yeah. Hmm. Very interesting. Even the moons have been thrown off their original orbits. Something odd happened here."

My Spidey sense tingled. "Could this be anything dangerous, Skippy?"

"I haven't completed a sensor scan yet, but there is no sign any ship is here, or ever has visited this system. There are no loose gases in orbit, like I would expect if a ship had picked up fuel here. No sign of ships here now, or any satellites. No, Joe, this isn't dangerous, it is merely curious. You should be happy; poking into the mystery of what happened here will keep me busy for a while."

"Busy is good. Tell the pilots which orbit you want us to put the ship in; I want us humans to fly the ship by ourselves. How long until we can launch the dropships?"

"Roughly thirteen hours. Our momentum is carrying us away from the planet; we will need to reverse course to slow down, then catch up to it before we can establish a stable orbit. I will have the rock cloud fully mapped by then."

"Pilots, follow Skippy's instructions."

I expected Skippy to protest that us flying the ship by ourselves was a waste of time; he must have been extra busy unravelling the mystery of the unexplained moon orbits, because he replied distractedly with "Uh huh, yeah, sure. Fine. Course plotted and transferred to navigation system. While we are waiting, we could- Uh oh. Wow! Joe, you need to see this!"

Before I could open my mouth to ask what was so exciting, Skippy replaced the main bridge display's status readouts with a sensor image of a moon. Or most of a moon, because a big piece of it was missing. "Whoa," was all I could say.

"That's a Death Star," Adams exclaimed excitedly. She was right. The moon was spherical, and a whitish gray in color. The surface was covered in the usual assortment of meteor craters; what made this moon different was the giant crater that had been scooped out of one hemisphere. This crater was bigger in diameter and deeper than the laser dish of a Death Star. The very bottom of the hole was flattened, like lava or something deep within the moon had flowed into the gap and filled part of it in.

"That thing is more like a *Dead* Star," I remarked without taking my eyes off the display. "Skippy, I am leaning toward jumping us the hell out of here right now."

"No need to do that, Joe!" He answered anxiously. "This solves the mystery of why there is a cloud of rocky debris around this planet. There is absolutely no indication of recent activity in this system. I am running back the orbits of the debris cloud, give me a moment here. Gosh, I used 78% of my processing capacity to perform those calculations quickly. The debris cloud was created millions of years ago."

My Spidey sense tingled hotly. "Millions of years, like around the time Newark was pushed out of orbit, and funky stuff happened to Elder sites?"

"Uh, hmm, exactly. At first, I thought two moons might have collided here, but when I ran the orbital mechanics backwards, I can see this was no natural event. There had to be Elder-level technology involved in blowing up that moon."

"This does not make me happy, Skippy."

"Me neither, Joe."

"I meant I am not happy about being here."

"Oh. I meant I am not happy that I did not predict this star system could potentially be host to an Elder site. I still do not understand why the Elders would have placed a facility on that moon. Since a big chunk of the moon is missing, I may never know."

"Sergeant Adams," I turned to look at her, "you are correct; that moon does look like a Death Star. But that crater is way bigger than the laser dish thing in Star Wars. Skippy?"

"This moon is three thousand miles in diameter," Skippy stated, "and the crater is almost one thousand miles across at the lip. The crater is only three hundred miles deep, still, the event which left that crater almost cracked that moon in half."

"You think maybe the Elder facility exploded somehow?" An accident would be the least alarming scenario I could think of right then.

"Nope. This was deliberate. There was hostile action here, Joe. I hasten to remind you this happened a very long time ago; it does not represent any threat to us today."

Great, I thought. The science team would be beating on me for permission to drop down to that moon to examine it. And they were right, we should not miss an opportunity to gather more information that might help explain what the hell had been going on in the Milky Way galaxy, after the Elders departed and before the Rindhalu developed space flight capability. Since I couldn't send a science team down by themselves, they would need an escort, and of course Major Smythe would want the opportunity to conduct low-gravity training on that moon. If the away team took a nuke with them, maybe Chotek would grant permission for a mission down to the moon. I doubted that, but I would ask anyway.

Hans Chotek surprised me again. He not only gave permission for the science team to land on the Dead Star moon, he wanted to go with them. Being aboard the relay station, he told me, had given him a different perspective. He had been able to think of the mission as a whole, rather than focusing only on the actions of the *Flying Dutchman*. "Besides," he told me with a slightly embarrassed shrug, "it would be a shame for me to return home, without having walked on something other than the deck of this ship."

Once he had made the decision to go down to the moon, Chotek was eager to get going; he left in one of our big Thuranin 'Condor' dropships as soon as we were close enough. To speed his journey, I asked the pilots to change course so we would swing close to the Dead Star. It's not that I was trying to get rid of Chotek as fast as I could, I- Oh, hell, that's exactly why I did it. It would be good to let someone else deal with him for a while. The away team took two dropships, two nukes, portable shelters and plenty of extra oxygen tanks. I almost asked Major Simms to pack stuff so they could make S'mores on their camping trip, but then I realized since he was an Austrian, Hans Chotek probably had never heard of a S'more. That was his loss.

Simms assured me she had packed plenty of Austrian chocolates aboard Chotek's dropship. I think she was happy to be staying aboard the ship this time.

Adams walked into the gym as I was finishing a workout. "Sergeant," I waved her over. "I didn't see your name on the list of people requesting to go down to the Dead Star."

"Yes, Sir. I had shore leave the first time you went down to Paradise," she meant the mission where we used Perkins' team to reactivate the buried maser projectors. "I want to give someone else an opportunity to get off the ship for a while."

"That's nonsense, Adams. You named the Dead Star," technically she called it the Death Star but close enough. "You should see it in person. There is plenty of space in the dropships," the away team was flying two of our large Thuranin dropships we called 'Condors', "and in the shelters. And we'll be rotating people back to the ship; this crazy refueling ops Skippy has planned is going to take a while. Also, with the science team going down there, I need some adults to supervise."

"It would be good to get off the ship for a change," Adams said, in a longing voice women usually reserve for the prospect of getting chocolate.

"You're a Marine, Adams," I teased her, "you're supposed to be deployed aboard a ship."

"Not all the time, Sir, not every. Freakin'. Day. And being deployed shipboard doesn't mean we enjoy that, it's just part of the job. I guess being out here has its benefits; I haven't been invited to any cookware or candle parties."

"Huh?" I had no idea what she meant, and wasn't sure I wanted to know.

She rolled her eyes. "One of those 'parties' where you go to some woman's house and they serve wine, and then get you to

buy a bunch of useless crap you don't need."

"Oh!" I laughed. "Yeah, my mother used to get dragged to those parties. Adams, that is one reason why being a guy is way better than being a woman. If one of my buddies invited me to, like, a fishing tackle party, I'd say: 'Get the fuck outa here. I'm not going to your stupid party. What the hell's wrong with you?' And that would be totally Ok, nobody would get hurt. Also, no guy would ever try *that* shit again. But you women can't do that."

"Sometimes you have to support your friends," she replied defensively.

"If one of my friends needs extra money, he can do something useful like replace the roof on my toolshed, or replace the brake pads on my truck. Don't try selling me a bunch of crap. Or I'll loan him cash."

"Being a man is so much easier," she admitted.

"Hey, you women make these social rules, you can change them."

"I'll get right on that, Sir. After we save the world-"

"Again," I finished the thought for her.

Adams walked off to the treadmills, while I picked up a dumbbell to do curls.

"Joe, are you *flexing* in front of that mirror?" Skippy chuckled.

"Checking out my guns, Skippy," I grunted while curling a weight, flexing my biceps. Sure, I wasn't in Olympic athlete condition compared to our SpecOps team, but-

"Ugh. Damn, it's a good thing there aren't many women in here to witness this travesty. It's supposed to be *beef*cake, Joe, not Spam cake."

A woman behind me laughed and I felt I needed to defend myself. Especially because the woman was a Chinese Night Tiger and she could kick my ass from one end of the ship to the other. "Hey, I'm not-"

"Maybe *tufo*cake, since it's you," Skippy mused. "Something soft and squishy."

I almost dropped the weight on my foot. Crap, maybe I needed to start working out in my tiny cabin.

"Explain this to me again, Skippy," I said as I ran a hand over the kludgy rig we had installed on one of our larger dropships. It looked like a cross between a high school science project and a yard sale. A lame science project like one of mine, not a project by one of the smart kids who actually knew what they were doing. While Chotek with most of the science and SpecOps teams were away on their fun-filled camping trip on the surface of the Dead Star, and Skippy's bots were busy skittering around repairing the ship as best they could, the *Flying Dutchman's* crew was supposed to be collecting fuel.

"Again?" Skippy sighed. "Joe, this is the third freakin' time! I explained it to you twice before. Were you not listening, or can your brain not comprehend even this tiny bit of my awesomeness?"

The truth was, I wanted him to explain it again, in order to delay launching two of our dropships on what I considered a dangerous mission of dubious value. "Both, Skippy. I have a meatsack brain and a short attention span. Humor me, please."

"Ugh," he sighed. "Fine. Most ships that refuel from a gas giant lower a special fuel-collection drogue into the atmosphere, at the end of a long cable. Star carriers do not refuel themselves, so we do not have a drogue. And before you ask me another stupid question, no, we did not have a drogue the last time we took on fuel either. Back then, we had a frigate," he meant our captured *Heavenly Morning Flower of Glorious Victory*, "that I could remotely dip into the atmosphere. Now all we have is a lifeboat that has no propulsion. So, my plan is to have two large dropships dip into the atmosphere, flying in formation with my super-duper fuel collection scoop gizmo suspended between them."

"Calling it a gizmo is not a great way to convince me you know what you are doing."

"I am not a salesman, Joe. Imagine I said it in a way that will convince you."

"*You* are not going to be flying one of these things, Skippy," I stood on my toes, reached up and rapped my knuckles on the cabin of the dropship. "The pressure vessel on this thing is, what, 2 millimeters thick? That is the only thing holding the air in, to protect the crew."

"More like one and half millimeters, Joe. You are correct that the pressure vessel is the only thing protecting the crew from the harsh vacuum of space. On this mission, holding air *in* will not be the problem. For my fueling gizmo to work efficiently, the dropships will need to get deep enough in the atmosphere that they will experience pressure equal to thirty times that on Earth's surface. If the pressure vessel ruptures, toxic gases will rapidly pour into the cabin, and the crew would be crushed."

"You are *filling* me with confidence, Skippy."

"If it makes you feel any better, the crew would be incinerated instantly before they got crushed. They should be wearing Kristang spacesuits as a precaution against minor problems. Kristang armored suits are made of tough material, as you know from your first space dive, however, in the event of a serious hull breach, it is possible those suits would not compensate quickly enough."

"That does not make me feel any better. It makes me feel worse, because I'll be staying aboard the ship, and ordering other people to take the risk." I was not qualified to fly the larger type of Thuranin dropship, and I wasn't the best pilot for the job anyway. I was probably the least-skilled pilot aboard our pirate ship. "We absolutely must have pilots aboard the dropships? You can't control the dropships remotely?"

"Not with a pair of dropships flying in formation, Joe. The latency issue caused by signal lag would make it impossible to control the dropships together. I would have to go aboard one of the dropships-"

"No! No, that is not an option," I declared. No way was I going to risk UNEF's greatest asset in a risky mission. If the dropship he was in suffered a failure, Skippy would helplessly plummet to the core of the gas giant planet, and effectively be lost to us forever. "Our pilots will fly the mission."

"We will arrive in the proper orbit shortly, Joe. If you have serious second thoughts, you should have expressed them *before* I went through all the trouble of building this very complicated fuel-collection scoop apparatus," Skippy said, sounding peeved. "And before the pilots wasted time practicing this mission in the simulator."

I was not concerned about pilots wasting their time; it kept them happy and busy, and that type of training might be useful in the future. My problem was guilt; I would be ordering pilots to take dropships into action they were not designed for, using an untested fuel-collection 'gizmo'. The guilt was not that the pilots would be taking a risk; they were Ok with that. No, my guilt was that we had time to dawdle in an uninhabited star system at all. If I or the command staff had been able to think up a good, workable plan to prevent the Ruhar from sending a ship to Earth, we would be implementing that plan rather than taking time to top off our fuel tanks. That meant if anyone was killed or injured while taking part in Skippy's Flying Circus, it would be partly my fault.

And if we didn't think up a plan to stop the Ruhar from reaching Earth, the extinction of my entire species might be *partly* my fault. Or entirely my fault, damn it. Crap, I needed to focus on what was most important. "Skippy, I know nothing about the technical details of refueling, so I have to trust you on this one."

"Joey, Joey, Joey. You trust your life to me with a million things every freakin' minute. *You* don't keep the reactors from exploding. I got this. Now, go, I don't know, try to do something useful. Are we Ok to proceed or not?"

"Yes. I'll tell the duty officer," I said with a final skeptical knock on Skippy's cobbled-together fuel collection device. "I don't suppose there is any point in asking Nagatha for a second opinion?"

"Oof," Skippy breathed a sigh of exasperation. "I told you, it, *she*, is a submind built for communications, not for any type of analysis or control. And if you asked her for a second opinion, she would tell you-

"I would tell Colonel Bishop that he has no choice but to trust you," Nagatha interrupted.

"Thank you," Skippy said smugly.

"He has no choice," she scolded, "because you don't tell him anything useful. Colonel, in this case, Skippy's analysis is correct, the refueling operation should proceed successfully. That is based on my verification of Skippy's analysis. Of course, if Skippy forgot to include something in his analysis, I would not know about it. I am, as Skippy reminded you, designed for communications and not crunching numbers."

"Thank you anyway, Nagatha. See, Skippy, you could try being nice sometimes."

"Ugh. I'd rather jump the ship into a black hole. Damn, I regret the day I loaded that submind into the relay station's computer."

Hans Chotek scrunched up his nose, closed his eyes tightly, and held his breath to suppress a sneeze inside the helmet of his spacesuit. He had sneezed before in training, the experience gave him confidence that a sneeze would not be disastrous as he first thought, it was still embarrassing. The inner surface of the helmet's visor was protected by some type of energy field, specifically to protect the visor from contamination that might obscure visibility. Even the moisture he exhaled with every breath had the potential to fog the visor and render it useless, if not for the amazing technology built into the helmet. If he did sneeze, the droplets would be caught by the force field, then drawn gently downward into a collection tray at the bottom of the visor; from there any foreign material was vacuumed into a holding tank near his left shoulder. Due to some magic Chotek did not remember from suit training, the tank never needed to be emptied or cleaned during a mission; the material was stripped down to its constituent elements and the useful parts like oxygen recycled. Chotek knew that Skippy's bots performed almost all of the maintenance tasks on the suits, so whatever service the holding tank required, it wasn't something humans took care of.

The urge to sneeze passed, and Chotek opened his eyes. He was not in a good place to be standing with eyes closed for an extended time; if he lost his balance he might fall and tumble head over heels for a long way. The suit's stabilizers should protect him from clumsily falling forward and Chotek had tested that function in training. He did not wish to trust his life to a mysterious, unseen technology that he did not understand.

Opening his eyes reminded him of where he was standing; at the lip of a vast crater that had been carved out of the moon millions of years ago. Literally carved, according to Skippy. The damage to the moon had not been caused by an explosion, instead a partial sphere of material extending deep into the moon had been scooped out and deposited in orbit around the gas giant. That material, free from the gravity of its host moon, had quickly broken up and now formed a partial ring around the planet. The relocation of such a large mass disrupted not only the host moon, but the orbits of all the moons circling the gas giant.

Chotek looked down in awe. The crater was so large that the far rim could only be recognized using the visor's handy magnification feature. Originally, when the crater was created, it was a perfect partial sphere. Quickly, material welling up from the moon's core had flowed in to fill the bottom of the void, and subsequent quakes and meteor impacts had covered the remaining surface with cracks and small craters. Being newer and consisting of material different from the moon's ancient surface, the crater was distinctly darker, making it appear even deeper when viewed from the lip.

"How are you doing, Sir?" Major Smythe called.

Chotek paused to take a breath. "Fine, Major. I'm standing on a moon in a star system thousands of lightyears from Earth, at the edge of a crater made by a force that could destroy our home planet, and the only thing keeping me alive is a spacesuit that is maintained by a shiny beer can."

"An *alien* spacesuit, Sir," Smythe reminded the mission leader. "A powered armor mech suit made by a species we are now fighting against. The science team tells me they do not understand half the technology in these suits. Regardless, they work splendidly. Without them, we would not be able to enjoy this view."

Chotek grunted. "I had expected this view to fill me with awe, but instead, I find myself depressed."

"Depressed?" Smythe could understand experiencing a wide variety of emotions while standing at the edge of an ancient cataclysm. Depression was not within that range.

"Yes. The technology that was used here, to scoop out such an enormous part of this moon, is awe-inspiring. And that is the problem. To the beings who caused this, the technology they used was well understood, maybe even taken for granted by them. That depresses me. Major, the beings who did this," he swept an arm to encompass the vast crater, "are so far beyond our comprehension, their technology might as well be magic to us. Even if we are able to complete our current mission to prevent a Ruhar ship from traveling to Earth, we- Even if by some miracle we are able to deal with all the *known* threats in this galaxy, there is some force out there we don't yet know about. Beings who could create a crater like this are a threat even to the Maxolhx and Rindhalu. How could we protect ourselves against such a threat?" He shook his head inside the helmet, forgetting that Smythe standing beside him could not see the gesture.

"I get your meaning, Sir," Smythe replied quietly, keeping the slight annoyance he was feeling out of his voice. He had come down to the Dead Star to get away from the ship for a while, for a change of scenery rather than the same passageway walls and bulkheads. He had come down for an opportunity to engage in surface combat training with his team. He had accompanied Chotek on a walk out to the rim of the crater, partly to get some private time with their mission commander, but mostly simply to stand in awe of a force beyond his comprehension. And now Hans Chotek had dragged Smythe's mind back to threat analysis. Was an hour of peace too much to ask for?

Chotek took a moment to suppress another sneeze. Had dust from the moon's surface gotten past the airlock filters of the portable shelters they were living in? That was unlikely; when Chotek had put on the helmet inside the shelter, it was sparklingly pristine. He had seen, touched and smelled moon dust in the science lab section of one shelter; it had a slightly burnt ozone smell that was not inside his helmet. The urge to sneeze passed again. Looking out through his helmet visor reminded him of how badly he wanted to stand on an alien world without a spacesuit and breathe unfiltered air. When Colonel Bishop went down to the surface of Paradise, twice, Chotek should have accompanied the team at least once. The first time, he had not dared leave the ship in case something went wrong. The second time, it had partly been his own arrogant stubbornness that kept him aboard the *Flying Dutchman*. He deeply regretted that now. Turning to his right, he looked into Smythe's visor. How many worlds had Smythe set foot on? Even counting only the planets, the British Special Air Services Major had walked on Newark, Paradise and Jumbo. Although, Jumbo's atmosphere had not been breathable, so the away team had been forced to live in their suits. "Major, what was it like on Newark?"

"Most of the time, it was like being in Scotland during the springtime, except summer was never coming. Not on that world." Sensing Chotek wanted to talk, Smythe told of his experience on Newark; not details of the successful military operation, but what it was like simply *being there*. To stand on an alien world wearing nothing but cold weather gear, to breathe the damp chilly air, to feel as if you could never get enough oxygen. When Chotek asked what it was like to stand in the chamber where the last sentient natives of Newark had spent their last days huddled against killing cold, Smythe told him. "As you said, there is an unknown force out there, Sir. Here, it scooped out this crater. On Newark, it pushed an entire habitable planet out of its orbit. It wiped out an entire sentient species. The people there, the natives, they knew what had happened to them. They didn't know why, or how, or who, but they knew their world was going to turn into a block of ice, and there was nothing they could do about it. No way they could survive." He turned to look in Chotek's visor. "Since Newark, I've asked myself if humanity could survive if something like that happened to Earth. The inhabitants of Newark had Bronze-age technology. We have nuclear reactors. Could we have survived deep in caves, or down deep in the oceans where the water didn't freeze?" Smythe looked at the crater. "I don't know. The beings who made this crater, I don't think they would leave anything to chance. If humanity tried to survive an event like Newark, I have a feeling we would be hit with an even worse disaster. What bothers me, Sir, is like you said; even if we deal with all the known threats, something like this is looming over our heads."

"Much as I hate to admit it," Chotek replied slowly, "I am beginning to agree with Colonel Bishop; we may need to investigate what happened to Newark, and here and other sites you found on the *Dutchman*'s second mission."

"There is a larger threat out there," Smythe agreed.

"What bothers me right now is the nature of that threat. We think it is a mystery because Skippy tells us it is a mystery to him. Newark was pushed out of orbit, and this crater was made, after the Elders left the galaxy, and before the Rindhalu developed capability for interstellar travel. That is only what Skippy tells us, and it is only what Skippy knows. Skippy admits his memories are incomplete and garbled. Major Smythe, how much do you trust Skippy?"

Smythe took a moment to consider his answer. "Originally, I trusted Skippy only where his interests aligned with ours. On my first mission with him, he wanted to find this Collective, whatever that is. Everything we did during the first half of that mission was for Skippy's benefit. Even going down to Newark and our actions there were to further Skippy's goals; he needed a place the crew could live while he repaired the ship, and he wanted us to take the comm node and AI from the Kristang scavenger group on Newark. Then something changed, and I don't know all the details, you would have to ask Colonel Bishop. The second half of that mission was all about stopping the Thuranin surveyor ship from traveling to Earth. Skippy helped us with that aspect of the mission, he did most of the work. Stopping that surveyor ship did not directly benefit Skippy. Preventing the Ruhar from sending a ship to Earth now also does not directly benefit him. Our recent actions to safeguard the future of UNEF on Paradise had no benefit to him that I can think of. He helped us anyway, he is continuing to help us. Part of why he helps us might be his friendship with Bishop," Smythe shrugged. "I find it difficult to believe a being like Skippy considers friendship with a monkey," one side of his mouth turned up in a wry smile, "to be as valuable as we think of friendships. We are not his peers, we never will be. Eventually, Skippy will insist on contacting the Collective. He has said before he does that, he needs answers for what happened in the galaxy while he was dormant. If we want to investigate the nature of the threat we're facing, then our goals align with Skippy's."

Hans Chotek took one last look down into the crater, and shivered despite the cozy warmth of the suit.

Desai wriggled in her somewhat ill-fitting Kristang powered armor suit, trying to get comfortable. She was not our shortest crew member, but she wasn't tall either, and the Kristang suits could be modified only so much. While Desai normally did not wear a suit, she had trained to wear one when she was flying a dropship, so she had a suit custom made for her. She still didn't like it, and I didn't blame her. I had worn a suit almost full-time during the mission to the heavy gravity planet Jumbo, and it got irritating after a while. The warrior ethos of the Kristang prevented them from making many concessions to the suit user's comfort; likely the lizards thought things like ergonomics and comfort were signs of weakness unbecoming a warrior.

"Are you comfy in there?" I asked, holding a helmet for her. We were outside her dropship in a docking bay, running a preflight check, although Skippy of course assured us everything was perfect with both dropships.

"Comfort is not the issue, Colonel," she replied as she shown a light into a thruster. Dropping her voice, she turned to me. "This is going to be difficult flying. I appreciate your faith in me, but as I have told you before, I am not the best pilot aboard the *Dutchman*. Someone else would be a better candidate to fly this fuel-collection run."

"Desai," I checked another thruster for her, and gave her a thumb's up gesture. "I know you are not our most technically skilled pilot. That is why I want you flying lead on the first mission."

"Sir?"

"Our best pilots know they are hotshots, and they might fly like it. I do not need any hotshot cowboy crap going on while you are flying in atmosphere that could crush these dropships. If it gets too dangerous down there, I expect you to abort the mission. We'll debrief, make adjustments, and try it again. The last thing we need is someone's ego making them push too hard."

"Yes, Sir," she said, this time with a little smile.

"Desai, you are an excellent pilot; and I know for damned sure you are cool under pressure. What I value most about you is your judgment. If all I wanted was a great stick jockey, I could have chosen any pilot. I want these dropships to come back; that means you fly lead."

"I might scuff the paint a bit, Sir," she laughed.

"Don't worry, it'll buff right out," I winked. "You come back safely, with or without fuel, understood?" I offered her a fist, and she bumped me.

"Got it."

CHAPTER SIX

Two of our big Thuranin dropships we called 'Condors' were away on their refueling mission, and I had nothing to do other than monitor their progress, drive the CIC crew crazy and worry myself sick. I went to the galley to get coffee, more because I needed something to do than because I needed a jolt of caffeine right then. Adams was sitting at a table, reading something on a tablet, so I took the opportunity to sit down across from her. "Sergeant, I want to show you something," I set my tablet on the table. "Hey, Skippy. You made our unit patches," I meant the pirate-paramecium logo for the Merry Band of Pirates.

"Yes, and I did a spectacular job on that, if I do say so myself."

"You always do say so yourself," I rolled my eyes. "Anyway, thanks for that. Two of our navy pilots-"

"They are called 'Naval Aviators', Joe."

"Whatever."

"Yeah, that's what I thought, too, but Nagatha told me I should be more respectful by using the correct terms. 'Pilot' is an Air Force term."

"Army too. We have pilots. Anyway, these *aviators* mentioned to me that we need a logo for the ship. So, I sketched this," I pulled up the image on my iPad and turned the display toward Adams. "What do you think?"

"Hmmm. Mmmm. In-ter-esting," Skippy stretched the word out. "It looks like while Van Gogh was cutting his ear off, he tripped over Picasso and spilled paint on a Disney sketch. What, um, what is that supposed to be?"

"It's a cool pirate monkey standing on a flying banana," I explained defensively. Damn it, I was proud of that sketch. It took me hours to make. "See, the ship is a flying banana, because we are monkeys, right? You see it, Adams?"

Adams tilted her head one way then the other. I could see her shoulders quiver as she suppressed a laugh. "Whatever you say, Sir."

"A banana?" Skippy did chuckle. "That's supposed to be a *banana*? Hmmm, I can see it is a sort of yellowish blob-"

"It *is* a freakin' banana!" I insisted.

"Ok, I can see how someone on *serious* drugs may think that thing on top might be a pirate monkey, but, um. Hmm, maybe you could replace the lower part of the sketch with text saying 'imagine a banana here'." He began laughing hysterically, and Adams joined in.

"You are *such* an asshole." I turned the iPad off.

"Don't get mad, Joe. This is really no different from any of your operational orders. After all the boring blah blah blah at the beginning, you could insert 'imagine a plan here'."

Adams was laughing so hard she had tears in her eyes. That was the last time I showed my artistic ability, or inability, to anyone.

I looked out one of the *Flying Dutchman's* two viewing stations, where a bubble of clear glass, plastic, crystal or maybe it was diamond, protruded in a dome above the skin of the ship. The viewing stations had not been designed for sightseeing, they were intended for an emergency backup method of guiding dropships into the docking bays. "Hey, Skippy, where's this fabulous nebula you promised to show me?" All I could see were smudges and stars, lots of stars.

"It's on the display anytime you want to look, dumdum," Skippy sounded distracted.

"I can look at stuff on a screen anytime. I want to *see* it, with my eyes. You told me this thing is huge!"

"Oh, for crying out- How come you bother me every single time I am busy doing something important?"

"Like what are you doing that's so important? You told me talking with us baboons hardly takes up any of your processing power."

"Talking with *you* specifically takes more of my resources than usual, because I have to waste time attempting to understand what you are trying to say with all the blah, blah, blah. If you must know, I am calibrating the jump drive coil assembly, monitoring the dropship fuel collection operation, and I am in the extremely delicate process of renewing the containment system of Reactor Three."

"Extremely delicate, huh?"

"Things could go 'Boom' rather easily, if my concentration slips."

"Got it. Show me this nebula, and I'll leave you alone."

"Aargh," he groaned in frustration. "Even from here, it is a dim object, Joe. Not dim like you, I mean the amount of light emitted."

"We're practically on top of it, you said!" I protested. One reason I had agreed to jump to this boring, crappy star system was that Skippy promised it was close to the North America Nebula, which I thought was a cool name.

"We are practically on top of it; less than twelve lightyears. It is, however, mostly on the other side of the star. And the planet is blocking part of the view at the moment. If you wait half an hour, our orbit will take us around, and you will have a better view. Joe, prepare to be disappointed. With the naked eye, even from here it's only going to be a hazy blob."

"Fine," I sighed. "I'll wait."

"What's bothering you, Joe? I know astronomy is not your greatest passion."

I did enjoy astronomy, but not as much as I enjoyed, for example, cheeseburgers. Or crinkle fries, the kind that have ridges to hold extra ketchup, you know? Or beer, of course, duh. "I'm worried sick about the fueling operation, that's all."

"Captain Desai and her team have reached target depth without incident, and have deployed the scoop; it will begin filtering the atmosphere within the next ten minutes. Relax, Joe, everything is under control."

"We're losing control!" Desai warned, trying to be calm while struggling with the dropship and the homemade fuel scoop. In the preflight briefing, Skippy had warned them about sudden wind gradients as they descended deeper in the gas giant's atmosphere. The pilots of the two dropships had been prepared for sudden changes in wind velocity and even direction; the layers in the atmosphere showed up clearly on the sensors of the dropships, and Skippy provided warning and guidance from the star carrier high above. Descending from orbit, the scoop had connected the two dropships, but with the fuel collection mechanism retracted it had not been difficult for the pair of Thuranin ships to fly in close formation. Skippy had designed the scoop so that it did not awkwardly hang between the two dropships; instead each ship had a nanofiber cable trailing them, with the furled scoop far behind at the end of the V-shaped cables. With the scoop furled, Desai found flying in formation no more difficult than in any other aircraft.

Once the two ships reached target depth, where the thickness of the atmosphere allowed the homemade scoop to function efficiently, the flying had become much more difficult. At first, Desai had almost been able to relax after the scoop was fully deployed. She had gotten used to the substantial drag caused by the unfurled scoop, finding she needed to increase power almost exactly as she had in the simulations programmed by

Skippy. Everything had been going as planned; the scoop was functioning as designed, fuel was being collected and pumped along tubes into the special tanks installed in each dropship's aft cargo holds, and the rate of fuel flow was three percent above Skippy's estimate.

Then a problem arose when the dropships flew through an area of turbulence, which Desai saw as a slightly more pink section of the purple clouds around them. The dropships did not have actual windows for the pilots to look through; windows would have degraded their stealth capabilities. Instead, in front of the pilots were curved displays that showed a view from cameras mounted in the nose. When they first dipped down into the clouds, Desai had followed Skippy's suggestion to set the displays for an image which removed most of the clouds, but Desai found that distracting and useless. So she switched to a plain image; it showed her only thick clouds and navigation data but was no different from flying in thick clouds on Earth. She found that images vaguely comforting while she piloted an alien dropship in the crushing pressure of a gas giant planet, almost two thousand lightyears from Earth.

The problem began with an almost imperceptible flutter traveling along the cables from the scoop. Desai did not notice the flutter at first, being occupied by the turbulence that was far worse that what Skippy had told her to expect. Her dropship was bouncing up and down fifty meters at a time, alternatingly forcing her down into her seat or suspended against the straps with her stomach doing flipflops. As the lead ship in the formation, she was not responsible for maintaining distance from the other ship; her task was to fly as smoothly as possible and hold to their programmed course. The other pilot then only needed to follow her lead. With the two ships lurching their way through the thick clouds, keeping the formation within the limits of the scoop was fairly difficult.

When fully extended, the scoop formed a circle large enough so its rim was wider than the distance between the two dropships. They towed the scoop behind and between them, at the ends of two nanofiber cables that stretched and flexed in the powerful, roiling wind. On its own, the scoop would have spun around the twin cables and destroyed itself within seconds. To prevent that, the scoop was capable of steering itself with guidance from Skippy, using sensor data from the ship and the dropships. Skippy controlled the flight of the scoop and the operation of the fuel collection mechanism; all he needed the dropships to do was tow the scoop like an airplane on Earth towing a banner.

That was Skippy's plan.

It wasn't working.

The flutter traveling up the cables became a shaking, hard enough for Desai to feel over the bouncing of the ship. It was growing worse by the second. Desai struggled with the controls, then heard her first flight instructor's words in her head. Never fight the controls, the instructor had told her, work with them. If you are trying to make the aircraft do something it can't, the controls will tell you. She relaxed slightly and listened to what the controls were telling her.

They were telling her the scoop's induced flutter was growing worse, feeding on itself. It is continued, the scoop would fail and might take both dropships down with it. "Cable status?" Desai inquired of her US Air Force copilot.

Alarmed, Samantha Reed in the copilot seat pointed to the strain gauge on the display; the stress on the mounts where the cable attached was already almost to the redline. The data feed from the second ship showed the same problem. "Almost critical," Reed reported tersely. "It's spiking." Her fingers flew over the controls, seeking a solution.

"Skippy!" Desai called. "We're losing the scoop!"

"I know that," the alien AI responded with a snarky tone. "There's too much flutter, I can't control it. Damn it! If we lose this scoop, it will take me too long to build another one. This is our only chance to do this. I'm working on it," Skippy admitted.

"Work faster," Desai silently pointed to the button that would sever the cable from both ships simultaneously.

Reed interrupted. "Ma'am, I think I can fly the scoop from here," she announced with calm confidence.

Desai raised an eyebrow without looking away from the controls. "Are you sure, Sami?"

"Yes. Skippy can't control the scoop from up there because of the signal lag. I can fly it from the console here."

"No you can't!" Skippy argued. "You monkeys' reaction time is way too slow for-"

"We are not monkeys," Desai declared without raising her voice. "What you're doing isn't working, so we're trying this before we have to sever the cables. Release control on my mark," her tone did not allow for any argument. "Three, two, one, mark!"

Desai had a moment of almost panicked regret, as the scoop jerked hard, and the dropship yawed to the side. "Sami!"

"Got it," Reed did not break her concentration. "I had to correct the flutter before I could make it fly right. It's smoother now."

It was smoother, the cable's vibration lessened, then settled down to a gentle, random pulsing. The vibration was no longer building on itself in a fatally sympathetic action. Desai cautiously lifted her hand away from the button that would sever the cables. She glanced away from the flight control displays to check the scoop's status. It was still rocking side to side and up and down, but it was bouncing around no more than the two ships that were towing it. "Skippy," Desai called, "the scoop is under control."

"Yeah," the ancient alien AI replied grumpily. "I can see that. Whoopee freakin' doo. Stupid monkeys."

"Ma'am," Reed felt confident enough for a quick look to her left, "I've got the feel of it now. It is," she added as a drop of sweat rolled down her forehead and off her nose, "not easy. I think when we have full tanks, we furl the scoop here before we climb out."

"You want to furl the scoop in this turbulence?" Desai asked, surprised.

"I know how to handle this turbulence. If we climb above this cloud layer, to where the wind direction and speed is different, I don't know if I can fly the scoop through the transition."

"Skippy?" Desai called. "Can we do that?"

"Yes. Lieutenant Reed is correct; it would be better to furl the scoop in conditions we know she can control. I have just uploaded revised software for the scoop to furl itself, while it is being flown from the dropship."

"Outstanding," Reed replied with an ear-to-ear grin. "Ma'am, on future missions, we need a third pilot. I can't both control the scoop and act as copilot."

"Agreed, I will inform Colonel Bishop," Desai acknowledged. "Skippy, we should add training on flying the scoop to the simulations; can you get people working on that now, so the next crew will be ready?"

"Yes, I am designing the simulation based on Lt. Reed's actions," Skippy replied sourly. "I have a question. You proved that monkeys can do something I couldn't do. Ugh. So, is Lt Reed ever going to wipe that grin off her face?"

Reed shared a laugh with the *Flying Dutchman's* lead pilot. "What do you think?"

"Shit. No," Skippy's voice almost choked. "To be fair, I would do the same thing. We can, um, keep this between us, right? No reason for the entire crew to know about this little incident?"

"*Little* incident?" Desai was amused. "You mean the incident where we were on the edge of mission failure, and possibly losing one or both ships, because you couldn't handle it?"

"Maybe I'll get lucky, and one of the reactors will explode before you get back up here," Skippy said hopefully.

I was in the docking bay to greet Desai's dropship when she returned. The condition of the super high-tech Thuranin dropships surprised me; they both looked scorched, their noses and leading surfaces caked with dark soot. And they smelled burnt. Not the pleasant wood-smoke scent of a campfire; this was the bitter stench of burning plastic. Despite my earlier joking with Desai, the damage to the skin of those dropships was not going to buff out; Skippy's bots would need to perform some heavy maintenance before we could use those dropships in any sort of stealth mission. Skippy assured me both ships were ready for another trip down into the atmosphere, and he was very pleased with the fuel collection process. Putting our dropships, which were *space* craft, deep enough in an atmosphere that they could be crushed made me uncomfortable. "They are *fine*, Joe. Trust me," Skippy said as we waited for the skin of both ships to stop radiating killing cold before I could approach.

"*You* are not down there with the pilots," I retorted.

"Fine. Don't take my word for it, then. The door is about to open, you can ask Desai."

"How was it?" I held out my hands to take her helmet and flight bag, she looked tired. Her hair was plastered to her head, and she had dark circles under her eyes. The dropship had a tiny bathroom, she and Reed could have removed their suits and washed up a bit after the dropship cleared the atmosphere. The fact neither of them had done that told me how exhausted and stressed they must be. Desai was tired and her copilot looked even worse.

"Challenging," she replied with a voice drained of emotion. "We can do it; the difficulty is flying in formation with a ship you can only see on sensors. The winds down there are more variable than Skippy told us to expect, or he has a different idea of what 'variable' means." She shook her head and pinched the bridge of her nose. "Sir, that was a six hour flight, with three hours collecting fuel. I recommend limiting flights to two hours in the atmosphere; three hours is pushing the limits of human concentration and endurance. And we need a third pilot, so the third pilot and the copilot can take turns flying the scoop. Reed did an outstanding job, but three hours of flying the scoop is too much; she is exhausted." Desai's own right hand was shaking slightly, she covered it with her left and clutched them tightly.

I did some quick math in my head; cutting fuel collection time by one third would mean we needed one additional mission. While that might not seem like much, it was another time crews needed to drop into a crushing atmosphere, an additional opportunity for something to go horribly wrong. "We will run two more missions as planned, then I will reassess whether to go down there again." As much as I hated the idea of sending more people down into the gas giant, we should top off the *Dutchman*'s fuel tanks while we could, and the fueling operation wasn't going to be any more safe in some other star system. "For now, get some food while you brief the pilots for the next flight." My hope was to turn the dropships around quickly and send another team out within two hours. I had assured Chotek this uninhabited star system was perfectly safe, and I was anxious to jump back out of there before something went wrong.

The problem was, jump to where?

We still did not have a plan to steal a Kristang starship. After days of off and on discussions, we had a grand total of nothing resembling a workable plan. The closest we had to a plan was a desperate dropship raid like the op we'd conducted when the original Merry Band of Pirates boarded and took the *Heavenly Morning Flower of Glorious Victory*. No way was Hans Chotek, or I, going to approve a sketchy op like that.

One problem we faced was that frigates seldom traveled on their own, they were escort vessels. Most of time, a frigate flew with other frigates, escorting destroyers or larger ships. Finding an isolated frigate was going to be very difficult.

Then Skippy had thrown a monkey wrench into the planning, when he weighed in with his opinion on one idea we were considering. "No, no, no, you idiots. I can't magically take over any Kristang warship whenever I want. That Thuranin nanovirus is a short-range, short-term technology. It degrades over time; a Kristang ship needs recent exposure to a Thuranin star carrier to be infected with viable nanomachines. You're going about this all wrong anyway, Joe."

I rolled my eyes. "Enlighten us, please, Oh Great One."

"You can't simply steal a warship," he sighed disgustedly. "A Kristang clan would not need to steal a frigate; they have plenty of them. If the Kristang know a frigate was stolen, and then a frigate attacks the Ruhar negotiators, the Kristang will know the attack wasn't by one of their clans. They will know the ship was stolen by an outside party who wants to stir up trouble within the Kristang. The whole thing could end up backfiring in your face by actually uniting the Kristang against a common enemy."

"An outside party?" I asked. "Like, if the Ruhar attacked their own negotiators?" That didn't make any sense to me.

"No, dumdum, not the Ruhar. An outside party like the Thuranin, or the Wurgalan; even the Torgalau or the Bosphuraq. The Kristang and the Wurgalan are supposed to be peers, and on the same side, but they *hate* each other."

"Oh, this is way too complicated," I groaned. "We have to steal a freakin' warship, without anyone knowing it was stolen? That is impossible!"

"Not impossible, Joe," Skippy replied cheerfully. "We got the *Flying Dutchman* that way, right? You clever monkeys will think of something. Because, you know, you kinda have to."

Skippy was entirely right; we had to think up a good plan, because the survival of our species depended on it. I felt like Skippy was not taking the situation seriously, so I went into my office and closed the door to have a talk with him. He promised to listen, and he kept his promise while I explained the importance of us working together.

"Ba ha ha!" Skippy chuckled suddenly, interrupting me.

"What? You think this is funny?" I asked, appalled.

"Huh? What? No, you dumdum. Sergeant Adams just said something funny. Hee hee."

"Adams? Jesus Chr- You promised you would pay attention to me?"

"Yeah, and I di- Oh, wait, you expected me to pay attention *the whole time*? For crying out loud, Joe, no one can do that. You blah, blah, blah so long, listening to every word you say would put me in a freakin' coma."

"But you responded while I was talking!?"

"Oh, that," he muttered. "Yeah, once I figured out what you were probably going to say, I created a quick submind to say stuff like 'Yes' and 'I agree' and 'Mmm hmm' while I was busy."

"Did you actually hear anything I said?"

"Sure, of course. Well, shmaybe? Let me play it back. Uh, apparently, uh, I'm skimming through it here, getting the high-level stuff. Damn, even running through it at high speed is putting me to sleep. Apparently it is something about bad guys, danger, monkeys in trouble, planetary extinction, yadda yadda yadda, is that about it?"

I kept bonking my head on the table.

He made a helpful observation. "Joe, if you keep hitting your head on the table like that, you could get a concussion. It's not like you have a surplus of brain cells."

"Thank you, Skippy."

"Oh, no problem, Joe," he said brightly, "always happy to help. Hey, while you're not busy-"

"Not busy?"

"Not doing anything useful, that's for sure. Anywho, I want to show you something."

"Show me wha- what in *the* hell is that?" I gasped as a holographic avatar popped into existence on my desktop.

"Isn't it magnificent?" His voice sounded entirely pleased with himself.

The avatar was less than a foot tall, with a small silver beer can for a body, and a large, round head, like an old bobblehead doll. He was wearing a costume, one I didn't remember from the batch Major Simms had given me. Skippy hated having costumes put on his can, so I had used costumes sparingly after our endless mission in the dropship. For example, I had dressed Skippy in a Red Sox uniform to celebrate the day of the Red Sox first home game of the season. Before that, he had been dressed up like a leprechaun for St Patrick's day. Man, he had totally *hated* that.

Now, his avatar was wearing a resplendent Navy blue, white and gold admiral's uniform, although the uniform was not from any naval service I knew of on Earth. His enormous ancient fore and aft hat had so much 'scrambled egg' gold braid and fringe that almost half the blue was hidden. The wide 'shoulders' had epaulets weighted down with stars.

"That's a," I had to bite my lip to keep from laughing. "That's a, very nice hat."

"You like it?" His chrome surfaces that were exposed glowed a happy light blue.

"It needs to, uh," digging a fingernail deep into my palm helped me not to snicker at him. "The hat should be a bit bigger."

The avatar's hat grew. "Like this?"

"Oh, yes. That is, very, uh, very impressive to all the hairless apes. Skippy, what's up with this getup?"

"Grand Admiral of the Fleet Lord Skippy, at your service, Joe."

"Grand Admiral of the Fleet, huh? Oh, and I see you are a, five, six," I counted, "*seven* star admiral. Interesting."

"Hmm. Should it be eight stars, then? To tell you the truth, I was kind of guessing. Your international military senior rank structures are confusing."

"No, seven stars should be plenty," I assured him.

"Do I look fierce, Joe?" He scowled, although it was hard to see his eyes under the giant, ridiculous hat. "I want my avatar to project authority."

"You are," this time I bit my lip so hard that I drew blood. "Definitely projecting, uh, something. Fierce might be one word for it." *Ridiculous* was a better word, I thought to myself. "Why did you pattern your avatar after a bobblehead doll?"

"Well, Joe, I noticed that your species creates bobbleheads for people who are respected and admired, like sports stars. This avatar should certainly get me respect, right?"

"Respect," damn it, I was almost biting through my lip. "That is one word for it, yes. Where did you get this, uh, uniform?" I figured he would not appreciate me calling it a 'costume.'

"I designed it myself. Pretty awesome, huh?"

"Awesome is not the word I would use," I answered with restraint. "You know us primitive cavemen can't truly appreciate the full scope of your awesomeness. I like you having an avatar, but I thought you hated dressing up?"

"Consider this uniform a preemptive strike, Joe. There is a holiday approaching, and I do not want you dressing my can like the Easter Bunny."

"OMG!" Until that moment, that idea had not occurred to me. "That is a *great* idea!"

"Shit. No, it is *not* a great idea!"

"Oh, come on, Skippy. Imagine how cute you will be, wearing a fuzzy pink-"

"Not happening!"

"Sergeant Adams would think you are absolutely adorable." I knew Skippy had a soft spot in his heart for our tough US Marine Corps Staff Sergeant.

"Really?"

"Skippy, Adams is a woman, you know."

"Maybe- No! No way. Not happening. Zero chance."

"You'll think about it?"

He sighed heavily. "Yes, I will think about it. Not for you, but for Margaret," he used Adams' first name. "Don't count on it. Keep in mind, Joe, the real Easter Bunny would hide delicious chocolate treats around the ship for everyone. The Skippy Bunny might have his bots sprinkle radioactive reactor waste instead."

"I will keep that in mind," I said distractedly, thinking of the costume I wanted Major Simms to make. Fuzzy pink fur to cover his beer can, floppy pink ears on top of his lid, a puffy tail in the back. He was going to be adorable. "Has anyone else seen this new avatar?"

"No," the avatar shook its oversized bobblehead with the towering hat. "I learned my lesson last time, Joe. Figured it is best to run it by you first."

"That was good judgment, Skippy. How about you keep your new avatar a secret until dinner tonight? I will announce that you have a new, uh, persona, and you can reveal your magnificent self to more than half the crew at one time."

"I like it!"

"Hey, uh, I have to go."

"What? You called me, Joe. What did you want in the first place?"

"At this point, I really don't remember. It couldn't be that important, huh?" I turned to leave, chuckling at the thought of Skippy's beer can dressed up as the Easter Bunny.

"Hey! Colonel, you are supposed to salute me," Skippy sounded miffed. "I do hugely outrank you."

I gave him a gesture that was, let's just say it was not quite a salute.

"I saw that!"

"Goodbye, Skippy."

I let it be known there would be an important announcement during dinner, so the galley was extra crowded. Normally, people drifted in and out of the galley over the two and half hours designated for dinner time; this time the place was packed right at 1800 hours. "As you all know, and some of you have seen," I looked at Adams, Simms and a couple others, "Skippy has been considering using a holographic avatar so we can communicate better with him. He experimented with different types of avatars, and today he showed me the, uh, design he has selected. I am certain that when you see it," I scowled at the assembled crew, hoping they caught my meaning, "you will appreciate that his avatar is *fierce* and commands *respect*. Certainly his new avatar is not any source of *amusement*."

"Respect, yes, Colonel Bishop," Chang said while looking quizzically at me. "Not amusing."

"Please welcome Grand Admiral of the Fleet, Lord Skippy." As soon as I said 'Skippy', his holographic avatar popped into existence on a table at the end of the galley.

Every morning, I get a status report from Lt. Colonel Chang. A lot of the data in the report comes from Skippy, or the CIC duty crew. It contains mundane info about critical ship systems, which no human was capable of doing anything about, but it was nice to know if Skippy had taken a defensive shield generator offline for maintenance. Major Simms contributed the logistics section of the report, detailing how many supplies had been consumed, how much of each item we had remaining and an estimate of how long until we ran out. There was the usual section of crew injuries; the inevitable minor sprains and bruises from SpecOps people training as intensely as they could.

Because Chang's report used a standard Chinese Army format, it contained a section on discipline issues. That section was blank, every single day. The Merry Band of Pirates were the elite of Earth's special forces; every one of them was supremely self-disciplined. If they were bored or frightened or pissed off at a fellow soldier, none of them showed it. They all knew we were on a dangerous, extremely important mission while stuck aboard an alien pirate ship, and that everyone needed to exhibit their best behavior to ensure unit cohesion and good morale. Also, none of our ultra-competitive people wanted to be the first to break discipline. Major Smythe had done an outstanding job blending five rival nations into one fighting force, but those rivalries were still there, just under the surface. And that sense of national pride ensured that no one wanted to bring shame upon their country by being the first to be reported as a disciplinary issue.

I mention this because, when Lord Skippy's avatar materialized, with his ridiculous giant hat and elaborate uniform, I witnessed our bad-ass special ops people struggling mightily not to burst out laughing. Some people were sitting rigidly, biting their lips or covering their faces with hands. Other people were rocking back and forth in their chairs, a hand over their mouths, doing their best not to burst out laughing, and losing the battle.

Sergeant Adams had it worst; tears were streaming down her face as she stared at her boots and bit down hard on a thumb. At any moment, someone was going to start laughing at Skippy. And it was probably going to be me. So I did the only thing I could do, while I still had enough breath in my lungs. "Hooray for Lord Skippy!" I shouted, pumping a fist in the air.

Everyone cheered, some of the exclamations were choked with laughter. A ragged cheer kept going as Skippy bowed, clueless to the general air of mirth in the galley. "Thank you, thank you," he responded. "I hope now that you monkeys see my new form, you will stop referring to me as a beer can."

"Oh, Skippy, I am sure," I declared, "that is *never* going to happen."

CHAPTER SEVEN

Because sitting around trying to dream up a plan produced nothing worthwhile, I declared a break and went to the gym; our SEALS team was in the middle of a grueling workout when I arrived. We finished around the same time, hit the showers and then the galley for a post-workout snack. When I walked into the galley, a half dozen people were already eating lunch. One of the SEALS named Jones saw a piece of chocolate cake sitting by itself on a table, and picked it up hungrily.

"Not worried about ruining your appetite by eating dessert first?" I asked jokingly.

"No, Sir," he grinned, taking a big bite of cake. "Aboard this ship, things change so fast, it's better to eat dessert first. You never know-"

"Hey!" A Ranger named Jeff Mychalchyk came over to the table with a tray full of food. "I was gonna eat that cake."

"You snooze, you lose," Jones mumbled as he stuffed the rest of the cake in his mouth. "Finders keepers, man. Consumption is, like, nine tenths of the law. Right, Colonel? Colonel?"

I was already back out the door, pulling my zPhone out. "Dr. Rose, meet me in my office ASAP."

When I got to my office, she was already waiting for me. "You got here fast," I noted, beginning to regret my haste in leaving the galley. After the rest of the SpecOps people descended on the galley like a horde of starving locusts, I would be lucky to lick crumbs off the floor for my lunch. Damn it. I should have at least grabbed a sandwich on my way out.

"I was in the CIC," Sarah pointed over her shoulder.

"CIC?" That surprised me.

"Dr. Friedlander suggested we shadow the flight crew, so we can fill in if needed. On the sensors and weapons stations, not the flight controls."

"Oh. That's a lot of work."

She held her hands up. "I'm a geologist and a chemist. It's not like I'm busy out here right now, especially now that my secret is out," she shook her head ruefully. "Besides, I think Friedlander is pissed at me right now. I don't blame him. He's a good man, I didn't like deceiving him. That's why I wasn't included in the science team exploring the Dead Star."

"It's not your fault, Sarah. It was your job to deceive all of us. I'm the one who should apologize to Friedlander; I knew about you and I chose not tell him." The only actual promise I had made to our friendly resident rocket scientist was that he would not be eaten by a space lizard, but lying to him still didn't sit right with me. I needed to schedule a time to speak with him one on one. "Anyway, I have an idea I want to run past you. And Skippy."

His avatar popped into existence on my table. "You are in luck, Joe, my Lordship happens to be free at this moment. With what do you propose to waste my time now?"

"A question, Skippy, but first, Dr. Rose. You said there are three ways to get a ship. Make one, buy one or steal one."

"You suggested 'fake one' as an option," she reminded me.

"That was more of an *alternative* to getting a ship, not another option for getting one."

"Yeah, and it was an epically stupid suggestion, Joe," Skippy said gleefully.

"Only because you failed to bend the laws of physics properly, Skippy, anyway-"

"Wha- what? *I* failed?" Skippy fumed indigently. "You flea-bitten, ignorant-"

I cut off his insult. "Skippy said if we steal a ship, we have to do it without anyone realizing it was stolen, which seems impossible to me. So, I was thinking there is a fourth option for getting a ship."

"Oh?" Sarah raised an eyebrow, in the gesture that usually means a guy is in trouble, but in this case it meant she was curious.

"Maybe it's a type of stealing. But I don't think so. We *find* a ship."

Her mouth formed a silent 'O'. "Finding is not stealing, I suppose, if-"

"Right," I nodded. "If the ship has been abandoned. According to maritime law on Earth, an abandoned vessel is subject to being salvaged, and taking control of an abandoned ship is not stealing. It's like the 'finders keepers' rule, only its written into law."

"Look at the big brain on Joe!" Skippy exclaimed. "How did you get all smart about law stuff?"

"I read 'Interstellar Law for Dummies' during breakfast this morning."

"Uh huh," Skippy did not sound convinced. "You want us to *find* a starship? How? I can assure you the Kristang do not leave the keys in their ships while they run into the 7-11 for a burrito. Ooooh, hey, or do you mean like a scavenger hunt? Cool! We could-"

"No scavenger hunts, Skippy."

"Damn. Just when I think things might finally be getting fun around here."

"Sorry, Skippy. You'll have to wait for karaoke night to have fun."

"Karaoke? I'm invited?" He asked, astonished. "Gosh, Joe, that's great. I can-"

Oh crap. We actually did have karaoke every other Tuesday night in the galley, and Skippy was right, he had never been invited. Because he epically *sucked* at singing. There was nothing Skippy enjoyed better than belting out show tunes, and there was nothing the crew hated worse than listening to Skippy sing. "Uh, yeah, great, let me, um, talk with Major Simms about fitting you into the schedule, Ok? What I meant by finding a ship is, there must be Kristang ships that have been abandoned due to battle damage, or things like that."

"Yes, there are. However, by definition, a ship abandoned because of battle damage is unable to fly, Joe. A ship like that would be useless to us, *duh*. And the Kristang typically scuttle their warships after they have been abandoned; they blow them to space dust."

"I don't mean only warships, Skippy. We can make an armed ship out of a transport vessel, the old term for that is a 'Q-ship'."

"Oh, great," his avatar rolled its eyes. "So I'm supposed to go searching the galaxy for ships that just happen to be-"

"No searching needed, Skippy. I hope not. I think you have all the info you need from this ship's database."

"Huh? Now you have completely lost me, Joe."

"You told me the previous crew of the *Flying Dutchman*, before we captured it, had dumped several overloaded Kristang transport ships in deep space, because the Kristang couldn't pay for their passage on a Thuranin star carrier. And by the time the Kristang scraped together enough money to pay the Thuranin, most of the lizards on those ships were dead."

"Yeah, so?"

"Are those transport ships still out there, or did the Thuranin pick up all of them?"

"Ohhhhh," he said with an amazed whistle. "I see what you did there, Joe. This isn't so much you being a clever monkey, you were using just your memory. Although that was pretty clever. The answer is yes. According to the Thuranin records, three transport ships were left behind, because everyone aboard was dead. And more importantly, they were left behind because the jump drive systems had been partially removed from those ships, in a desperate attempt to get one other ship to a habitable planet. The three ships were in bad condition even before they were overloaded with refugees."

"Understood. Would it be possible to fix those ships, even if we have to cannibalize two of them to get one in flyable condition?"

"I, hmm." Skippy when silent for a moment, and his avatar froze for a moment. "I do not know, Joe, the Thuranin did not bother to record that data. Even if they did, it doesn't matter. Didn't you listen to me? Those three ships had the jump drives stripped out. Before you ask a stupid question, no, I can't use three busted jump drives to make one good one."

"The Q-ship only needs to make a single jump, Skippy. It needs to jump in near the Ruhar negotiators' ship, launch an attack and then get blown up, or self-destruct. One single jump. There is no way to do that?"

"With what? Despite what you hairless apes think, you can't make everything with mud and sticks."

"What about if we add duct tape?"

"Oh, well, then, in that case, NO! A jump drive is an incredibly-"

"Yeah, blah, blah, monkeys can't understand technology, blah, blah," I waved my hand dismissively. "Look, Skippy, all I'm asking is, can we take a couple jump drive coils from the *Dutchman* and install them in one of the Kristang ships?"

"No, of course you can't do- Hmm. Maybe. Shmaybe, let me- Damn. Yes. Yes we can. We can, but we shouldn't. Joe, we do not have an unlimited supply of jump drive coils. Quite the opposite. The quantity aboard is severely limited and cannot be replaced."

"Hey, you know what else can't be replaced, Skippy? Earth. It does us no good to preserve the *Dutchman*'s jump capability, if the Ruhar go to Earth and tell the whole galaxy that humans are flying around with a device that can control Elder wormholes."

"It's not so easy, Joe. No, I can't simply use some of the *Dutchman*'s drive coils to jump a Kristang ship. We would also need to install capacitors to provide power to the coils. And the Thuranin coils leave a jump signature that is distinctly different from that of Kristang coils."

"Oh," I stuck out my lower lip and frowned in feigned disappointment, hoping Skippy would be clueless about me manipulating him. "If it's too difficult even for you, then-"

"Hey!" Skippy said indignantly, his avatar's hands on its hips. "I didn't say that I couldn't do it. It's me, Joe; expect the impossible."

"Expect the impossible?" I asked with arched eyebrow. "Is that going to replace 'Trust the Awesomeness' as our unofficial unit motto?"

"Sadly, no. All right, yes, we can remove drive coils and capacitors from the *Dutchman* and install them in a Kristang ship, and I can monkey, pun intended, with the signature of our coils to make the jump drive appear to be a genuine Kristang piece of crap . For control, control, hmm, I need to think about that, hmm. Kristang jump computers are notoriously crappy. No, I'll need to control the jump remotely from the *Dutchman*."

"Excuse me," Sarah interrupted. "Those Kristang transport ships; are they abandoned, or did the Kristang blow them apart? You said the Kristang self-destruct the ships if they have to abandon them."

Oh, crap. I hadn't considered that. My whole plan could fall apart right there. Fortunately for me and my image, Skippy rescued me. "Nope," he assured us, "those ships did not get blown up. Ordinarily, you are correct, those ships would have been destroyed, even after they had been stripped of everything useful. The Thuranin did not allow these particular ships to be destroyed, because of their location. The place where the Thuranin dropped those ships is close to a strategically important wormhole cluster, and experiences heavy traffic. While drifting ships can be tracked and avoided, having debris floating around unpredictably creates a serious navigation hazard."

"Huh." A thought popped into my head. "Is that why the Elders put their wormholes in deep interstellar space; because there is not a lot of space junk floating out there?"

"That is one reason, yes. Ships emerging from a wormhole are temporarily blind and their shields are disrupted by passing through the wormhole's event horizon, so they are vulnerable to impacts with, as you said, space junk," Skippy explained with the tone people use when talking to small children. "There is a more important reason the Elders put their wormholes in deep interstellar space; being far away from gravity wells reduces the power required to keep a wormhole stable."

"I will keep that in mind when I'm building my first wormhole," I chuckled. "We have a plan, then; we will jump to the location where the Thuranin last reported those ships. You can predict where the ships have drifted since then?"

"Easy peasy, Joe. They didn't travel far from where the Thuranin left them, I can predict their current locations within three kilometers, and the Thuranin attached navigation beacons to each of them. The ships have drifted apart, it will require our dropships to fly between them."

"Drifted?" Sarah asked. "I don't understand. Why didn't the Kristang ships leave the area after they had been stranded by the Thuranin?"

"To go where?" Skippy asked sarcastically.

"They couldn't go anywhere," I explained, shooting Skippy an unhappy look. If it entertained Skippy to insult me, I was Ok with that. Berating my crew was not Ok. "Kristang ships can't usually travel between stars; their jump drives take so long to recharge, they overall travel slower than light."

"Yeah, and their crappy jump drives would wear out long before the lizards got halfway to a star," Skippy added.

"Yes, but," Sarah held up her hands. "They did not even make an attempt?"

"Oh, I assume 'they' did," I made air quotes with my fingers. "Right, Skippy?"

"If by 'they', you mean the crews of all the ships, then yes, they did," Skippy confirmed. "The crews, all males, of course, stripped critical components from the other ships to keep a single ship functioning. They left the passengers of all other ships, mostly females, to die when the environmental systems failed. Their plan, if their comrades failed to come up with payment for the Thuranin, was to take that one ship through the nearby wormhole and attempt to reach a habitable planet. To do that, they would have needed to replace their jump drive components many times, which is why they stripped the drives out of the other ships. Personally, I think that one ship would have failed along the way, and those hateful, cowardly MFers would have died in deep space like they deserved. Instead, their clan paid the Thuranin just enough for one ship, and their ship got picked up by a star carrier. Their cowardice allowed them to survive, while the others died."

I could see Sarah's knuckles grow white as she squeezed her fist in anger. "We can make Q-ships out of these transports?"

"Hopefully more than one," I replied.

"I wouldn't count on more than one, Joe," Skippy cautioned, "but we can try."

"Great! Even Count Chocula can't argue with this plan," I was gloating. "We jump in, cobble together one or two Q-ships, take them aboard the *Dutchman*'s hardpoints, and intercept that Ruhar negotiation team."

"Yes!" Skippy agreed. "Except for, you know, the teensy weensy little complication."

My heart skipped a beat. "What complication?"

"Well, heh, heh, Joe, there are so, so very many complications," Skippy chuckled.

Complication Number One was, of course, Hans freakin' Chotek. While he wasn't quite as stiff as when he came aboard, he was still ate up with following UNEF Command's orders to the letter. I wonder if he was more concerned about getting blamed for taking initiative, than he was about aliens raining hellfire down on our home planet. "Q-ships?" He asked skeptically, after we discussed the plan with Skippy, in exhaustive detail.

"Yes, Sir. This is much less risky," I cringed as the words came out of my mouth. I should have said picking up the stranded transports represented no risk at all. Since my idiotic brain had told my mouth to say the wrong thing, I had to do damage control. "There is almost no risk to this proposed operation. These transport ships have been abandoned; they are hanging dead in space, in the middle of nowhere." That was not quite true, as the ships had been stranded near an Elder wormhole cluster. "We do not know their exact condition, however Skippy is confident he could bring one or more of them back to operational status." I was using big words to conceal my nervousness. "Skippy has completed most of the necessary repairs to the *Dutchman*; he can work on the remaining issues while we are under way. We should depart immediately."

Chotek gave an exaggerated sigh. Whatever new perspective he found while gazing down from the lip of that crater on the Dead Star had not made him any more trusting of me. "Colonel Bishop, I am aware of the expectation that once a mission has begun, it acquires a momentum that becomes impossible to stop."

"Sir," I held my tongue from the acid remark I wanted to say. "At this point, all I am asking is that we proceed toward these abandoned transport ships. You can abort the mission at any point. If we think of a better plan before we arrive at the transports, I will be very happy to turn the ship around. If we do not leave soon, we could be wasting valuable time we cannot get back later. As you mentioned, the clock is ticking."

Chotek frowned, looking at the outline of my plan on his tablet. "This is a rather complicated operation, simply to pick up three abandoned, unarmed ships."

"The complications are Skippy's contribution, and he assures me they are all necessary."

Count Chocula surprised me again. "Very well," he pushed his tablet face down on the desk, "we will proceed toward the objective with all possible speed. Colonel, I wish for your rather," he searched for a word, "*inventive* mind, to continue searching for alternatives."

"Yes, Sir. I will inform the duty officer to break orbit."

Damn it, I hated when Skippy did his weaselly 'well heh heh', because I knew it meant nothing but trouble for me.

When he said 'many complications', my Spidey sense tingled, and for good reason. Complication Number One, Hans Chotek, I had been able to deal with. The rest were going to be a problem. "There is no other way to do this, Skippy?" I asked, knowing the answer.

"There are many other ways to do this, Joe, and I know that because you and Chocula and the usual gang of idiots made me go through every freakin' possible option in nauseating detail, before our friendly Count reluctantly approved this forehead-slappingly obvious plan. There is no other *good* way to do this, Joey."

"Well, crap. Pilot, are we ready?"

Captain Desai didn't even bother to turn in her seat. She was standing by, but for this maneuver, she was letting a Chinese act as Pilot In Command. "Affirmative. Everything is green across the board, Colonel." Desai acknowledged calmly, but I could see the tension in her shoulders.

The 'complications' Skippy mentioned were serious problems. Any thought I had of easily swooping in, taking up two or three abandoned transport ships, and jumping away to some place where we could take our time working on them, went out the window when Skippy dumped his gloomy info on us.

Those Kristang transports were drifting near a strategically important wormhole cluster that was closely monitored by the Thuranin. Two Elder wormholes materialized in that area regularly, providing the Thuranin with quick and easy access to far-flung points across the sector. The transport ships were stranded in deep space, but not in the middle of nowhere, the entire area was covered by a sensor network. There was also a lot of Thuranin traffic coming in and out of the two wormholes. Worse, there would be starships hanging around, waiting for the wormholes to open. Hanging around, with nothing better to do than to scan the area, and see an unusual-looking, unidentified Thuranin star carrier that would certainly be worth investigating.

We could not do what I wanted; jump in near the wormholes, take the three ships aboard and jump away quickly. Skippy explained that a ship jumping in near the wormholes, hanging around for a while and then jumping away without going through one of the wormholes would be very suspicious. And we could not go through either of those wormholes to the other ends, especially not in our unique star carrier, and not with three battered Kristang transports on our three hardpoint docking platforms. The other ends of those two wormholes were deep inside Thuranin territory, and near star systems with heavy military presences. There was too much risk of us encountering Thuranin ships on the other ends of those wormholes. The last time we encountered Thuranin ships had not been healthy for the *Flying Dutchman*.

So, we needed to come through the wormhole from the other side. Then we could jump away without exhibiting odd behavior. Except, the other sides of those wormholes were in territory too dangerous for us. That left us the option of Skippy using our Elder wormhole controller module to get us through the wormhole from another point in space. "Skippy, are you sure this won't cause us more trouble than we're already in? You warned us against monkeying with wormholes unless we absolutely have to. If the Thuranin notice either of these wormholes are behaving strangely-"

"That will not happen, Joe, I explained that to you."

"Yes, but you also said these wormholes see a lot of traffic, and there could be many ships on the other ends, waiting to go through. That might be too many witnesses."

He sighed. "All that is true, and all that is irrelevant. I *told* you, I will temporarily adjust the connection of one wormhole, during a gap in its sequence. By the time the wormhole is supposed to resume its sequence, I will have magically restored its function. You are welcome, by the way."

Skippy had explained that, because the area of space near the stranded Kristang transports had two wormholes whose patterns overlapped each other, the wormhole network coordinated the actions of that pair of wormholes so they did not interfere. Avoiding interference required one or the other wormhole to pause between emergence points, during which time the wormhole was temporarily dormant. It was normally temporarily dormant, except this time Skippy was going to wake it up and make it connect to a different wormhole where the *Flying Dutchman* was parked. "Ok, I trust you the Thuranin on the other end won't notice a gap in the sequence-"

"And it is unlikely there will be Thuranin ships hanging around the target end of the wormhole, Joe. They expect that wormhole to be temporarily dormant at that location, to there is no point to a ship waiting there. Any ship desiring to go through the wormhole will jump to the next emergence point."

"Yes, but-"

"Chill! Joe, take a chill pill, please. Nothing in life is without risk. The risk in this case is minimal. For going through the wormhole, I mean. A whole lot of bad shit may happen after we go through, as I warned you."

"Yeah," I took a deep breath to calm myself. Everything our friendly beer can said made sense. Then why did this *feel* like we were jumping into another ambush? Hell, I couldn't run the ship based on my feelings, and this wasn't my Spidey sense tingling; it was more of a nagging fear. "Pilot, take us through the wormhole," I ordered in a voice that was not as confident as I intended to project. "If we detect anything squirrely on the other side, you punch it and jump us away, don't wait for me."

"Understood," Desai nodded without turning to look at me; she was still stiff with tension.

My shoulders were knotted up also.

The *Flying Dutchman* went through the wormhole, emerging from the far side event horizon almost blind and with our defensive shield and stealth field temporarily weakened. We had our sensor field set on maximum range, not that it mattered. The sensor field was so distorted by passing through whatever weird physics happened inside a wormhole, that it could not have detected a battleship right in front of us. All ships were briefly defenseless and blind after emerging from a wormhole; fortunately, we had a chrome-plated beer can on our side. "No enemy ships in range," he reported after a brief pause. Even Skippy could not shrug off the effect of going instantaneously from one point in space to another.

"No *enemy* ships?" I asked, confused. Confusion about the punchline of a joke could be awkward. Confusion about the tactical situation could be fatal. "There are no friendly ships *anywhere*, Skippy." Saying that gave me a pang in the pit of my stomach, thinking just how totally alone we were in the galaxy.

"Uh, sorry about, Colonel," he replied, chastened. Skippy could be completely serious when he wanted to, and when he was paying attention. That rarely happened. "Perhaps I should have said no ships which represent a threat, or a concern. I do detect the three Kristang transport ships, close to where I expected them to be."

"That fast?" It seemed suspiciously quick, even for our magical beer can.

He sighed. "Technically, I do not yet detect them; they are too far away. What I did was query the local sensor network; they accepted our identifications codes, and responded to my question about potential navigation hazards in the area."

"Oh."

"Joe, you complain when I give you too much detail, then you complain when I skip the details," he said with a sniff. "Make up your mind, please."

"My fault, Skippy. I'm a little, uh," it would not be good for the captain of the ship to mention his fears aloud. "It's a tense situation."

"The quicker we get to it, the quicker we can get out of here," he reminded me.

"Agreed. You can reset the wormhole back to its original connections?"

"Doing that now," he replied, and the wormhole symbol on the main bridge display blinked out. "Done. It will proceed to the next emergence point without any change in timing. The Thuranin should not notice anything strange happened."

"Great. Thank you for your awesomeness." The first of Skippy's 'complications' was going through the wormhole, without being detected by the Thuranin. That was successfully accomplished.

The next 'complication' was the extensive Thuranin sensor network around this wormhole emergence point. According to Skippy, we had passed the first hurdle: the network accepted the fake ID code provided by Skippy. That code, he warned, would not pass close scrutiny by Thuranin command. Before we could park the ship near the Kristang transports to work on them, he needed to worm his way into the sensor network and take partial control. "How long will it take for you to get into the sensor network, Skippy?" Before we went through the wormhole, Skippy had only been able to guess how long it would take him to hack in; too many unknown variables, he said.

"Doing it now," he said in that distracted voice that I hated. "This could take a while, even in meatsack caveman time, Joe. The network is widely distributed; the problem is the far nodes of the network are responding at the painfully slow speed of light. We're good for now, I'm doing some unauthorized things with the laws of physics that you don't need to know about."

"We're good?"

"Yes. By the time we reach the Kristang ships, I will have full control of the sensor network. If a Thuranin ship arrives before then, we will have to jump away whether I'm in control of the network or not."

"Fair enough. Colonel Chang, our payload is still secure?"

"Confirmed. We had some flaking off the surfaces, nothing significant." He referred to the three asteroids we carried on the *Dutchman*'s remaining hardpoint docking platforms. Yes, one of Skippy's delightful surprises was that along the way, we had to stop in a crappy, uninhabited star system to pick up a trio of asteroids. And not just any three random asteroids, oh, no. That would be *way* too easy. Instead, we poked around the boring star system what seemed like forever while Skippy scanned for just the right three asteroids, like he was Goldi-freakin'-locks and the bears weren't coming home any time soon. The asteroids could not be too big, or too small. They could not be made of rock too soft or metal too dense. I swear, waiting for Skippy to select three asteroids was like waiting while a girlfriend tries on shoes. In my experience, she looks at and tries a hundred pairs of shoes, and it takes hours while you slowly lose your will to live, and in the end she leaves the store with either nothing, or a pair of shoes *exactly* like the ones she was already wearing.

Not that I'm still bitter about it.

Securing those bulky, inert chunks of rock to the *Dutchman*'s three docking platforms had been an enormous pain in the ass. To make room for the rocks, we had to leave Nagatha and the relay station/lifeboat behind. If the operation went according to plan, we would pick up Nagatha either on our way back, or after the mock attack on the Ruhar negotiating team. If we took all three Kristang transports, we wouldn't have room for Nagatha until we dropped one of the transports.

When Skippy proposed that we bring a trio of asteroids with us, I couldn't believe it. The rocks were not to help us take the transports, they were necessary to maintain our cover after the mock attack on the Ruhar. After the attack, we did not want anyone poking around, trying to figure out where our Q-ships came from. Skippy's hacking into the Thuranin sensor network would mostly cover our tracks. He could erase any evidence of us having come through the wormhole at a time when the wormhole was not scheduled to be open. He could wipe records showing data about a strange-looking Thuranin star carrier that wasn't listed in their fleet database. And he could prevent the Thuranin from seeing us taking aboard the Kristang transports and jumping away with them. With the awesome awesomeness of Skippy, the Thuranin would never know the *Flying Dutchman* was ever there.

What Skippy could not do was permanently change the laws of physics. After we left, the changes he had made to the programming of the sensor network satellites would gradually be overwritten as the code was updated by passing ships. After the network was restored to full functioning, it would still be unable to report that the *Flying Dutchman* had been there, because Skippy would have erased that data. But the sensors would be able to report that the mass of one or more Kristang transports in the area was suddenly missing. And that would start the Thuranin asking uncomfortable questions about why those stranded hulks of ships had been taken, by who, and where they had gone. It would not take the Thuranin long to realize the missing ships were involved in the attack on the Ruhar negotiators.

Which would not be good for us, or humanity.

To avoid that, we needed to prevent the Thuranin from ever discovering the hulks of those ships had gone anywhere. We needed to leave a mass equal to the mass of each ship, we needed to remove the navigation beacons from the ships and attach them to the asteroids. And we needed to shroud the asteroids. Yes, we had to cover the asteroids in an inflatable sort of balloon. Skippy assured us the Thuranin were not paying close attention to those worthless ships; but if those distant objects suddenly became more, or less, large or shiny than they used to be, that would attract attention. Thus, the need to surround the asteroids in a balloon that was the same size and shape of the ships, and as shiny as the hulls of the ships were.

When Skippy had explained that we needed to replace each transport ship with something of equal mass, I knew exactly what he meant. “Oh yeah,” I said confidently. “I saw that in that old *Indiana Jones* movie! He steals a golden statue, and replaces it with a bag of rocks or something. Is that what you plan to do?”

“It was a bag of sand, Joe. And yes, I plan to do something like that.”

“Hmm. I remember that didn’t work out so well for Indiana Jones.”

“I will be much more careful, Joe. I promise.”

“Good. Because if a giant rock starts rolling after me, I’m throwing you under it.”

CHAPTER EIGHT

Skippy's need for an Indiana Jones-type trick is why we came through the wormhole with three asteroids attached to the *Dutchman*, and why I was pleased we lost only minors bits of rock along the way.

"Excellent," I acknowledged Chang's report. A minor amount of material flaking off the asteroids we could live with; we had carved up three asteroids until they were slightly more massive than the stranded transport ships. When we reached the ships and got good sensor data about their mass, we would trim each asteroid to the proper mass with the *Dutchman*'s maser cannons. I would have greatly preferred to cut the asteroids to size and install the balloon around them before going through the wormhole, but Skippy insisted he did not have accurate data on their masses and 'albedo', which I learned is a fancy sciency word for how shiny something is. I did not know why scientists couldn't just use a normal word like 'shininess'. "Pilot," I ordered, "take us over to the nearest Kristang transport. And step on it."

The reason I wanted us to reach the target transports quickly became apparent ninety seven minutes later, when one of the local wormholes was scheduled to emerge into that part of space. Skippy had completed his scans of all three ships, and we were ready for the next phase of the operation, to tackle the next in Skippy's list of 'complications'. Before we could proceed with the next phase, we had to shut down everything but our stealth field, and tuck the *Dutchman* in behind one of the transports. Desai had the *Dutchman*'s nose practically touching one of the transports, with our pirate ship's long, skinny hull stretched out facing away from the wormhole. To be safe, I ordered the ship into position thirty minutes early, in case we ran into last-minute glitches like a balky thruster.

And it was a damned good thing we hid our pirate ship, because four minutes after the Elder wormhole popped into existence, two Thuranin star carriers came through. Between the two star carriers, they were transporting two battleships, four cruisers, a light cruiser and eight destroyers. I shuddered when I saw the destroyers, remembering how a squadron of those ships had nearly trapped and destroyed the *Flying Dutchman*. "That is a lot of firepower," I said quietly, swallowing hard.

"It is, Joe," Skippy's own voice was quieter than usual. "Right now, just one of those destroyers could tear this us apart. I rebuilt our pirate ship as best I could, but it's kind of held together now with duct tape and a prayer."

"Thank you for boosting our confidence there, Skippy. Any chance those ships see us?"

"Zippy chance of that," he scoffed. "None of those ships are even actively scanning the area; they are relying on a feed from the local sensor network, and I control that. If they bother to look in this direction, what those ships are seeing over here are the dead hulks of three Kristang transports, and nothing else. My only concern was whether a ship might energize its active sensors, to tune them after coming through the wormhole. But these ships just left a Thuranin fleet shipyard, and they are in optimal condition. There is no reason for those ships to bother looking around. I am, hmm, that's interesting."

"What?" Out where we were, 'interesting' was rarely 'good'.

"Joe, I just decrypted data from one of the star-"

"Skippy! You promised you would not go poking around in the databases of those ships. They might detect something out here is spying on them."

"Cool your jets, Joe. I am not poking around anywhere. One of the star carriers transmitted their secret mission orders to the other carrier, and I intercepted the message. I have gotten better at decrypting Thuranin military transmissions, and this particular one was no challenge for me. What I find interesting is the objective in their orders; that pair of star carriers are going to join four others for an assault on a Jeraptha-controlled wormhole cluster. My question to you is whether it might benefit us to somehow pass that intelligence to the Jeraptha."

"Uh," I looked at Chotek, who was standing in the CIC. "We'll have to think about that, Skippy. It would depend on whether preventing a successful Thuranin attack would benefit us."

"*And*," Chotek emphasized the word, "whether passing along that data poses a risk of revealing our presence."

"A risk? Ha! Oh, no way, dude!" Skippy chortled. "As if! I could include the data in a freakin' birthday message to Jeraptha Fleet Command, and they would still have no idea where it came from. Chocula, since you are supposed to be the grand strategic thinker here, I expected you would see the value to humanity of the Jeraptha further securing their recent military gains in this sector. The more secure the Jeraptha are, the more peaceful this sector is, and that is all good for humans on both Earth and Paradise."

"I will," Chotek replied with irritation, "consider it. *After* we complete the present operation. How long will those ships remain here?"

"Not long," Skippy's voice sounded seriously peeved. He had offered what he thought was a valuable piece of information, and Chotek had dismissed it as a distraction.

"Skippy," I hurried to assure our friendly beer can, "that is excellent info, and an outstanding effort. You dug into that transmission on your own initiative, I appreciate it." Hopefully, he would notice the use of 'I' rather than 'we'. "How long is 'not long'?"

"Those carriers are already accelerating away from the wormhole, and using their shields to clear space in front of them for a jump. If they follow standard Thuranin procedure, they will jump away within eighteen minutes; shortly after the Elder wormhole closes."

I looked back to the CIC. "Colonel Chang, tell the away teams to be ready for departure in twenty minutes. I want us to get the hell out of here as fast as we can."

The next 'complication' in Skippy's grand list of complications was trimming the asteroids to match the mass of the transport ships, then covering the rocks in the balloons and inflating them. This was sort of his Indiana Jones trick. Once the balloons were in place, their shells would harden, and Skippy could adjust the color of the shells to match the reflectivity of the ship hulls. At the distance the transports had drifted from the satellites of the sensor network, we didn't need the balloon shells to look like the ships, just to reflect a similar amount of faint starlight in a roughly similar shape.

Skippy, his bots and the CIC crew could handle carving up the asteroids, dispersing the debris, and installing the shrouds. Some of Skippy's bots could also assist in the other 'complication' I was most worried about; locating and removing the booby traps.

Skippy had explained that, because the Thuranin had not allowed the Kristang to self-destruct their abandoned ships, the lizards had very likely planted booby traps to prevent anyone from easily messing with them. Soon after we arrived at the first ship, Skippy's scans had detected several explosive devices aboard, and he warned there were probably many more that external scans could not detect. We could not risk taking booby-trapped ships aboard the *Dutchman*'s docking platforms, so the explosives needed to be cleared first. With his bots, Skippy could help, but he did not have enough bots available to clear ships quickly enough. So, Major Smythe's SpecOps team would have to suit up and go aboard the ships to clear the booby traps. It would be dangerous, and it would be necessary, and it needed to be done quickly. There was too much traffic through those two wormholes for us to take our time clearing the ships of explosives.

Skippy had learned the Thuranin were launching a major operation to stabilize their losses in the sector; that meant the pair of wormholes would be experiencing extra traffic; both fresh ships coming from fleet shipyards, and ships in need of heavy maintenance returning to base. Ships coming in through the wormhole were not a serious danger to us; Skippy knew exactly when the wormholes were scheduled to be open, so we shut down operations twenty minutes before each wormhole appearance. Incoming ships did not linger long after coming through the wormholes; we waited ten minutes after each inbound ship departed, just to be safe.

Ships seeking to go through the wormhole from our side were a serious threat, and a threat we could not predict. Ships jumped in from way beyond even Skippy's sensor range, and they jumped in without any warning. We could not even rely on ships jumping in only shortly before one of the wormholes opened, because sometimes ships arrived hours before a wormhole emergence. Skippy tried to assure me that ships would rely on data from the sensor network he controlled, rather than looking around with their own sensor fields. I was still greatly concerned that during the time enemy ships were lingering; some ship's ambitious sensor officer could try for the Employee of the Month award by nosily poking around the area with sensors, double-checking the feed from the local sensor network. The *Dutchman* had its stealth field operational 24/7, and any of our dropships flying around used a stealth field also, protecting us from being discovered by a casual sensor scan. Any sort of serious scan with a military-grade sensor field would certainly not miss the presence of our shrunken but still massive star carrier. The unexplained presence of a very odd-looking, stealthed Thuranin star carrier would prompt an immediate investigation by any Thuranin warship in the area, no matter what line of bullshit Skippy tried to feed the local sensor network.

"Ready?" I asked the pilot of the dropship.

"Yes, Colonel," the French pilot acknowledged.

"Punch it," I ordered, and gripped the too-small Thuranin seat with both hands. It was unworthy of me as a commander to wish I had Desai flying the dropship, rather than the Frenchman. Gustov Renaud was a fine pilot, having flown the hottest Rafale fighters the French had in their inventory, and Desai had given him high marks on his evaluation. Still, I always felt more comfortable with Desai at the controls.

The dropship rocketed out of the *Flying Dutchman*'s docking bay at the maximum acceleration its human occupants could stand, headed directly for the second Kristang transport ship. To prevent our activities from being discovered by Thuranin ships jumping in, we moved between our star carrier and the Kristang ships as quickly as possible, limiting our exposure time. That technique protected the away teams from being detected. To protect humanity, in case the Thuranin somehow did notice something funky going on near the stranded Kristang transports, each away team brought along an old friend of mine: Mr. Nukey. Our dropship's tactical nuke was strapped into the seat beside me, happily emitting stray neutrons, but otherwise silently enjoying a chance to get away from the *Dutchman* and explore the universe. Join UN ExForce, I thought. See the galaxy, meet new people, and nuke them!

Maybe that slogan needed some work.

In case our pirate ship was detected by the Thuranin and had to jump away, an away team trapped aboard a Kristang transport was expected to trigger their nuke, to destroy all evidence of humans flying around the galaxy on our own. It sucked, and I wished there was a way around that unpleasant necessity, but I didn't see an option. My personal plan, if I got trapped with nosy and pissed-off Thuranin approaching, was to wait until a

Thuranin dropship got close enough, and let Mr. Nukey do what he did best. At least we would take some little green MFers with us.

"Flight path is nominal," Captain Renaud said in a French accent that my American ear found unintentionally snobbish, like he was looking down his nose at me. I don't know why I still felt that way; I knew plenty of French Canadiens from living in Maine and they were good people. Of course, Canadians had a reputation of being as polite as the French reputation for being rude. "Cutting thrust now."

My stomach did a flipflop as the dropship was momentarily in zero-gee, then the pilot kicked thrust on hard to decelerate. "Approaching target," he said, his voice reflecting the strain of forces five times Earth normal gravity. This was the tricky part of getting the away team into the docking bay of a Kristang transport. Skippy's bots had cleared booby traps from a docking bay, and manually cranked the doors open. Our pilot needed to fly the dropship into the bay as quickly as possible, with no external guidance, and no safety margin from capture mechanisms in the bay. The ship ahead of us was dead, without even any reserve power. There may be a powercell or two still active aboard; they weren't providing any power to the docking bay. We were trading the risk of crashing in the docking bay, with the risk of being exposed in empty space if a Thuranin ship jumped in and decided to look around. Since our pilots could mostly control the risk of crashing, I opted to let them fly and trust their skill and judgment.

I looked over at Mr. Nukey, who some jokers had painted with a big purple Barney flipping the bird and saying 'Greetings from Earth, MFers!' with a moronic Barney grin.

The greeting did not seem sincere to me. I was totally Ok with that.

Our pilot must have thought he was landing a Rafale fighter on the deck of a carrier, because we came to a very abrupt halt that rattled my teeth. On the display in front of me, I could see we had still been moving at a good speed when the dropship's tail entered the transport's docking bay, and we had briefly pulled over eight gees to arrest our progress. Renaud was either very, very good, or he was showing off. Or both. Now the dropship wobbled slightly, then settled to the deck with a clanging sound as our skids clamped on firmly to the alien deck. "Thank you for flying Air France," the pilot said smoothly. "There is a comment card under your seat, please feel free to ignore it."

I decided right then that Gustov Renaud was a damned good pilot.

The giant docking bay doors, open to cold space, were on the side of the ship facing away from the wormholes so we didn't have to worry about being detected once we were in the bay. To speed our exit, the doors were left open, which left the bay open to vacuum. That didn't matter; everyone in the away team was wearing Kristang powered armor suits except the two pilots in the cockpit. They sealed the cockpit doors, then we popped open the dropship's large rear ramp and let the air rush out. We couldn't wait to cycle through the dropship's airlock four people at a time, and the dropship had plenty of oxygen onboard. It was a credit to the professionalism of our SpecOps team that I did not see anything, not even a stray candy wrapper blowing around when we let the air out in a rush.

Skippy's bots had cleared the docking bay, and the inner airlock door, before he had to recall the bots to work on trimming the asteroids and installing their shrouds. We had two bots with us in the dropship; they were available because Skippy's scans had determined one of the transports was in such bad condition, it wasn't even useful as spare parts. That left only two ships to clear of booby traps, and we would only be able to make one functional Q-ship out of those two hulks. It was disappointing that we had come all the way out here, taken substantial risks and were expending a lot of effort, to make just one Q-ship.

With only two bots available to our away team, our plan was for people to locate booby traps, and for Skippy to use the bots to disarm those IEDs. Skippy had already remotely rendered the larger booby traps inert, but he wasn't able to do much about the crude, manually triggered devices the Kristang crews had cobbled together before they abandoned the ships and left their terrified passengers behind to die.

By 'locate' booby traps, I did not mean for us to stumble across them and have them go 'Boom' in our faces. We had portable scanners that could see through doors, decks and bulkheads at short range. That's a damned good thing, because sure enough, the inner airlock door had an IED that would explode if the door slid aside and pulled a wire with it. Seeing that on the scanner made me roll my eyes. I had dealt with more sophisticated IEDs in Nigeria, and I found it ironic that an advanced starfaring species like the Kristang relied on such crude devices. Crude did not mean ineffective, of course, that bomb could have killed the half dozen people of the SpecOps team. Instead, they reported their scanner's findings to Skippy, and he had one of the bots drill a hole through a bulkhead, then reach a skinny tentacle around and disarm that IED. One door down, a hundred more to go, I thought to myself. We had to clear the entire ship, compartment by compartment, before it would be safe to take the transport on one of the *Dutchman*'s docking platforms. Our already shaky pirate ship could not afford to take any more damage.

"Inner door is clear!" An Indian paratrooper reported. "Opening it manually now."

"Let's move," I said, unbuckling my seat restraints and standing up carefully, reminding myself that Kristang starships do not have artificial gravity even when they have power.

"Are you sure, Colonel?" The question came from one of my babysitters, an Army Ranger named Paul Rodriguez. He and my semi-permanent shadow Lauren Poole had unofficially been assigned by Major Smythe to keep me out of trouble. Smythe probably thought that, me being US Army, I might feel more comfortable with Rangers. Or he thought I would protest less and be less of a whiny pain in the ass if my babysitters were Rangers. Either way, I was stuck with them and they were stuck with me.

"Yes, I'm sure," I tried being polite with my babysitters. All three of them, which included United States Marine Corps Staff Sergeant Margaret Adams. Whereas Major Smythe had assigned Rodriguez and Poole to babysit me, Skippy had arranged for Adams to accompany me.

"We could wait for the forward team to clear the first passageway, Sir," Adams suggested, in a voice that implied it was not quite a suggestion.

"Adams," I responded while swimming through vacuum toward the open rear ramp, "I know Skippy assigned you to keep me out of trouble. But you were supposed to keep Skippy out of trouble when we took the relay station, and you got into one hell of a firefight with the Thuranin."

"Yes, Sir," Adams was not deterred. "That was one time. Skippy knows for sure that *you* are a magnet for trouble everywhere you go."

That was a statement I could not argue with. "Fine. Then your job is to keep me out of trouble, *while* we clear the ship of IEDs. This op is all hands on deck, Adams, I'm not going to sit on my ass aboard the *Dutchman*."

"Yes, Sir," she replied unhappily. She wasn't the only person unhappy about me going aboard a Kristang transport, most of the command crew had strongly urged me to remain aboard our pirate ship. I had vetoed that idea. This wasn't Star Trek, I had told them, where the captain had to remain aboard the ship while an away team took all the risk. Colonel Chang was perfectly capable of running the ship in my absence, and Skippy wanted me on an away team, in case we ran into a situation that required, as Skippy put it, 'a monkey-brain idea'.

I took that as a compliment.

"Colonel Bishop?" Lt Sodhi of the Indian team called over the link in my suit helmet. "Sir, could you come up here, please? I think you should see this."

"Make a hole, people," I called over the broadcast channel. Adams propelled herself along right on my heels, with the two Rangers close behind. The Rangers were special forces, and they both outranked her, and Margaret Adams had made it crystal clear that she didn't give a shit about any of that. My safety was her responsibility; the Rangers were welcome to tag along if they stayed out of her way.

When I got to the inner airlock door, four soldiers were floating, hugging the airlock door frame. They turned to look at me, saying nothing as I pulled myself forward with slightly less grace than the special forces had. We had all been practicing zero gee combat maneuvers in our Kristang powered armor suits; I had devoted extra hours to that part of the training, as I didn't want to let the team down if we went into action together. In combat, it was unlikely I would be able to do anything useful with a weapon compared to the SpecOps team, but being capable of handling myself in zero gee meant the professionals could concentrate on their jobs and not worry about me. It was the least I could do, since I had not made the sacrifices and commitment to qualify for special forces. And I wasn't good enough anyway.

"What is it, Lieutenant?"

Sodhi pointed to his left, then his right, silently.

They were visible as soon as my helmet came through the airlock. On both sides, floating randomly in the passageway. Kristang bodies. They looked desiccated, like mummies. Before we arrived, Skippy had speculated that the lack of oxygen and bitter cold inside the ships would have preserved the bodies in some fashion; a possibility I had asked him not to discuss with anyone else. The bodies had been floating undisturbed for a long time, until we forced opened the airlock door and sucked out whatever atmosphere remained. Now, exposed to extreme cold and hard vacuum, the exposed lizard skin had crazed and cracked, freezing and burning at the same time. It was ugly.

Women and children. Kristang females and their young. Mostly. I saw only four adult males, in civilian clothing. Or they were wearing what I thought was Kristang civilian clothing; I knew it was not the black and yellow of Kristang military uniforms.

"God." I didn't know what else to say. I couldn't say anything else. Yes, we all knew the transports had been overloaded with civilian refugees, and we knew the Thuranin would not have allowed the Kristang to eject the bodies, because bodies would create a risk of ships smacking into them after coming through a wormhole. So we knew the ships would be full of bodies. Maybe the SpecOps people were ready for what they saw. I wasn't.

"Sir," Sodhi drew my attention to an adult female. I knew she was a female due to her small size. "Gunshot wounds."

Looking closer, I saw he was right about the wounds. It wasn't only that one Kristang; now that I knew what to look for, I saw many of the adults had wounds characteristic of bullet holes. In fact, all three of the adult males, all civilians, had more than one gunshot wound. "They killed them."

"Yes, Colonel," Sodhi nodded, I could see his helmet bobbing up and down. "My guess is this ship's crew stripped their ship of everything useful, then retreated to the docking bay," he pointed back through the airlock. "The passengers must have panicked when they saw they were being abandoned. I know I would. The crew killed them if they got in the way."

"Holy mother of God." The passageway was only maybe thirty meters long, and it was crammed with mummified bodies. I wondered in horror whether the entire ship was like this; Kristang stacked on top of each other like cordwood. Skippy had told us the transports were ‘grossly overloaded’ with refugees, and that the ship’s environmental systems had struggled to provide enough oxygen. I should have asked him for a better definition of ‘grossly overloaded’ before we came aboard.

My team seeing their commander stunned into inaction was not helpful. Everyone was feeling the same way; my job was to keep us focused on making sure humanity did not suffer the fate of these dead Kristang. “Lieutenant, if the passengers rushed toward the docking bays, it makes sense this part of the ship would be packed with people. Hopefully the rest of the ship isn’t like this. Get your scanning teams to clear this passageway in both directions, in case the crew booby trapped the bodies,” I had known militia crazies to do that in Nigeria. “We will work our way compartment by compartment, until we have identified all IEDs so Skippy can disarm them. I want teams limited to two-hour shifts; we need to be razor sharp and focused. Teams not active will return to the dropship to remove suits and get some R&R.”

“Yes, Sir,” Sodhi agreed immediately, which surprised me. I had expected a hard-core special forces leader to insist his team did not need rest. Major Smythe must have impressed upon his SpecOps team that I would not tolerate any gung-ho cowboy bullshit. Or Sodhi simply understood we could not take any risks aboard these unfamiliar alien vessels. “We will need to move these bodies out of the way to get access farther into the ship.”

“Right.” I called Captain Renaud in the dropship. “Captain, we need space in here, so we will be bringing, uh, bodies, into the docking bay. Get the outer doors closed so the bodies aren’t floating out into space.”

“Colonel, may I suggest another idea?” Renaud asked. “We have netting in our gear locker. I suggest that I move the dropship to the end of the docking bay, and we stretch netting across the bay to contain, whatever it is you need to move into the bay.”

“Good thinking, Captain.” I related the plan to Sodhi. “As you work your way down the passageway and verify there are no booby traps, pass the bodies back down through the airlock, and we’ll secure them.”

I volunteered my team to set up the netting across the docking bay, and we formed a human chain to accomplish the grim task of passing mummified bodies along. After the passageway was cleared, blessedly none of the bodies had IEDs attached, we split up into teams of four, each team having two hand-held scanners. In our team, Rangers Poole and Rodriguez operated the scanners, while Adams and I tagged areas with verified or suspected IEDs, and used fancy Thuranin spray cans to paint a fluorescent orange check mark on compartments we had cleared.

It was a tough job. Not physically, because our powered armor suits and the lack of gravity made moving around almost effortless. It was tough emotionally. The first ‘compartment’ we cleared was more of a storage locker, barely large enough to hold two sets of powered armor; we found a scene that almost made me have to take off my helmet in the vacuum. Because I almost puked and cried at the same time.

In the locker was a Kristang female. A lizard. A member of the species that would wipe humanity off the face of the Earth without a second thought.

This female was huddled in the locker, clutching three young Kristang, the four of them hugging each other. Even though her face was mummified, and now cracked from exposure to harsh vacuum, I thought I could sense the hopelessness and terror in her eyeless sockets.

She must have taken shelter in the locker, clutching her children to her, as the food, water and oxygen ran out, as the crew stripped everything useful out of the ship, as the power died and darkness closed in. She had tried to comfort her children as best she could, knowing for certain there was nothing she could do for them. Knowing they were all going to die horribly of suffocation and frostbite.

I reminded myself that Kristang females had been genetically engineered to be small, weak, docile and less intelligent. The creature, the *woman*, I saw in that locker had done her best to take care of her children, in the only way she knew, the only way she could. The only way she was allowed to by her murderous species.

Adams backed away, bent over double. She was also struggling not to lose her breakfast on the inside of her helmet.

"Breathe deep, Sergeant," I suggested. A glance at our two Rangers told me they were not having an easy time of it either. Telling Adams to take deep, calming breaths helped me do the same, and focusing on the three members of my team distracted me from my own disgusted nausea.

"Yes, Sir." Adams straightened up, her face pale inside the helmet. "No excuses, Colonel." Droplets of tears floated freely in her helmet, some beading up on the faceplate.

I held her shoulders and pressed my faceplate against hers, looking her directly in the eyes. "No excuse *needed*, Staff Sergeant. If you are not emotionally affected by this," I gestured to the dead family in the locker, "then I don't need you in my crew. These Kristang, these *people*, are not our enemies. Their warrior caste is. Not these civilians. Not defenseless women and children."

"Yes, Sir," she shook her head, but she shook it angrily. And she gently pushed herself away from me. "I'm all right, Colonel."

"None of us are all right, Adams. We're doing our job anyway, because we have to."

"Colonel Bishop," Poole called. "These people were stranded here by the Thuranin crew of our ship? The *Flying Dutchman*?"

"Yes," I confirmed. "Our ship didn't have a name back then, but yes. Our ship did this."

"Because the Kristang couldn't *pay*?" She asked incredulously.

"Because their clan couldn't pay for passage aboard a star carrier. Skippy told me the story is, the Kristang were evacuating a planet; they packed these ships full of refugees. The Thuranin picked up these transports, but halfway to their destination, the Thuranin learned the Kristang clan couldn't come up with payment. If the Thuranin support a Kristang military operation, they transport the warships and support vessels for free. Apparently, if the Kristang want transport that doesn't directly support Thuranin interests, the clan has to pay for the ride." I looked down the passageway, to the dozens of doors to compartments and lockers we needed to clear. "By the time the clan scraped together the cash or whatever they sue for payment, most of the people aboard these transports were dead. Thousands of them."

Poole took a deep breath, loud enough that I could hear it over the comm system. "Colonel, during the pre-mission briefing on Earth, we went over the records of your first two missions aboard the *Dutchman*. One of the topics was the incident when you put the Thuranin crew in a container, and jumped them inside a gas giant planet. Sir," she looked at me, the lights on the side of her helmet illuminating my face. "There was some discussion about whether you committed a war crime by killing those sleeping Thuranin."

"I have wondered that myself," I admitted. At the time, I was so fearful about the Thuranin, I did not consider too deeply the morality of what I did. Later, I had been able to rationalize my actions as necessary at the time. The incident did keep me awake some nights. "Maybe I could have kept them locked up somewhere, until we got to Earth and UNEF Command could take them as prisoners of war. But at the time, we had just seized an alien starship, and I didn't know if we would ever see Earth again-"

"Maybe you should stop thinking about it, Sir," Poole declared emphatically. "The former crew of the *Dutchman* got better treatment than they deserved." I could see she had a tear welling up in the corner of one eye.

"There is a higher authority that will judge me for that, Poole." By 'higher authority', I didn't just mean Chotek, Skippy, UNEF Command or the United States Army. "This locker is clear," I closed the door and sprayed an orange check mark on it. "Let's keep moving."

I was in the process of suiting up again in the dropship, getting ready for another two hour shift clearing IEDs, when Skippy pinged me. "Trouble, Joe. Five Thuranin ships just jumped in, and the next wormhole emergence isn't for another eight hours and sixteen minutes. We already ceased operations on trimming and covering the two asteroids, before you ask."

Damn it! Five ships that would have nothing to do for over eight hours. What if one of them got bored and decided to scan the area, or even fly over to check out the dead hulks of three Kristang transports? "What type of ships?" I prayed they were unarmed transports. No such luck.

"Two battlecruisers and three light cruisers."

Crap. I checked my zPhone; the app to activate Mr. Nukey was on the second screen. According to the status, Nukey was ready to go at any time. If he needed to do his job, I would not be able to give him a performance evaluation afterward. "Is there any indication they are going to do anything other than wait for the wormhole to open?"

"No, Joe. They are just maintaining formation. All ships queried the sensor network, and they are all satisfied with the data I fed them."

"This isn't good, but I don't see that we can do anything other than continue clearing these ships of booby traps, and hope those little green MFers go through the wormhole."

"I agree. Hey, Joe?"

"Yeah?"

"You be extra, extra careful over there, please?"

"I'm touched, Skippy. Thank you for caring about me. You're a good guy."

"Oh. Uh, I was going to say that if you do something stupid and an IED explodes now and the Thuranin see it, we're all screwed. But let's go with me being a good guy."

"Asshole."

I told the teams of both ships about the Thuranin ships, and reminded them all to be extra super-duper awesomely careful. As if they needed to be told to be careful around explosives; especially crude, hurriedly-built amateur explosive devices that just might decide to detonate on their own because they were bored and lonely.

CHAPTER NINE

Clearing both ships of IEDs took 30 percent longer than we estimated, although we had been making a wild guess. The other transport ship was declared free of booby traps twenty eight minutes before the ship I had been working on; I like to think me being on the team didn't slow us down. It didn't matter anyway, because those five Thuranin warships were still hanging around, and the wormhole wasn't going to open for more than an hour. With nothing else to do, I ordered downtime for everyone. We ate and rested as best we could; some of the SpecOps people actually took naps. One of them, a Ranger whose name shall not be mentioned except it rhymes with 'Slauren Spoole', might have snored a bit. Or more than a bit.

It's funny how when you drool in your sleep, and you are in zero gravity, it doesn't run down your chin, it floats in front of your face.

We waited until the wormhole was scheduled to open. We waited five minutes, then five minutes more. Skippy did not give us the All Clear signal, or any signal at all. Finally, I broke communications silence and pinged the *Dutchman* on a low-power, tightbeam laser burst transmission that lasted half a nanosecond. Skippy had assured me there was a near-zero chance of the Thuranin detecting the transmission; I still felt unprofessional breaking silence. The way I justified it to myself was that if the Thuranin were on their way toward us and I needed to activate Mr. Nukey, I wanted time to make a boring and useless speech to the crew. I'm sure they would have preferred to let Nukey do the talking for us. "Skippy, what the hell is happening out there?"

"I do not know, Joe. Those five ships are powered up, but they are not maneuvering into position to go through the wormhole."

"Oh, for crying out loud. Did one of them get a flat tire or something?"

"Again, I do not know. I would know, if you didn't have a hissy fit about the idea of me poking around in their databases, you knucklehead."

"I do not have hissy fits, Skippy. I have, uh, legitimate concerns."

"Uh huh. They just *sound* like hissy fits."

"I- Can you guess what those ships are doing?"

"Maybe they ordered a pizza and they're waiting for it to be delivered through the wormhole? How the hell should I know? Oh, hey, here's a crazy idea; I could dip into the navigational database of one ship, and-"

"No! N-O. Do *not* do that."

"I can spell, Joe. You're the grammar challenged one. We- wait, there's a new development."

"What?"

"Will you *please* shut your crumb catcher for a minute?"

I shut up. To burn off nervous energy, I checked the connection to Nukey on my zPhone. Then I flipped open the cover of Nukey's status panel to check again. That drew alarmed looks from the crew, proving once again that I am an idiot.

"Ok, good news, Joe," Skippy announced. "The reason five ships were holding back is because three star carriers just came in through the wormhole. Now the five ships are maneuvering to go through. I intercepted a transmission between the two groups of ships; these three star carriers are in a hurry, and will be jumping away within ten minutes."

I breathed a sigh of relief and closed Nukey's status panel cover. Half an hour later, our dropship was headed back to the *Flying Dutchman* at high acceleration. And within the hour, I was freshly showered and on the bridge as I watched the duty officer, Major Simms, monitor the process of taking the first Kristang transport aboard one of our three docking platforms. One of our asteroids was now in the exact position that transport had occupied, with the hardened balloon shroud in place with the correct shape and level of shininess. Skippy had removed the beacon from the transport and attached it to the asteroid. With any luck at all, the Thuranin would never know we had just stolen, or technically salvaged, two Kristang transports ships.

It took another three hours until the second transport ship was firmly secured to a docking platform, and its replacement asteroid was in position. We not only needed to make sure the asteroid had the same mass as the ship it was replacing, within one percent. We had to make sure the shroud balloon was the same size, and reflected the same amount of dim starlight as the ship we had just salvaged. And before we left, the asteroid had to be moving in the same direction and speed as the ship, plus the asteroid had to be tumbling at the exact same rate. Overall, this simple operation to pick up two transport ships no one wanted was *way* too freakin' complicated. According to Skippy, he thought it very likely those shrouded asteroids would drift onward, alone, until the end of time. If, hundreds of years from now, anyone ever investigated the one remaining transport ship and the two asteroids, they would have one hell of an intriguing mystery to explore.

We had debated the wisdom of accelerating the ship a significant distance before we jumped; so that if Thuranin ships arrived shortly after we jumped, they would not wonder why there was a remnant jump signature close to what was supposed to be three dead Kristang transports. We could not use quantum resonators to help disguise where we jumped to, because using resonators would be like holding up a huge sign saying 'Highly Suspicious Activity Here'. Also, we did not have many resonators aboard the ship anyway. In the end, I decided remaining in the area longer was the greater risk, so I ordered Chang to jump us away as soon as possible.

"All decks and systems report ready for jump," an officer in the CIC reported.

Lt. Colonel Chang, the duty officer in the command chair, acknowledged the report with a curt nod, and spoke without checking with me. I approved of that; Chang was in command of the ship right then, and he should not feel he needed to clear everything with me. "Pilot," he ordered, "jump us away."

"Aye, Sir," the lead duty pilot replied. Our two pilots, a British guy and a French woman, exchanged quiet words, then a button was pressed, and the starfield shifted. "Jump completed successfully. We are within," the Brit checked his display, "one hundred ninety two meters of our target jump coordinates."

"One ninety two? That's sloppy, you're slipping, Skippy," I teased.

"Ahh, we were in a hurry to get out of there, so I didn't have time to factor in the exact masses of our two new ships," he said with a defensive tone.

"I was just busting your balls, Skippy. That was remarkable, as always."

"The most remarkable thing about me, is how I make the remarkable seem ordinary."

"Yeah, that's it," I rolled my eyes. "Colonel Chang?"

He ran the crew through the preparation for another jump, and the ship distorted spacetime again. We wanted to get far away from the wormhole cluster, in case Thuranin ships jumped in shortly after we left, and saw the distinctive remnants of our jump wormhole. A ship with a bored or curious captain, or a captain hoping for a promotion, might decide to pursue us to investigate. Hopefully even a very ambitious captain would give up after one jump.

"Where to now, Skippy?" I asked.

"First, we eject that third asteroid that we don't need. Then, ugh, I guess we should swing by and pick up your girlfriend in the lifeboat-"

"Nagatha is not my girlfriend, Skippy."

"That's what *you* think, she would have another opinion about that."

"Fine. Those are the obvious moves. What about after that? You need some place to work on converting the transports into something useful for the attack."

"I do, and interstellar space is not convenient. The hulls of those ships have been cold-soaking for too long, they need to be warmed up before I can make major modifications and get their systems operational again. There is an uninhabited star system we could get to by transiting a wormhole; I would need to connect it to a wormhole that has been dormant. This star system is a safe place to work; according to all the survey data I have, no one has ever been there."

"Ever? Never ever?" I asked skeptically.

"Never, Joe. I just told you, the wormhole near that system is dormant, so no one can get there. It's another boring red dwarf, no one wants to go there. I'll send the data to you and Chotek. Before we go to work on building a Q-ship, we should stop by a Ruhar data node, to check if anything has changed with the negotiations."

"A data node?" Chang turned in the command chair to look at me. "Is that like a relay station? It will not be dangerous for us to approach?" I knew Chang was thinking back to the difficult, complicated and dangerous operation it took for us to capture a Thuranin data relay station. We could not take the risk, and did not have the time, for another op like that one.

"Sort of," Skippy explained. "The Ruhar have many types of data nodes, the one I'm thinking of is an automated signal transfer station; it is unmanned and used to relay signals from a star system to the Oort Cloud region where Jeraptha ships transit. The data node I have in mind is near the edge of a star system where the Ruhar have recently established a colony; the system does not have a permanent military presence. We jump in, I ping the data node with authentication codes, and download the data we need."

"Just like that?"

"Just like that, Joe. Easy peasy. We don't need to do any crazy shit like stuffing a dropship inside a comet, or capturing a relay station. This time, we are not trying to get military secrets from the Thuranin, all we need is Ruhar federal government communications. The negotiation with the Fire Dragons is not a closely-held secret, now that federal government has approved the talks to proceed."

"You can do some awesome Skippy magic thing, make this data node think we are a Jeraptha or Ruhar ship?"

"Oh, yeah, no problemo. I'll use the IFF codes of a Ruhar ship to contact the data node, then instruct the node to erase its memory of us after we leave. This will be easy, Joe. Trust me."

Crap. Now I needed to persuade Hans Chotek to approve us visiting a Ruhar-inhabited star system, and approve us screwing with a dormant wormhole so Skippy Claus and his little helper elfbots could take our salvaged transports ships to Santa's Workshop. Checking the main bridge display, I saw the countdown timer indicated we could not jump again for thirty seven minutes. "I'll talk with Chotek. In the meantime, Colonel Chang, eject that asteroid and move us away, I don't want that thing anywhere near us when we jump." We did not need another incident of a large mass distorting our jump wormhole.

One thing that bugged the hell out of me about Hans Chotek was- Ok, there were a lot of things about him that bugged the hell out of me. This time, specifically, it was my total lack of ability to predict his mood, or what he would do. On my way to his office, I stopped to splash water on my face and tidy up my Army Combat Uniform. I regretted that camo pattern was the uniform of the day aboard the ship. For a discussion with Chotek, I wanted to be wearing at least my Class B Army Service Uniform, because I figured that would make him take me more seriously as a senior officer. Changing uniforms now would only tell Chotek that I was nervous.

My uniform top was stuck to my back from the sweat of nervous tension. There wasn't time for a shower; I took my top off, tossed it in a bin, and got an identical top from a closet. Skippy would get his Magical Laundry Fairy bots working on cleaning my dirty clothes, and they would be back in the closet or drawers the next morning.

Before walking into his office, I mentally prepared my arguments in favor of contacting a Ruhar data node and then taking the ship to an unknown, unexplored star system where Skippy could set up Santa's Workshop. Organizing my thoughts was not a strength for me, but I did the best I could in the time available. Knocking on the doorframe, I saw he was head-down at his desk, reading something on a tablet. "Mr. Chotek?"

To my surprise, he pushed the tablet aside, stood up, and offered me a handshake. An enthusiastic, arm-pumping handshake. "Colonel Bishop," he grinned. "Congratulations to you, and to your crew. That was a truly outstanding operation, *outstanding*," he emphasized. Maybe he thought 'outstanding' was something the US military said a lot, I had to remember his native language was German.

"Thank you, Sir."

He released my hand, gestured for me to sit, and plopped back down in his chair with a satisfied smile. "Colonel, when you presented me what seemed like an overly complicated plan to pick up several discarded starships, I was skeptical. More than skeptical. But we did it! We have two alien starships to work with, and there was no risk to us or our mission."

"We may only get one Q-ship out of those two transports, Sir," I reminded him.

He waved a hand dismissively. Nothing could ruin his good mood. "Mr. Skippy will handle that, I suppose." My impression was he was so relieved the operation had not been a disaster, he wasn't letting anything kill his buzz. "You wanted to speak with me, Colonel?"

"Yes, Sir." I launched into Phase One of my argument in favor of pinging a Ruhar data node. As I finished and was taking a breath to plunge forward with Phase Two, he interrupted.

"Good, good. We should get updated intelligence before we proceed, I was going to suggest we do something like that."

Maybe it was hard for me to take an unexpected 'Yes' and run with it, or maybe I'm just an idiot, because my brain locked up and I heard myself saying "Skippy assures me there is minimal risk in us contacting this data node." Idiot! I told myself. I should have kept my mouth shut and run out of his office as soon as he said 'Yes'.

Chotek's eyes narrowed and his smile slipped just a bit. "You disagree? You think the risk is substantial?"

"No! No, I agree with Skippy's analysis. I, um," I gave him that weak, awkward goofy smile that was on my face every time someone took a photo of me. "Sir, I had a whole persuasive argument thought out. You caught me off guard," I admitted.

That restored Chotek's sunny mood. "Is that all?"

"No, Sir. After we update our intel, assuming the negotiations are still on, Skippy wants us to go to an uninhabited red dwarf star system so he can work on a Q-ship. Or ships." I explained about Skippy needing to awaken a dormant Elder wormhole, and that the star system was totally unexplored. My fear was Chotek would hear the word 'unexplored' and panic, fearing that entering a star system we knew little about was too risky.

He surprised me again. "Unexplored? Hmm. That sounds good. If no one has ever been there, no one will be there now to threaten us. Ask Skippy to send me whatever data he has on this star system. I can make a final decision, after we contact the data node and confirm the negotiation conference is still on schedule. Again, Colonel Bishop, please convey my congratulations to your crew."

His uncharacteristic bubbly mood was infectious. "Sir, tomorrow is our formal dinner," the night when all the military people wore formal uniforms to dinner. "I think the crew would appreciate you giving them congratulations yourself. We shouldn't break out the champagne until we know the Ruhar aren't sending a ship to earth, but we could celebrate completing this phase of the mission with a nice bottle of wine?" One thing I knew about Hans Chotek was that he loved a good bottle of wine; Major Simms had brought aboard several cases of wines that were known to be Chotek's favorites. While I usually preferred beer, I could drink a glass of wine with our fearless leader, if it meant Chotek's good mood would continue.

"Thank you, Colonel. Yes, I would like that. I will address the crew at dinner tomorrow."

"Outstanding, Sir," I mimicked his words on purpose. The next thing I needed to do was check that the Indian team which was galley duty the next day, cooked something that Chotek enjoyed. And that went well with his favorite wine.

On the way to the Ruhar data node, we made a detour to pick up our lifeboat and perhaps more importantly, Nagatha. "Hello, Nagatha," I greeted her as Desai was in the tricky process of maneuvering the ship to take the lifeboat back aboard. Because the lifeboat had almost no means of moving itself, we had to move our entire star carrier to get the bulky lifeboat onto a docking platform. I stayed in my office to chat with Nagatha, while Chang handled the command chair. "We have been busy." I was eager to tell her the adventures we had gone through just to pick up two junk spaceships that no one wanted.

"Oh my goodness, yes you have. It must have been quite exciting. I am very pleased that no one was injured by the booby traps in those ships."

"That was scary for a while- wait. You already know what happened?"

"Of course, dear. Skippy told me all about it a few milliseconds after you jumped in. It all sounds dreadfully frightening."

Damn it. I had been looking forward to telling her about the mission, and I didn't consider that Nagatha is an AI who communicates at lightspeed. That is how pathetic my life had become; I looked forward to telling my story to a computer. It made me feel like a little boy running home from to tell Mommy about his day at school. "It was, uh, yeah. It was, you know," I felt deflated. "It actually wasn't all that exciting. A lot of bad things could have happened, but they didn't. It was exciting at the time," that sounded lame as I was saying it.

"Dear," she said in a motherly tone, "did Skippy ruin your surprise by telling me? He made it sound like you monkeys, I'm sorry, you humans, would have been lost without him. He always says that, I should know better than to listen to him."

"Skippy is Skippy, we couldn't have done it without him-"

"-and he lets you know that."

"Yes," I laughed, "he does." I wondered what Nagatha's conversations with Skippy were like. Did they have conversations, or did they only exchange data files? Someday, I needed to ask her about that.

Skippy's avatar popped into existence above my desk. "Hey, Joe, FYI, while we have some downtime-"

"Downtime?" We were in a typical jump, recharge, jump cycle on our way to the Ruhar data node. Most of the crew were intensively training for our upcoming pitch-black operation, even though hopefully there would be nothing for us to actually do. I was participating in as much special ops and pilot training as I had time for, and at night, I found it difficult to fall asleep because I was so worried about getting the entire crew killed. Or exposing the presence of humans flying around the galaxy, which might get our entire species wiped out by pissed-off aliens. Other than that, I was sleeping just great. "What downtime?"

"Relatively, I mean. I have a submind running most of the ship for me right now. Ok, so the downtime is mostly mine, whatever. While I'm not real busy, I want to try something. I was thinking about that dead AI we found on Newark."

"What about, uh, him?" Since we were talking about what used to be an Elder AI, Skippy might not appreciate me using the pronoun 'it'. The gang of Kristang scavengers on Newark had dug up an Elder AI, a shiny chrome beer can just like Skippy. We stole that AI- Hmm, technically, we didn't steal it, since by the time we took possession of it, the Kristang were all dead. Ok, I guess that is still stealing. But it wasn't like the Kristang had a legal right to 'own' a sentient AI, so sue me. Anyway, I vividly remembered how sad, disappointed, and frightened Skippy had been when we brought that other beer can aboard, and Skippy determined the canister was empty. Something bad had happened to the AI in there, something Skippy could not understand, something that scared him badly. "Again, I'm sorry about that. I know you were looking forward to talking to another of your kind."

"That, too, but I was mostly hoping that AI could give us answers we need. Whatever happened to Newark, an AI there should know who did it. Joe, when we get done saving Earth, *again*, we need to get some answers about what the hell has been going on in the galaxy."

"Skippy, I agree," I ran a hand through my hair in frustration. "I'm not the person you need to convince. Chotek is the mission commander; he doesn't see that flying around the galaxy looking for clues to ancient mysteries is worth the risk to Earth. There is too much danger of our presence out here becoming exposed."

"Hfff," Skippy sniffed. "We found Elder sites that had been obliterated, by Elder technology. We found an intelligent species that was wiped out because Elder-level technology pushed their planet out of orbit. We don't know how this happened, or who could have done it, because all this mysterious stuff happened after the Elders left the galaxy and before the Rindhalu had spaceflight capability. There is an unknown actor in the galaxy, and Count Chocula thinks this is not a threat that is worth investigating?"

"Damn, Skippy, you are preaching to the choir. I agree with you, we need answers." Even if humans didn't have any immediate practical need to know what happened to Newark, we owed it to Skippy to help him find out about those events. And how he came to be buried in the dirt on Paradise. And why he can't contact the Collective. And the more basic question: who Skippy truly was. Since UNEF Command on Earth already didn't trust Skippy, I think they should very much want to know his true nature.

But I could also see Chotek's point of view. UNEF Command on Earth knew the *Flying Dutchman* was humanity's only way of learning about new alien threats to Earth. Our stolen pirate ship was also our only prayer to halt those threats. Our current mission starkly demonstrated that there were immediate threats to Earth from aliens we already knew about. Until we could secure our home planet's survival in at least the medium term, we should not go looking for even bigger trouble.

Unless acting now was the only way to prevent even bigger trouble later. Damn, I really, really hated my job some days. "Anyway, Skippy, what about this AI? You said it, uh, *he*, is dead as a doornail."

"Joe, I do not understand why, of all inanimate objects on Earth, your species singled out the lowly doornail as a sterling example of deadness, but, yes, the AI is certainly dead. What I want to do is load part of myself in that canister, so I can examine it in detail. I am hoping I can determine the nature of the AI; was it like me, or different. And what happened to it?"

I did not like the sound of that. "You want to load part of yourself, in an AI container that might be defective?"

"It's not defective, Joe. The canister is just fine, what I want to know is what is inside it. There might be residual traces of the AI that resided in there, I mean the part of the AI anchored in local spacetime. If I can understand the nature of the AI, I might be able to get some clues about what happened to it. Because it frightens me terribly that something could have destroyed an AI like me."

"Uh huh, it frightens me too, which is why I don't like the idea of you poking around in dark scary places all by yourself." Sometimes, it was easy to forget that Skippy was an incredibly advanced being who spanned beyond our spacetime. All I could think of was how small and vulnerable he looked, and how much he needed someone to protect him. Too often, Skippy lacked common sense, and he was so absent-minded, I was concerned he would go poking around in there, and forget what he was doing. "This is like a horror movie where one of the characters wants to open a door and go down into the dark, creepy basement, and the audience is all yelling 'Don't go in there'! But of course the stupid character goes down the steps, and the light goes off, and the monster or spiders or serial killer is right there. So, if you're asking for my permission to-"

"Joe, I was being polite, because Nagatha insisted. Why would I need permission from *you*?"

"Skippy," I let out an exasperated breath. "You reminded me that you should be on the crew roster, because you are a sentient being and vital to the operation of the ship."

"Yes, and I see you still have my rank in the roster listed as 'Asshole First Class'."

"Let's not get into that right now," I said quickly. "My point is that if you are a member of the crew, you are subject to my authority as captain of the ship." Technically, he was also subject to Colonel Chang's authority as executive officer; I wasn't going to push the issue right then.

"Oh sure, as if." He chuckled. "Oh, wait, you're *serious*?"

"Duh."

"Crap. Double crap! So, my choices are that either I am considered a shipboard system like a toaster, or I am part of the crew and have to listen to monkeys tell me what to do?" His voice reflected disbelief.

"What part of military chain of command do you not understand? The *Flying Dutchman* is a warship, we're not on a pleasure cruise out here. This is a Special Operations mission under the authority of UNEF Command."

"Technically, this is a stolen alien pirate ship that only functions because I do all the work around here," Skippy grumbled with sarcasm. "Fine. Whatever. What. Eh. *Ver*. Colonel Bishop, do I have permission to examine the empty AI canister? Pretty please, with sugar in it?"

"You are certain there is no danger to you, or to the ship?"

"Joe. Come on. It's *me*."

"Exactly what I am worried about." I rolled my eyes. "What if I say no? You will leave that AI canister alone, you won't go behind my back and do it anyway?"

"Sure, let's go with that."

"Skippy!"

"Let's also pretend I haven't already been examining the canister for the past twelve freakin' minutes, while you've been blah, blah, blahing me to death. I started before I even mentioned it to you. Does that make you feel better?"

"Oh, crap. No, it does not make me feel better."

"One way for you to feel better, Joe, is to avoid asking questions where the answers might upset you," he suggested helpfully.

"A captain is supposed to know what is going on aboard his ship," I clenched my teeth. Sometimes I wanted to strangle him.

"I did say this was more of an FYI, Joe."

"Oh, that makes me feel *so* much better," I sighed. Skippy was going to do whatever he wanted, whether I liked it or not. Ordering him to stop would only erode what little sense of authority I had. "Ok, fine, do what you want, but please, please, be careful? When you go poking around in dark corners, bring a flashlight with you, so when the monster kills the lights, you can still see."

"Hmmf. What good will a flashlight do against a monster? Whatever. Yes, I promise to be extra careful. I will keep you updated. So far, what I have found in there is a whole lot of nothing; just a big, empty space. I might as well be exploring the inside of your skull, Joe."

After what he cluelessly perceived as a very positive and respectful response when he revealed his Grand Admiral Lord Skippy avatar to the crew, Skippy had been pestering me to let him perform at karaoke night. I put it off as long as possible, but after he was so helpful during our successful operation to salvage two derelict starships, I relented. The crew universally groaned at the thought of listening to Skippy warbling off-key, and I was almost forced to voluntold some people to fill the galley for the occasion. Chang suggested if I was going to assign mandatory fun, it might be a good idea to open the liquor cabinet for the evening. That was a great idea because once I made that announcement, the galley was standing room only.

Skippy's avatar was especially resplendent and sparkly, like he had rolled himself in stripper glitter. Anyway, he led off with the theme song from an old James Bond movie, it was the one about nuclear submarines, or maybe the one about space shuttles; I forget. Except that, Skippy being Skippy, he changed the lyrics to fit his arrogant asshole self. "*Nobody does it better, makes me sad for the rest. Nobody does it half as good as meeeeeeee, baby I'm the best-*".

Simms leaned over to me with a harsh whisper. "The correct lyrics are 'Nobody does it half as good as *you,* baby *you're* the best'."

"Shhh," I shushed her. "He's happy and not causing any trouble for the moment."

"True."

Next, Skippy performed an old Beyoncé song. "*You can feel my halo, halo. You can see my halo, halo-*". That also was not quite how I remembered the original lyrics, but I wisely kept my mouth shut.

Skippy's karaoke singing went on for twenty minutes, with the well-disciplined and well-lubricated crowd clapping enthusiastically. The alcohol may have helped the enthusiasm of the audience, I know it helped me. Really, although the little beer can's voice was beyond horrible, his performance was so unintentionally amusing, we all had an uproariously great time.

"Bravo! Bravo!" I stood, clapping so hard my hands hurt.

"Why thank you, Joe, I'm touched. For my next number-"

"No!" I stood up and waved my arms. "No, Skippy, you need to give someone else a turn. Although, hey," I looked around at the crowd, "who would want to follow such a remarkable performance?"

The answer turned out to be me, Staff Sergeant Adams and Lt. Williams of our SEALS team singing 'Lollipop'. As my singing voice was even worse than Skippy's, my only part was to do the 'pop' sound with a finger in my mouth.

I crushed it.

Counting down for the final jump that would take us near the Ruhar data node, Skippy threw me a curveball. "Hey, Joe. Before we contact the data node, we should talk about that thing first."

"Thing?" With the corner of my eye, I saw Chotek shoot me a look of annoyance. No doubt he was wondering what crucial detail I had failed to tell him about before, so I could spring it on him at the last minute.

"Yeah, you know, the, uh, the thing."

The beer can was not helping me at all. "What *thing*, Skippy?"

"Oof," he sighed. "That intel I got from the Thuranin ships at the wormhole cluster. You know, about those little green MFers planning a major offensive against the Jeraptha? You said we would talk about it later. This is later. If that intel is going to do any good for the Jeraptha, I need to pass the info along to them soon. Like, now."

"Oh," I breathed a sigh of relief and looked at Chotek. "Sir, we did tell Skippy we would address that issue. I had forgotten about it," I admitted with a lame smile.

Chotek looked briefly unhappy. He had forgotten about it too. "How would you pass the intel to the Jeraptha, without them knowing the message came from us? And why would the Jeraptha trust intelligence that fell into their laps?"

"Oh, please," Skippy scoffed. "Dude, I am Skippy the Magnificent. This is child's play for me. I will load a file into a Ruhar message, that will route itself to a Jeraptha data node in the sector the Thuranin are planning to hit. When the Jeraptha pick up the file, it will unpack itself, infiltrate the ship's computer system, and convince the computer the message is legit orders from Jeraptha Fleet Headquarters. By the time the message gets to the Jeraptha ships, they won't have time to contact Fleet HQ and get a confirmation. They will have to act, and they will."

"Ok," I shared a look with Chotek. "They won't be able to authenticate the message before the battle, but afterwards, their Fleet HQ will know for sure they didn't send those orders, or have that intel. Somebody will be wondering where that intel came from."

"Joe, your lack of faith in me hurts. Trust the awesomeness. The file will erase its tracks along the way, no way will the Jeraptha be able to trace it back to that data relay. And yeah, of course Jeraptha Fleet HQ will go crazy trying to figure who passed that crucial intel to them. The prime suspect will be the Bosphuraq."

"The Bosphuraq?" Chotek asked, confused. "They are peers of the Thuranin, in the Maxolhx coalition, correct?"

"Peers in terms of being clients of the Maxolhx, and in terms of rough technological equivalence with the Thuranin. The Bosphuraq would dearly love an opportunity to screw with the Thuranin; anything that hurts the Thuranin moves the Bosphuraq up a peg in the hierarchy. There is no love lost between any member of the Maxolhx coalition. Remember, Joe, the Maxolhx encourage competition, even conflict, between their client species. Having their clients fighting weakens those clients and decreases the potential for those species to ever threaten their Maxolhx patrons."

"Damn it," I swore. "Is there anyone under the Maxolhx who are *not* trying to stab everyone else in the back?"

"In this local sector of the galaxy, I guess that would be the Urgar. They are clients of the Wurgalan, but due to their harsh treatment by the Wurgalan, the Urgar are nearly extinct. The Urgar are busy simply trying to survive, they don't have the time or energy to harm anyone else," Skippy explained, as if he were describing the menu at Denny's rather than the politics of a murderous group of alien MFers. "Anywho, the intel reaching the Jeraptha ships in the target sector is easily explainable. The question is, yes or no? We jump in near the data node in eighteen minutes, I need an answer quickly."

"What would be the benefit to humanity, of passing this intel to the Jeraptha?" Chotek asked. "I don't see how two alien species fighting one battle in a very long war affects Earth."

"That's simple. And complex," Skippy responded. "Right now, Paradise is in a region firmly under the control of the Jeraptha. The Ruhar are stationing a battlegroup at Paradise, mostly because they hope to find Elder artifacts there, but also because the region around that planet is protected by their patrons, the Jeraptha. Without strong support by the Jeraptha, the Ruhar could not hold Paradise for long. If the Jeraptha suffer a serious military setback in this sector, they might pull their forces back from the area around Paradise. Now that we made everyone think Paradise might be a treasure trove of Elder goodies, the Thuranin may be interested in taking that planet for themselves. I'm sure you can see how that would be bad for the humans on Paradise."

"Jesus Christ," I pounded a fist on the arm of the command chair. "We just got done rescuing UNEF there. When is it going to be enough?"

"I'm sure our resident diplomat could tell you," Skippy said with dry humor, "resolving one crisis leads you right into the next one."

Chotek nodded, with a smile creasing the corner of his mouth. He and Skippy had just found common ground on something, I guess that was progress. "Skippy," I asked, "you got any more good news for us?"

"Sure, Joe," he replied with cheer. "Right now, the wormhole near Earth that we shut down is in a region at the edge of Thuranin-controlled territory, and remote from any of their large military bases. With their current weakness, the Thuranin are not much interested in that area, or that wormhole. But if the Thuranin are able to score significant victories against the Jeraptha, they might want to exploit the area around that deactivated wormhole, and they eventually will investigate why that wormhole shut down. So, to keep Earth safe, we should ensure the Thuranin remain weak in this sector."

"Great," I said. What I thought to myself was that we had yet another freakin' thing to worry about. When this current mission was over, I was going to raid Major Simms' secret stash of bourbon and get drunk for a week, at least. "Is there any downside to us telling the Jeraptha about the Thuranin's plan to hit them?"

"Downside? Mmm, no. No, I can't think of any. I'm not the strategic military genius here, Joe. That's supposed to be your job. But I can't think of any downside to giving the Jeraptha advanced warning of an attack. Chotek, if you are holding out hope of eventually becoming allies of the Ruhar and Jeraptha, then giving the Jeraptha this intel would be a nice gesture."

That last remark sold Hans Chotek on the idea. "I agree. Very well, Mr. Skippy, do your awesome magic and send the intel to the Jeraptha."

"My pleasure," Skippy said happily, without even bothering to throw a casual insult at our mission commander. My guess was, Chotek was learning how to flatter Skippy.

It was only much later we realized that giving the Jeraptha a warning about the attack was a terrible, awful, no good idea.

CHAPTER TEN

Communications Specialist First Class Hanst Bo of the Jeraptha's 98th Fleet nearly choked when he read the header of the decrypted message. Hoping no one had noticed, he put the message in a temporary holding folder, and pulled up the original, encrypted transmission. It had been carried by a fast packet ship, one of the small ships dedicated to delivering messages from Fleet Headquarters to the various units and bases across the far-flung territory of the Jeraptha. Their already expansive territory had recently grown substantially, through resounding defeats the Jeraptha Home Fleet had inflected on the Thuranin.

Having priority messages delivered by a fast packet ship was not anything unusual. What was unusual was this message designated itself as Flash Gold traffic; the highest Fleet priority. But when Hanst Bo had initially scanned the flood of messages transmitted by the packet ship as soon as it had jumped in, the summary file had not listed any of the messages as Flash Gold, or Flash at all. Or, he thought none of the messages had been listed as Flash, because when he went back to the original summary file and ran it through the decryption process, there was a message blinking boldly at the top, demanding immediate attention.

How could he have missed that?! Bo shivered, and not just because the Communications chamber had air conditioning that seemed to be powered directly from a fusion reactor. Swallowing hard, Bo ran the Flash message through the decryption again, silently hoping it had not, in fact, been designated as Flash Gold by Fleet HQ. While he waited agonizing seconds for the multi-layered decryption process to complete, he reminded himself to remain and act calm, including making sure his antennas did not droop suspiciously.

His console 'binged' when the decryption was complete, which by itself was odd. The first time he had run the message through decryption, the computer took longer, even seeming to have trouble reading the file. This second time, the decryption algorithm move at lightning speed. When Bo saw the 'Flash Gold' designation at the top, and that it was addressed directly to the Admiral of Blue Squadron, 98th Fleet, Bo tore the flimsy message slip out of its slot and dashed out the door, his four legs scrambling to find purchase on the ship's deck. When he rounded a corner and reached a straight stretch of passageway, he reared up on his back two legs and raced as fast as he could, using his two front legs only for balance. "Make way! Make way!" He shouted.

Admiral Tashallo of the Jeraptha Blue Squadron, 98th Fleet, was engaged in casual conversation with the captains of his flagship and the three other battleships under his command. The five had enjoyed a sumptuous meal provided by the admiral's staff, an event which occurred every fifteen days whenever the Fleet was in port. Sometimes more frequently, depending on the admiral's mood, which depended on his luck with the wagers he loved to participate in. When there was not a battle looming to be wagered upon, Tashallo arranged for ships to race each other, or for two stealthed ships to hunt each other. It was good practice for the crews, it was good for morale within the 98th, and it provided decent action for a fleet mostly assigned to dull garrison duty.

The 98th was responsible for defense of the Glark star system where the Blue Squadron was based, a star system that provided fuel and warship servicing facilities for a quarter of the sector. The system had one habitable planet, though the people who live there and crews who took shore leave on that world, considered the term 'habitable' to be somewhat questionable. The planet had been a boiling hell when the Jeraptha first took control of the star system. The planet's gravity was thirty two percent greater than was normal for the Jeraptha. The thick carbon dioxide atmosphere had trapped heat, making the surface hot enough to boil water even at the poles. Because the planet rotated so slowly, one side faced the star long enough to almost melt soft metals. Over thousands of years, Jeraptha engineers had worked to make the world habitable. They had seeded the thick clouds with algae that ate the carbon dioxide and released free oxygen. They speeded up the planet's rotation and reduced the surface gravity, by flinging parts of the planet's core into space using enormous railguns. Now, according to the planetary government, it was a delightful garden world, a wonderful place to live and enjoy shore leave. Except for the equator, where it was still hot enough to fry the proteins of a Jeraptha brain. And except for that burnt metallic smell that filled the air whenever the winds blew from the equator.

The planet had been made habitable because of the other assets the system possessed. An extensive asteroid field, rich in metals and other elements that were rare in other systems. Two gas giant planets with weak magnetic fields and small moons, which were ideal conditions for extracting fuel. The Jeraptha had constructed permanent fuel collection facilities based on small moons that had been towed into low orbits. And the largest gas giant had four large spacedocks to provide heavy servicing of warships, spacedocks that were almost capable of building a small warship from raw materials extracted from easily-mined asteroids.

All the assets in the system paled in comparison to its location; the star was near the center of three strategically important wormholes, two of which were clusters of wormholes. The five Fleets of the Blue Squadron all relied on the star system for supplies, maintenance and repairs, and staging. Admiral Tashallo's 98th Fleet had drawn the unlucky duty of acting as the Home Guard force for the Glark system. Acting as a garrison force was boring and provided hardly action, and Tashallo couldn't wait until he could bid on a better assignment.

Communications Specialist First Class Hanst Bo burst in on the admiral and four senior captains. "Admiral, begging your indulgence, we just received a Flash Gold message. Fleet Intelligence has discovered an imminent threat to the Glark system."

Rather than being alarmed, Tashallo was annoyed. "Of course, our Fleet Intelligence group is never wrong," Tashallo's antenna shook with mirth, and the command staff broke into gales of laughter.

"Fleet Intelligence is offering sixty to one odds on this," Bo read quietly.

"*Sixty to one*?" Tashallo gasped. Then he tilted his head and rolled his eyes dramatically. "How many points are they taking?" he asked with a chuckle. Sixty to one was unheard of, unprecedented coming from Fleet Intelligence. Those indecisive desk jockeys never offered more than five to four odds on their predictions of enemy intentions. And they always insisted on taking points.

"None, Admiral. No points," Bo replied after checking the message twice.

"Let me see that," Tashallo demanded, snatching the flimsy message slip from the subensign's hand. When the admiral touched the slip, additional information became available, scrolling up from the bottom.

What he read made him gasp and his antenna stand straight up.

The 98th Fleet was equipped for strong defense of valuable static targets; that is why Tashallo's force included five heavy but relatively slow and short-range battleships. With five battleships supplementing the Strategic Defense satellites in the system, any attack by the Thuranin, Bosphuraq or a combination of the two would need to commit two entire fleets to an attack, and the enemy had never wanted to pay that steep a price. The purpose of the 98th Fleet was not to do anything by itself; it was to take away the enemy's incentive to do something.

The Flash Gold message stated the enemy had decided to pay the price of hitting the Glark system. Two Thuranin fleets were on their way; they would strike soon. Fortunately, Fleet Intelligence somehow knew exactly when, where and how the Thuranin planned to strike. Tashallo's mind considered all his options quickly; that is why he had risen to the rank of admiral. "Captain Dahmen, signal that fast packet to proceed to this ship at best speed, I need to borrow it to confer with Admiral Sashell. Get the 98th ready to move out; load the battleships onto star carriers. We can't afford to have slow ships delaying us."

"Sir?" Captain Dahmen burned with curiosity to know what the message slip stated was such a terrible threat that Tashallo wanted the 98th moved out of the star system the fleet was designed to defend. Battleships could be accommodated on the docking platforms of a star carrier, but a single battleship took up two or three platforms by itself, and while burdened with the massive bulk of a battleship a star carrier could only transport two or three other ships. "Should we wait for confirmation? What if Fleet Intelligence is wrong?" If the intel was wrong and Tashallo pulled the 98th away from the Glark system, the critical facilities there would have their defenses cut in half.

"Dahmen, those credit-pinching thieves at Fleet Intelligence are offering sixty to one odds this information is accurate, and they're not asking for any points. It is more likely Glark's star will go supernova tomorrow, than this info to be wrong. I don't know how, but Fleet Intelligence stumbled across a gold mine, and I'm going to act on it. Get me a dropship; I need to get aboard that fast packet immediately."

Nine hours later, the fast packet carrying Admiral Tashallo emerged from jump close to the flagship of Admiral Sashell's 67th Fleet. Breaking all safety protocols, a dropship brought Tashallo aboard the battlecruiser *You Want a Piece of This?* and the two admirals quickly read through the extensive data in the Flash Gold message. "I agree," Sashell said when he was able to recover his wits from the shock of the astonishing message. The idea of the Thuranin rolling the dice to attack the critical Blue Squadron facilities at Glark was not what shocked Sashell; the Thuranin were known to be desperate after their recent military setbacks. Sashell would have bet against the Thuranin launching a major offensive operation in the sector for at least three months. With a pained wince, Sashell remembered he *had* wagered against such a Thuranin offense, though he could not remember the exact terms of the wager. As soon as he and Tashallo were done talking, he needed to speak with the 67th Fleet's Action Officer, the woman responsible for recording wagers and setting odds. "This is a tempting opportunity to hit the Thuranin hard, make their little green noses bloody. Fleet Intelligence would not have sent this," he flapped the flimsy slip in the air, "unless they knew it is solid gold. Sixty to one sounds good, but I will not be betting against them," Sashell chuckled, and Tashallo joined him.

The decision was thus made; Tashallo slightly outranked Sashell due to more time as an admiral, although they operated independent commands. Keeping in mind the different strengths and capabilities of their two fleets, the two admirals quickly made a plan, dividing the three enemy targets between them after a reasonable and expected amount of argument. The fast packet ship was then dispatched back to Fleet HQ, carrying a request for validation of the Flash Gold message, and the intentions of the 67th and 98th Fleets to counter the enemy's attack.

Then the two admirals got down to the more important business of handicapping the wagers between themselves, and between their two fleets. Shortly after Tashallo returned to his flagship, a second fast packet ship was dispatched, this one carrying messages far more important than keeping Fleet HQ informed of the activities of two powerful Fleets of the Blue Squadron. Every Jeraptha in the two Fleets who could scrape together or borrow a single credit, had bet the limit on the results of the upcoming battle, and the second packet ship carried records of those wagers. Also official records of the wager Admirals Tashallo and Sashell had made with each other, their side bets, and every side bet of the entire crew, no matter how odd. One example was a wager between the chief navigator and second engineering officer of a battlecruiser, on which type of Thuranin ship would be the first to fall victim to the battlecruiser's big railguns. Any such wager needed to be recorded by the ship's Action Officer, and sent to be registered at Fleet HQ.

No one in either Fleet could resist such juicy action. And not a single person bet against Fleet Intelligence. Sixty to one! That message rang throughout the hull of every ship in the two fleets, astonishing everyone who heard it. More than one wager was recorded that Fleet Intelligence must have discovered practical time travel; a way to see into the future. And more than one witty Jeraptha had commented that, even if Fleet Intelligence could see flawlessly into the future, of course those gutless cowards only offered sixty to one odds.

Twenty six hours after the Flash Gold message was received, the 98th Fleet disappeared in blinding flashes of gamma rays, as they sortied out to meet the Thuranin.

The *Flying Dutchman* completed another jump, and our pirate ship was now hanging in deep interstellar space, waiting for the drive coils to charge up for another jump. We only needed two more jumps, to reach the uninhabited star system Skippy had chosen for creating a Q-ship from our two salvaged transports. His detailed examination of both ships had not changed his mind; we would only get one Q-ship from the two junkers we were carrying. He also warned me that an attack by a single armed transport ship would not be considered a credible threat by the Ruhar negotiation party; no Kristang clan would launch an attack that weak. That was a problem I would need to deal with, after I dealt with all the other problems.

I had waited out the latest jump from my office, rather than hanging around the bridge and making the duty crew nervous. Me being in my office during a jump was my way of showing confidence in the Merry Band of Pirates. While being right around the corner in case anything went wrong and I was needed on the bridge.

"Nailed it, Joe!" Skippy exulted, his avatar coming to life and holding up an index finger. "I'm number one, baby. We emerged from that jump within twenty six meters of the target, that is my best accuracy yet."

"That is amazing, Skippy," I replied without bothering to refresh my memory of how far we had jumped. It was far, that's all I needed to know.

"Yup. And I did it even though I am somewhat distracted by my investigation of that AI canister."

"Oh, yeah." He had not given me an update on his messing around with the dead AI since he first told me about it. "How's that going?" I needed him to finish screwing around with that AI canister before he started work on building our Q-ship.

"Mostly dull," he admitted. "I have been careful like you asked, even though there is nothing in there that could harm me, duh. I did find something interesting, intriguing, even. You made me go slower than I wanted, otherwise I would have found it much soon-"

"Found what?" Now he had my interest. I had asked him not to go poking around in dark corners by himself.

No answer. And his avatar was frozen in place on my desktop.

"Skippy? What is it? What did you find in there?" I tried to project amusement in my voice.

Still no answer. And the avatar blinked out.

"Skippy? Come on, I know you're pissed at me for asking you to go slowly and be careful; sue me for caring about you. What did you find in there? Can you tell me, pretty please?" I added, in case his ego needed soothing.

Nothing. Now I was trying to decide between being alarmed that something had happened to Skippy, or being pissed that he was ignoring me.

I called Adams. Skippy liked her; she didn't take any crap from him, and he respected that. "Sergeant, could you contact Skippy for me? He's giving me the silent treatment," I explained.

"Sir, I was just in the middle of a conversation with him, and he stopped talking," she replied, confused.

Oh shit.

My blood ran cold; I used to think that was only an expression. "Nagatha?" I looked at the speaker in the ceiling, as if that would help. She didn't answer. Pulling out my zPhone, I stared at it, realizing that I had no idea how to call Skippy or Nagatha. I had never actually called them; I spoke and they always answered. It wasn't like either of them had a phone number, or an entry in my zPhone's address list. "Nagatha? Skippy?"

The lights flickered, and the familiar sounds of a working starship faded away. No air faintly hissing out of ducts, no bots rolling or crawling along the decks. And there was none of the subsonic rumbling sound that I associated with the reactors, even though the reactors were far away at the aft end of the star carrier's still long spine.

I dashed around the corner to the bridge, aware from my bouncing steps that the artificial gravity was fading. Plenty of sound was being generated there, all of it human voices in a state of alarm and confusion. Gustov Renaud was the duty officer in the command chair. "Colonel, we have lost power; all three reactors have executed emergency shutdown procedure," he pointed to the main display, where the three reactors were outlined in blinking red on a schematic of the ship. "It appears we are running on backup power. We can't contact Skippy."

"Environmental systems are functional," I observed in a shaky voice. Good. We would not suffocate from lack of oxygen, or freeze to death as the ship's residual heat radiated away into the bitter cold of space. "Captain Renaud, keep, doing, uh," I couldn't think of anything useful he or anyone else could do at that moment. "Send someone to the lifeboat," I meant the Thuranin relay station that was attached to one of our docking platforms. "Get a status of the lifeboat's systems, and see if anyone can contact Nagatha there." I was not optimistic. Skippy had warned me that as a submind, she was an integral part of his being or matrix or whatever you wanted to call it. Nagatha had functioned on her own aboard the relay station while our pirate ship was away, but she had outgrown the capacity of the Thuranin computers there, and Skippy had pulled most of her functioning inside his own. My hope was that part of Nagatha still remained aboard the lifeboat; enough to communicate with us. I didn't need witty conversation, a text message would be Ok with me.

"Yes, Sir. Colonel, where are you going?" Renaud asked as I spun and headed back out the door, running carefully as the main display on the bridge had indicated the artificial gravity was adjusting down to its minimum, low-power setting. If it shut off completely, we were going to have problems, as many systems humans used aboard the ship were poorly adapted to zero gravity. Most importantly, the humans ourselves.

"I'm going to check on Skippy," I explained. The ship schematic on the display showed the icon for Skippy's escape pod was still attached to the ship; I was hoping there had been some glitch or accident, and Skippy wasn't communicating because he was actually spinning off into space with the escape pod. That was a bogus hope, because physical separation of a few hundred yards, or a few million miles, would not stop Skippy from being able to contact us. If bogus hope was all I had to cling to, I was going with it.

No such luck. The escape pod was where it always was, with the hatch open. Inside, his motionless beer can was strapped into a seat. "Skippy?" I called out, feeling foolish, as if I needed to be in the escape pod for him to hear me. "If this is a practical joke, it is not funny even one tiny bit."

There was no response. Cautiously, I tapped his lid with a finger, then I pressed a fingertip against his smooth, shiny surface. He was warm, almost hot. Whatever was wrong with Skippy, he was still in there, and something was going on inside that can. I debated ducking back through the hatch and ejecting the escape pod, then had a better idea. I pulled him out of the straps, and squeezed back through the hatch into the passageway, where a crowd had gathered. As we were aboard a ship, I should have used the Navy term 'gangway' but since I am Army, I said "Make a hole, people," as I ran with unusually long strides back to the bridge. "Renaud, I'm taking Skippy away from here in a dropship. Get the ship moving in the other direction if you can."

"Where are you going, Sir?" Renaud asked anxiously.

"Skippy's can is warm and growing hot," I explained. "I'm getting him away from the ship, in case he explodes or loses containment or something."

I got a dropship launched within seven minutes of securing the airlock door; it took longer than a typical emergency launch because I had to do everything manually. We kept one of the smaller Thuranin Falcon dropships on Zulu alert as a ready bird, so all I needed to do was hop in and close the hatch; it was already powered up. Fortunately, all the controls and displays aboard the dropship were in English; I had been fearing that without Skippy they would revert to their native Thuranin script. The big docking bay doors responded to my command to open, even though I had to hit the override twice since the bay was still partially pressurized. I did regret the loss of breathable air aboard a ship with environmental systems operating on backup power, and I balanced that against the risk of Skippy exploding and losing the entire ship.

As soon as the dropship cleared the doors, I punched the throttle and accelerated away at three and a half Gees, then went to a sustained five Gees. All I cared about was getting away from the *Dutchman* as fast as possible, in empty interstellar space there wasn't any particular direction for me to go anyway. I picked a star at random and set the autopilot to aim for it. When we passed a hundred thousand kilometers from the ship, I cut thrust and let the dropship coast outward at high speed. One hundred thousand klicks was not any scientific measurement of a safe distance in case Skippy exploded, it was just a nice round number and I could not take five gravities of load on my body any longer. My back was killing me; it would have been better for me to have taken two seconds to get comfortable in the seat before engaging the main engines.

What really mattered was that Skippy had not exploded and destroyed the *Flying Dutchman*. Unstrapping from my seat, I floated over to the little guy and checked his temperature. "*Dutchman*, this is Bishop," I called through the dropship's comm system. "Skippy is still warm, he may be warmer than he was before, I can't tell. No response from him yet. Have you been able to access the lifeboat, or contact Nagatha?"

Chang replied after a brief pause; the ship was already far enough away that signal lag was noticeably already. "A team just entered the relay station from a docking bay, they report backup power is engaged because the reactor there also shut down. Nagatha is not responding there or here. The science team was able to get artificial gravity cut off here six minutes ago; we couldn't take the power drain, so now we're all floating in zero gee. Dr. Friedlander has his teams working to assure the environmental systems continue to run on backup power, then he will concentrate on restarting one of the reactors."

"Is he confident he can do that without blowing up the ship?" I asked, without intending any kind of a joke.

"He doesn't not know yet. Sir, if we can't get a reactor restarted-" He didn't finish the thought because he didn't need to.

"Yeah, I know. Do the best you can over there, I will monitor Skippy here." At some point soon, I would have to decelerate so I didn't get too far from the ship. If Skippy woke up, I wanted to get him back aboard the *Dutchman* as quickly as possible.

"Understood. Colonel Bishop? Mister Chotek wishes to speak with you."

Of course he did. An already crappy day was getting better every minute. No doubt Chotek was going to blame the incident on me. Better that he take his anger and fear out on me via voice communication, than making life miserable for people aboard the ship. I took a deep breath. "Mister Chotek?"

Smythe called me six hours later; the crew had been taking turns calling me every hour. "How are you doing out there, Colonel?"

"I am not well chuffed, Major. You might even say I am not close to being chuffed at all." With the timelag in the transmissions, the conversation was awkward.

"It's not your fault, Sir," he assured me, because much of the crew had heard Chotek berating me.

"I know. Skippy was going to go poking around in that dead AI canister whether I approved of it or not. We don't even know if that was related to him going AWOL or not," I said, although that coincidence was tough to argue against. "What bothers me now is that we are completely out of options. Humanity, I mean."

"How so, Sir?" I took the tone of his question to mean genuine interest, he was not merely humoring me as I sped away into the void.

"Chotek's backup plan, if the Ruhar reach Earth and our secret gets out, is to hand over Skippy and the Elder wormhole controller module. Unless Skippy comes back to life, or by some miracle Friedlander finds a way to fly us to civilization, Earth will have the worst of all possible options. After the Ruhar return with info about Earth, both sides of the war will quickly learn humans have been screwing with Elder wormholes, but UNEF Command won't be able to offer a wormhole controller, or an Elder AI to make it work. Earth won't even be able to give a hint where to find us. Aliens will tear our little planet apart to find whatever they think we're hiding."

"That would certainly bollocks things up," Smythe agreed. "I'm sure you'll think of something, Sir."

I couldn't tell if he was joking, or trying to cheer me up. "Has Dr. Friedlander made any progress?"

"He thinks we could eventually restore normal space propulsion, right now Lt. Colonel Chang has them working on restarting one of the reactors. Chang said the ability to fly in normal space is useless without a place to go, and we'd be draining the capacitors for nothing. The jump drive coils are charged enough for one jump, that's not enough to get us anywhere useful. From here, we can't even jump to a place where we could signal either side to surrender. By the time our signal reached anyone, everyone aboard the ship would be dead."

That got me thinking. Certainly, everyone aboard the ship would be dead, but if we sent a signal to the Ruhar or Jeraptha, the signal could tell them to come pick up an Elder wormhole controller, and possibly an Elder AI if Skippy was functional again by then. My hope was such an offer might give Earth a tiny bit of consideration from the Rindhalu, if they or the Maxolhx hadn't already ransacked Earth, searching for a device humans used to screw with Elder wormholes.

I would keep that idea to myself, until it became our only option. Or our best option, which would be the same thing at that point.

Smythe and I talked for a while longer; neither of us were good at small talk so the conversation petered out. "Any change in Skippy?" He asked.

"No," I replied. "He's still sitting there, not responding. The good news is he has not gotten any warmer." I had feared Skippy's beer can would grow so hot that I would need to toss him out an airlock. Part of me had selfishly hoped he would explode. That would kill me instantly, and save me the trouble of suffocating or freezing to death aboard the *Dutchman* with everyone else. It looked like I would not be taking the easy way out.

"He is a safe distance from the ship now, Sir. What are your plans?"

I knew Smythe meant when would I give up, leave Skippy there in space, and fly the dropship back to our slowly dying pirate starship? The answer was, I was in no hurry to do that. The dropship had enough food aboard to sustain one person for a month; that had been my idea after I had once gotten trapped aboard a dropship with hardly any food. In my opinion, there would be no point to my flying back to the *Dutchman* without a functioning Skippy. As that little shithead was fond of mentioning, I could barely figure out how shoelaces worked; I would be useless in trying to get the reactors or jump drive functioning. The best thing I could do for the Merry Band of Pirates was to stay a safe distance away from the ship with Skippy. That way, if he did wake up, I could bring him back to the ship as quickly as possible. Checking the rations aboard, I calculated I could stretch the food to six weeks before I became too weak to fly the dropship. Considering my math skills, maybe I'd be dead by then. Whatever.

Smythe signed off with a promise to contact me again with a status report every hour. I appreciated it, and asked him to tell Chang to concentrate on the ship and crew, rather than speaking uselessly with me.

From what I had heard so far, the science team was not accomplishing much useful aboard the ship anyway.

Twelve hours and some minutes had gone by since Skippy went AWOL on us. I had just finished talking with Sergeant Adams, she drew the short straw to be the one to check in with me at the hour mark. I shouldn't have said that, that was unfair to her. She was nice and didn't make the conversation any more awkward that it had to be; with her aboard a dying ship and me floating in space two hundred fifty thousand miles away. I had decelerated the dropship to keep a constant distance from the *Flying Dutchman*; a distance I hoped was far enough away for the ship to survive if Skippy lost containment and exploded. The science team was still sort of working on getting a reactor restarted, but they had put that on a lower priority, as Dr. Friedlander thought it unlikely they could successfully restart a reactor before the backup power failed and carbon dioxide began building up inside the ship. If, or when, that happened, part of the crew could get into dropships and survive there for nearly a month. Others could use Kristang spacesuits to survive for a short time; neither option was truly a solution. What Friedlander had his team working on was using the jump drive capacitors to power the life support system. Heat and lights would be great, what the ship really needed was to restore power to the fancy Thuranin system that cracked carbon away from carbon dioxide molecules and provided breathable free oxygen. Our science team understood the basic theory of how that oxygen recycling system worked, all they needed to do was supply power. The jump drive capacitors apparently did not store power using the electromagnetic force in any way we monkeys could understand, and the power was not designed to flow out of the capacitors into the ship. Despite the obstacles, Friedlander's team thought reversing the power flow was a more realistic option than attempting to restart an advanced alien reactor. Adams told me Chang was considering the idea, if the science team had confidence they could extract power from the capacitors in a controlled manner, and not blow up the ship in a blinding flash of light. The concept sounded crazy to me, but as I was not the commander on the scene and Chang was, I kept my mouth shut. This was a case where we had to trust Friedlander and his team; no one else aboard truly had the knowledge base to make a judgment call. Adams assured me Friedlander did not want to even attempt to screw with the unholy power in a jump drive capacitor, until backup power was below fifty percent.

After ending the call with Adams, I floated in the dropship's cabin, looking out a tiny window, trying to see the *Dutchman* with a naked eye. Our star carrier, even in its new shrunken form, was massive though spindly. The skinny spine could not be seen from that distance, and the docking platforms were also relatively slender. The best I could hope for was to be watching as the bulk of the forward section, the aft power and propulsion module, or the relay station we had brought along as a lifeboat would pass in front of a distant star, and I would see that star dim briefly. During the minutes I watched, I didn't see anything, so I gave up and checked the *Dutchman* using the dropship's sensors. The ship was easy to see with Thuranin optical technology, rather than the old Mark One eyeball. Since the stealth field was powered down, I got a good look at our pirate ship. It was beat up, and it was beautiful, an oasis of breathable air in the cold dark of interstellar space. Until that air ran out.

I floated over to a supply cabinet, poking around the food containers without enthusiasm. There was plenty of food for me, and I knew I should eat something, I just wasn't hungry. There was also a bottle of magical pills Skippy had created that would counteract the negative effects of long-term zero gravity on the human body. I shook the bottle, then put it back. If I was in the dropship long enough for my eyes to be affected and my muscles to atrophy, then a bottle of pills would not solve the big problem.

Skippy. I closed the cabinet door and floated over to the chair he was strapped into. He was warm, though no warmer than he had been for the past eleven hours, since I figured out how to use the glove of a Kristang spacesuit as a temperature gauge. In a totally useless move, I touched his can with a bare finger. Definitely warm, something was going on in there. Whether Skippy was still in there, I had no way of knowing.

In another totally useless move, I unstrapped him and picked him up. In zero gee he didn't weigh anything, he still had mass and I thought maybe he was lighter than before. That was another thing I should have checked.

Then I got tears in my eyes, which is damned inconvenient in zero gravity. Tear droplets don't run down your cheeks, they well up and float in front of you, sometimes getting caught on your eyelashes where they get drawn back into your eyes and sting again. Skippy, the Asshole Almighty, and my friend. Skippy had lamented that his first ever friend was a monkey; my best friend was a beer can. Cradled in my hands, he looked so small, so vulnerable, lost and alone. If something had happened to him and he was truly gone, then he had survived millions of years of loneliness only to die after a short time awake. He never did contact the Collective, whatever the hell that was. And he died completely alone, possibly the last of his kind and not knowing.

Holding him in my hands was useless, not that I had anything else to do. Except I should have used the abundant free time to try thinking of a way to fix the problem. The way I justified cradling his beer can was that perhaps me touching him and getting teary-eyed would be so disgusting to him, that he would come back from wherever he had gone.

After a couple minutes of self-indulgence, I strapped him back in and wracked my brain for a way out of our dilemma. Four hours later, I had a grand total of nothing.

Hans Chotek returned to his office after a grim meeting with Dr. Friedlander. The science team was pessimistic about the prospect of even short-term survival aboard the ship; with main power cut off, carbon dioxide was already double the normal level. Thuranin technology used some sort of power-intensive magical technology to strip carbon away from CO2 molecules and produce breathable oxygen, the ship didn't have a backup system like lithium hydroxide filters. On the recommendation of Friedlander, half the crew had been moved into dropships, which had their own life support systems. That desperate measure would only be useful for a short time. Unless main power could be restored, the entire crew was doomed to die in the cold wasteland of interstellar space. Chotek met Major Smythe striding down a passageway, and waved the SAS soldier into his office. "Major, Dr. Friedlander tells me he is not optimistic about getting a reactor restarted. I should have insisted that Skippy train the science team to fully operate the ship, even if only the emergency systems. No. I should have insisted that Colonel Bishop order Skippy to train the crew more effectively."

"Sir," Smythe sat still in his seat, having trained himself not to wriggle when uncomfortable. "Whatever happened to Skippy, it cannot be blamed on Colonel Bishop."

"Can't it?" Chotek asked with raised eyebrows. "Bishop knows our alien AI far better than any of us do; I find it difficult to believe he did not know Skippy was having some sort of problem before he went silent. Or that Skippy was taking some type of ill-advised risk. It is at times like this, Major, I am convinced more than ever that Bishop is too young and inexperienced to be entrusted with such a vital responsibility."

"The fault is not in our stars, but in ourselves," Smythe intoned.

Chotek raised an eyebrow. "Quoting Shakespeare to me, Major?"

"Yes, Sir. Also, bloody hell, proving my teachers were right all along; I told them studying the classics would be useless for me. Perhaps the problem is not that Bishop is too young, but that *we* expect someone with his level of responsibility to be older. The issue may be with us, not him."

Hans Chotek did not like being accused of allowing personal bias to affect his ability to make decisions; his diplomatic training had emphasized the importance of recognizing and avoiding personal bias. Chotek knew he was not the only person who considered Joe Bishop too young to command an important, a vital, mission. UNEF Command specifically stated that Bishop's lack of experience was an unacceptable risk factor. "Bishop has proven himself to be brave, and clever and inventive. The military has a distinction between staff officers and commanders, I believe. Bishop could be an excellent staff officer, responsible for developing plans; it does not automatically follow that he is a good commander. He still has a tendency, an instinct, to take unnecessary risks."

"You approved all of our operations so far, Sir," Smythe said evenly.

"I did approve the operations being conducted, according to my instructions for minimizing risk. If left to himself, Bishop may have successfully taken control of the relay station, and also secured UNEF's future on Paradise. But if he failed, the results would have been worse than the limited damage that I allowed for. And, Major Smythe, I do not know how many riskier plans Bishop did not even mention to me, because he knew I would not approve them. He may very well have done something rash, if he did not have guidance from more experienced leaders," Chotek looked Smythe straight in the eye as he spoke. Smythe understood the implication: UNEF Command expected Smythe to act as a check on Bishop's risk-taking instincts. When Smythe did not reply, Chotek pressed his point. "If the Kristang had not insisted that Bishop be promoted as a public relations stunt,

I believe he would still be a sergeant on Paradise now. A good sergeant, most likely. But certainly not a colonel."

Smythe nodded, but his words did not please UNEF Command's chosen leader. "If the Kristang hadn't gotten Bishop promoted, Earth would still be under the control of the Kristang, and you and I might be dead. You see, Sir," Smythe stared Chotek directly in the eye, "I have a different perspective on risk. The SAS motto is 'Who Dares Wins'. What we're trying to win out here is the survival of our species. There is risk in action. There is also risk in *not* acting."

Chotek sighed inwardly, mentally crossing Major Smythe of 22 Special Air Service Regiment off the list of people who could be relied on to provide a cool head in a crisis. Maybe it didn't matter anyway, if the *Flying Dutchman* remained drifting powerless in interstellar space until the end of time.

CHAPTER ELEVEN

Seventeen hours, seven minutes and twelve seconds after Skippy went missing, he picked up exactly where he left off. "-er. But no, I had to be extra super careful, because little Joey watched too many crappy horror movies where the dumb kids don't know to- Hey! Joe! What in *the* hell are we doing way out in the middle of freakin' nowhere?"

"Skippy!" I shouted, getting tears in my eyes. The sudden sound of his voice in the empty, echoing silence had startled me so badly I almost pulled a muscle in my neck. "You're back!"

"Duh. I never left. What the hell did you do?"

"I didn't do anything," I protested gently. I was so happy, I didn't have the heart to banter back with him.

"Oof," he breathed that exasperated, disgusted sigh that I hated. "Come on, Joe. *Somebody* did something stupid, and what are the odds that it *wasn't* you?"

"Skippy, I would ordinarily agree with you a thousand percent, but not this time. You went silent on us for over seventeen hours."

"Ha! As if! No way, Jose."

"Check the dropship's time code. Or the orbits of planets, or motion of the starfield, however you tell time."

"Holy shit," he breathed a moment later. His avatar popped into life, hovering a couple inches above the copilot seat. "Joe, what happened?" He sounded frightened. Right then, I regretted his ridiculously oversized admiral's hat, because it was not appropriate for the seriousness of the situation.

"We do not know. When you disappeared, you were telling me about how you were poking around in that other AI canister. Hold a moment, I'm signaling the *Dutchman* that Skippy the Magnificent is back in action. You, uh, are back to your old self, right?"

"Never better. Although, huh. Hmm. My reserves of metallic helium 3 have been noticeably depleted. I must have been running on internal power. That is troubling."

"Yeah it is. Hang on," I started the process of powering up the dropship's main engines.

"Like I can hang on, you dumdum," his avatar pointed back to his motionless beer can form, still strapped into a seat. "I don't have hands."

"Yup," I said with an ear-to-ear grin. "Skippy is back!"

"Everyone, calm down, please," Skippy appealed for quiet in the *Dutchman*'s conference room. "This was not a big deal, not for me. I was not in any danger, and it won't happen again. All that happened was, I lost track of time while I was examining that dead AI canister. You know my sense of time is radically different from the way you meatsacks think of time. Most of the time, the vast majority of my consciousness is dormant, because it isn't needed. If my entire being stays awake all the time, I use too much power, and I would go crazy from boredom. So, when part of my consciousness went in there, I didn't realize how time was going by on the outside, and the remainder of me shut down temporarily."

I did not know whether to believe him or not. "Why did the entire ship shut down? And the lifeboat's reactor shut down also. You have left the ship before, and it continued operating."

"That's because I planned to leave the ship those other times, so I left preprogrammed operating instructions. Those only work for a limited time; I can't perform maintenance or calibrate the jump drive coils unless I'm here. This time, the onboard systems timed out after they couldn't contact me; they shut down as a safety measure. I will create an automated process for the ship to follow if onboard systems are not able to contact me, but, again, those systems can only run the ship by themselves for a limited time. Don't worry," he chuckled, "I didn't plan to go missing."

"How can you be sure this will not happen again?" I asked.

"Joe, the next time I go poking around in dark corners, I will bring a watch in addition to a flashlight. I didn't miss anything exciting, did I?"

"Our jump is delayed," Chotek glared at him. "The entire crew was subject to unnecessary stress."

"Ok, true. On the other hand, your science team had an opportunity to attempt running the ship without me. How'd what work for you monkeys, by the way?" He said in a sarcastic tone.

"You know exactly how it worked," Chotek replied, his face red.

"Uh huh, I thought so. By the way, your science team's loony idea to reverse the power flow from the jump drive capacitors would have made the ship go BOOM. There would have been monkey parts flying in every direction. More like monkey dust, actually. Listen to me, I have said this before and you apparently did not listen. There are a lot of delicate systems aboard this ship that could cause a disaster if you screw with them, so please do not touch anything more complicated than shoelaces."

"We would not have had to consider touching anything, if you had not left us drifting with no power to run the life support systems," Chotek scolded while wagging a finger at Skippy's avatar.

"Oh, for-" Skippy's avatar folded its arms across its chest. "I *said* I was sorry. How many times do I need to say it? Hey, Joe, how about I put 'I am very sorry and it will not happen again' on a loop and run it until, oh, the end of time? Will that work for you? I can set it to music if you like."

"I would not like. Skippy, your apology is accepted," I said so we could move on.

Chotek was really fuming. "Colonel Bishop, Skippy's reckless actions-"

"Mister Chotek, I am captain of this ship, and a shipboard system had a glitch," I cut him off before he antagonized Skippy further and we got stuck in an argument all day. "What happened is my responsibility, and we can discuss it privately, if you wish."

Skippy blessedly took that as a cue to end the conversation. "Well, much as I'd simply *love* to stay here and listen to Count Chocula scolding me, I have reactors to restart, jump drive coils to calibrate and a jump to program. Unless you apes want to handle that for me? No? Didn't think so." His avatar gave a flamboyantly disdainful salute in Chotek's direction and disappeared.

"Colonel Bishop-" Chotek turned his anger at me.

"Yes, Sir. I will speak with him. In the meantime, we should continue preparations for a jump?"

"Yes," Chotek said unhappily. My impression was he wanted more time to yell at me. "Mr. Bishop, the next time your beer can decides to go on holiday, please tell him to leave the ship running."

"Joe, can you keep a secret?" Skippy said over my zPhone. I was in my cabin, reading a report before I turned out the light. Or, I was supposed to be reading a report, but I couldn't concentrate, so I was playing solitaire. And losing, every time. I noticed he didn't use his avatar this time; that told me he wanted to be completely serious for a change. "Depends," I turned the tablet off and put it on the floor. "On what the secret is, and who I'm keeping it from. Also," I thought for a moment, "if a friend tells you a secret, but the secret is that they are about to do something self-destructive, you might be obligated to break the secret for their sake."

"I guess that's fair. This friendship thing is still new to me, Joe. The secret is about me, and we're keeping the secret from Count Chocula."

"In that case, bring it on, homeboy." Since waking up from, wherever he had gone, Skippy had been extra disdainful of Hans Chotek. Privately, I was pissed off at Chotek also. That pompous ass had berated me mercilessly about something I had no control over, and I took that as a sign of weakness. A strong commander would have been quietly calm, and focused on resolving the problem rather than assigning blame. Chewing me out in front of the crew had only eroded my authority; you dress people down in private, not in public. "What's the big secret? Have you discovered," I sucked in a breath dramatically, "that you are an asshole?"

"I'm trying to be serious, Joe."

"Sorry. You can understand how I'd be confused."

"I'm working on that. The secret is that I was not entirely truthful about what happened when I went missing. You might even say I lied my ass off."

"Might?"

"Ok, I did. In my defense, I am scared out of my mind."

I took my mother's advice to breathe deeply and count to three so I wouldn't explode at him. Getting upset wasn't going to help anyone. "Skippy, anything that can scare you must be awful. What happened?"

"It is true that I lost track of time, but the reason I didn't notice time going by was that my higher functions were offline. Since I woke up, I've been piecing together what happened. At first, I loaded a submind into the matrix of that AI canister, but each submind lasted only a short time; they quickly became unstable. That was no big surprise; without knowing the exact nature of the matrix in there, I wasn't able to prepare each submind to adapt to the changing conditions. And the subminds were not smart or fast enough to adjust with sufficient speed on their own. Since I was able to determine there was nothing in there that posed a danger to the subminds, I extended part of my consciousness into the matrix to examine it closely. Everything went fine for a while, it was boring, really. Then, and this happened really fast while I was talking with you, I was hit by a surprise attack. Not physically, of course; this was- Hmmm. You wouldn't understand it. To put it in very crude terms that you can relate to, this was like a computer worm."

"Uh, Ok, sure." I had little idea what a 'computer worm' is. "Malware, right? Like a virus?"

"Yes, except that on Earth, a computer worm is different from a virus in that worms are designed to replicate and spread. The worm that attacked me, like I said, it's not a worm, that's the best analogy I can give you. This worm replicated itself many times, to keep attacking while my internal systems defended my higher-level consciousness. Every time the worm was hunted down and neutralized, it popped up again somewhere else."

"Sounds frightening."

"You haven't heard the scary part yet, Joe. The worm should have killed me, rendered me inert, whatever you want to call it. It locked up my conscious mind in a loop so I was not aware of anything, not even of time passing. I was helpless; it could have taken me apart and erased me, like it erased the AI that used to occupy that canister. The only reason I survived, Joe, was that I had sort of antibodies to fight the worm. At some point in my past, I must have encountered a worm like that before, although I probably had outside help to fight it back then. During that fight, long ago, I built antibodies to destroy that worm, and those antibodies have been waiting inside me all this time. My conscious memories have no record of that first incident, I didn't even know they existed, but now I estimate these antibodies make up almost two and a half percent of my memory. That is a huge amount of my capacity. When this worm attacked me, my antibody subroutines protected me, firewalled off my consciousness, and attacked the worm."

"Whoa." I took a moment to process that. "Where did this worm come from?" I asked anxiously. If something that dangerous was floating around the galaxy, we could be in big trouble. Any computer worm that could overwhelm Skippy, could crush the computers aboard the *Flying Dutchman*. Probably infiltrate and take over a Maxolhx computer also.

"I do not know. I don't know where it came from, I don't know who built it, or whether it evolved from a simpler system. It was in an Elder AI canister, and that AI was wiped out a long time ago, that is the only thing I am certain of."

"So, what? The worm has been hiding in there all this time, waiting for another Elder AI to come along and start poking around in dark corners?"

"No, Joe. The worm has not been waiting or hiding, not consciously. It is not sentient, it is a weapon. It was not aware of time passing. It was designed to destroy an Elder AI; after it accomplished that, it went dormant. It would have remained dormant, if I had not gone into that canister."

"This worm was designed to destroy an *Elder* AI? Not just any type of AI?"

"Yes, it was built to destroy an Elder AI."

"How do you know that?"

Skippy ordinarily would have scolded me for asking a stupid question. This time, he didn't even give a sigh of exasperation. "It is capable of destroying lesser AIs, but the impressive capabilities of this worm would only be fully needed against an Elder AI such as myself. Any lesser worm would not have affected me, so it seems pretty obvious to me this thing was built to kill me."

"Skippy, you say your memories are foggy. How sure are you that you are an Elder AI?" He was speechless for such a long time, the hairs in the back of my neck rose, fearing he had gone AWOL again. "Skippy?"

"Sorry, Joe. I was thinking about what you said. You know that I often disparage your intelligence-"

"You can apologize any time you want," I said smugly, waiting to hear him grovel.

"Huh? What? Why would I- Joe, I am *totally* justified in disparaging your intelligence. What do you mean, how do I know I am an Elder AI? I have capabilities far beyond those of the Rindhalu or Maxolhx. My memories contain data only available to the Elder. *Duh*."

He wasn't getting away that easily. "How do you know those are *your* memories?"

"Oh, man, you are- Huh. Hmmm. The monkey may have a point there," he added under his breath. "Shit. Now you've given me another thing to worry about. Great! Just freakin' great! Here I am getting four reactors restarted-"

"Four?"

"Four including the one in the lifeboat, yes. I already have enough crap to think about, and you throw me a goshdarned curveball. Damn it!" He sputtered in frustration. "The truth is, I do *not* know with absolute certainty that I am an Elder AI. In fact," he muttered something I couldn't quite hear. "I have been disturbed by something else I found in that canister; whatever AI was in there was fundamentally different from me. That was a surprise, and, hmmm, now that I think about it, trying to understand why my matrix is so different from that dead AI absorbed almost all of my attention. If I hadn't been working on that puzzle, maybe the worm would not have been able to sneak up on me."

"Is the other AI's matrix different because it was corrupted by the worm? Could that explain the difference?"

"Uh, no. Not, not even close. It's embarrassing, really. Sometimes your profound ignorance is cute, Joe."

"Great, thank you. Talking with you is a huge confidence-booster for me, as always."

"No problem, Joe."

Several jumps later, we arrived near a boring, ordinary, nothing-special M-class red dwarf star that absolutely no one would care about. According to Skippy, there were over one hundred *billion* red dwarf stars in the Milky Way galaxy. The starlight would make it easier for us to work on the Kristang ships. And if we encountered a threat, we could jump in near the star, where other ships could not form a jump field.

I was just happy to see a star that was not a tiny dot. This red dwarf was not impressive from twenty million miles away; it was still a distinctive disk, not a pinpoint. After a while, the romance of being in deep interstellar space got old for me; I wanted sunlight on my face, even through a porthole.

"Joe," Skippy called me only a couple minutes later. "I found something interesting."

My Spidey sense tingled. "Interesting in an oh-shit-we-are-in-huge-trouble-again way, or interesting in a nerdy science way?"

"Science is not nerdy, Joe," he sniffed. "You should try it some time."

"Sorry, Skippy, I didn't mean any offense. So, no immediate danger?"

"Nope, no danger at all. Joe, you once asked me whether a planet orbiting a red dwarf star could be habitable."

"Uh huh, yeah, I remember that." At the time, I had been vaguely insulted to learn that Earth's star, The Sun, was considered a yellow dwarf star. A dwarf! I found that insulting. "You told me that conditions around a red dwarf have to be absolutely perfect for a planet there to be habitable. You found one here?" I asked excitedly.

"Um, no. Close enough, in this case. I did find a rocky planet in this star's Goldilocks zone, but this planet cannot actually support human life. The atmosphere has too much carbon dioxide, and almost no free oxygen. The good news is that because of the carbon dioxide, the atmosphere is reasonably thick, about ninety percent of sea-level normal on Earth. And the greenhouse effect from all that carbon dioxide trapping heat keeps surface temperatures at the terminator from freezing."

"Terminator?" When I heard 'Terminator', I automatically thought of the killer robot movies.

"This planet is so close to the star, it is tidally locked; one side always faces the star, like the way Earth's moon always shows one side facing your planet," Skippy explained with unexpected patience. "The side facing the star gets baked by solar radiation, while the far side is frozen in eternal darkness. The edge of the planet, between the daylight side and the night side, is called the 'terminator'."

"Oh. Sorry, I should have remembered that. Being between the hot side and the cold side, wouldn't the terminator area have strong winds?" Somewhere in high school, I had read that what we call 'weather' is a mechanism for distributing heat across the surface of a planet. Also I remember that 'meteor-ology' is not about meteors, but about weather. That made no sense to me back then, and it still puzzled me.

"Very good, Joe!" Skippy said in the tone of voice parents use when a small child has done something simple. "Yes, there are strong winds there. Anyway, I thought you would be interested to know about this planet. It was mentioned in the Thuranin long-range survey data about this star system, however, that data is almost two thousand years old and I did not know whether conditions had changed. A single solar flare could have significantly altered the nature of the planet's atmosphere, but it still looks good. Gravity is 78 percent of Earth normal."

Skippy had told us this system was uninhabited, that is why Chotek had agreed to come here. "You don't see any sign the Thuranin, or anyone else, had been here recently?"

"Nope," Skippy confirmed.

I sighed, because I knew what was going to happen next; while Skippy was working on building a Q-ship from our two salvaged transports, Major Smythe would want his team to go down to the surface for training. And the science team would be eager to go there also. And I would have to argue with Chotek for permission to send teams to the planet.

Or not. Hans Chotek had been surprisingly adventurous recently. Maybe he would like to go down to the surface himself, so he could tell people he had walked on another planet instead of just an airless moon, when he got back to Earth.

Before any talk about anyone going down to the surface for a picnic outing, we had what I hoped would be a brief meeting to review Skippy's latest info on our two salvaged transport ships. I was anxious to get them refitted for the mock attack operation.

"Let's get it over with," Skippy announced as I was sitting down. "we can get only one usable ship out of these two hulks. Uh!" He shushed me as I was opening my mouth. "Please shut your crumb catcher and let me talk, or this will go on all freakin' day. In order to make a believable Q-ship, it needs to have shields much better than a typical transport is fitted with. The shield generators of both these ships are in terrible, horrible, no-good, unforgivable condition. I don't know how these ships managed to survive as long as they did, Joe. One of the reasons the ship you cleared was selected to be abandoned is, a micrometeorite impact damaged its reactor shielding, because the energy shields were so weak. I will have to strip shield generators and reactor components out of both ships, and even then, our Q-ship will barely be capable of conducting a believable attack on the Ruhar negotiators. The shield generators I can work with; with modifications, they will last for a short battle and no more. The reactors are complete scrap; the best I can do is to make them hot and fill them with radiation so they appear to be operating on a sensor scan. To power the ship, I will need to use capacitors, and that will require pulling capacitors from the *Dutchman*. I did warn you about this before we started this whole operation; the condition of the transports was an unknown. Now I know, and what I've found is the ships are in very poor condition. It will be stretching our resources to get even one ship ready for the mock attack."

The room, or technically aboard a ship it is a 'compartment', was silent. "Hello?" Skippy called out. "What, no monkey is going to challenge my data?"

"It's not your data we would challenge, Skippy," I explained. "If we challenged anything, it would be the conclusions you drew from the data." As I spoke, I patted myself on the back for using such fancy words. "And," I looked at the blank faces around the table, "we got nothing there. We have to trust your judgment. It is," I let out a sigh everyone was feeling, "disappointing that we went through so much effort, to get only one Q-ship."

"One barely capable Q-ship, Joe. Seriously, the ship we end up with is going to quickly get pounded into dust by the Ruhar or the Kristang or both. It is dicey whether an attack by our Q-ship would be perceived as a credible threat by the Ruhar. And I did warn you about that."

"I know, Skippy, I know. Mr. Chotek, I recommend that Skippy proceed with modifying one ship, whichever one he thinks best."

Chotek sat stiffly upright; I could tell he was disappointed also. And worried, deeply worried. "I agree. Mr. Skippy, please proceed as you see fit."

"Colonel Bishop?" Margaret Adams spoke from the other end of the conference table. She technically wasn't senior staff; I had invited her to the meeting because she had been involved in clearing one transport, and I knew she was deeply emotionally invested in the operation. "What will happen to the Kristang aboard the ships?"

Oh shit. I knew what she meant. I should have mentioned that upfront.

Before I could answer, Skippy unhelpfully replied. "That is a good point. The Ruhar and Kristang will scan the debris, after our Q-ship is destroyed. We will need Kristang bodies, male of course, as part of the debris. To make the attack believable, we can't have any females or children, so-"

Before he could continue, I interrupted. "That is not the point, Skippy. We do need to keep some male Kristang corpses aboard the Q-ship. The remainder of the, remains," I cringed at the word, "we will treat with care and respect. The Kristang aboard those ships were civilians. We need to-" To what? What could we do with thousands of dead Kristang?

Skippy surprised me. Again. "Colonel Bishop, I do understand your meaning. As you stated, the Kristang civilians aboard those ships were not our enemy. I propose that when I am finished building our Q-ship, we jump the *Flying Dutchman* closer to the star, and send the Kristang remains aboard the other transport ship, on a trajectory down into the gravity well. A burial in space; going out in a blaze of glory, I believe is the expression. No pun was intended."

"Staff Sergeant?" I directed my question to Adams. "Is that acceptable?"

Adams thought a moment. I knew that female and her three children, huddled in a locker, were in her mind. "That is acceptable. For now."

"For now?" Skippy asked, puzzled. "What could we do after the burial?"

"Payback," Adams said simply. "Not tomorrow, not the day after that, but someday. No matter how long it takes. I'm a Marine, Sir," she looked directly at me. "*Semper* Fidelis. The lizards need to learn what payback means, someday."

"Someday, Staff Sergeant." I felt the same way.

Someday was going to be a long, long time away.

"Hey, uh, Joe?" Skippy called me when I got back to my office. His holographic avatar didn't activate, so I assumed he wanted to talk seriously about something.

"What is it, Skippy?"

"This is probably a conversation you and I should have in private."

"Got it." I pressed the button to close the door of my tiny office.

"This is an unpleasant subject. I mentioned that we need several bodies of adult male Kristang aboard the Q-ship. The ship will self-destruct following the attack, and the Kristang will certainly scan the debris. They will expect that whatever clan conducted the attack will have been careful not to leave behind any clues pointing to them, so searching the debris will mostly be an exercise for the benefit of the Ruhar. It would be highly suspicious if there were no traces of Kristang DNA from the crew in the debris field."

"Uh huh, you did mention that." The adult male bodies aboard the transports were civilians, except for one crew member who had apparently been caught by a mob and stabbed to death. His body for sure was going aboard our Q-ship, along with three others. I had privately instructed Skippy to set aside more adult male bodies, in case we somehow acquired another ship for the attack. "I don't like using civilian bodies for the attack, but we have to do it."

"Hmm. Something that is morally distastefully, but necessary, can be acceptable? You know my moral compass does not always align with yours, Joe."

Oh, crap. "It depends, Skippy. Those civilians are victims, and I do not like the idea of using their remains in an action against their own people, but I will do it to protect my own people. What is necessary, beyond what we have already talked about?"

"This is the part where the conversation needs to be kept private. You promised Sergeant Adams to treat the remains with respect, except for the adult males we need to leave behind as evidence of a Kristang clan being involved. The problem is, the attack will not be seen as the action of a Kristang clan, if the debris contains only *male* DNA."

"Oh shit."

"If a Kristang clan conducted such an attack, the crew would be volunteers for a suicide mission. These are typically criminals, or disgraced warriors sent by their families to atone for their crimes. Or they often are younger sons who have limited prospects, and hope their sacrifice will elevate the standing of their family within the clan. These suicide volunteers are provided females to, uh, 'comfort' them during their final mission."

"Damn it," I spat.

"Joe, it would be suspicious if some female Kristang DNA were not found among the debris. I do not like it, but I do think it is necessary."

"I don't like it either."

"Sergeant Adams is very much not going to like it. Joe, I wish you had this discussion with me, before you promised Adams to give all the remains a respectful burial in space."

I wish the beer can had mentioned needing female DNA aboard the Q-ship, before my conversation with Adams! "Adams is not going to know about this."

"But-"

"But nothing. Skippy, this is what we call a 'lie of omission'. For some reason I am not an expert about, not telling a person something, is considered morally superior to than telling them a lie. We are simply not going to tell her, or tell anyone else, got it? You can use your bots to collect female remains, and hide them somewhere aboard the Q-ship? And enough for a second ship, if we can get one. Do not tell me how many female bodies we need, please, I don't want to know." My mind flashed back to high school history class, when I heard about kings being buried with their servants, while those servants were alive. I could not imagine the terror of a Kristang woman, already living a life of miserable slavery, knowing she was being used as 'comfort' on a suicide mission. Humanity were not the only people who needed to pay back the Kristang warrior caste; their own people needed a measure of retribution.

Right then, I had enough other problems to deal with.

"I can do that, Joe. I did consider doing it without telling anyone at all, but I felt the need to check with you on the morality of such action."

"You are always right to check with me, Skippy, and don't be concerned about my feelings. As the commander, I need to deal with this shit, so my people don't have to."

"Technically, Joe, Count Chocula is in command of the mission."

"You didn't tell him, did you?" I asked, alarmed.

"Phhhht!" Skippy made a raspberry sound. "No way would I ask Chocky-boy's advice on anything important. The less he is involved with a mission, the more likely we are to succeed. He talks to me all the freakin' time, and I tell him the minimum he needs to know. Or I ignore him. When I, uh, went on vacation for seventeen hours, Chotek didn't notice until the ship's power cut out, because he is used to me ignoring him."

It would be better for everyone if Skippy developed at least a cordial working relationship with Chotek; someday he might need Chotek's good will. "Skippy, please, I know you can't stand the guy, but can you dig down into your endless well of patience and try to work with him? Please?"

"I can try, but you'd better have a bottomless well of patience with me, because Earth's sun will be a cold, dark cinder before Hans Chotek and I get along."

"The guy will be dead by then, Skippy."

"Exactly."

Major Smythe did indeed want his teams to go down to the surface for training. Hans Chotek also wished to go, but resisted the temptation. My guess was he didn't trust me to handle the ship by myself. And maybe he was worried Skippy would take another 'vacation'. The science team was torn between wanting to see what Skippy's bots were doing to convert two derelict transports into a Q-ship, and wanting to explore a planet that orbited a red dwarf. We compromised on members of the science team splitting their time on the surface and on the ship. To make sure we could evacuate the entire surface team in one trip, I limited the number of people on the surface to the number that could be transported in the two dropships assigned to stay on the surface. For pilot training, dropships shuttled from the ship to the surface and back, but two were always near the ground teams, ready to whisk them away on short notice. Also, the ground teams had portable shelters that they could live in for several weeks if needed, and stealth netting to conceal the shelters.

I was patting myself on the back for having thought of all possible problems, when I happened to look at my tablet. In the center of the display was the planet. Next to the planet were a dot representing our pirate ship, and two adjacent dots for the salvaged transports attached to our docking platforms.

Then I had a bad thought. "Skippy, uh, it is possible you could work on those transports somewhere else? Like, away from the ship and the planet?"

"Um, maybe, why? Is being close to my awesomeness making you swoon, Joe?"

"Not even a little. I'm concerned that if you have another, you know, episode, it could be bad for the *Dutchman*. And the planet."

"I am not going to explode, Joe," he declared with sarcasm. "And if I do, I should be way, way far from the planet. That atmosphere there is reasonably thick, but it will not protect the landing party from me exploding. Even if I was on the other side of the star, the planet wouldn't be safe. Gravity waves would cause the star to send out intense solar flares that would fry the planet's near side."

"Exploding is not the only potential problem," I insisted. "You once told me that if you were to lose containment, your full mass is about a quarter that of the planet Paradise. Having that much mass suddenly pop into this spacetime would disrupt the orbit of the planet, and cause quakes down there that could kill the away teams." Too late, I realized that almost the entire science team, who were the people we needed if Skippy went AWOL again, were down on the planet. That was poor planning by some idiot named Joe Bishop. The United States Army had a lot of explaining to do, why they put *that* moron in charge of anything more complicated than emptying a trash can.

"Hmmm. Joe, I am mildly impressed that you consider the effect of my mass upon the planet. However, to avoid negative effects on the planet in the extremely unlikely event I were to lose containment, I would need to be on the outer edge of this star system, which would ruin the whole reason we came all the way here in the first place. Settle down, Joe, I am not going anywhere. Trust me, I got this. I am right in the middle of a very delicate operation on the Q-ship, so please leave me alone for a while to do my job."

CHAPTER TWELVE

Skippy did not, in fact, explode, or lose containment or go AWOL while he was working on the Q-ship. Despite my worries, work on the Q-ship proceeded smoothly and ahead of schedule. When he finished, we carefully and respectfully packed most of the dead Kristang into the other transport, and cast it down into the star. Although Skippy wanted to get moving, I held the *Dutchman* in orbit, until we saw the transport burn up in the star's photosphere.

"Excellent! We have a Q-ship," Chotek announced happily as we prepared to break orbit. "What's wrong?" He added after seeing the expression on my face.

"Sir, that's the problem. We have 'a', as in one ship. And 'Q-ship' as in not a real warship. I am concerned that our mock attack, with a single old converted transport ship, will not be perceived as a serious threat. We will only get one chance at scaring those Ruhar negotiators. It would be a shame to waste all this effort, Sir. It would be worse than a shame; if the mock attack doesn't succeed in breaking the negotiations, we will have ruined our best, maybe our only, chance to keep aliens away from Earth."

Chotek ran a hand through his hair, I could tell he was forcing himself to be patient. As he made that gesture, I realized my timing could not have been worse. He was in a good mood, an almost celebratory mood. He had approved my plan for a mock attack on the Ruhar, rather than his preference of approaching the Ruhar openly to offer an alliance. He had suffered through an incredibly complicated operation to pick up two derelict starships. Now we had a Q-ship to use in the mock attack, and instead of acting pleased, I was throwing cold water on the whole idea. My timing sucked. I should have had this discussion while Skippy was working on the Q-ship. Or before. "You want to get *another* starship?" He asked quietly, in a tone with more than a hint of exasperation.

"Yes, Sir. If we can."

"You have an idea of how we could do that?" His skeptical expression implied that if I had such an idea, we should have done it already. Perhaps we should have done it instead of constructing a Q-ship out of discarded transports.

"We're working on concepts, Sir. If we have to, we will go with the single Q-ship. For now, we should proceed toward the nearest Elder wormhole; that will take us two days. Once we get there, you can decide where to go. Skippy says we have plenty of time before the Ruhar arrive at the negotiation site."

Back in my office, Skippy's avatar popped to life. "Joe, I heard your conversation with Count Chocula. I do agree that hitting the Ruhar with our one Q-ship is unlikely to make the hamsters pull out of the negotiations. However, you were wrong about one thing; it will take us *five* days to get to a wormhole, not two," Skippy chided me.

"Really?" I flipped my tablet open and pulled up the star chart app Skippy had supplied. It was constantly updated with the ship's position, so the little pirate-monkey-on-a-flying-banana icon for the *Flying Dutchman* was always in the center. "There's a wormhole, like, two days from here," I tapped the screen, leaving a smudge mark.

"Ugh, you smudged the screen again, Joe. I hate it when you don't wash your hands after eating potato chips, it makes extra work for my cleaning bots."

"Huh," I had been wondering how my iPad screen was always squeaky clean every morning. Feeling guilty, I absent-mindedly wiped my hands on my pants.

"Damn it! Don't clean your hands on your pants, Joe!"

"Don't worry, Skippy, the uniform of the day is Army Combat Uni, so on this camo, a couple greasy chip stains actually improves the digital pattern."

"*You* don't have to do your own laundry," he said in a huff.

"Yeah, thank you for that." Like the entire crew, I dropped dirty clothes in a bin, and the next day, they reappeared, cleaned and folded, tucked into drawers or the closet in my cabin. Skippy's Magical Cleaning Fairy bots took care of most domestic chores aboard the ship. Somehow, he knew exactly which clothing belonged to which person, even Army-issue socks that looked identical to me. I had tried putting my dirty T-shirts in a bin far from my cabin, and the next day, my T-shirts were back in a drawer in my cabin. Skippy never said anything about me testing him, and I wasn't going to mention it. "So, like I said, there's a wormhole two days from here."

"Yup, wow, you can read a star chart. Do you want a trophy?"

"No trophy needed, how about you give me an explanation instead?"

"Me explain hyperspatial navigation to you? Ugh. I should get a trophy for that. All right, here goes nothing. Yes, Joe, there is a wormhole only two days from here. We can't risk using that wormhole, we need to use the wormhole that is five days away."

"Incredible. Gosh, that was so difficult for me to understand, Skippy. Me caveman, hmm, two days not same as five days? Huuh? Me primitive mind blown! How about you, oh, I don't know. What the hell, let's go crazy; how about you explain *why* we can't use the wormhole that is three days closer to us? You can manipulate wormholes to change their connections, right?" In one of our cargo bays was a 'magic bean stalk', an Elder wormhole controller module we had stolen from a Kristang asteroid research base during our first mission. Skippy could use it to shut down a wormhole, which is how the Thuranin and Kristang no longer had access to Earth. He had discovered that he could also use it to temporarily change which distant wormhole a nearby wormhole connected to. That had been my idea, by the way. Being able to temporarily change local wormhole connections saved the Merry Band of Pirates a tremendous amount of time, because we could use a single wormhole to get to our destination, rather than hopscotching from one wormhole to another like all other ships in the galaxy had to. We could go directly from, say, Atlanta to Duluth, instead of going Atlanta-Dallas-Chicago-Detroit-Duluth. Except, of course, there is no reason for anyone to ever to go to Duluth.

Oh, crap! Now I'm going to get flooded with angry messages from the Duluth Chamber of Commerce. All I can say is, get in line behind the people from Newark, after I maligned their fair city by naming a miserable planet 'Newark'. Anyway, bite me. "Before you tell me how stupid I am, I do know that each wormhole can only connect to a limited number of wormholes, and the potential connections don't all make sense." Like, a wormhole could be made to connect to another wormhole a thousand lightyears away, but it could not connect to a wormhole ten lightyears away. Skippy said the reason was complicated, which was his way of saying that he didn't understand it.

"Yup. That is not the reason why we can't use the wormhole that is only two lightyears away. There is actually another wormhole that is only half a lightyear away from here, Joe, I didn't show that closer wormhole on the display because it is dormant, and its potential connections do not go in the direction we need to travel. The reason we can't use the closest active wormhole is I have become concerned that my messing with wormholes is dangerous. The more times I screw with wormholes, the more likely it is that someone will notice abnormal wormhole behavior, and attract the attention of the Maxolhx and Rindhalu. That has already happened; on our last mission, a pair of Thuranin ships were waiting for a wormhole that never appeared, so they had to jump to another wormhole emergence point and wait there. That was only one anomaly, but wormholes are predictable as a sunrise; even one hiccup is deeply troubling to the species who use them."

"Shit! Skippy, you didn't tell me the Thuranin noticed us messing with wormholes."

"It was only that one incident, Joe. Uh, well, one that I know of," he admitted. "I have tried to avoid messing with heavily-traveled wormholes, for that reason. The more traffic a wormhole has, the more likely it is that anomalous behavior will be noticed."

"Okaaaay," I kept my breathing even. Crap. An idea I thought was a great timesaver for us, a major tactical advantage, might give away our presence and endanger our home planet. Maybe I should stop trying to think up clever ideas. "We should only use wormholes that don't get much traffic, then?"

"Yes. There is another problem, an even worse problem. There are three wormholes we have manipulated more than once, because they can be adjusted to provide convenient routes to Earth or Paradise. Each time I alter one of those wormholes, I notice their connection to the network is slightly less stable. And all wormholes in the surrounding local area become less stable. The level of instability increases on a roughly logarithmic scale, I won't bother attempting to explain the math to you. To put it simply, I am concerned about destabilizing the entire wormhole network in this sector, and causing a shift. Another shift could undo everything we have accomplished out here. It could make it impractical for the Ruhar to base a battlegroup at Paradise; forcing them to abandon that planet and leaving UNEF at the mercy of the Kristang. Another shift could also give the Kristang access to Earth again. As I told you, the wormhole I shut down is not the closest one to Earth. This could be a major, major problem."

"Shit. Oh, shit. Should we stop messing with wormholes completely?"

"I do not think that is necessary. Not yet. Some wormholes can be safely manipulated; for example the one five days away has never been adjusted, and it is on a local network we have never used. When I say it is 'safe', I mean in terms of not inadvertently causing a catastrophic wormhole shift. We will always run the risk of someone noticing that wormhole behavior has changed."

"Great. Just great." We have a huge tactical advantage, and now we couldn't use it. "So, I'm thinking the rule is you only mess with wormholes if it's an emergency?" Crap. When was the Merry Band of Pirates ever *not* responding to an emergency?

"That would be prudent, Joe."

"I will tell the crew." Crap. Count Chocula was absolutely going to *love* hearing this news. Especially the part about the ship's captain, me, not knowing about this danger until it came up in a casual conversation with our absent-minded alien AI. "Skippy, you need to tell me about these type of things."

"I figured there was no reason to worry you about it, Joe, until it became an actual problem."

"You figured wrong. As captain, I need to know about potential problems, so we can avoid making them into actual problems."

"Hmm. Um, I should probably tell you about Reactor Two, then-"

A few minutes later, I wished he hadn't told me. Thc ship was in even worse condition than I thought.

Because I had learned that bad news does not improve with age, I went to see Chotek, while the ship accelerated away from the planet. Chotek had left his office and was in the conference room, talking about some boring thing with Simms and a few other people. When I told him we needed to talk about the condition of Reactor Two, he summoned me to sit down. What I told him was not good news.

"Mister Skippy," Chotek said, studiously avoiding looking at Skippy's avatar. "Records from your second mission indicate you rebuilt the ship from raw materials. Can you not do that again?"

"Correct, I cannot do that again."

Chotek and I shared a look. I bailed out my boss. "Skippy, that expression means-"

"I know what it means, dumdum," he said with his avatar's hands on its hips. "I meant what I said. I can't do that again. Yes, last time I used raw materials, but those only supplemented the materials and equipment on hand. I had to cannibalize parts of the ship to fix other, more critical parts. The equipment remaining aboard the ship is not sufficient to repair or rebuild most of the sophisticated systems that are wearing out. The *Flying Dutchman* is not a Von Neumann machine, you know, it- Oh, boy. Now I have to explain what a 'Von Neumann Machine' is to you."

I was puzzled by the reference, so I guessed. "A '70s progressive rock band?"

"No," the avatar buried its face in its hands. "This is hopeless-"

"Oh, sorry, duh," I said, embarrassed. "Hey, is Von Neumann the guy who wrote that song 'I Love L.A.'? What does that have to do with-"

"No, that was *Randy* Newman! Oh, why do I bother trying to explain anything to you? And you, Chocula, put your hand down, stop feeling so smug. Just because you know what a Von Neumann machine is does not make you smart; you're like a four year old who is proud that he can go potty by himself. That is not a major accomplishment. For your education, Joe, a Von Neumann machine is a device that can make a copy of itself, using only raw materials from the environment."

That didn't sound like any big deal to me. "So, it's a woman?"

"What?" Skippy sputtered. "No, you-"

"Because any woman can do *that*," I observed, getting an appreciative look from Major Simms.

"No, it's not a wom-"

"Women do need a little help-" I started to say.

"*Very* little help," Simms rolled her eyes, and made air quotes with her fingers when she said 'help'.

"We men call that the 'fun part'," I laughed.

"Joe!" The beer can avatar was hopping up and down on the tabletop. "Focus! Please," Skippy broke down sobbing, "*please*, try to focus. Oh, why do I even bother? I'm on a pirate ship full of ignorant monkeys." The avatar got on its knees, face in its hands. "I'm doomed, doomed, *doomed*."

"Wow, sorry, Skippy. You were saying that the ship can't make a baby," I suggested. "or, something like that?"

"You totally missed my point as usual, Joe," the avatar shook its head sadly, but at least it was standing up again. "The ship can't fix itself, because it is not capable of making the machinery needed to create replacement parts. The Thuranin fleet does include support ships with extensive fabrication facilities, but even those ships can't produce certain items, like atomic compression warheads. Or the exotic matter in superconducting magnets used for reactor containment systems."

"Got it," I thought I understood him. "Even your magnificent awesomeness can only do so much, with the crappy equipment you have to work with."

"Exactly!"

Chotek had gotten irritated by my back-and-forth with Skippy. UNEF Command should have included a sense of humor in their requirements for a mission commander, but they hadn't, so we were stuck with Hans Chotek. To be fair, he wasn't as stiff as when he first came aboard, but he could still be a major dick sometimes. Most of the time. "Mister Skippy, we appreciate that this ship can't continue flying forever, without access to a Thuranin shipyard. How long can we fly, until the ship becomes permanently disabled?"

"Even I can't answer that, Chocky," Skippy said as his avatar put a hand on its chin thoughtfully. "There are too many variables; the number and distance of jumps we make, whether we engage in combat again, all that. Even flying through normal space creates wear and tear on the shield generators, to prevent impacts from space junk and protect the crew from radiation. The stealth field is the system that is most likely to fail without being repairable; I am using my own capabilities to enhance our stealthiness, so we can use the ship's stealth field at a lower power level. The jump drive coils are the most critical system we have aboard; as they wear out, we can't replace them. If you ask me to guess, and of course you will, I would say that Reactor Number Two will be the first to fail. The good news is that when I have to shut down Two, I can cannibalize it to keep One and Three online longer. At our current tempo of operations, Reactor Two will likely fail within seventy four days."

Based on the shocked faces around the table, seventy four days was much less than the crew expected. If they had even thought of the ship as something that could wear out at all. With Skippy's magical, largely unseen bots handling all the maintenance, most people aboard tended not to think of the *Flying Dutchman*'s systems at all; it was like air on Earth. You breathed without thinking about it, and never considered free atmospheric oxygen as something that needed to be renewed. I had the most frequent contact with Skippy, and even I often took our stolen star carrier's smooth operation for granted. "Sir," I looked at Chotek, "in a way, this makes decision-making simpler."

"Simpler? How?"

"We have all been thinking, in the back of our minds, that whatever our current mission is, we need to make sure the *Dutchman* is available for future missions, indefinitely. Now, instead of planning missions with the idea of preserving the *Flying Dutchman* as a resource available to UNEF Command, we need to think of the ship as a use-it-or-lose-it proposition. Our pirate ship has a limited life remaining, so we need to make the most of it, before some critical system fails and leaves us stranded dead in space."

"Colonel," Chotek said with a troubled expression, "I hear you. However, I believe we should not give up on this ship, until we have considered all alternatives. Mister Skippy, Earth has considerable industrial resources. Is it possible that an extended stay at Earth could allow you to construct the equipment needed to keep the ship functional?" As he spoke, I could almost see the wheels turning in his head. He was hoping humans could build facilities to create advanced technologies that would not only repair the *Dutchman* under Skippy's direction, but also be available for humans to construct our own ships in the future. Our own totally human-controlled ships, that would not require Skippy to operate. UNEF Command would love to break our reliance on an untrustworthy alien AI.

"Uh, no." Skippy's avatar rolled its eyes. "Earth does not have industrial resources anywhere near the level of development that would be useful in repairing this ship. And before you ask, the answer is no; I can't give you the technology needed. Right now, I am already skating on the thin edge of having to shut myself down by talking with you. You know that my programming prevents me from revealing my presence to technologically advanced species. Humanity's level of technology is still pitiful, but you being aboard a Thuranin star carrier, simply operating basic flight controls, or sensor and weapon systems in the CIC, has me on the verge of shutting down. I am having to fight with some of my internal systems, and that causes conflicts that make me create workarounds. The next dumb question you are going to ask me," the avatar looked directly at Chotek, hands on its tiny 'hips', "is whether I could give you a data dump of technology you need, so that even though that will cause me to go silent, you would be able to operate the ship on your own. The answer is no, and hell no. I know this, because I have tried doing that already."

"You did?" I asked, surprised. "When was this?" He had not mentioned it to me before.

"On our second mission, when we got jumped by that squadron of Thuranin destroyers. If you remember, I heroically volunteered to sacrifice myself for this troop of flea-infested monkeys-"

"I do remember, and I remember that was a terrible, awful plan, Skippy."

"Ok, so maybe it wasn't the best idea I ever thought of, but still, I valiantly offered to lead the Thuranin away so you could escape-"

"Which would not have worked."

"Joe, I already said it wasn't a good plan. Anywho, when I thought you would tragically be deprived of my awesomeness, I attempted to put critical data into a file for you, Joe."

"Oh, that was very thoughtful of you, Skippy," I said, genuinely touched.

"Ah, in this case, it has to be the thought that counts, because it didn't work. My internal systems prevented me from assembling the data. If I want to give you a gift in the future, you'll have to settle for a fruit basket."

"I like pineapple."

"I will keep that in mind Joe. Bottom line is, I can't offer any sort of significant upgrade to humanity's technology level. You will have to do it the hard way, on your own."

"Or we do it the easy way, like all other species seem to do in this galaxy: we steal it."

"I'm not following you, Joe," the avatar tilted its cap up.

"We have a Kristang troop ship at Earth, or close enough. Back home, they should be taking that apart soon, to figure out how it works. If we can get the *Dutchman* home, even if it can never fly again, we can try to reverse engineer Thuranin technology."

"Good luck with that," Skippy scoffed. "Joe, understanding the theory behind how something works is only the first step. To make the theory useful, you have to be able to make it work. While we have been talking, I ran some rough estimates of how long it would take for Earth industry to create something relatively simple, like magnets for a crude reactor containment system. The best guess I can make is eighty years, Joe. Eighty years, and that assumes I am directing the effort, which I can't do. On your own, it could take three hundred years to build the infrastructure to create stable exotic matter."

"I don't think humanity has any important appointments over the next three hundred years, Skippy; we can concentrate on understanding this technology and building up our defenses. What the Merry Band of Pirates need to do keep is aliens away from our home, so Earth has time to develop technology."

"Oh yeah," Skippy said, his voice dripping with even more condescension than usual. "Good luck with that, monkeys."

During our five-day journey out to the wormhole, Simms was in my office when Skippy called me. "Joe," Skippy's avatar hopped up and down on my desk and waved its arms to get my attention. "I know where we can pick up a Kristang frigate cheap."

"What? Where?" I asked, assuming this was one of Skippy's jokes.

In a blink, his avatar changed to fat guy wearing a cheap plaid suit and what my grandfather used to call the 'Full Cleveland' outfit: white belt and matching white shoes. Hey, that was my grandfather's expression, so the Cleveland Chamber of Commerce can direct hate mail to him, not me. I looked closely, the avatar even had crumbs on its chin and some sort of grease stain on its shirt and tie. Skippy really nailed the used car salesman image.

Oh, and the National Association of Pre-Owned Car Salespersons can bite me too.

"Joey, Joey, you are in luck, my boy," the avatar said smarmily. "This frigate is a real cream-puff, only a zillion lightyears on it, all highway mileage. We're having a Labor Day blowout sale-"

"It's not Labor Day," Simms whispered to me.

"Don't bother him with facts, he's on a roll," I whispered back.

"-and for you, oh, my sales manager is going to *kill* me for saying this," the avatar said with a conspiratorial wink. "We'll even throw in our guaranteed rustproofing package."

"There's no rust in space," I rolled my eyes.

"That's why it's guaranteed. So, what would it take to get you into a quality warship like this, today? By 'what will it take you', I mean other than the special ops assault team that will be needed to capture it."

It still wasn't clear to me if he was joking or not. "What are you offering for financing? I doubt if my credit card works out here."

"Joey, Joey, Joey. With Skippy's Used Starship Emporium, your job is your credit. Although, hmm, your job is only going to last until your next major screwup, so maybe I should insist on a cash transaction."

"Are you being serious, Skippy? You know where there is a Kristang frigate we could take?"

"Yup, dead serious. And, as a bonus, you already sort of know this ship."

"I do?" My mind raced through the limited number of Kristang ships I had encountered. The troop transport that had brought me outbound from Earth? No, Skippy said this ship was a frigate. The *Flower* had been a frigate, but Skippy had taken that ship apart to repair the *Dutchman*. Several of the ships we had jumped into a gas giant planet had been frigates, the key phrase being 'had been'. Those ships were unorganized particles now. And when we arrived at Earth the first time, Skippy had jumped a Kristang frigate into the Sun. So, my mind was coming up blank. "Sorry, Skippy, my dumdum brain can't understand what you mean. Which frigate is this?"

"The '*To Seek Glory in Battle is Glorious*', of course."

"Holy shit," I gasped. I did know that ship, or knew of that ship. It had been a thorn in the side of Commodore Ferlant's task force at Paradise, and later the *Glory* had joined Admiral Kekrando's battlegroup. We had never actually encountered that ship during our first mission there to reactivate maser projectors, nor on our later mission to plant fake Elder artifacts. But from mission reports Skippy hacked from both sides, we sure as hell knew all about the *Glory*. Based on those reports, I almost had to admire the crew of that stubborn little ship that refused to die. Almost. What dampened my admiration was knowing the *Glory* had used her maser cannons to burn out fields of human crops in Lemuria, killing humans in the process. At one point, I had considered suggesting to Chotek that we should take out the *Glory*, if we could do that without risk to our mission. I never made that suggestion, because I knew the ever-overly-cautious Count Chocula would reject my idea, and that would give him even more reason to distrust my judgment. "I thought the *Glory* was declared lost during the final battle, before the cease fire took effect."

"Rumors of that ship's death had been greatly exaggerated, Joe. I suspected Admiral Kekrando was lying about how many ships he had left at the time of the cease fire, I just never had an opportunity to investigate. If you remember, we were kind of busy."

"How do you know about it now?"

"That Ruhar data node contained an interesting report that the *Glory* recently surrendered to the Ruhar; that ship really didn't have any choice, after Major Perkins destroyed the Kristang commando team the *Glory* was supposed to retrieve."

"Perkins? *Perkins*- what the hell?" I sputtered. "What commando team?"

"Joe, after we left, there was, um, trouble on Paradise." While Simms and I listened with mouths gaping open in astonishment, Skippy gave a brief account of what had happened within the first few weeks after we left Paradise behind.

"*Shauna NUKED an island*?!" There was another phrase I never thought would ever be coming out of my mouth.

"Uh huh. What is left of that formerly peaceful tropical isle has been renamed 'Jarrett Island'. From the limited data in the file, I do not think your former squeeze Shauna considers that to be much of an honor. Although, she sure did blow the hell out of it, so it is mostly her fault."

"Holy *shit*," I slumped in my chair, sharing an amazed look with Simms. "Goddamn it. I figured Shauna and the rest of them would be, I don't know, growing tomatoes or something peaceful."

"Apparently, United States Army personnel have a talent for finding trouble."

"That's our job, Skippy. We find trouble and take care of it, before trouble can find civilians."

"You, and people who know you, seem to have an uncanny ability to attract trouble," Skippy's voice dripped sarcasm. "Maybe being around you rubbed off onto them, Joe?"

"I hope not. But, wow, Goddamn. They couldn't stay out of trouble for one freakin' month? Uh, I'm glad Perkins and her team were able to stop that commando attack."

"Me too. It gave the Burgermeister an excuse to ensure better treatment of UNEF. They even have chocolate now! So, anyway, back to the subject. The *Glory* surrendered, and her crew have been interred by the Ruhar; they will likely be traded for Ruhar prisoners of war later. The ship itself is being prepped for a short voyage out to rendezvous with a Jeraptha star carrier. The *Glory* will be waiting just beyond the outer edge of the Paradise system, alone and with only a skeleton crew of four Ruhar technicians."

"A sitting duck," I said with appreciation. "Hmmm. That is what I call a tempting target. Damn, Skippy, that is a good deal. Tell you what, I'll take this creampuff, I don't even need rustproofing."

"You never did need rustproofing, Joe. I do highly recommend our special interior detailing and air freshener package. That ship's air filters haven't been changed in four months, and a group of scared, sweaty lizards were packed in there for way too long."

"Ugh. We'll keep our suits on. Ok, I need to brief Chotek on this."

"Really, Joe? Count Chocula is only going to say 'no', and you know it."

"What am I supposed to do, Skippy? Run a secret op behind his back, and tell him the *Glory* just happened to latch onto us like a lost puppy?"

"That's not a bad idea, Joe. You think he would buy it?" Skippy asked hopefully.

"Not a chance, Skippy. Ah, crap, I have to think of a way to persuade Chotek to approve an attack on a UNEF ally."

"The Ruhar are not officially, or knowingly, our allies, Joe. They are only allies of UNEF on Paradise. And the operation doesn't need to be an attack; we only need to take the ship away from an almost defenseless skeleton crew. That shouldn't be too difficult for our bad-ass team of SpecOps warriors."

"You're forgetting that we need to make sure this skeleton crew of Ruhar don't learn, or even suspect, that humans were involved. Other than making those four hamsters into actual skeletons, I don't know how we could do that."

"Joe, I am confident that you and Sarah Rose will cook up a sufficiently devious plan between the two of you."

"Oh, great. Major," I said to Simms, "it looks like I'm going to be busy." I picked up my phone to call Dr. Rose. Before I proposed anything to Chotek, I needed to have a solid plan. Then I set the zPhone back on the desk; I needed more info before I called Sarah. "How long will the *Glory* be sitting there, all by itself, before a Jeraptha star carrier picks it up?"

"According to the schedule in the file, nineteen hours. The schedule is padded because the delivery crew is not confident in the ability of the *Glory*'s jump drive to get them to the rendezvous point on time."

"Nineteen hours? Damn. That's a pretty tight window."

"Nineteen hours, if the *Glory*'s crappy jump drive doesn't cause any delays. I would count on there being at least one delay."

I whistled in dismay. "That is cutting it pretty close, Skippy."

"Come on, Joe, we've done operations way more complicated than this. The reward for this op is a freakin' alien warship, for crying out loud. You have to at least try to think up a plan."

"Yeah, you're right. Is there any chance you can use the Thuranin nanovirus thingy to take control of the *Glory* for us?"

"No," he sighed disgustedly. "I already told you, that nanovirus is a short-range, short-term technology, Joe. It is designed to protect Thuranin star carriers from being attacked by Kristang ships the carrier is transporting. The *Glory* has been operating away from a Thuranin ship for long enough that the nanovirus aboard her would have gone discoherent."

"Ah, crap." The nanovirus wouldn't have helped us deal with the Ruhar crew anyway. "Hey, one more question for you, Skippy. It will take four days to get to Paradise from here? How long until we have to change course to go back to Paradise?"

"It will be twenty six hours until we jump through the next wormhole. At that point, we have to go toward Paradise, or continue on to intercept the Ruhar negotiators."

"Yeah, but we have plenty of time for that, right? No change to that timeline, is there? We could divert to Paradise, pick up the *Glory*, and still be at the negotiator's rendezvous point with plenty of time?"

"Oh, certainly, Joe, no problem. Even stopping by Paradise to implement whatever lame-brained plan you cook up, we will be sitting around waiting four days for the Ruhar negotiation team to arrive."

I picked up my zPhone again. "Great, so now I have twenty six hours-"

"Twenty five hours, forty two minutes and fifteen seconds-"

"-to dream up a plan, and persuade Chotek we should take the risk. Wonderful."

"You should hop to it, then, Joe. Considering how slowly your brain works, you will need every second."

CHAPTER THIRTEEN

To give my brain a break, I went back to Cargo Bay Six that we used as a shooting range. It was one of the ship's two longest cargo bays, not as big as the docking bays used for dropships, but those were fully occupied and we couldn't have any shooting in there. The fact that we could fire live weapons inside a starship had been a surprise to me, I had asked Sergeant Adams to work with Skippy to set up some sort of training range, and my expectation had been a type of simulator. Our shooting range was a simulator, a really good one. At the far end, Skippy projected very realistic-looking holographic targets, moving targets that could shoot simulated rounds back at us. We mostly practiced against holographic Kristang, occasionally Thuranin. Sometimes we 'fought' simulated Ruhar, not because we expected to go into combat against hamsters, but because it was useful to learn their preferred weapons and tactics.

The holographic enemies all fired simulated rounds, or maser beams, or whatever weapons their species used in combat. We fired live rounds, although our rounds did not use the explosive tips that were standard issue in action. We shot at either holographic targets or regular bullseye targets, and the really cool thing was the rounds did not impact the far wall to ricochet all over the cargo bay. Skippy installed some sort of magic energy field that took the momentum of our practice rounds and dispersed the energy in multiple directions. When a round entered the field, it was enveloped in some exotic effect that turned part of the round's kinetic energy into negative energy. Instead of all the kinetic energy moving the round forward, part of the energy wanted the round to go backwards, some left, right, up and down. The net effect was the round came almost to a stop before it impacted the padded far wall, where it gently dropped into a tray on the floor. Skippy controlled and fine-tuned the field in real-time so he arrested the flight of rounds individually. The incredible technological magic of the field in our firing range was based on the same technology as the defensive energy field that protected the ship from kinetic weapons like missiles, railguns and some of the effects of particle beams. We had another type of defensive shield to deflect energy beams like masers; this energy shield acted like a stealth field to bend incoming maser beams around the ship. The energy shield was interlaced with the kinetic shield, and used the same projectors.

Anyway, that is how we could use live-fire weapons aboard a starship without blowing holes in the hull and sucking all the air out, or hitting some vital ship component that did not deal well with being shot at, like energy conduits. Or, you know, people.

When I walked into the firing range, there were no holographic enemies, just bullseye targets. Most of the crew were eating lunch in the galley, I wanted to squeeze off a couple rounds while I considered what to do that day, shooting relaxes me because it focuses my mind on one thing. Skippy is right, most of the time I am a scatter-brain and my thoughts are a jumble. The only people in the firing range were my Ranger babysitter Lauren Poole, and Doctor Friedlander. Following the incident where Chotek was trapped aboard the relay station, I had decided everyone aboard the ship should have at least minimal weapons training. To my surprise, Friedlander and his team had taken to the training with great enthusiasm. Part of the fun was being able to fire advanced alien weapons; everything we used was Kristang gear we had taken from the troopship in Earth orbit. We had standard Kristang infantry rifles, a heavy rifle that we rarely found a use for, rockets, grenades and of course Zinger antiaircraft missiles. "Having fun, Doctor?" I asked with a grin.

"Yes," his grin was even wider than mine. "I shot .22 rifles in the Boy Scouts, but this," he held up a Kristang rifle, "is an amazing weapon."

"Poole?" I asked. "Is the good doctor a good student?"

"Yes, Sir." She said with pride.

"Look," Friedlander was eager to show me. "It's easy, this rifle is very well designed, it is easy to use. You press this button, there's one on either side, that ejects the ammo clip-"

"The magazine," I corrected him. "It's an ammunition magazine, not a 'clip'."

Friedlander tilted his head at me. "I've heard you refer to it as a 'clip' before."

"Yes, that's because I'm a total dumbass," I explained. "I can't tell you how many times I got punishment duty for using the wrong terms, don't make the same mistakes I do. Like, I use 'Special Forces' instead of the proper terms 'Special Operations'. 'Special Forces' is a particular unit in the US Army; the teams we have aboard are dedicated Special Operations troops. Anyway, go ahead, you ejected the magazine."

Friedlander demonstrated that he was familiar with a Kristang infantry rifle, and that he knew how to shoot it also; Poole told me our friendly local rocket scientist had been practicing every opportunity he had, when the firing range wasn't scheduled by Major Smythe for his teams. I felt the need to uphold my honor by firing off a magazine one round at time, making holes in the holographic target and racking up a decent score. When I was done, the three of us chatted while cleaning our weapons and putting them away on the rack. Kristang rifles don't need much in the way of cleaning; they mostly use magnetic fields rather than lubrication, and their ammo fires so cleanly there is almost no residue. Regular maintenance was taken care of by Major Smythe's teams, and Skippy's bots handled heavy maintenance like replacing magnets periodically. Still, taking care of your weapons is a good habit for a soldier. "That was good shooting, Doctor," I told Friedlander.

"Thank you. When I'm not shooting at bullseyes, I practice against a holographic space lizard Skippy created for me. I promised my wife," he hefted his rifle, "that I am *not* being eaten by space lizard."

"My brain hurts," Sarah said four hours, eighteen minutes later.

"Mine too," Skippy agreed, with his avatar yawning and stretching. "Listening to you two come up with one moronic idea after another is killing me. After four hours, you still don't have a workable plan?"

"We have several workable plans, Skippy," I objected, mostly on behalf of Dr. Rose. "We're trying to create a plan that Chotek might actually approve."

"Ha! Good luck with that one."

"Mister Skippy, do you have any suggestions for us?" Sarah asked while she was looking at me.

"Yes! Go to the gym. Or bake cookies, or take a nap. Do anything other than sitting in Joe's office, lowering my opinion of human intelligence."

"Whoa!" I clutched my chest, feigning shock. "I thought it wasn't possible for your opinion to get any lower?"

"It's close to rock bottom already, Joe; I wouldn't push it, if I were you."

We took Skippy's suggestion. Usually, stepping away from a problem helps me think. This time, it didn't work. We ate a late lunch, separately because otherwise the two of us would continue to think about the problem if we were together. The whole point of stepping away was to not think about the problem, and let our subconscious minds work on it. Or something like that, I'm not a psychologist. Or it is a psychiatrist? I know it's not a psychic; those are the women on late-night TV who will tell your future if you just give them your credit card. Which always made me wonder; wouldn't a real psychic already know your credit card number?

What was I saying? Oh, yeah, eating lunch didn't help. Working out at the gym wasn't useful either; I had gone to the gym that morning and didn't need another weight-lifting session, and I had done a tough cardio workout the day before. So I jogged on the treadmill until an Indian paratrooper made me feel guilty about hogging the machine. Disappointed that my brain hadn't magically dreamed up a solution, I thought about going to Cargo Bay Three, where our SEALS team was practicing hand to hand combat against the Chinese team. While hand to hand combat was probably mostly useless in space, it kept the teams' skills sharp, and it was good for morale. After watching SEALS sparring against Night Tigers, I slunk out the door silently. Even the controlled moves they were using were beyond my skills and conditioning; I would have gotten my ass kicked and accomplished nothing other than taking training time away from the professionals.

A nap didn't help; I got a solid twenty minutes of shut-eye, which usually refreshes me. I woke feeling better physically; mentally I was irritated that my foggy brain hadn't done the job for me. In the corridor outside my cabin, I ran into Hans Chotek. "Colonel Bishop, I hear you have been in your office with Dr. Rose most of the day. Would you care to tell me what you are working on?"

Crap. No, I did not care to tell him anything at all. "Sir, I would rather not discuss what we're working on, until we have thought it through, and it is ready to present for your consideration."

From Chotek's expression, that was the wrong thing for me to say. Now he was on guard, prepared to shoot down any proposal I brought to him. "Colonel, I hope you appreciate that we have taken on enough risk already."

"Yes, Sir," I replied with a touch of sleep-induced irritation.

No sooner had I sat down in my office with a cup of coffee, when Sarah walked in. "Anything?" She asked hopefully as she sat down. If she had thought of an idea, she would have mentioned that first.

"No," I took a sip of coffee to jolt my brain into action.

"You're kidding me," Skippy's avatar said as it popped into existence on the desk. "Nothing? Between the two of you? I practically hand an alien warship to you on a silver platter, and you can't figure out how to take it?"

"Sorry, Skippy," I gave Sarah a guilty look. She was helping, but it was my responsibility to think of, or at least review and approve, a plan.

"What is the problem?" Skippy demanded. "I stopped listening to your conversation a while ago, to avoid contaminating my logic circuits."

"We have a plan, a good, workable plan, to take the *Glory*. We can deal with her crew, I think. The real problem is that we can't be certain the Ruhar won't learn that we are humans. We will use our tallest people for the boarding party, wearing Kristang armor suits, but Chotek is going to insist that the Ruhar don't detect even one strand of human DNA. If the Ruhar crew discover they have been boarded by humans, then we will have to either kill them, or take them aboard the *Dutchman* as prisoners, forever. Kidnapping is almost as bad as killing them; Chotek would never approve that."

"Dammit, I wish you had told me this problem before," Skippy replied with disgust. "The DNA issue is no problem, Joe. Yes, every surface aboard the *Flying Dutchman* has been contaminated by human DNA by now, including the exterior of the Kristang armored suits. Yuck, by the way. We can deal with that problem, easily. Once people are wearing their suits in the airlock of the dropship, I can use the airlock's decontamination procedure before the outer door opens. Usually, the decon procedure is used when someone is coming *into* a dropship; it does work just as well when someone is leaving. The standard decon equipment of a Kristang dropship doesn't work reliably; I can supplement it with Thuranin upgrades. So, there will not be an issue with human DNA on the outside of the boarding party's armored suits."

"That's great, Skippy; we still have the problem that if there is any fighting, there might be human blood in the air."

"All of the Ruhar crew are civilians, Joe, only two likely have weapons."

"I know that. I also know Chotek, he will not like *any* degree of risk. If capturing the *Glory* poses a risk of our DNA exposing the fact that humans are flying around the galaxy, then-"

"No problem, Joe; that ship has sailed."

"What?" Sarah and I gasped at the same time. I didn't trust Skippy to understand human expressions. "Skippy, the expression 'that ship has sailed' means-"

"I know what it means, dumdum," he scoffed. "The train has left the station. The bird has flown. The fat lady has sung. However you want to say it, I mean that you no longer need to be overly concerned about leaving your DNA behind. Other humans are flying around the galaxy now. Or, at least, they were, recently."

That blew my mind. Sarah must have been just as shocked, because she was also momentarily speechless. "Skippy," I asked when I could speak again. "What the hell are you talking about? There is another Merry Band of Pirates out there?" That would completely shock me, because it implied that another group of humans had encountered *another* AI like Skippy.

"Huh? Of course not! Monkeys can't fly a starship without me, you know that," he chuckled. "Monkeys flying a starship, hee hee, that's a good one."

"Yeah, I, uh, thought you meant there was, uh, another Skippy out there. Another," I hastened to add, "type of Elder AI," because Skippy had said many times he was unique.

"Ha! As if! No, Joe, perhaps I misspoke. Other humans are not technically flying around the galaxy, not even mindlessly pressing buttons like this troops of monkeys does," he cluelessly insulted every hotshot pilot aboard the *Flying Dutchman*. "The humans I'm talking about are not even hitching a ride, they are more like prisoners. Or slaves, which is how the Kristang certainly think of them."

"Slaves? From where? Earth?"

"From Paradise, Joe." And he explained that nearly seven thousand 'Keepers of the Faith' had left Paradise with the Kristang, when Admiral Kekrando's battlegroup departed. An initial group of eight hundred had gone with the first wave of Kristang ships, with the remainder scheduled to follow soon after. By now, those Keepers should be on their way to, wherever they were going. Even Skippy did not yet know what the Kristang planned to do with the entire group of humans, but he did know the first eight hundred had been sold to other Kristang clans, and the remaining Keepers would likely share the same fate. The information available to Skippy was incomplete but disturbing. Some of the Keepers would be used for hunting, with humans as the prey. Some Keepers would be used as 'sparring partners' for young Kristang warriors; the humans would be forced to fight until they were inevitably killed. Skippy suspected most Keepers were intended to be used in suicide missions; desperate assaults normally carried out by Kristang who were disgraced or criminals. Clans would actually consider using human troops as a sick kind of status symbol. "What matters, Joe, is that now if human DNA is found someplace other than Earth or Paradise, it will not be completely unexplainable."

"Holy shit," I said as Sarah and I had the same idea at the same time. "This totally changes the planning for future operations. We don't need to be completely sterile to avoid leaving DNA behind?"

"Duh, Joe, that's why I mentioned it," Skippy's voice dripped with derision. "Does that solve your problem of taking the *Glory*?"

"Forget the freakin' *Glory* for now! When did you find out about the Keepers leaving Paradise?" I demanded.

"Hmm, when we were at that Ruhar data node? For sure, that is. I picked up a rumor about it back when we were hooked up to the relay station."

"And you did not think this information was something important I needed to know?!"

"Well, I know you're busy, Joe. Your brain is already overloaded with stopping the Ruhar from going to Earth, and, you know, keeping your shoes tied and stuff like that."

"Arrgh!" I mimed putting my hands around the neck of his avatar and squeezing, but the holographic image popped out of existence and reappeared on the other side of the table.

"Joe," he asked innocently, "would it help if I fabricated a Skippy voodoo doll, that you could strangle when my awesomeness overwhelms you?"

"Yes! Yes! That would be fantastic," I shouted. "Could you also arrange to, I don't know, how about you plunge to your death into a black hole? That would be super awesomely helpful to me right now."

"I'm sensing you are miffed about something, Joe. I would try to guess what, but that would require me to care, so-"

Bonking my head on the table was my only response, even in front of our friendly neighborhood CIA officer.

"Colonel?" Dr. Rose spoke. "If I could make a suggestion?"

"Please. Anything," I mumbled with my face in my hands.

"There is nothing aboard the ship that can hurt Skippy, and we do have a firing range in Cargo Bay Six-"

"Whoa! Hold your horses right there, missy," Skippy's avatar held its hands out in a halt gesture. "You want Joe to shoot at me, just to release his frustrations?"

I pulled my head up. "Sarah, that is a *great* id-"

"No, that is a *terrible* idea," Skippy declared. "Uh oh, gosh, Joe, hmm, I just found a problem with the air supply in Cargo Bay Six. Slight air leak. Don't worry, I sounded the alarm and the people in there are evacuating now."

"Not funn-"

"Ha ha," he chuckled with glee. "I disagree, Joe. Whoohoo! You should see those monkeys scurrying out of there. Run, monkeys, run!"

"Skippy, if I drop the idea of people using you for target practice, will you please, please stop the air leak?"

"Deal. Hmm, looks like that air leak was a false alarm. I hate it when that happens."

"I bet you do. Will you also promise to tell me important information as soon as you know about it?"

"Joey, Joey, Joey. There is no way I can guess what information you might think is important. I can't tell you every single thing I know, your little monkey brain is already *dangerously* close to capacity. If you have more thought like 'I am hungry' or 'Mmmm beer', you could lock up and then I'd have to reboot you."

"How about if I worry about that risk, Skippy? I will trust your judgment. If it involves humans, anywhere in the galaxy, I want to know about it."

"Uh huh, you say that now, but when I start flooding you with info-"

"We will worry about that later, Ok? Right now Dr. Rose and I have work to do. While we are putting the finishing touches on our plan to capture the *Glory*, please inform Chotek, and Chang and the rest of the commanders about the Keepers."

"You don't want to tell Chotek about the Keepers yourself, Joe? I thought you would appreciate the opportunity to bring important information to your boss."

"If I learned about it when you did, five days ago, yeah. Now, I prefer he yells at you, instead of me."

"Ugh. I have to endure another hour of Count Chocula berating me? Crap. Is the option of me falling into a black hole still open?"

"Uh, that is a no. Take your punishment like a," I was going to say 'man', "beer can."

"Shit. Well, hmm, I just discovered an air leak in Chotek's office-"

"Talk to you later, Skippy."

Chotek sat quietly while he considered the issue. He could do that; sit silently, without nervously feeling he needed to fill the awkward silence with chitchat. He also expected the rest of us would not interrupt his thinking by talking amongst ourselves. Hans Ernst Chotek was naturally used to being in authority; he had been all his life. He was born into a wealthy, accomplished family, and he went to only the best schools. After college, he moved easily into positions of authority in business, government and then worked his way up the UN bureaucracy. He was accustomed to people waiting quietly for him to speak.

By contrast, I was a grunt who was lucky to have finished high school with a 'B' average, and only got promoted to colonel as a publicity stunt to please oppressive hateful alien MFers. Command came naturally to Chotek; I still felt like a fraud. I kept waiting to wake up in a tent in Nigeria and discover the whole thing; alien invasion, meeting Skippy, me being promoted, had all been a dream.

Except, if this was a dream, I should be getting laid a lot more.

And there should be more cheeseburgers.

"Mister Skippy," Chotek finally spoke. "You learned about the *Glory*, by picking up an encrypted Ruhar file?"

"Uh huh, yeah, did I mumble? That's what I said."

Chotek ignored Skippy's insult. Along with developing a natural authority, he had a thick skin. "How can you be sure the message in the file is not a trap for the Kristang? The message states a captured Kristang ship will be alone in deep space; that would be a tempting target to the Kristang. They surely would not like the idea of the Ruhar military taking apart one of their ships and getting an intimate view of their technology. I am concerned this *Glory* frigate will be surrounded by stealthed Ruhar warships, waiting to ambush any Kristang ships who come to retake, or destroy, the Glory."

Crap. Hans Chotek was the most nit-picky, micromananging boss I ever had. He was also absolutely right to ask annoying questions. Damn it, I should have asked that question, when Skippy told me how he found out the *Glory* would be parked in deep space, all by itself. Now that I thought about it, the whole situation was way too convenient.

I felt like a freakin' idiot.

Skippy, though, was not intimidated by Count Chocula. "Nuh uh, no way, dude," he scoffed. "The encryption in the message can't be broken by the Kristang, because the encryption was provided by the Jeraptha; it's not something the Ruhar developed on their own. The message is from the Ruhar to the Jeraptha, notifying the Jeraptha that the Ruhar want a star carrier to pick up the *Glory*. This is an encryption scheme the Jeraptha allow the Ruhar to use only when they are communicating with the Jeraptha. The Kristang can't break that encryption, and if the Kristang gave the file to the Thuranin to crack the encryption, the Thuranin would tell the lizards to go screw themselves. If the Ruhar were using that message as bait, they would have used one of their own encryption schemes, one that they know the Kristang are capable of breaking. Duh."

Chotek's face reddened slightly. Despite his diplomatically-trained thick skin, he hated it when Skippy belittled him. Maybe it was being insulted by a beer can that got him upset. To avoid a distracting argument between the two of them, I spoke before Chotek could open his mouth. "Skippy, if we jumped in before the *Glory* arrived at the rendezvous point, could we scan the area closely enough to be certain there aren't any ships waiting to set up an ambush?"

"Yes, we could do that," Skippy said flippantly. "With my awesomeness, that is no problemo, Joe. In my opinion, doing that would be a waste of time, but what do I know? I am only a super smart being who manipulates spacetime as a hobby."

"Sir," I addressed Chotek, "that was a good question, and I apologize; I should have considered that possibility. We can verify that Skippy is correct by arriving at the rendezvous site early and scanning the area. If there is any threat, we jump away immediately. That way, we can minimize the risk."

Chotek thought for a minute in his quiet, deliberative way. "I agree scanning the area could minimize that particular risk. There is another risk you have not mentioned. Colonel Bishop, your plan is to seize the *Glory*, without killing or injuring the four Ruhar aboard?"

"Yes, Sir. You made it clear we are not to risk hostile action against a potential future ally."

"Your plan takes admirable care not to harm those four Ruhar. My question is; would the Kristang be so careful with their enemies?"

"Sir?"

"The plan relies on the Ruhar crew believing our boarding party is Kristang," Chotek observed. "If our boarding party behaves like polite Boy Scouts, the Ruhar will not believe we are Kristang."

Crap! He was right again. The Kristang would not leave four Ruhar alive when they recaptured the *Glory*. They would either kill the Ruhar, or take them prisoner. Chotek had forbidden us to do either, and I didn't like the idea of killing or kidnapping four hamsters anyway. I was trained by the military, and I abided by a military code of conduct, and I had a military sense of right and wrong. If someone is an enemy of my country, or in this case, an enemy of my species, I could take direct action to neutralize that threat. Meaning, I could kill them in most cases with a clear conscience. My drill instructor in Basic Training told me the job of an army, any army, is to kill the enemy and take territory away from them. If anyone couldn't stomach that idea, they didn't belong in the army.

The idea of killing four Ruhar, just to maintain our cover, made me sick. Dr. Rose, with her different set of sensibilities, might consider four Ruhar lives to be reasonable collateral damage in a covert operation. I couldn't do that, not yet.

In all the hours Dr. Rose and I had spent thinking about how to take the *Glory*, we had never considered that our boarding party, disguised in Kristang armored suits, needed to behave like Kristang. Real Kristang would never leave four Ruhar alive behind them.

Unless.

Unless the Kristang had a good reason for doing just that.

Great. Now all I needed was to think of a reason why a Kristang boarding party would not kill or capture the four Ruhar crew.

The good news was, I had a couple days to think of a reason for Kristang to behave that way.

All that flashed through my mind in a heartbeat, after my boss asked the question. "Yes," I replied to Chotek, "we will need to provide a rationale for the Kristang leaving four Ruhar alive and free. We have several possibilities for such a cover plan," I lied outrageously, "and we wish to refine those possibilities before presenting them to you. Sir, at this point, the sole decision that needs to be made is whether we continue along our present course, or divert to Paradise. If we divert to Paradise, we will have time to refine our plans to capture the *Glory*, and we can always abort that operation at any time. Diverting to Paradise will not pose any risk to us arriving at the negotiator rendezvous point on time."

"Colonel, you are asking me for more time to turn in your homework assignment?" Chotek asked with a raised eyebrow.

"I'm embarrassed to say, but, yes." Crap. With the homework comment, he made me feel like I was a dumb high school kid again. And knowing Hans Chotek, the diplomat skilled in manipulating people, that is exactly what he intended.

Chotek took a deep breath. "If nothing else, this will be another interesting test of your inventive planning skills. Colonel Bishop, you may divert the ship toward the Paradise system. I do not want us within one lightyear of Paradise, until I have reviewed and approved a plan to capture the *Glory*. If I do not approve a plan, we let the *Glory* go on its way, and we proceed to the mock attack with our Q-ship by itself."

"Understood, Sir."

Before going back to my office, I stopped by a supply cabinet and requisitioned a particular item, then went to visit Skippy in his escape pod mancave. "Hello, Skippy."

"Hi, Joe. Hey, what, what is that?"

I pulled a foil package out of a pocket and tore it open; it was something I had gotten from the Supply cargo bay.

"Is that a *rubber*?" He shouted.

"In your case, Skippy, it's a CAN-dom," I said with a grin.

"Oh, very funny, Joe. You'd better not- Hey!" He screamed as I stretched it over his lid. "Get that off of me!"

"You scared people when you faked that air leak in Cargo Bay Six. That was a dick move, Skippy. You were being a dick, and this is what goes on a di-"

"NOT FUNNY!"

I stepped back. His new costume wasn't as cute as some others, and I only put it in halfway, so the other half with the tip flopped down in front of him. "I don't know," I laughed so hard I almost blew a snot bubble on the deck. "It's funny to me."

"Ooooh, you better get this off of me RIGHT NOW!"

"If you want to be a dick, this is what you wear."

"Joe, you get this disgusting thing off me right now or-"

"Or what, Skippy? You can't move, remember?" My zPhone beeped.

"Uh, hey, Colonel Bishop?" The voice was hesitant, it was one of our US Air Force pilots.

"Yeah?" I was almost choking with laughter.

"Um, this is Lieutenant Reed, I'm in Cargo Bay Two, and, um, one of our nukes just went active? It's showing a ninety second countdown to detonation. I, uh, I thought you should know, Sir. Uh, hmm, now they're all active. You didn't, uh, plan this?" Her voice ended in a squeak.

I pressed the button to mute my phone. "SKIPPY!"

"What?"

"You know damned well 'what'? Deactivate. The. Nuclear. Warheads." I could not believe that was something I would ever have to say. Holy shit my life had gotten way off track somehow.

His voice was muffled. "Sorry, Joe, I can't hear you, I'm wrapped in a can-dom. Major Simms and I have a hot date tonight."

"Not funny. About the nukes or Simms. Stop it."

"You stop it. You started it, you big jerk."

"*You* started-" I could tell this kindergarten conversation wasn't going anywhere. "Did you learn your lesson not to be a dick?"

"Fine," he huffed. "Yes, I learned that *you* can be a dick, but I'm not allowed to."

"Close enough." I pulled the offending item off his shiny beer can. "The nukes?"

"The nukes are sleeping soundly again. I just have to check that their timers are functioning properly every once in a while, Joe."

"Uh huh. Why do I not believe you?"

"Because you're still hurt that your parents lied about Santa, so you don't trust anyone?"

I gasped. "Santa's not real?"

"Oh, shit," Skippy groaned. "Did I ruin that for you? I'm sorry, Joe, I didn't mean to-hey, wait! You're laughing. You *jerk*! You already knew about Santa!"

"Ya think?"

"Ooooh, that makes me so mad. Who's the dick now?"

"Can we call it even, Skippy?"

"Sure, why not?" He sighed. "Otherwise, this will go on all day. Damn, I should have suspected something was going on when you pulled a rubber out of the supply cabinet. I was hoping you would make a balloon animal; there is certainly nothing else useful *you* can do with one of those things."

"Talk to you later, Skippy."

CHAPTER FOURTEEN

"Colonel?" Sarah asked quietly when we got back to my office. "We have a plan for why the boarding party will not be acting like typical Kristang?"

"Ha!" Skippy's avatar danced on the table, bent over with laughter. "No way! Joe is a lying dog. He lies like a rug! Joe, when Chocula asked that question, you panicked, right?"

"Absolute panic," I admitted, giving Sarah a weak smile.

"I knew it! But, Joe, it took you only a moment to recover. You totally pulled that one out of your ass, and you did it in a split second. Oh, ho!" the avatar danced joyously. "Damn! Once in a while, your brain somehow manages to move at lightspeed."

I appreciated the rare praise. "Thank you, Skip-"

"Why does your brain normally work like a freakin' glacier, then? A glacier with a busted leg. Moving through quicksand. And dragging a-"

"We get the idea, Skippy."

"I'm just sayin', why-"

"We get the idea. Do *you* have an idea for why a Kristang boarding party would be nice to the Ruhar?"

"Huh? Me? No way, Jose! This is your problem, monkeyboy. This reminds me of that 'Far Side' cartoon of the cowboy on a horse, being chased by indians. The cowboy wants the horse to run faster, and the horse says 'Hey, they're not chasing *me*'. Hee hee! Your home planet getting wiped out by pissed off aliens would be a disaster for you, but only mildly inconvenient for me. Hmm, now that I think about it, that might just possibly be entertaining for me, in a sort of-"

"Skippy! Not funny."

"Oh, I wasn't joking. Anywho, I told you the *Glory* will be all alone and vulnerable. Figuring out how to take that ship is your problem, cowboy."

"You don't have any suggestions for us?" I asked with little hope.

"Try holding your breath, Joe? If you're not breathing, you can use *both* of your brain cells to think with."

Sarah burst out laughing, waving a hand at me to apologize.

And my day just kept getting better and better.

Since neither Sarah nor I could think of why a group of Kristang would not act like murderous hateful MFers, we split up to think about it. She went back to the science lab, even though things there were awkward now that everyone knew she was a CIA officer. I went to the galley to get a cup of coffee, more to burn time that for any other reason. Also, I needed a change of scenery; my cramped little office was not inspiring me to think up a brilliant idea.

Of course, I got there as Margaret Adams was emptying the last dregs of the coffee pot into her mug. "They're making more, Sir," she nodded toward the British team that was in charge of staffing the galley that day.

"Don't the British drink tea?"

"They drink coffee also," she replied with an amused smile. Staff Sergeant Adams often had an amused smile when talking with me, like I was still a dumb recruit and she needed to make sure I didn't blow my foot off with a rifle.

"You like our new coffee mugs?" I held up my mug, which had the pirate-monkey-on-a-flying-banana logo that was now the official symbol for the *Flying Dutchman*.

"Yes, they're nice," she had a twinkle in her eyes, remembering my original crude sketch for the logo. "That reminds me, Sir, we talked about an official motto for the Merry Band of Pirates, but we never did anything about it."

"A motto?" Somehow, I did not picture Adams as someone who cared about mottos, or mission statements or anything like that.

"Every unit has a motto," she replied with a shrug.

Skippy's voice came from the zPhone on my belt. "Clearly the motto of the Merry Band of Pirates should be 'Trust the Awesomeness'."

"Uh, no. I like 'Climb to Glory'," I suggested.

Adams gave me a look that my mother used to give me. "That is the motto of the Army 10th Infantry Division. You shouldn't favor your old unit, Sir."

"Uh, you're probably right," I admitted, stung.

"How about 'Striving for Competence'?" Skippy suggested.

"No."

Skippy sighed. "You're right, Joe, nobody would believe that this outfit would even dream of competence. Maybe something like 'Less fun than a barrel of monkeys'?"

"No."

"Uh, 'I made potty all by myself'?"

"NO!"

"Or 'I'm not wearing any pants'?"

"Oh boy." It went downhill from there. And that is how we ended up with 'Trust the Awesomeness' as our unit motto.

When Adams finished laughing and was able to speak again, she poured coffee into my mug and changed the subject. "I heard we have a plan to capture this Kristang frigate, the *Glory*, but there is some problem? Is there anything I can help you with?"

"No, I-" Why not ask her advice? I lowered my voice and gestured her over to an empty table. "Our resident spy and I have been trying to think of a reason why a group of Kristang would *not* act like typical Kristang."

"How's that?"

"If we send a boarding party over to seize the *Glory*, Chotek insists we not harm the Ruhar crew, and we can't kidnap them either," I explained. "I agree with him, but it makes the operation impossible. Any real Kristang boarding party would kill the Ruhar, or take them prisoner. That's why I say we need a reason why Kristang would not act like Kristang."

Adams gave me another one of those infuriating smiles, and sipped her coffee. "You're asking the wrong question."

"I am?" Damn it, the question of why our boarding party could not act like Kristang has been Chotek's idea, but I had bought into it.

"Sir, the question is not why a group of Kristang would not act like Kristang. The correct question is, why would they act the way you need the boarding party to act?"

"Uh," that sounded like the exact same thing to me.

"A Kristang warship was captured by the enemy, and a group of Kristang are taking it back. The boarding party leaves the Ruhar crew behind, as witnesses, right?"

"Right." *Witnesses*. The Kristang boarding party would leave the Ruhar behind as witnesses. "Right!" I got it. "The Kristang who take back the *Glory* are not the same group of knuckleheads who lost the ship to the enemy."

"No, they are not," Adams seemed pleased that I had caught onto her idea, like I was puppy who learned a new trick. "The boarding party is a group of Kristang who want to humiliate the punk-ass Swift Arrow clan who let the ship be captured by the enemy. They want the Ruhar crew to report who took the ship back, so everyone knows."

"Brilliant! All we need is for the boarding party to wear insignia of a clan that is a rival to the Swift Arrows. Skippy?"

"I have been listening," his voice came from the zPhone on my belt. "Sergeant Adams, that was very good thinking, I applaud you. Joe, how long did you wrack your brain about this problem, without any result? You should be ashamed of yourself."

"Oh, shut up," I was feeling humiliated in front of Adams. "Ok, if you're so freakin' smart, which clan should the boarding party pretend to be? Which clan is the biggest rival of the Swift Arrows?"

"That would be the Great Claw clan."

"Great, then-"

"Ah! You didn't let me finish, Joe. The Great Claws and the Swift Arrows hate each other with a passion that is intense even for Kristang. However, the Paradise system is far from Great Claw territory; it is rather unlikely the Great Claws would or could go all the way there just to pick up a beat-up old frigate. My suggestion is the boarding party pretend to be members of the Razor Tail clan. The Razor Tails are a very ambitious minor clan, that has recently been quite reckless in order to position themselves to benefit from a potential civil war."

"Razor Tails, huh? Ok, sounds good. And you know what their clan insignia looks like?"

"Joe, please, you insult me. I am already fabricating Razor Tail insignias for our suits."

"Problem solved, then," I said happily.

"You're going to tell Mr. Chotek now?" Adams gulped the last of her coffee.

Crap. "Uh, Sergeant, it would be best if you kept quiet about this. I, uh, I sort of told Chotek that I already had a plan."

"Your secret is safe with me," she said with a wink.

"Thank you. Um, this is all great, except the Razor Tails will know they did not, in fact, recapture the *Glory*. And they sure won't be bringing that ship back as a trophy."

Adams tilted her head. "Why is that a problem? No way would the Razor Tails miss the opportunity to take credit for it anyway. With the *Glory* being in bad condition, it won't be surprising if it disappears along the way."

I explained our brilliant plan to Hans Chotek. A Kristang frigate would be hanging in empty space, all by itself, with only a skeleton crew of four Ruhar. It was a prize easily taken, and we had a solid plan to minimize the risk.

Chotek still didn't like it. "Colonel, I commend you and your team for developing a plan to minimize the risk. There is still risk, and I am uncomfortable with that."

Dammit. Chotek was ate up with following the letter of UNEF Command's orders. "Sir, risk is a relative term. If this mission fails, there is a *hundred* percent certainty that we lose Earth. Any risk below a hundred percent is worth it. And this plan," I tapped the display, "carries a low level of risk with it."

"We have our Q-ship, we can proceed with the mock attack."

"Skippy had analyzed Ruhar psychology, and he strongly believes that a mock attack by a single armed merchant ship would not be perceived as a credible threat, Sir. We need a second ship, preferably a warship. A small, older warship that a clan would consider expendable. The *Glory* is perfect for this purpose."

He was still hesitant. He picked up his tablet and examined the details of the plan again.

I pressed him to make a decision. "We can abort the plan at any point, up until the boarding party's dropship enters their docking bay. Even at that point, the *Flying Dutchman* can jump away to safety if anything goes wrong."

He didn't reply immediately, and I knew to keep my mouth shut and wait. Hans Chotek needed to reach the decision on his own; if I tried to sell him on the idea, he would reject it.

He tapped the screen of his tablet. "The four Ruhar crew will not be harmed?"

Crap. I couldn't openly lie to his face about the subject. "If they start shooting, I can't guarantee no one will be harmed, Sir. Before we board the *Glory*, we will announce our intentions, and explain that all we want is the ship. That we *want* the Ruhar to survive. If there is any fighting, that is on the Ruhar. If the Ruhar do start shooting, my orders to the boarding team are to retreat and try negotiating again. Frankly, I think it is about fifty-fifty that one of the Ruhar gets an itchy trigger finger; that does happen in tense situations. The Ruhar know they ordinarily have no reason to trust the Kristang. My hope is the Ruhar will be persuaded by the fact that our boarding party does everything that can *not* to start a fight."

His expression was still maddeningly unreadable. I suppose masking his emotions was part of his diplomatic training. Skippy probably could monitor Chocula's pulse, blood pressure, skin temperature, brain waves and whatever else might provide a clue to what our official mission commander was thinking and feeling. I had no idea. The silence made me uncomfortable. This was the best plan we had been able to dream up and it was a damned good plan, an excellent plan. An imaginative plan. We had addressed every roadblock Chotek threw in our path, and still he hesitated. "Sir," I shifted uncomfortable in my chair. "This is a lot to think about, it's a big responsibility. We won't need a decision for another six hours; after that the schedules of the wormholes we have to go through make it difficult for us to keep on schedule. I'll be in the training bay, watching Major Smythe's teams practice the boarding operation."

"Very well, Colonel." He didn't even tell me I was dismissed, he didn't even look up from the tablet. I let myself out quietly. "I will consider the operation, and inform you of my decision before the end of the day."

I later learned Chotek had called in Chang, Smythe and Adams to get their perspective on the plan. The three of them didn't tell me about it, because Chotek ordered them not to; Skippy told me. Chotek had to know Skippy would tell me, so I don't know what he thought he was accomplishing with the attempted secrecy. Or maybe secrecy wasn't the point; maybe he wanted me to know he was getting second opinions because he didn't trust my judgment. Either way, I did not care, because he approved the plan without a single change. We jumped with two hours left in the deadline.

We were going to steal *another* alien starship!

Damn, as much as I hate my job sometimes, I do freakin' love being a pirate.

The Thuranin plan to hit the Jerpatha was bold, and required aggressiveness and precise timing. Near the Glark system was one wormhole, and two clusters of two wormholes each. The Thuranin force came through three wormholes simultaneously, at points when the wormholes were almost the farthest distance from Glark in the figure-8 paths they had traced for millions of years. While the Jeraptha had sensor nets and a small force of picket ships guarding the areas where the wormholes were at their closest approach to Glark, it was not practical to cover all the other emergence points. The Thuranin plan did not depend on emerging as close to Glark as possible; it depended on their three groups of ships coming through wormholes at the same time. With five wormholes to choose from, the mission planners had at first assumed it would be easy to coordinate the timing of the three task forces. To their great frustration, they were wrong. During many of the times when three wormholes were open simultaneously, one or more wormhole was at or near the closest approach to Glark. That meant a task force emerging there would immediately be detected, and attacked while the ships were nearly blind and defenseless after coming through a wormhole. It took several AIs more than an hour to determine when three wormholes would be open and also none of them close to Glark. The analysis showed such a result was rare, almost as if the Elders who built the wormhole network had planned to protect the Glark system. The next time three wormholes were available was distressingly soon; Thuranin Naval Command had to scramble to pull enough ships together to launch the operation before the window of opportunity closed for another four months. Ships had been pulled out of spacedock with only partial repairs completed to battle damage, some ships departed with only half their typical missile load. The mission to hit Glark was important enough that risks had to be taken. Destroying Glark's spacedocks and fueling facilities would severely hurt the Jeraptha's ability to control that part of the sector, requiring the nasty beetles to pull back from other areas where their fleet was pressing the Thuranin back with every passing day. To achieve such a result, to hit the Jeraptha in such a critical area, Thuranin Naval Command was willing to sacrifice the ships in the three task forces; the best result expected to lose half of their ships in the operation.

That grim information was not directly shared with the commanders and crew in the three task forces. Knowing the strength of their target, the crews could calculate their odds of survival by themselves.

The three task forces did not send all their ships through the wormholes in one continuous line. First, each task force sent two unlucky destroyers through, to scan the area and report on any threats. Waiting for the sensors of the destroyers to recover from the disruption of passing through the wormhole burned valuable time, and waiting for those sensor fields to expand at the slow speed of light, then report their results at the same slow speed, was agonizing for the task force commanders. Every second they delayed going through the wormholes was another second ticking away until the wormhole closed. The three task forces could not talk to each other or share sensor data; each task forced feared they would be going in to attack Glark alone, if the other two task forces had been detected.

All three pairs of destroyers reported the area around their wormholes were clear, and the task forces began to come through, two massive star carriers at a time. Pairs of star carriers, heavily laden with battlecruisers, cruisers, destroyers and frigates, streamed through nearly nose to tail. As soon as the first pair of star carriers emerged from each wormhole and moved aside to clear navigation space for the next pair, one destroyer jumped away to scan deeper into space, in case a stealthed Jeraptha force was waiting just beyond immediate sensor range. As none of the three destroyers jumped back warning of danger, the task forces continued to stream through, with the ships maneuvering to clear jump space and allowing time for their defensive shields and sensors to recover from the wormhole's spatial disruption.

Twenty two minutes was the goal time for the ships in each task force to pass through the wormholes, reset their systems, and ready their jump drives for the high-speed approach to Glark. Because of the inevitable glitches and delays with such large forces, the planners had allotted an extra three minutes before the initial jumps. Each of the three task force commanders were proud their ships had completed the wormhole transition at least two minutes ahead of schedule. All that remained was for the massive star carriers to spread out so their jump wormholes did not damage each other, and that phase of the operation was also slightly ahead of schedule. Much danger lay ahead, but the critical passage through the wormholes was completed successfully. The only anomaly detected was a cloud of pebbles dispersed around each wormhole. Such rocks should not be in deep interstellar space; only individual hydrogen atoms were typically found so far from a star system. If the three task forces had been able to communicate, they might have been mildly alarmed that all three wormholes were surrounded by anomalous clouds of pebbles. As it was, each task force dismissed the pebbles as interesting phenomena to note in their navigation charts, but not at all dangerous.

Then the Thuranin in the three task forces began to have a very, very bad day.

Admiral Tashallo, commander of Blue Squadron's 98th Fleet, touched an antenna to the pocket where he kept the original flimsy message slip, and resisted the temptation to take it out and read it for the hundredth time. The information provided by Fleet Intelligence was either accurate or it was not, reading the message again obsessively would not change reality. Having the crew see their admiral constantly checking the message was bad for morale, so Tashallo used the antenna to tuck the slip deeper into the pocket, then tried to forget about it. If the information was wrong, then Admiral Tashallo had dangerously depleted the Glark system's defenses, and he would know about it too late to prevent the enemy from hitting critical Fleet facilities.

At the last moment, just in case Fleet Intelligence was wrong and Tashallo had ruined his career, he took a wager at sixty to one odds against Fleet Intelligence. If the information was wrong, he could at least spend his forced retirement in relative comfort. If the information was correct, Tashallo would consider the lost wager to be a guarantee of success.

Normally, detecting enemy ship formations in deep space was difficult, and taking action before an enemy could jump away even more difficult. The Flash Gold message had provided the exact time and place Thuranin task forces would come through three wormholes. From long experience, Tashallo knew approximately how long it would take before a Thuranin task force could assemble and jump. And he knew when the wormhole opened; surely the Thuranin would send their ships through as quickly as possible. He therefore knew exactly where the enemy would be, and for how long, within a seven minute window. *If you know where the enemy is*, his first tactical training instructor had told him, *you can hit them*. Tashallo knew where the enemy was, and he planned to hit them hard. "-three, two, one, jump!"

Each Thuranin task force was suddenly and simultaneously surrounded by an overwhelming number of Jeraptha warships, and damping fields propagated outward to prevent the Thuranin from jumping away. One star carrier, taking a chance before the multiple overlapping damping fields became firmly established, initiated a jump. It was still too close to the massive bulk of its companion star carrier, and the damping field grew stronger with each nanosecond. That star carrier's jump field failed catastrophically, releasing the energy stored in its drive coils, and the star carrier disappeared along with the eight warships it was carrying. The waves of spatial distortion from its failed jump snapped the spine of its companion star carrier, causing that ship to lose all power except in the aft third of the spine. Without power, the defense and stealth shields blinked out, leaving the star carrier and its attached warships vulnerable to massed maser and railgun fire. The Jeraptha wasted no time taking advantage of their good fortune; within sixteen seconds, all the warships attached to that star carrier were disabled and useless.

The Thuranin task force commander ordered all her star carriers to eject their warships in an emergency separation maneuver; an act of pure desperation. While attached to a star carrier, a warship could not activate its own stealth and defensive shields, and with the intense firepower of the Jeraptha hammering the star carriers, none of those giant space trucks would survive for long. Warships broke free of their docking platforms, some being ejected by their host ship, others firing engines and tearing themselves loose, regardless of the damage. A few warships, unable to detach from their docking platform in time, ripped their platform away from the star carrier's spine. Those ships trailed sparks and debris, rendering their attempts to form a stealth field useless.

The Thuranin task force commander, aboard a battlecruiser that was itself being pounded by accurate maser and railgun fire, saw with shocked dismay that all attempts to use stealth were for nothing; somehow the enemy knew exactly where each one of her ships were, even before the Jeraptha sensor fields had time to propagate and send targeting data back to their motherships. She could not understand what was happening. It was as if the Jeraptha had been surveilling the Thuranin ships before they jumped in, which was imposs-

Pebbles. Too late, she remembered the cloud of pebbles.

"The data feed is becoming incoherent," a Jeraptha sensor technician reported.

Tashallo laughed. Loss of critical sensor data from the cloud of smart pebbles was not a laughing matter, the admiral's glee was due to the reason the sensor feed was failing. Space around the Thuranin task force was becoming so cluttered with hard radiation, high-energy particles and debris flying off at near-relativistic speed that ships could not interpret data fed back by their own sensor fields, and the passive sensors of the smart pebbles had become nearly useless. The pebbles had served their purpose; silently and passively recording the location of every enemy ship, and transmitting that data when ordered by Tashallo's ships. Once the battle started, the pebble network was no longer needed.

Most of the debris flying around, so much that it was becoming a hazard to ships on both sides, was pieces of the Thuranin task force. In the first minute of fighting, half the ships in the Thuranin task force had been disabled or destroyed completely, another thirty percent had their combat power reduced to the point where their only option was to run for the wormhole before it closed. Tashallo ordered one of his battleships moved into position to block escape through the wormhole. The giant ship slowly turned and accelerated with painful slowness, Tashallo could see six enemy ships burning hard for the wormhole, missiles on their tails. More enemy ships had gotten the message to retreat or had made that decision on their own. The battleship would not arrive in time to prevent the first six enemy ships from transiting the wormhole, so Tashallo offered an incentive. "Three to one odds at least one of those enemy ships escapes," he told his own task force.

Almost instantly, the task force's Action Officer reported seven Jeraptha ships had taken the wager. Those seven ships broke formation and burned at full emergency thrust for the wormhole, while other ships in the task force furiously wagered with or against them. Before the seven ships could engage, missiles claimed two of the six enemy ships, and the Action Officer updated her handicapping in real-time. She knew that two ships falling victim to missiles, before the seven wagerers could reach cannon range, would be the subject of endless arguments after the battle, and would likely be submitted to the Fleet Action Board for a final ruling. That was a problem for another day.

The seven ships reached targeting range and launched missiles, letting those weapons run on ahead under their own guidance. It was unlikely the missiles would score a damaging hit by themselves but they would tie up enemy defenses, and force those ships to maneuver away from a direct path to the wormhole.

When the enemy was in effective range of maser cannons and railguns, the Jeraptha fired those weapons, and Thuranin ships began to slow and stagger as they took hits. The enemy was not waiting for death, they hit back, concentrating all their fire on the cruiser *Never Tell Me The Odds*, knocking back that ship's shields and forcing it to break away. Knowing the nature of the Jeraptha, the Thuranin ships continued firing at the cruiser even after it had altered course. The Thuranin knew the crew of the *Odds* had wagered none of the Thuranin ships would escape, and that ship's wager would be considered null and void if the *Odds* backed away from the conflict.

As the Thuranin predicted, the cruiser swung back onto her original course, after a quick internal debate about whether the wager action was worth risking their very lives. Of course it was worth it! The ships of the 98th Fleet had not seen action this hot in years, no way could they resist taking part. The *Odds* signaled its intention to rejoin the fight.

"Admiral," the Action Officer of the 98th called, "we are now offering five to seven against the *Never Tell Me The Odds* surviving the battle. Do you want in?"

"No. Aargh!" Tashallo grunted in frustration. While he was sorely tempted, and while it would be legal for him to take either side of such a wager, it would be bad for good order and discipline within the 98th. "I have to let this one play out on its own. Although, blast it! I would love to get in on this one."

"Me too, Sir," the Action Officer agreed unhappily. By Fleet regulation, she was prohibited from wagering. Sometimes, that made her want to quit her lucrative job.

The cruiser *Odds* survived; sustaining heavy damage before the two remaining enemy ships plunged through the wormhole. The damage the cruiser took, and its brave or foolhardy return to the battle, ensured the ship's crew would be allocated a cut of the pot, if the wager was successful.

But two enemy ships had escaped through the wormhole.

And three overzealous Jeraptha ships, still burning at full emergency power, followed them.

"Admiral, the wormhole is scheduled to close in sixty four seconds," the battleship's second officer warned. "We will lose contact."

"Understood," Tashallo studied the tactical display. Other than the lucky two ships who went back through the wormhole, every enemy ship had been disabled or destroyed. Tashallo's task force, having the advantage of surprise and initial targeting data, had scored a resounding success. Two Jeraptha ships had been destroyed, four disabled, and seven others had battle damage serious enough to require a star carrier to bring them back to the Glark spacedocks. In anyone's book, that was an overwhelming victory, but Tashallo's face was a mask of unhappiness. He had boastfully and perhaps unwisely wagered with Admiral Sashell, and with Captain Dahmen who temporarily commanded the third task force, that not a single Thuranin ship would escape. Minutes ago, he had offered the other side of that bet to his task force, as extra incentive for them to crush remaining resistance. If no enemy ships escaped, he would lose that recent wager, but come out ahead overall. And more important, he would win the bet against the much-too-smug Admiral Sashell of the 67th Fleet. "Tell all units to stand down and affect repairs. I wish to return to Glark with all possible speed." Then he waited, along with the entire task force. The battered cruiser *Never Tell Me The Odds* anxiously took up position close to the wormhole, in hope that the last two enemy ships had been destroyed, and knowing that hope was extremely unlikely. The 98th's Action Officer continued to update her handicapping even as the wormhole counted down toward closure.

"Wormhole closing in seven, six," the battleship's second in command said in a voice drained of emotion. "Five, four-"

And three Jeraptha ships came flying through the wormhole, just before it closed behind them. One of the ships was trailing fire, sparks and smoke, and another ship's shields were flickering alarmingly. No one in the task force cared, least of all the triumphant crews of the three ships. The ships transmitted sensor recordings to prove they had killed the last two enemy ships. They had won their wager and as the ships most active in achieving the result, they would split most of the winnings between them. Those in the task force who had bet against them could not help congratulating the victors, while silently cursing their own bad luck.

The crew of the cruiser *Never Tell Me The Odds* also rejoiced. Their share of the winnings would be reduced, but they knew a far larger prize awaited. As the *Odds* had acted to help Admiral Tashallo win his wager against Admiral Sashell, they would be cut in on the action.

And nothing was better than that.

Admiral Tashallo's task force was the last to reach the spacedocks and refueling stations of Glark, but his task force was the most successful. Though he had given one of his powerful battleships to Sashell's force, and two to the force temporarily commanded by Captain Dahmen, no enemy ship had escaped from Tashallo. Two had managed to get away cleanly from Sashell, and one from Dahmen. Sashell was already arguing that because he had only one battleship, the points system should have been weighted more in his favor. This despite the fact that Sashell's 67th Fleet had three powerful battlecruisers that were faster than any battleship, and despite the fact that the points and odds had been worked out in heated discussions before the operation commenced. Tashallo sighed. This matter would take months to sort out by the Fleet Action Board. Then Tashallo sighed. The people on the Fleet Action Board, all retired combat commanders, were widely known to reward success in combat regardless of other circumstances. There was no way anyone could argue with the results Tashallo had achieved. The Thuranin had been hurt badly, enough that Fleet Command needed to be careful about their next move. While the Jeraptha now had the ability to push the Thuranin back anywhere in the sector, they could only push so hard and so far. If the Thuranin were pushed to the point of collapse, their Maxolhx patrons might step in directly by hitting the Jeraptha. While the Maxolhx did not seem to mind a limited amount of weakness in their client species, they also would not tolerate outright defeat. None of the Jeraptha, nor the Thuranin, wanted the Maxolhx or Rindhalu to become involved directly. It was an unwritten Rule in the endless conflict that species fought other species with roughly comparable technology, rather than beating up on those with lesser technology. Tashallo thought adhering to that unwritten rule was an excellent idea.

The Thuranin would be reeling, both from their crushing defeat, and from the certain knowledge that the Jeraptha had somehow known exactly when and where to attack. Tashallo burned with curiosity to know how Fleet Intelligence had acquired such accurate information about enemy plans. Who had betrayed the Thuranin? Was it their rivals the Bosphuraq? Or could it have been the duplicitous Maxolhx? Tashallo knew finding the answer to that question would consume Thuranin intelligence officers.

No one considered that the information may have come from a shiny beer can.

CHAPTER FIFTEEN

Of the current Merry Band of Pirates, only me, Chang, Giraud, Desai, Simms and Adams were from the original crew that escaped from Paradise. In the operation to seize the *Heavenly Morning Flower of Glorious Victory*, Desai had piloted our stolen Ruhar 'Dodo' dropship, and the other five of us had been in the boarding party. Because we had lost the *Flower* on our second mission, many of the current crew had never been aboard a Kristang frigate, and I wanted our boarding party to know exactly what the interior of a frigate looked like. We could not afford to have our supposedly Kristang boarding party stumbling around in front of the Ruhar, not knowing where to go on one of their own ships. We also needed the boarding party to be comprised of tall people, who would be believable as members of the Kristang warrior caste. That should have excluded me, as I am only six feet three inches tall, but no way was I sitting this one out. Technically, I was sitting during the operation; unless something went very wrong, I would be remaining aboard the dropship as Desai's copilot, and hopefully I would not be leaving my seat until the Ruhar crew had left. One way I justified going on the away mission was that I was one of a handful of people qualified to fly a Kristang frigate, even though my skills were probably marginal.

Chotek did not argue when I told him I would be in the boarding party; he was likely thinking that, as the lunatic plan was mine, I should take the risk personally. He may also have been happy to see me away from the ship for a while.

Anyway, the boarding party was me and Desai as pilots, with Smythe, a Chinese and a Ranger actually going aboard the ship. If everything went according to plan, we would never meet the Ruhar crew. Because we were the Merry Band of Pirates and therefore almost nothing ever went exactly according to plan, we were prepared for problems. Chotek had laid down the rules of engagement: if the Ruhar crew resisted or threatened to blow up the ship, we were to back off. The only way we would be authorized to shoot is if we were already aboard the ship, and the Ruhar shot first.

We had no way to confirm the *To Seek Glory in Battle is Glorious* was at the rendezvous point, we had to trust Skippy's data was accurate. The pilots had the *Flying Dutchman* on a hair trigger to jump away, in case Chotek's suspicions were correct and the *Glory* was being used as bait to lure Kristang ships to their doom. We jumped in, immediately reestablished our stealth field, and Skippy did some magic to make it appear as if our ship was an unstealthed Kristang battlecruiser. It had something to do with projecting an image through our field, and Skippy warned the effect would not be convincing if the Ruhar had good sensors. Since the Ruhar were aboard a beat-up Kristang piece of junk, I thought it probable their best set of sensors would be eyeballs looking out a porthole.

"How's it going, Skippy?" I asked, struggling to keep my voice calm. I was sitting in the copilot seat of a Kristang dropship, wearing a powered armor suit, and sweating enough the suit was having to chill the air to prevent trickles of sweat from dripping down my back.

"Okey-dokey, Joey. I'm talking with the Ruhar now."

"Are they planning to give us any trouble?"

"Nope. No, I tapped into their internal communications, and they just about peed their pants when they saw our bad-ass battlecruiser jump in on top of them. All four of them are eager to get off the *Glory*, particularly since the ship's environmental system is going haywire. Parts of the ship are below freezing, and other compartments are uncomfortably hot. The oxygen recycling system is broken, so the Ruhar are wearing breathing masks.

Also, interestingly, these four are all civilian contractors. The admiral in command of the battlegroup stationed at Paradise wanted to keep the *Glory* as a prize, or use it for target practice. When he learned some jackass at Fleet headquarters wants to bring to *Glory* to their home planet, the admiral refused to assign any of his personnel to the task. His people checked that the *Glory*'s reactor and jump drive met minimum safety standards, and that's it. So Fleet headquarters had to contract with civilians to bring the ship out to meet a Jeraptha star carrier."

"Cool!" I gave a thumb's up to Desai. "So, these guys don't want any trouble, and they will leave the ship to us?"

"They are not all guys, Joe, two of them are female hamsters. They most definitely do not want any trouble; one of them is former military, and she was the first to say they should hand over the ship to us."

"But?" Something in Skippy's tone told me there was more to the story.

"But what, Joe?" His fake innocent voice wasn't convincing anyone.

"There is always a *but*, Skippy. Nothing we do is this easy. There has to be a catch."

"Oh yee of little faith. Why does there have to be a catch? Once in a while, there is a pot of gold at the end of the rain- Oh, forget it. Not even I could sell this line of BS. There is a teensy weensy complication. The plan was that we jump in, the Ruhar get scared by our super duper battlecruiser, they fly off in their dropship and leave the ship to us."

"Yeah, so? You said the battlecruiser image did impress them, and they want to leave. What is the problem?"

"The problem is, they don't have a dropship."

"What the f- How can they not have a dropship? Ruhar Fleet protocol requires all crewed ships to have- Oh, damn it. These guys aren't part of the Fleet, they're civilians."

"Egg-zactly, Joe. Thus, the teensy weensy problem."

"Crap. Hold a minute, I need to call Count Chocula." Oh, this was sure to be more fun than a barrel of monkeys. Once again, I had to tell my boss that a plan I developed had run into a problem. I pressed a button on the copilot console to call Chotek. "Sir, we have a problem. The Ruhar want to leave the ship peacefully, but they don't have a dropship with them."

I could hear Chotek give a weary sigh. "*Of course* they don't have a dropship! Can we, can we give them one of ours? We have plenty of them." He meant we had removed all the dropships from the two transport ships we salvaged. Most of them were junk, but Skippy's bots were able to cobble together enough parts to make several flyable units. We had plenty of space in the *Dutchman*'s docking bays, and I felt better having more equipment that less.

"We shouldn't do that. Those dropships are covered with human DNA inside and out, from us working on them," I explained. "Trace amounts of our DNA might be explainable, now that we know the Kristang took Keepers away from Paradise, but we can't give the Ruhar a dropship coated with human DNA. We have to go with Plan B."

"Do what you think is best. We've come this far, and the Ruhar are willing to leave the ship to us."

"Yes, Sir." My finger poised over the button to end the conversation.

Chotek had other ideas. "Colonel? Please remind your team that I will not tolerate any itchy trigger fingers."

"Understood."

The Ruhar opened the doors to a docking bay for us, and Desai flew us in, with me in the copilot seat calling out fore and aft clearance. Since we were in the smaller Dragon-A type of Kristang dropship, we had plenty of room. We used the landing skids to secure the ship to the floor of the docking bay, but did not engage with the clamps on the cradle. If we had to get out of there in a hurry, I didn't want balky clamps slowing us down.

The large doors cycled closed slowly, with one of them sticking halfway and needing to be pulled back before it slid into the fully closed and locked position. A light came on, indicating the doors were locked, and our ship's sensors detected air being pumped into the bay. "I think we keep our suits on," I said to Smythe. "There is a lot of carbon dioxide in the air. And I don't trust the seal on those doors." Air pressure in the bay was increasing much less quickly than normal for a Kristang frigate; either there was a leak somewhere, or the air pumps needed servicing. My suspicions were confirmed when air pressure reached normal, but the pumps had to keep running.

The airlock door opened, and a female Ruhar peeked her head around the door. She was wearing a soft-shelled spacesuit, but rather than a helmet she wore an oxygen mask, and waved hesitantly. "Hello?" In the enhanced view from our Dragon's cameras, I could see her hand was shaking slightly.

"Major, put her at ease," I ordered. "I don't want any misunderstandings that lead to a firefight."

"A firefight in a confined space would not be my first choice, Colonel," Smythe acknowledged. I watched through his helmet camera as he opened our airlock doors, leaving both of them open in case his team needed to get back aboard quickly. He stepped down the set of stairs that extended from the bottom of the airlock, trying to walk softly in his heavy armored suit, with his boots adhering to the deck in the zero gravity. Although a distinctive Kristang rifle was slung across his chest, he held up both hands and turned to face the Ruhar woman. Through my console, I heard the translation of the Ruhar words that issued from his helmet speakers. "Hey, how you doin', huh? Ah, excuse me, I knew I shouldn't have eaten that burrito this morning." Smythe's voice said. "I just flew here from Rigel, and boy are my arms tired."

"Skippy! What the hell?!" I shouted. Our beer can was supposed to handle the translating for us, rather than trusting the limited abilities of the suit computer.

"Ah, relax, Joe. I was spicing it up for your benefit. All Smythe said was 'hello'. Damn, I try to inject a bit of fun into this job, and I get yelled at."

"Just the straight translation, please," I said through gritted teeth, while to my left, Desai was laughing so hard she had tears in her eyes.

"Ok, Ok. Fine."

"-harm us?" The Ruhar was saying.

In his armored suit, Smythe was a good six inches taller than the hamster woman, he leaned forward to tower over her menacingly, as a Kristang warrior would. "If we wished to harm you, you would already be dead. Our assignment," he said as he took a step backward, "is to recover this ship, which our brothers the Swift Arrow clan disgracefully lost."

"Oh," her eyes grew wider, and she peered at the clan insignia on Smythe's suit. "You wish us to report which clan recovered this ship, to atone for the disgrace? We can do that. You are welcome to have this ship. It is not in good condition."

"It does not have to be," Smythe declared, and waved his team forward. They walked around to the back of the Dragon, where the back ramp was lowering. When it was fully down, they unstrapped a bulky package and wrestled it into a clear space behind the dropship. The package was a Kristang emergency shelter that had been aboard our former frigate the *Flower*. Smythe instructed the woman to bring her companions into the docking bay, and to don their spacesuit helmets.

Plan B was for us to inflate the portable shelter, put the four Ruhar in it, and push it out of the docking bay. Push it gently to avoid jostling the occupants, push it hard enough to drift away before we fired up the *Glory*'s engines and flew far enough away for a safe jump.

It was a minor miracle that nothing further went wrong with the operation. The four Ruhar were visibly nervous, even with Smythe's repeated assurances. When two of them hesitated to enter the inflated shelter, Smythe became slightly exasperated. "I told your companion that, although I would be pleased to kill your entire dishonorable species, that is not my purpose here today."

"You want us as witnesses?" One of the Ruhar squeaked, cowering away from Smythe. "You only need *one* witness."

"That is correct," Smythe patted his rifle. "I suggest you enter the shelter immediately, as I do not need all four of you alive."

That settled the issue, the two lagging Ruhar fairly dived into the shelter. Smythe's team got the shelter sealed, confirmed the air inside was breathable and the shelter functioning optimally.

"We are ready," the hamster woman said, and in the cockpit, I pressed a button to suck air out of the bay, then cycle the big doors open. One of the damned doors got stuck, I had to cycle it back and forth until it finally slid out of the way. The three SpecOps men gently picked up the shelter and tossed it out the door.

"Skippy, cut their comms," I ordered.

"Done. They can't see or hear anything outside that shelter. Their suits will run out of oxygen in ten hours, the shelter will keep them alive until well after the Jeraptha star carrier is scheduled to arrive. I suggest you get moving, hint, hint."

We did not need any urging to move as fast as we could, none of us wanted to be in a beat-up Kristang frigate if a Jeraptha or even a Ruhar warship jumped in unexpectedly. Skippy ran diagnostics on the jump drive, while Desai and I hurried to the bridge. We moved the *Glory* away from the drifting shelter, first using only thrusters until we were far enough away to fire up the main engines.

"Hoo, boy, this thing is a *total* POS," Skippy announced with great disgust when he completed his analysis. "How the hell did the Kristang almost sneak up on Paradise in this thing? That does not say good things about Ruhar sensor technology. And it is a miracle this shitbox managed to jump all the way out here without exploding. Anywho, thanks to the magic of Skippy the Magnificent, you can use the drive for a single jump; I have it programmed into the nav system. After we get this hunk of junk on one of the *Dutchman*'s docking platforms, my bots are going to be super busy getting this ship ready for a mock attack on the Ruhar. It is a damned good thing you aren't counting on this piece of crap to make a real attack."

"Thank you, Skippy, that is great," I replied while I tightened the straps on the couch I was in. "Desai, jump us when ready."

"You should do it, Sir," she said with a smile.

"You sure?"

"This may be our last opportunity to perform a jump in a Kristang frigate," she noted. "The honor should be yours."

I grinned. "Yeah, you're just thinking that if this thing breaks, you don't want the blame."

She grinned back. "That, too."

A Jeraptha fast packet ship jumped into orbit of the Glark system's largest gas giant planet, where the main spacedock servicing facilities floated. The ship's unexpected arrival, far inside the legal inbound jump zone, set off alarms on every ship and station in the immediate area, and nearly resulted in the fast packet ship being blown to dust by the Strategic Defense satellite network. Only because the ship broadcasted very high-level authentication codes was it allowed to survive, although it was not allowed to approach the spacedock which included the 98th Fleet Command offices.

"Admiral Tashallo," Communications Specialist First Class Hanst Bo's voice was shaky as he approached the Fleet commander. "The ship that just arrived is transporting an Inquisitor. She is requesting," Bo checked the message flimsy, "*demanding*, clearance to dock immediately."

"An Inquisitor?" Tashallo's antenna stood straight up and turned red. "What- did the message say why she is here?" All of his wagers were within the rules, he was certain, and his behavior was exemplary. He had acted in the best interest of the Jeraptha, regardless of the consequences to the positions he had taken on various wagers. Why would an Inquisitor venture all the way to the Glark system? Tashallo's mind was racing through possibilities, including whether he could book a quick prop bet on the purpose of the Inquisitor's visit, when he realized Bo had asked him a question. "What?"

"Sir, I asked whether I should signal clearance to the Inquisitor." Bo thought the answer was fairly obvious, as no one stood in the way of an Inquisitor.

"No," Admiral Tashallo declared with a combination smile and grimace. "Signal that ship to hold position at the inner marker. It is not to approach this facility. Also signal the Ready Guard force to send two ships to escort that fast packet back beyond the outer markers. Please tell the Inquisitor that if her mission is urgent, a dropship would be her quickest option, regardless." Seeing the shocked and questioning look on Bo's face, the admiral leaned back on his couch and added "If the Inquisitor finds fault with my actions, it is not because I allowed a strange ship access to a critical Fleet facility."

"Inquisitor Shone," Admiral Tashallo bowed his antenna in respect. "If you wish to conduct a review of our actions during the recent engagement, Captain Dahmen is available here, on this ship. Admiral Sashell departed with the 67th Fleet only two days ago. You could-"

"I have no questions for Admiral Sashell. Nor Captain Dahmen," the Inquisitor said simply. "My purpose here is to inquire about the message you reported receiving, the message which stated the Thuranin intended to attack."

This time, Tashallo was not able to fully conceal his surprise. The message he *reported* receiving? Was the Inquisitor questioning the authenticity of a message from Fleet Intelligence? A chill struck Tashallo's thorax, then he quickly recovered. He had not risen to his lofty position by being rattled by unexpected developments. "Yes. I admit I was initially skeptical that Fleet Intelligence had acquired information so precise; the exact locations and times when the enemy would come through three wormholes. It was the fact of Fleet Intelligence offering sixty to one odds, and no points taken, that convinced me the information must be accurate. You will note I did not wager against Fleet Intelligence at first."

"I have so noted."

"Immediately upon reaching the decision to act on the information contained in the message, I issued orders to prepare the 98th Fleet to depart the Glark system, and I took a fast packet to confer with Admiral Sashell. We were able to-"

The Inquisitor cleared her throat. "Admiral Tashallo, I read your report. Your actions were exemplary, as were those of Admiral Sashell, Captain Dahmen and the crews of all three task forces. You will all receive commendations, and I can tell you in confidence, Admiral Sashell's claim to reset the handicapping of your wager post-battle will be rejected."

Tashallo smiled outwardly and groaned inwardly. A quick ruling in his favor could only mean that some people at Fleet Headquarters expected to get cut in on the 98th Fleet's action. Damn it, Tashallo thought to himself, any time you get a major score, there are a hundred hands out looking for a taste. Fine, he would give them a taste of the vig, and the admiral commanding the Blue Squadron would expect to be paid his 'tax' although Blue Headquarters had not known about the battle until it was well over.

The Inquisitor no doubt knew exactly what thoughts were racing through Tashallo's mind, for she paused before continuing. "Congratulations to you, Admiral. I have been instructed to convey the gratitude of Fleet Headquarters, and of Admiral Mavanne in particular."

"I am grateful, for their, gratitude," Tashallo stumbled.

"That is not why I am here."

"Then, why?"

"Fleet Intelligence reports that message, with its extremely accurate data on enemy intentions, did not originate with them."

"Wha-*what*?" For a moment, Tashallo was rattled.

"Fleet Intelligence was shocked to hear of the battle you fought, they had no idea the Thuranin planned any kind of offensive. Indeed, they were about to issue an estimate stating the enemy was unlikely to mount any offensive operations for the next seven months."

In spite of his own shock, Tashallo automatically asked "What odds were they giving on that estimate?"

The Inquisitor actually smiled briefly. "Four to six. Of course."

"If the message did not originate with Fleet Intelligence, then where did the packet ship pick up that message?" Tashallo assumed the message had been traced back to its origin.

"We do not know. That ship was halted and thoroughly inspected. Its records indicate the message was received from a relay station near the Margulo system. That relay station's records indicate it received the message from another packet ship, and according to the records of that other packet ship, it picked up the message *directly* from Fleet Intelligence Headquarters. The computers at Fleet Intelligence have no record of sending such a message, although it contained all the proper authentication codes, as you know. Somehow, one of those packet ships received a message it has no record of, and the records of both ships have been altered."

Tashallo's head was spinning. "How is this possible?"

"Admiral Tashallo," the Inquisitor smiled, and Tashallo realized *she* was rattled. "That is why I am here."

After all the planning and preparation to set up our mock attack, once every possible thing was done and all we needed to do was wait, the waiting was driving me crazy. Everything was great. We had two ships prepped and ready for our mock attack on the Ruhar negotiation team. We had solid intel, and everything was proceeding on schedule and according to plan. Even better for me, Chotek had not raised any new objections or questions, and no one had thought up a better plan. The *Glory* and our Q-ship were going to jump into action, without any risk to the *Flying Dutchman*. Soon, I hoped, the Merry Band of Pirates would be enjoying a leisurely and uneventful ride home to Earth.

And still I worried constantly that I had forgotten something important. "Skippy, there isn't any possibility human DNA will be detected in the debris, after we self-destruct our two ships?"

"No. I told you that like twice already," his avatar had hands on its hips, shaking its head at me. "The only time humans went aboard the *Glory*, the boarding team was wearing Kristang armor that had been thoroughly scrubbed to remove all traces of DNA, or anything else that might possibly tie back to Earth. My bots did all the work after that, so the *Glory* is clean. And my bots scrubbed and decontaminated the Q-ship also."

"Great, thank you. Hey, uh, I've been thinking."

"Is that what you call it? Joe, the word 'thinking' in the dictionary just filed a defamation lawsuit against you."

"Oh, you are freakin' hilarious. Listen, we'll be leaving behind DNA from adult male and female Kristang in the debris. My question is, should we also leave at least a little hint about which clan conducted the attack? Like, uh, the Black Tree clan? You told us the Black Trees are the biggest rivals of the Fire Dragons."

"The Black Trees are bitter enemies of the Fire Dragons, true. I also told you that no clan would wish to be blamed for an attack on an alien negotiation team, so they would be extremely careful not to leave any evidence behind. The DNA is not a problem, because clans do not share DNA databases."

"Oh," I felt foolish. "Sorry to have-"

"However, ugh, I hate to say this; you might be onto something. Let me think a moment. Hmm. If we were able to leave behind evidence pointing to a clan, and make it look like someone had tried very hard to avoid leaving that evidence behind, that might be believable. If we could do that, and I emphasize *if*, then the best thing to do would be to point the finger not at the Black Trees, but at a minor clan within the Fire Dragon coalition."

"What?"

"When I speak of the 'Fire Dragon clan', I usually mean all the various groups belonging to or officially allied with the Fire Dragons. Major clans all have acquired minor clans, or prominent families within the Fire Dragons have split off to form their own minor clans. My point is, there are likely many minor clans within the Fire Dragon coalition who are eager to move up in the hierarchy, and a civil war would be their best opportunity to gain advantage over their rivals. Many of these minor clans would welcome a wide-scale Kristang civil war, and they might scheme to prevent the Fire Dragon leaders from reaching a deal with the Ruhar to send a ship to Earth. It is also true that some minor clans do not like the idea of the Fire Dragons absorbing the assets of the White Wind clan, because bringing the White Wind into the coalition would knock some clans further down the hierarchy."

"Holy crap, Skippy, how do you keep track of all this freakin' politics?" The situation of the Kristang reminded me of an old TV show my sister found and binge-watched; you needed a spreadsheet to keep track of the characters, and everyone dies anyway. "Damn, the Kristang must waste half their time worrying about getting stabbed in the back."

"They do, Joe. If you are a member of the warrior caste, you constantly must watch your back, or there will be a knife in it. Internal strife is the greatest weakness of the Kristang. Well, that and their warrior caste's foolish disregard of any technology that does not directly involve weapons."

"My heart bleeds for them, Skippy."

"I suspect you are not sincere about that, Joe. While you wasted time bitching about Kristang politics, I have been analyzing the idea of blaming the mock attack on a minor clan within the Fire Dragon coalition, that was *my* idea by the way. Joe, I like it! Damn, sometimes I am so freakin' smart that I amaze myself. Yes, we can do this, and we should do this. This solves a problem I have been concerned about."

"A problem? What problem?" I asked suspiciously. "You didn't mention any problem to me!"

"No I didn't, because then little Joey would have gone running to tell Count Chocula all about it, like a good and stupid little boy."

"Skippy, Chotek is the designated mission commander, I report to him. I have to inform him about possible risks to the mission. Crap, what is it this time?"

"The Ruhar negotiation party are aboard a cruiser, escorted by two destroyers. They will also be protected by at least a dozen Kristang warships. To make our attack by two relatively weak ships seem credible, we will need to jump them in close enough to the target, so they aren't blasted out of space before they can fire a shot."

"Uh huh, yeah, we discussed all that with the entire team. The magic of Skippy will make it easy to jump those ships in close, right?"

"Correct. That is not a problem, just another example of my awesomeness, Joe. The problem is; how will the attackers get the intel to know exactly where the Ruhar ships are? Other clans know the Fire Dragons are talking with the Ruhar, and they may know roughly where, but how do we explain that our supposedly Kristang ships know *exactly* where to jump in to hit the Ruhar?"

"Crap. You should have mentioned this before! I understand the problem now. Yeah," I mentally kicked myself for not considering that issue, "how *do* we explain where the attacking ships get tactical intel like that?" Unless the attack was believed to be the work of a Kristang clan, the whole operation was a waste of time and energy.

"Easy, Joe, thanks to my brilliant idea. I will plant evidence aboard the ships, leading the Fire Dragons to conclude the attack was carried out by a subclan in their own coalition. They will think they were betrayed by insiders, which happens often enough so it is not a big surprise. Framing a minor Fire Dragon clan for the attack will explain how the attackers got tactical intel, it will reinforce the Ruhar's thinking that the Fire Dragons can't be trusted to deliver on any deal, and it will weaken the Fire Dragon leadership. We don't want the Fire Dragons regrouping and making another offer to the Ruhar in the future. In fact," he paused, "yeah, this is great. If the Fire Dragon leadership thinks they have a subclan acting against them, they might decide to strike first and start a civil war, before their internal strife weakens them. Yeah!" He exulted. "Who da man? I'm da man!"

"You da man, Skippy," I rolled my eyes because his brilliant idea had started with me. "No one can argue with that. Is this something you can do quick, without Chotek knowing about it?" Unlike my increasing nervousness, Chotek had been super calm since he gave thc final approval for the attack. He had been almost jovial, even attending the recent movie night, and mingling with the crew for snacks and coffee after the movie. The last thing I wanted was to approach him now to ask permission for something I should have thought of weeks ago.

"The Count does not need to worry the chocolaty goodness in his pretty little head about it, Joe. I'm handling it right now, loading revised software into the operating systems of the *Glory*'s escape pods. Miraculously, one of the escape pods will survive the destruction of the ship; I'll damage it so it's not obviously a plant. The new software will point to the Top Hill subclan, and the Fire Dragon leadership will be furious. They will also be cautious, because the Top Hills have been increasing their influence in the last decade, and many subclans have begun look to the Top Hills for leadership. This will totally be believable, because the Top Hills have a well-deserved reputation for recklessness."

"Outstanding. There are no other potential problems you are keeping secret from me?"

"No. Hmm, let me check. No, nope. Not that I can think of at the moment. Soon as I think of one, Joe, I will tell you first," he offered cheerily.

"Great. That's fantastic, Skippy." I contemplated my empty coffee cup and decided against refilling it. My nerves and my stomach didn't need any more coffee. Checking the countdown clock on my tablet, I saw there was more than eleven hours before we launched our attack. The attack would commence at 0235 ship time, and no way was I going to get any sleep tonight. There were many days when I wished I was still a grunt with a rifle and a simple mission to perform. This was one of those days.

CHAPTER SIXTEEN

It was a good thing I didn't try to lie down for an hour or two of sleep. At 1923 Hours, Skippy's voice boomed out of the speaker in my office. "The Ruhar jumped in early, Joe, they're at the rendezvous point already!"

I asked Chotek to join me, then ran out the door and around the corner to the bridge. Major Simms was the duty officer, she vacated the command chair for me. "What does this mean, Skippy?"

"Well, they didn't jump in early to get a good parking spot," Skippy said with sarcasm. "It means the Ruhar do not trust the operational security of the Kristang, Joe, that's all. The Ruhar force is a cruiser and two destroyers, just like the intel expected. The Kristang ships have formed a defensive screen around the Ruhar, and, yup. All ships just activated damping fields. No ships on either side will be jumping away."

Chotek had come into the bridge right behind me, so he heard everything Skippy said. "Colonel Bishop, what is your recommendation?"

Hans Chotek was a royal pain in my ass most of the time, but he knew to defer to the military on military matters. "Sir," I replied, "I recommend we move up the attack. Go now. We're ready. If we attack now, that will reinforce in the Ruhar's minds that the Fire Dragons can't be trusted with operational security."

"Or be trusted with anything else," Chotek nodded. "Our sensor coverage is active; the microwormholes are in position?"

"Yes," I got out of the chair and pointed to a line of moving white dots on the main bridge display. To provide a real-time view of the battle, and so Skippy could adjust the actions of our attacking ships as needed, he had created a series of microwormholes. The near ends of those microwormholes were parked a kilometer away from the *Flying Dutchman*. The far ends had been loaded aboard a Kristang dropship and sent toward the rendezvous point at high acceleration. The unpiloted dropship had gently ejected one microwormhole after another as it continued to accelerate, then the dropship altered course and shut down. That dropship was on its way out of the Milky Way galaxy, and would drift onward through empty space until the end of time. The string of microwormholes were passing through the rendezvous area at high speed, one after the other. As one microwormhole went out of range, the next would be approaching the rendezvous. According to Skippy, we would have continuous and awesomely accurate real-time sensor data, extending eight hours before and thirty seven hours after the Zero Hour for our planned attack. With the Ruhar crashing the party early, it was a damned good thing we had sensor coverage already. "The third microwormhole will be at its closest approach to the Ruhar ship in sixteen minutes, and the fourth one is already within sensor range. There is no indication the Kristang have detected the microwormholes." I knew that because if the Kristang had detected one of Skippy's incredible spacetime tricks, the symbol for that microwormhole would be blinking red rather than white.

"Very well, Colonel," Chotek said as he took a step behind the command chair, and clasped his hands behind his back. "This is your show."

Suppressing a smile, I sat back in the chair. "Skippy, execute."

If the attack had been planned by a Kristang clan, they would not have relied on the relatively weak weapons aboard our two ships. They would have jumped both ships in as close as possible to the Ruhar cruiser, with the attacking ships on a collision course. With the attacking ships almost certain to get pounded by the heavy weapons of Ruhar and

Kristang warships, ramming was the best chance of inflicting damage on the negotiators before the attackers were disabled or destroyed.

Jumping in on a collision course was what an attacking Kristang would try to do, and since our goal was for the Ruhar to think it was a Kristang attack, that is what we did. The difference is that the awesomeness of Skippy allowed even the crappy jump drives of our two ships to emerge from jump within half a kilometer of the target, while a Kristang-programmed jump would be nowhere near that precise. Although Skippy grumbled about being deliberately inaccurate, he jumped our two ships in believably off target. The Q-ship emerged on the wrong side of the Ruhar cruiser, with its momentum carrying it away from the target. Immediately, the Q-ship launched weapons and burned its engines to bring it back toward the cruiser.

The *Glory* emerged on the correct side of the cruiser, although our little frigate was moving fast and would fly right by the Ruhar without making contact. That was good, we wanted it to look like the attackers intended to ram the Ruhar cruiser, but we didn't want to actually impact the negotiators' ship. The *Glory* burned its engines in a desperate attempt to avoid flying past the cruiser, a maneuver that the laws of physics were not going to allow. Our frigate also launched missiles and fired its masers.

"Two direct hits!" Skippy shouted excitedly.

"Chill, Skippy," I ordered. "You can't have the *Glory*'s weapons fire be too accurate. It's supposed to be flown by Kristang, remember?"

"Yeah, yeah," he grumbled. "Crap, Ok, it just missed the next three shots. It's not me, Joe, that's the way I programmed the subminds running those ships. All missiles are away, tubes are empty on both ships. The Q-ship is- uh, the Q-ship just took hits from five maser cannons and a pair of railgun darts. Engines are disabled, shields are holding for the moment. Eleven missiles are now targeting the Q-ship. Interesting. Only two missiles are from the Ruhar, the other nine are Kristang. Ha! The Kristang commander is assuring the Ruhar this attack is not by the Fire Dragon clan. The Ruhar are replying that anyone can see the *Glory* is a Kristang frigate. Hee hee, let's see the Fire Dragons talk their way out of that mess, huh?"

"Should we self-destruct the Q-ship," I asked anxiously, "or let the missiles destroy it?"

"Both, I think," Skippy answered. "I'll set it to self-destruct just before the first missiles impact. A real Kristang suicide team would wait until the last second."

I turned to catch Chotek's eye; he didn't intervene, so I turned my attention back to the display. "Do that, Skippy. The *Glory* is taking hits now?"

"Yes, my submind had it zigzagging nicely, but I had to let the Kristang score a hit or they would suspect something is odd with our frigate. Portside shields are getting pounded by maser cannons, the submind is rolling the ship to take hits on the starboard shields. One of the Ruhar destroyers is turning to unmask its railgun, and- Whoa! Wow. Direct hit with a railgun penetrator, went right through the *Glory*'s hull. Damn! Ha ha! Wow! What are the odds of that, the freakin' railgun didn't hit anything vital."

On the display, the *Glory* staggered, then thrusters flared and the little ship righted itself and continued to desperately burn toward the cruiser, which was accelerating to get away. The projected course on the display showed the *Glory* had no chance to crash into the cruiser unless the cruiser stupidly flew in the wrong direction. I opened my mouth to ask a question, when the image on the display flared white hot. The *To Seek Glory in Battle is Glorious*, the unlucky little frigate that had survived too long against the odds, was finally gone. "Was that your doing, Skippy?"

"No, I never had time to activate the self-destruct mechanism. The *Glory* took two Kristang maser cannon hits at the same time as a Ruhar railgun dart ran through her from bow to stern. Her reactor exploded. I have released control of the Q-ship self-destruct to her submind; I won't have time to react before- There she goes," he added quietly. The Q-ship flared on the display, even more brightly than the *Glory*'s death fires.

"What was the damage to the Ruhar?" Chotek demanded as his hands grasped the back of my chair.

"Minor," Skippy reported, blessedly sticking to the facts rather than insulting Chotek. "We scored nine maser hits total, and two missiles impacted the cruiser's shields. Five more of our missiles are still inbound to the target, but they are being fired upon by both sides, and I expect them all to be destroyed. The worst damage to the Ruhar was caused by the *Glory* exploding; some of that high-speed debris almost overloaded the cruiser's shields."

Following the destruction of our two ships in the mock attack, we hung around the area, monitoring the aftermath through the microwormholes that were still coasting through the area. Chotek was exultant because ten minutes after our Q-ship exploded, the Ruhar cruiser began accelerating toward the edge of the Kristang damping field. The Kristang ships moved out of the way to give the Ruhar plenty of space, and the two Ruhar destroyers stayed behind to continue projecting their own damping fields, so no Kristang ships could jump away. A lot of message traffic was flying back and forth between the Ruhar and the Fire Dragons. The Fire Dragons apologized profusely, to the point where Skippy said they must truly be desperate, because they were humiliating themselves in a very un-Kristang-like way. The Fire Dragons assured the Ruhar they were not involved in the attack, and vowed to both investigate who conducted the dastardly attack, and punish the perpetrators. The Ruhar replied that they needed to reassess the situation; Skippy told us the language they used was not the mealy-mouthed diplomatic speech which indicated the negotiations had a prayer of continuing. To my surprise, instead of being insulted by Skippy's characterization of diplomats, Chotek was pleased. He had been involved in many difficult negotiations in his career, and he advised me that if the Ruhar's language did not leave the door open for future talks, then future talks were unlikely.

Hans Chotek was not the only person aboard the ship in a near-jubilant mood; Major Simms reported to me that Chotek had asked her to have bottles of champagne chilled and ready for when the Ruhar officially declared the negotiations cancelled. I was in the unusual position of having to caution him to control his enthusiasm. The last thing I wanted was for the Merry Band of Pirates' hopes to be crushed again.

Around nineteen hours after our attack, Skippy called me while I was trying to relax in my cabin. "Hey, Joe, are you asleep?"

"You know I'm not, Skippy." My intention had been to sneak in a quick nap, but sleep had eluded me, so I was reading a book. Not a report, not another PowerPoint slide, a real book. It was keeping me from spending all my time worrying. We learned the Ruhar cruiser had not returned home, it had only jumped one lighthour away, and was simply hanging in space. That development was troubling; until the Ruhar jumped for home, there was a possibility of the negotiations resuming. "What's up?"

"Just intercepted a transmission from the Kristang destroyer that recovered a damaged escape pod from the *Glory*. They completed their analysis, and they are not happy. Some of the software code buried in the escape pod's operating system points to the attack having been conducted by the Top Hill subclan. Apparently the software was supposed to erase itself, but the damage to the pod interrupted the erasure process. The Fire Dragon leaders over there are furious; it seems the Top Hills have some 'splainin' to do, hee hee. There is a debate going on about whether to tell the Ruhar who was responsible for the attack. Some of the leaders are saying that revealing the attacker were a subclan of the Fire Dragons makes them look weak and hurts their negotiating posture. Other leaders think that being honest would surprise the Ruhar, and demonstrate how serious the Fire Dragons are about reaching a deal. This faction also states the Ruhar are not stupid; the attack happened so soon after they arrived, so the Ruhar already suspect the attackers must have had inside information."

"Hmmm. What do you think? Should we somehow let the Ruhar know about it?"

"I do not know, Joe. I hate to say this, but Chotck would be the best person to ask. He would have the best perspective on how this information might affect the negotiations."

"Crap. We can't tell him now; he would demand to know how that software came to be in the escape pod."

"I could tell him I did that on my own initiative, Joe," Skippy suggested.

"No," I tossed my tablet on the bed in disgust. "He wouldn't believe you did that without asking me. And it would only make him even more distrustful of you."

"You may be right about that. If it makes you feel any better, Chotek may be an expert on negotiating, but he knows little about Kristang or Ruhar psychology. I am an expert in those fields, and right now, even I cannot predict how the Ruhar would react to learning the Top Hill clan carried out the attack."

"Ok, then we wait." I wasn't happy about passively waiting for the Fire Dragons to make a decision; most of my unhappiness was because I knew I should have thought through what to do when the Kristang discovered the evidence Skippy had planted. This was an example of what Chotek said was my worst failing as a commander; I reacted to events, rather than thinking ahead and controlling my own fate. In this case, I had to agree with Chotek.

My angst about what to do didn't last long; Skippy reported the Fire Dragons had decided to tell the Ruhar about the Top Hill clan's involvement. Shortly after, one of the Ruhar destroyers sent a long, encrypted transmission to their cruiser that was waiting one lighthour away. The cruiser replied, but it didn't leave. Skippy, of course, decrypted the messages; we learned the Ruhar were still evaluating the situation. By now, even Chotek's jubilant mood was growing impatient. The champagne was on hold.

As the last of our microwormholes was speeding onward out of range, the two Ruhar destroyers still had not moved, and their cruiser was holding position one lighthour away. That was odd, I thought to myself. One of the Kristang destroyers had broken formation, flown to the edge of the damping field, and jumped away six hours before, and Skippy later detected a gamma ray burst from a Thuranin ship jumping in near where that Kristang destroyer had gone. I was on the bridge, crowded in with Chotek, Smythe and Simms. Chang was the duty officer in the command chair, being good-natured about the visitors squashed together around him. Chotek brushed past me to trace a fingertip on the main display. "When this last microwormhole passes out of range, we will have no way to know the status of the ships, or to intercept communications?"

Skippy answered before I could speak. "We will have limited data on the position of the ships. That data will be thirty seven minutes old, and will only contain data from the *Dutchman*'s passive sensors." Our current position was thirty seven lightminutes from the cluster of Ruhar and Kristang ships, that was about the closest safe approach we would make. "As to intercepting communications, not even I can do that from here. Both sides are using tightbeam transmissions; I have been picking up the backscatter. We're too far away for that without the wormholes."

"Is there any way we can turn the microwormholes around, or get new ones to the area?" Chotek put his arms across his chest in frustration.

"By 'we', you mean 'me', right?" Skippy was annoyed. "No, dumdum, I can't turn the wormholes around; I told you that. I could transmit power through them that would eventually change their course, even make them turn around. That would take months, and the wormholes would be visible the whole time. As to more wormholes, we could shoot the far ends into position with our railguns, except, oops, took our railgun apart because I needed the materials to fix the ship on our last mission. We'll need to use another dropship."

We had plenty of dropships, that didn't mean I wanted to waste them. And dropship, even unmanned, accelerated too slowly to be useful. "Skippy," I asked, "what about using missiles to carry wormholes over there?" He used a missile to position a microwormhole above the planet Newark on our last mission.

"We would need one missile for each wormhole," Skippy cautioned me. "Each wormhole will provide about ninety minutes of coverage. We don't have a lot of missiles aboard, Joe, and I can't make more of them without a lot of time and materials."

"Sir," I turned to Chotek. "When we launched the original set of wormholes, we didn't expect the Ruhar would still be trying to make a decision after three days. I think we can live with gaps in coverage, as long as we get the big picture. I recommend that we fire six missiles, spaced one hour apart. That will give us another fourteen hours of coverage," I concluded, hoping I had gotten the math right in my head. "If we have used the six missiles and still do not know the status of the negotiations, we will have to consider alternative means of monitoring the situation. We can't use up all our missiles."

Chotek considered for a moment, then nodded. "Agreed. We need to know whether your mock attack plan gave us the desired results. Proceed."

I noticed that he referred to the attack as *my* plan, now that he was no longer confident of its success. Clearly, Hans Chotek was not taking any blame if we failed. "Skippy, get the first microwormhole loaded into a missile. Have you figured out yet why that Thuranin ship jumped in near the Fire Dragon's destroyer?"

"No," his voice was discouraged. "Clearly, the Thuranin are talking to that destroyer. So far, the destroyer has not transmitted a message to the ships at the negotiation site. If I have to make a guess, I think the Thuranin likely demanded to know what the hell went wrong; how the Fire Dragons screwed things up this time."

We fired three missiles, and had a fourth ready in the launch tube, when Skippy called me in my office. His avatar popped into life on my desk. "Joe, the Kristang destroyer that met with the Thuranin ship just jumped. I assume it jumped back to the negotiation site, but a gap in coverage just began sixteen minutes ago, so we won't have any intel from the negotiation site for thirty eight minutes."

"Crap. Launch the ready missile now," I ordered.

"That missile is not due to launch for another-"

"I know. Do it anyway, do it now."

"I need to contact the CIC to press the button. Ok, missile is away. Light from the negotiation site will reach the missile first, so we will know whether that destroyer jumped there in twenty six minutes. Wormhole coverage will begin in forty minutes."

That gap in coverage, which had been a calculated risk by me, was maddening, and it was the best Skippy could do. "I'll tell Chotek personally."

When the ready missile carrying a microwormhole got close enough to the negotiation site, it picked up signals that Skippy was able to decrypt. "Hmmm," the beer can said quietly. "Ooooh, that's not good."

"What's not good?" I asked, not needing to look at Hans Chotek to know he was already glaring at me. "Are the negotiations going to continue or not?"

"The negotiations will not continue, Joe." I was about to pump a fist in the air when Skippy continued. "They don't need to continue, because the negotiations have already concluded."

"What happened?" I forced myself to be calm, while fearing the worst.

"Well, heh, heh," Skippy began, and everyone's hair stood on end. We all knew what it meant when that asshole beer can said those three words. "This is a funny story-"

"Funny like ha ha, or like planetary extinction?" I asked the question on everyone's minds.

"The, uh, second one. I guess that's not so funny after all, huh?"

"What the hell happened?" I caught Chotek glaring daggers at me out of the corner of my eye.

"Gosh, you know the Law of Unintended Consequences? That's not a physical law, like thermodynamics or the law of gravity. Of course, your primitive species only thinks those are laws because you don't understand the basic principles of-"

"Skippy," I said through clenched teeth. "Get to the point, please. What unintended consequences?"

"Joe," his voice was nervous. "Remember you told me to pass intel to the Jeraptha, warning them about the Thuranin offensive?"

"Yeah. Why? Was the intel you gave them bogus?"

"Bogus? No way, dude. Please. You're talking about Skippy the Magnificent. Bogus intel," he chuckled. "That's a good one. No, the intel was solid, it told the Jeraptha exactly when and where the Thuranin would be launching the offensive."

"What happened? The Thuranin won the battle anyway?"

"No, of course not," snarkiness was creeping back into Skippy's voice, and his avatar was standing up straighter. "The Thuranin got their asses handed to them on a platter. They got *crushed*, Joe. They lost almost all of the ships in all three task forces assigned to the operation. The Jeraptha even bagged the star carriers the Thuranin thought would be at a safe distance from the battle. The only drawback to the Jeraptha is their two admirals involved are in a heated argument over whose ships should get credit for which kills; each of them wagered a substantial amount on the outcome and now they have sent for a neutral arbiter to determine who won the bet. Anywho, the reason this matters to us is the Thuranin got their asses kicked so soundly, their whole defensive posture in the sector is in danger of collapse. And, hee, hee, this is why it's kind of a funny story," Skippy giggled nervously. "I mean like 'ha ha' funny, if you think about it. It's ironic, in the true definition of the word, not the stupid way hipsters say 'ironic'."

"Please, Skippy, get to the point. What is ironic?"

"Remember when I said I could not think of any possible downside to giving that intel to the Jeraptha? It turns out I was, what's the word I'm looking for?"

"Wrong?" I guessed.

"Yeah, that's it. The Thuranin got beat up so badly they can't afford their clients to be distracted by a civil war right now, so the Thuranin instructed the Fire Dragons to make a very tempting offer to the Ruhar, backed by assets and guarantees of the Thuranin. The Ruhar were pleasantly surprised, and they accepted."

"Holy shit," I slumped back in my chair. "We screwed ourselves by passing that intel to the Jeraptha?"

"Uh huh, yeah," Skippy said in a cheery tone. "That's why I said it was an unintended consequence, Joe. Hee hee. Ain't life funny sometimes?" He chuckled and I felt like strangling him. "As a result of the disastrous battle, the Thuranin are now willing to make a deal to delay a Kristang civil war, while they scramble to pull back and consolidate their forces across the sector. Those little green MFers are now willing to trade away assets that are at risk of being taken by force in the Jeraptha offensive that is sure to follow."

Chotek was rubbing his temples, a sure sign he had a headache coming on. He was avoiding my eyes; that told me I was going to catch hell later. "Is there anything we can do to derail the negotiations at this point? Are they final?"

"The acceptance is not formal yet; the Ruhar negotiation team needs to brief their federal government, and then the Jeraptha will need to sign off on the deal. But it is pretty much a done deal at this point; the Fire Dragons offered a valuable wormhole cluster that connects to three planets the Ruhar want badly."

"The Thuranin and Fire Dragons are willing to give up a wormhole cluster and three planets, in exchange for a ride to Earth?" I was incredulous. Planets are big things. Who the hell would trade even one planet for a road trip?

"And back, Joe. A ride to Earth and *back*. These are three planets the Thuranin have told the Fire Dragons they will likely lose anyway, when the Jeraptha begin pushing the Thuranin back in that area. The Fire Dragons are hoping a delay of a civil war will position them well when the war does inevitably start, and they could take far more than three planets away from rival clans. The Thuranin and Fire Dragons are accepting reality and making the best deal they can get at this point. When you think about, this deal is win-win for everyone. Except you humans, of course, you are *scuh-reeeewed*, dude."

CHAPTER SEVENTEEN

"That's it, then." Chotek was sitting in his office chair, looking thoroughly deflated. "The Ruhar will be sending a ship to Earth, and there is no way for us to stop it, without the Ruhar becoming suspicious and revealing our secret. Colonel, at this point, I suppose we should set course for Earth."

"No, Sir. We have a Plan B."

"A Plan B?" Chotek's raised eyebrows quickly fell into a scowl directed at me. "When were you going to present this alternative plan to me?"

"When we needed it. It's not a plan I want to implement."

"The Ruhar are sending a ship to Earth, and we can't stop it without the Ruhar knowing someone doesn't want them going to our home planet. What is your Plan B, Colonel?"

"It's fairly obvious, Mr. Chotek," Adams said quietly.

"Obvious?" Chotek turned his wrath toward her. She didn't flinch. "It's not obvious to me."

"Colonel?" Adams looked me straight in the eye. "I'm sure you're thinking the same thing I am. Tell him."

I nodded. "The whole purpose of the Fire Dragons paying the Thuranin to send a surveyor ship to Earth, and now making a deal with the Ruhar, is to delay a civil war. So, we give them a civil war, now."

I never saw Hans Chotek so shocked. "You want us to provoke a civil war," he said very slowly, "between Kristang clans?"

"Yes." Following the example of Staff Sergeant Adams, I wasn't backing down one bit. If a Marine wasn't fazed by Chotek's scathing words, I wasn't letting the Army down either. "Once the Fire Dragons are involved in a full-scale civil war, they won't be able to devote resources for an expedition to Earth. And they won't care about the White Wind clan leadership on Earth; they will be too busy fighting for advantage, maybe for survival. Getting the Kristang involved in a wide-ranging civil war weakens the Kristang overall, reduces their threat to Earth and to Paradise, and *permanently* removes any incentive the Kristang have for traveling to Earth." I emphasized the word 'permanent'. I figured Chotek would pick up on that.

"How long have you had this Plan B in your pocket, Colonel?"

"Since our mission to stop that surveyor ship, Sir," I explained matter-of-factly. "By the time we discovered the Fire Dragons were paying for a mission to Earth, the surveyor ship was already on its way, and couldn't be recalled even if the Fire Dragons changed their minds. As you know, we destroyed that surveyor ship." At the time, I thought that operation was horribly complicated. Now that seemed incredibly simple. "But it got me thinking what we could do, long-term, to prevent the Kristang from wanting to send an expedition to Earth. You said we need to think long-term, and I agree. We could provoke a civil war among the Kristang, *and* influence the outcome so that when the fighting is over, the most powerful factions of the lizards are less of a threat to us."

I don't know what shocked Chotek more; knowing I had an alternative plan ready, or that my plan was to start an interstellar war. "You are proposing we interfere with another species, to start a war that will kill thousands, perhaps millions, of sentient beings," Chotek said with a horrified expression.

Before I could defend myself, Skippy interjected. "Not really. Any civil war among the Kristang will kill a lot of lizards, sure, and mostly women and children because they get caught in the middle. If you are worried about having those deaths on your conscience, don't. A Kristang civil war is a matter of *when*, not *if*. They have a war between clans on average every eighty years, that's a rough number. Their last major inter-clan conflict was ninety three years ago, so they're overdue for one. Whether you start a war next week, or one starts on its own next year, the same number of lizards will die," Skippy said confidently. "Joe is right, though, if we provoke a war, we should influence the outcome so that the winners pose less of a threat to humanity." And then, because Skippy did not know when to shut up, he added "See what I did there, Joe? To show I am being serious, I said 'humanity' instead of 'monkeykind'."

"Yeah, that was great, Skippy, thanks. You make a good point," I looked toward Chotek hopefully. "He does make a good point, Sir."

"Does he?" Chotek asked sadly. "I've heard this argument before, Colonel. If Archduke Ferdinand had not been assassinated in June 1914, the First World War would have happened regardless, because of tensions between the great powers of Europe. Wars always kill more of the innocent than the combatants. I was trained as a diplomat to prevent conflicts that are supposed to be inevitable."

"With the Kristang, war is truly inevitable," Skippy said unhelpfully. "Their warrior caste can't exist without war. If it makes you feel any better, the Thuranin have provoked civil wars among the Kristang, when the Thuranin felt the Kristang were too strong and unified."

"It does not make me feel better to be compared to the Thuranin," Chotek replied with indignant anger.

"Well, you-"

"Skippy, you gave us a lot of good information," I said in what I hoped was a soothing tone. "I think now you need to let us primitive humans sort this out. It needs to be our decision."

"The survival of your species is at stake, so you had better sort things out quickly," he advised. "Whatever you decide, do it fast; the clock is ticking."

Chotek squared his shoulders and his nostrils flared as he took a deep breath. "Colonel, are you now going to tell me you have a plan for provoking a war?"

"No, Sir, you need to plan that with Skippy."

"*Me*?" Chotek was stunned.

I could tell he was completely surprised that I expected him to plan the war for us. "Yes. I can work with Major Smythe to plan the tactical implementation of whatever plan you develop," I used big fancy words to impress Chotek. "But figuring out what type of action would provoke the clans into war, and how to do that so the end result of the war enhances our security, I have no idea how to do that," I admitted. And I wasn't just feeding Hans Chotek's ego so he would take ownership of the planning; I was being sincere. "Sir, you mentioned Archduke Ferdinand, how one bullet started a world war. If you can tell me where to shoot, I can get that bullet to its target. I have no idea how to get the clans fighting each other, nor any idea which clan or group of clans we want to come out on top. That kind of great power diplomacy stuff is your area of, uh, expertise. Skippy has a lot of information about the clans, their relationships and history, and he can tell you about Kristang psychology. We need you to take all that info, analyze it, and tell us if we have a prayer of pulling this off."

"*Starting* wars was not part of my diplomatic training," he retorted, but he didn't sound angry. He sounded thoughtful. "Starting wars is your area, Colonel."

"No, Sir," I shook my head, and Chang, Smythe, Simms and lot of other people were doing the same. "We *fight* the wars. Politicians *start* them."

Chotek nodded, and sighed heavily. "And diplomats end wars. All right, Colonel Bishop, I will entertain the idea. I must admit, it will be intriguing to be on the other side of the equation for a change."

"Can you get started soon?" I asked. "As Skippy said, time is running out. We need a full-blown war raging before the Fire Dragons hand over those planets to the Ruhar. There is not a lot of time to develop a strategy, and then a tactical plan to implement it."

"I may need to borrow our resident spy, Dr. Rose," Chotek announced while rubbing his chin, half lost in thought already.

"You can ask, but I think her experience is on the tactical level like mine," I noted. "Although she certainly knows a lot more about political intrigue than I do."

I later asked Skippy if he and Chotek were making progress on identifying targets we could hit to spark a Kristang civil war, but he refused to say. "Darn it Joe, for a change I am actually able to tolerate Count Chocula, and I can say he is enjoying himself immensely, although he certainly wouldn't admit it. He is surprisingly knowledgeable about Kristang clan politics, which answers the question of what he has been doing with his time on this mission. So, I am not going to spoil the surprise; he will tell you."

Chotek called me into his office two days later, much faster than I expected. "Colonel Bishop, come in, please. Sit down."

"Thank you, Sir. You have a strategy for us?" Crap. I should have made some small talk first. In my defense, I sucked at small talk, and time was seriously running out. Major Smythe, Dr. Rose and I needed to slam an operational plan together fast, and we didn't even know our target yet. Now I knew how Hans Chotek felt, when he was waiting for me to tell him whatever outlandish plan I had cooked up.

"Before we start, how is the crew dealing with the prospect of another unexpected operation?"

I knew this was small talk; Hans Chotek didn't need me to tell him about morale of the crew, because he had a daily meeting with Chang. The team had been disappointed, when our enormously complicated operation to conduct the mock attack had not prevented the Fire Dragons from reaching a deal with the Ruhar. Now the team was pumped about the prospect of taking direct action against the Kristang. Major Smythe, Chang and I had cautioned everyone that, whatever action we took, still needed to be completely clandestine and the team understood that; it was nothing new. What was new was the very real possibility of us hitting the Kristang directly, hitting them hard. Starting a war that would kill a lot of Kristang warriors, and get a measure of payback for what they had done to Earth. For a couple minutes, I told Chotek what the crew had told me. My mother told me small talk was important because it established a bond between the people speaking. Even a useless comment like 'nice weather today' was an attempt to open a discussion, make a connection with another person. As I said, I sucked at small talk, but if there was anyone I needed to establish at least some level of personal bond with, it was Hans Chotek. So I worked at it. "Everyone wants to get back home to Earth, of course," I concluded. "And they all want to finish the mission, so we can go home."

"Can we ever truly finish this mission?" Chotek asked, speaking half to me and half to himself.

"I know what you mean," I grimaced. "In a galaxy full of hostile aliens, we will never be able to assume Earth is safe."

Chotek consulted his tablet, started to turn it toward me, hesitated, then seemed to make a decision about something. "Colonel Bishop, have you ever wondered why UNEF Command sent me on this mission?"

"Oh, uh," his question caught me off guard. "I assume it was because you're not a citizen of the five nations that make up the UN Expeditionary Force. So, you're neutral, sort of?"

"Yes, that also," clearly my answer wasn't what he was looking for. "My question was whether you know why UNEF didn't assign a senior military officer."

Scratching the back of my neck, I offered a guess. "Well, uh, Skippy forced their hand when he demanded that I be captain of the ship," although he had screwed that one up big time. UNEF agreed to make me captain of the ship, then assigned a mission commander over me.

"That also." Chotek acknowledged. "My point is, UNEF did not assign a military officer to command the mission, because they do not see that ensuring the long-term security of Earth has a military solution."

That, I thought to myself, plus the fact that Earth had no military of any consequence. "You got the assignment because of your diplomatic experience?"

"Yes. Colonel, my mission out here is not merely to prevent you from pursuing rash military adventures," he flashed a smile I took as genuine. "Part of my mission is to determine the political situation in the galaxy, if the word 'political' applies to aliens with technology beyond our imagination. You argued against us offering alliance with the Ruhar, and you made a strong argument. Your argument was that if Earth's secret became known to the Maxolhx and the Rindhalu, our little planet would be in grave danger, if only as collateral damage. I can tell you now that, personally, I agree with you."

"What?" I blurted out. "Sir? Sorry."

"No need to be sorry, I knew I would startle you with that revelation. Colonel, the topic of whether to approach the Ruhar, or even to contact the Rindhalu directly, was extensively and hotly debated before we left Earth. Opinions among the nations of UNEF, and the wider UN Security Council, are deeply divided on the subject. My orders are for us to avoid doing anything out here that would preclude us from pursuing a future alliance with the Ruhar. Your plan for a mock attack caused me much heartburn," he admitted.

"But we are Ok to take action against the Kristang?"

"As the expression goes, that ship has sailed." He didn't smile. "Maintaining secrecy is still paramount. However, I have become convinced, or I have convinced myself over the past few days, that keeping the Kristang busy fighting between their clans can only be a good thing for humanity."

I agree, I thought to myself. On the other hand, we thought warning the Jeraptha about a Thuranin attack held only upside for us, and that totally backfired in our faces. That was a sentiment I kept to myself. "You have identified a way for us to spark a war between clans?"

"We are confident that we know which levers to pull, where the pressure points are," he was speaking through a frown. "Colonel, this was an uncomfortable experience for me. As you stated, politicians start wars, which you in the military have to fight. My career has been about avoiding violence, or ending violence once it starts. Diplomats are supposed to be the people who prevent the military from fighting unnecessary wars. People like me are supposed to prevent people like you from being sent into harm's way." He looked me straight in the eye. "Now I find myself on the verge of ordering you into combat, to start a war that will kill millions. It goes against everything I have worked for my entire career. And yet, and yet," he seemed to be talking to himself, his gaze on the wall behind me. "I see no alternative. Colonel Bishop," he glanced at the silver eagles on my uniform, as if he still could not believe I was an officer. "Skippy will provide the details on the target we identified; you will of course need to create a tactical plan to attack the target. Without the Kristang ever knowing we were involved. Or that *any* third party was involved; my reading of Kristang culture indicates that if they suspected a third party was inciting the clans to fight, that would pull the clans together."

"Yes, Sir. I will talk with Skippy."

Chotek wasn't done with me. "Colonel," he looked at me sharply. "I suspect part of your motivation, in requesting that I determine how best to spark a Kristang civil war, was so that I would feel ownership of the resulting plan. You sought to manipulate me."

There wasn't any point in denying it. "Yes, partly. I did want you to buy into the concept," I looked straight at him. "Mostly, though, Mr. Chotek, politics is not my wheelhouse. If you point me toward a target, I can figure out how best to hit it, and I can do it. But knowing what type of action would get all the Kristang clans fighting each other," I dropped my gaze and shrugged, "I would be guessing."

"I don't blame you for attempting to manipulate me," he stated simply. "If you do it in the future, I have a suggestion for you."

"What's that, Sir?"

"Don't be so obvious about it."

CHAPTER EIGHTEEN

After I left Chotek's office, I stopped by the galley for coffee, decided to get iced tea instead, and brought it back to my office. "Hey, Skippy, Chotek tells me the two of you have identified optimal targets, for getting a civil war started throughout Kristang-occupied space."

"Hey, Joe," his avatar sparkled into existence above my desktop. "That is true. Three of us, to be accurate, Dr. Rose did help. Our local CIA officer has a devious and inventive mind, Joe. If you ever decide to give up this saving the world business and become a criminal mastermind, you should consider a partnership with her."

"Uh, yeah, I'll think about it."

"Also, I now have a tiny bit less disdain for our fearless leader."

"Enough to stop calling him 'Count Chocula'?"

"Pbbbbbt," Skippy blew a raspberry. I was grateful his avatar was a hologram, or I would have been covered with spit. "No way! For one, I'm having way too much fun with that. Besides, I'm sure by now he considers it only a nickname."

"I don't know about that, Skippy." After Chotek approved the successful missions to seize a Thuranin relay station, and rescue UNEF on Paradise, the crew's respect for our official mission commander went up a notch. People still ate Count Chocula cereal for breakfast, but I had requested those little chocolate sugar bombs be put in plain plastic containers rather than the original colorful cardboard packaging.

"That's his problem," Skippy grumbled. "As a mission commander, he is too inflexible and indecisive. However, he does understand political structures, even in alien societies. I must admit, the heavy work on how to spark a civil war was done by Chotek and Sarah Rose; I mostly provided historical background info, and ran wargame scenarios for them."

"Chocul-" I caught myself. "Chotek asked you to run a war game?"

"Joe, I meant 'wargame it' in the sense that I modeled various scenarios. We ran simulations, to determine which actions would most likely result in a widespread civil war breaking out. For us to only spark a local conflict between two clans would be a waste of our time. We need a big, full-scale conflict across Kristang space, that draws in all clans."

"Great. Ok, so, explain this genius strategy to me. I need to create a tactical plan, and I don't even know the target."

"Before I start, let me make sure you understand the background material," he said, and I mentally prepared myself for a lecture from Professor Nerdnik. "There are two major clans that currently dominate Kristang society; the Fire Dragons and the Black Trees."

"The Black Trees? The same clan that was the first to occupy Paradise, and took away all the Elder goodies?"

"Very good, Joey! You are my star pupil today, get yourself a juicebox. The Black Tree clan took all the Elder goodies away from Paradise, except the most important one: me!" He chuckled. "Stupid lizards. The hamsters weren't any smarter."

"Uh huh. Yup, truly, it is ironic that, of all the advanced species in the galaxy, only us lowly monkeys are capable of appreciating your awesomeness," I suppressed a gagging sound, trying to build up brownie points with our alien beer can.

"Ironic? Pathetic is a better word for it," he sighed. "Yes, the Black Tree clan was the first to occupy Paradise. They surrendered it peacefully to the Ruhar, because the Black Trees thought they had stripped that planet of anything useful."

"Whenever I hear 'Black Trees' I think of like a new age music group, not a bloodthirsty clan of lizards. That's kind of a lame name for a clan."

"Joe, you are *so* ignorant," his avatar put hands over its eyes and shook its head, the giant hat bobbing comically. "The name 'Black Trees' is a reference to ancient Kristang mythology. Back when the Kristang were barely able to use fire and their most deadly weapon was a wooden club, they were hunter-gatherers living mostly in forests. There were larger, more dangerous predators living in dense areas of the forests where trees with black bark grew. The Kristang knew to avoid those areas, but as their society developed, it was a rite of passage for young males to go among the black trees overnight. Those who survived were accepted as warriors. Even today, there are game preserves on many Kristang-occupied planets; these game preserves have thick forests of black trees, and many types of fearsome predators. Warriors test themselves by going into these forests armed only with a knife, and whatever weapons they can make from the forest. Over the years, some of the predators have been bred specially to be more deadly and harder to kill. To go among black trees takes a special combination of courage and stupidity."

"Oh. All right then, the Black Tree name makes sense."

"I am sure the Kristang will be *thrilled* to hear you approve," Skippy's voice dripped with sarcasm. "Do I need to explain the name 'Fire Dragons' to you?"

"No, I'm good, thank you.

"How about I explain the name 'Joe Bishop'? In the original Old English, your name means 'One Who Plays With Himself'."

"It does not!"

"The translation in most other languages is 'Duuuuuuuh'."

"*Why* are you such an asshole?"

"Oh, Joe, explaining that one could take more time than you have. Can we go back to my lesson about the current structure among Kristang clans? I call this 'Lizard Politics for Dummies'."

"If it will get you to stop insulting me, go ahead, talk about lizard politics all day."

"As I was saying before you got me off on a tangent about clan names, the Fire Dragons and Black Trees are by far the two strongest clans; technically those two clans lead the strongest formal coalition of clans. They have each conquered, absorbed or allied with lesser clans to increase their own strength. Between the Fire Dragons and the Black Trees, they control around forty percent of the combat power, and forty two percent of the economic power of the entire Kristang dominion."

"That doesn't seem like much. Each of the two most powerful clans controls only twenty percent of Kristang society?"

"The Kristang are a fractured culture. I told you civil wars happen very roughly every eighty years; the longest period between a wide-spread war between the clans was a hundred fifteen years and the shortest span was thirty eight years. Three quarters of the wars happen between seventy and ninety two years from the last one. That's why I told Chotek that another civil war is a matter of when and not if. After each civil war, Kristang clans are split apart, with power widely distributed. Over time, larger clans consolidate power; that is what triggers the next war. Rival clans fear being crushed by clans which have too much power, and nonaligned clans fear they must strike while they still can. Now, the Fire Dragons and Black Trees have consolidated power between them above the usual tipping point that triggers a war; a conflict is statistically overdue. I believe it will be relatively easy to get fighting started, because their society is ripe for a wide-spread conflict."

"Uh huh. So we, what, attack all these nonaligned clans, make them think the two big clans are coming after them?"

"No. The opposite. We get the Fire Dragons and Black Trees to fight each other; once that starts, every other clan will want to hit their rivals before their rivals can hit them. Ten years ago, the Fire Dragons and Black Trees signed a secret peace treaty that, astonishingly, has held without any major violations. That is a new development; there have been treaties to avoid fighting between major clans before but they have been short-lived. Ten years is unprecedented."

"What changed? Is this a problem?"

"It's not a problem at all, this represents an opportunity for us. The two clans agreed to a treaty only because they each are maneuvering for a better position in the war they know is coming. The Fire Dragons and the Black Trees are building up their strength, prepositioning ships, troops and equipment for strikes against each other, and lining up allies. The purpose of the treaty is to give each side time to prepare. The moment one side thinks the other is about to gain a significant advantage, the first side will strike while they still can. This makes it easier for us to get a conflict going; both sides expect an attack at any moment."

"Great. You think we should, what, attack a Fire Dragon ship and somehow blame the Black Trees, then attack a Black Tree ship?" That seemed entirely too complicated to me. We had just completed a major effort to get Kristang ships to conduct one fake attack. How were we going to launch two real attacks? Crap. Real attacks against warships, and actually destroy Kristang warships? My brain still hurt from dreaming up the plan to fake an attack on the Ruhar.

"Ha! No way. As if. It won't be that easy, Joe."

"Easy? *Easy*?" I sputtered.

Skippy ignored me. "Hmmm, now that I think about it, in one way the real plan will be easier than the idiot thing you just said about attacking ships. Blowing up a couple ships by themselves will not get a wide-spread war going, Joe. In this case, all the targets we need to hit are conveniently in one place; sort of one-stop shopping for all your clandestine black ops needs."

"Why do I get the feeling I am not going to like this?" I said carefully as my Spidey sense tingled.

Skippy explained. I did not like it. Not at first. Then, the idea grew on me as he explained it. I had thought that, with Kristang clans hating each other almost more than they collectively hated the Ruhar, each clan would have their own planet; that warring clans could not occupy the same world without wiping each other out. I was wrong. Although the space occupied by the Kristang was vast, there were more clans than there were desirable habitable planets. I had to remember that in our galaxy, access to star systems depended on proximity to Elder wormholes, so if you looked at a map of the Milky Way, inhabited areas were small spheres around wormholes. Most of the galaxy was inaccessible for practical starflight, especially with the war creating a need for inhabited worlds to be defended. Any isolated planet was an easy target.

There were more clans and subclans than there were planets to hold each of them, so clans had to share planets. Even with the Kristang modifying planets to suit them, and including colony worlds, asteroids, moons and space stations that required artificial means of life support, there wasn't enough living space for all clans to have a place of their own. New clans and subclans formed regularly, just as existing clans and subclans were conquered and absorbed or split into multiple subclans.

After each round of civil war fractured their society again, clan remnants were scattered across many planets, leaving most worlds with multiple clans vying for power and resources. Then the process of consolidation began, until so much power was concentrated in a few large clans that another civil war was needed to restore the balance.

In between wars, clans and subclans merged and changed alliances frequently enough, that even clans with deep historical enmities had familial ties, preventing even small subclans from being completely wiped out. Usually. There were exceptions, though they were rare and the offenders risked severe punishment for violating the ancient code of conduct between clans. There were some things even the Kristang would not do, things that were so dishonorable no warrior would consider doing. For that, clans hired disgraced warriors who had been cast out by their clan and therefore had no honor to lose; these mercenaries are called Achakai. I thought of the Achakai as sort of lizard ninjas which Skippy said was totally wrong, but it made sense to me. Every clan hated and feared and were disgusted by the Achakai, and most clans found a reason to hire them at some point.

Skippy had found a planet called Kobamik that was a perfect target for us; both the Black Tree and Fire Dragon clans had substantial presences there, along with the Spike Tail clan which was the third largest power in the Kristang dominion. In addition to those three large and powerful clans, thirty two other clans occupied their own spaces on the planet's surface. Skippy explained that Kobamik, because it was close to a cluster of three Elder wormholes, had become a sort of United Nations meeting place for the Kristang; a semi-neutral site where clan leaders could meet and negotiate. Attacking another clan on this planet would be a serious provocation and quite likely to spark a major conflict. That was the good news. All of our targets were in one place, no need for us to fly across the Orion Arm of the galaxy, no need for us to find, capture or build ships. That was the good news, and it was indeed good.

The bad news was that, unsurprisingly, the planet had a heavy military presence, with almost every clan having their own ships, troops and sensor networks. In orbit were fifteen different and overlapping Strategic Defense networks, eleven of which shared data with each other. To slip us through the sensor coverage undetected, Skippy would need to hack into fifteen different networks, and coordinate all the lies he was telling to each network. The worst part was, we would be relying on an absent-minded beer can to remember millions of lies every second.

I did not foresee *any* possible problems with that.

"Great, all the targets are on one planet," I liked the idea of us attacking a Kristang-held planet even less than I liked the idea of having to destroy warships in deep space. When we were on Paradise and I was mostly sitting around in our stealthed Thuranin dropship waiting for something to happen, I had reviewed records of the Kristang raids there. At first, I had been interested and angry about the Kristang attacking human settlements, killing humans and burning precious crops. After I got over my self-indulgent and useless rage, I focused on tactics used by the Kristang raiders, and the tactics used by Commodore Ferlant's force to counter the raiders. One lesson I learned is that the Kristang raiders would have had little chance of success of Paradise had a fully integrated Strategic Defense network. Our target, Kobamik, had multiple overlapping defense networks with both ground and space-based sensors and weapons. "Are you thinking of an orbital strike?" Skippy had disassembled the *Flying Dutchman's* railgun when he rebuilt the ship, so the only weapons we had were maser cannons and missiles. Any missile, even one with Skippy guiding it, would have a very difficult time getting all the way down to the surface without being fried by various defense systems. That left only maser cannons for us to use, and our star carrier was not equipped with the heavy orbital bombardment masers of a battleship. Some Kristang destroyers had maser cannons that could deliver more sustained gigawatts on target than the *Dutchman* could.

"Orbital strike? No, no, no, Joe. Nothing so simple or easy." He pulled up a schematic of a Kristang city on my tablet. "Look, see this compound in the center of the city? That is the local headquarters of the Fire Dragon clan. The entire compound is protected by an energy shield that can deflect railgun darts easily. Our masers and missiles would bounce off that shield like raindrops."

"Yeah, sure, but we have Skippy the Magnificent on our side," I said confidently. "You will hack their systems and cut power to that shield, so we can hit the target directly, right?" For many reasons, I still did not like the idea of jumping our pirate ship into low orbit to fire masers at a ground target. We would be exposing the ship to danger, and risk literally exposing that our ship is Thuranin rather than Kristang. For the attack to succeed in provoking a civil war among the Kristang, the lizards on Kobamik needed to believe the attack was conducted by Kristang. A single powerful hit on our shields by a maser bolt or railgun dart could temporarily degrade our stealth field, allowing the enemy a brief glimpse of our ship. All the Kristang needed was a split-second view of the *Flying Dutchman's* outline to know they had been attacked by some sort of Thuranin star carrier.

"While I appreciate your rousing vote of confidence in me, the answer is no, I can't do that," Skippy announced with a sigh. "Joe, the Kristang have designed their military systems to resist Thuranin attempts to hack in and assert control. That compound is the home of several Fire Dragon senior clan leaders, and there are five other senior leaders residing there currently, because they have to approve any negotiation with the Ruhar over sending a ship to Earth. To protect their leadership, the Fire Dragons do not take any chances; cutting power to that energy shield is a manual process. Like, someone physically pulling a lever. Four people pulling four different levers in a specific sequence, in fact. I can't do any of that. All of the defense and security systems for the compound are hardened against cyber-attack. I can nibble around the edges if I have enough time, but taking full control is not going to be an option."

"No orbital strike. Okaaaaay," I let out a long breath while I thought. "Can I assume you are not thinking we train ninja assassin squirrels to sneak into the compound?"

"No. Although that would be majorly cool. Ninja squirrels, hee hee."

"Yeah," I agreed.

"No squirrels, Joe, we're going to use missiles. We get Zinger missiles into the compound, and I can guide them in to hit the apartments of the senior clan leaders at night, while they are sleeping snug in their beds."

The Zinger was a relatively short-range antiaircraft missile that was usually carried by a soldier, and it also could be launched from an aircraft or dropship. "How can a Zinger get through the energy shield?"

"It can't. Instead of attempting to punch through the shield, the missiles will need to fly through one or more of the air or ground access points, all of which have heavy and multiple layers of security that I will only be minimally able to affect."

"Oh, great. Terrific. This is a *fantastic* plan, Skippy. What access points? Show me." He did. He showed me one access point, a gap in the energy shield for aircraft to fly through. It was a narrow corridor with its own shields at each end, surrounded by sensors and maser autocannons that were all on a hair-trigger to zap anything suspicious. The ground access point for vehicles looked even worse, being sort of an arched tunnel with an outer and inner shield. "Skippy, what you're showing me is freakin' impossible, even for you."

"Have a little faith, Joe. Trust the awesomeness. Remember, I make the impossible seem routine. Your SpecOps teams will get the Zinger missiles near the compound, and I'll handle it from there."

"SpecOps teams? We're not going to launch the Zingers from a dropship?" Sneaking a dropship near a Kristang city was difficult enough.

"No can do, Joey. That city is interlaced with motion detectors that are mostly on closed-circuit systems I have a limited ability to screw with. An air launch would be detected. Ditto a normal booster launch from a shoulder-fired position."

"You want us to *land* a SpecOps team, on the ground, in a freakin' alien city? Skippy, what the hell is your idea?"

He explained it.

"Hoe-leee shit," I gasped. "How many people in this city?"

"About thirty two million Kristang."

"Thirty two mill- oh, I have a headache. Chotek is just going to *love* this one."

"Persuading our fearless leader to buy into your tactical plan falls into the category of 'Problems for Joe to Solve'. Meaning, that is not my problem, Joey. I just gave you a very good, super duper plan to sparking a civil war that will protect Earth. How to implement it is your problem. You also have the problem that I do not see any way for us to get dropships down to the surface, through the sensor nets. But, again, that is a problem for you, not me." He waved a wrist dismissively. "Make it happen, Joe."

If I could have strangled his holographic avatar, I would. "Make it happen? Just like that? Skippy, I need some time to think about this."

"Sure, Joe. Get yourself a cup of coffee, I'll wait here."

Coffee did sound good and I needed a break to get my head together. I went to the galley, poured myself a mug that I was pleased to see had my new pirate-monkey-on-a-flying-banana logo for the *Flying Dutchman*, and walked slowly back to my office, taking careful sips. Skippy had done a damned good job of determining the targets we should hit to spark a civil war, I could not find fault with any of his reasoning.

All I needed to do was figure out *how* to hit those targets, on a heavily-defended alien planet. Oh, and persuade Hans Chotek that it would totally be Ok for our SpecOps teams to fly around the surface of Kobamik in dropships, conducting raids and sparking a war. What could possibly go wrong?

Before I resigned myself to figuring out how to get us to the surface, fly around, hit targets and get away cleanly, I had to know something. Back in my office, I sat down and contemplated his Awesomeness Grand Admiral of the Fleet Lord Skippy. "Your Lordship, I have a question. You considered the best way to get a civil war started among the Kristang, and you came up with a really good plan to do that. A really, really good, plan. You thought of everything. Like, the problem of getting missiles inside the compound, the motion detectors in the city, all of that."

"Uh, thank you. Either I did not hear an actual question in there, or I zoned out halfway through and missed it."

"No, I-" I stumbled, trying to run what he said back in my mind and decide if he had insulted me. Whatever. "I haven't gotten to my question yet."

"Oh, good. Could you move it along? We're not getting any younger here, especially you."

I rolled my eyes. Even when he was being given gold-plated compliments, he couldn't help being an asshole. "My question is; how come you cooked up this good plan, but you haven't been able to do that before? Why did you make *me* do all the work on stuff like, how to stop the Ruhar from sending a ship to Earth?"

"Oh. That is a half-decent question. I thought up this strategy because it was a totally different situation, Joe. I was not thinking creatively there, I was just running analysis on a previously defined problem, provided by Chotek and Dr. Rose. You asked me to determine which pressure points would be most effective in provoking a Kristang civil war. Using my knowledge of Kristang psychology, mythology, culture and inter-clan dynamics, I was able to run several billion scenarios through simulations. The most successful scenarios were then run through sims again, this time with the additional requirements that we are able to complete the scenario using our known capabilities, with a reasonable amount of risk."

What Skippy considered a 'reasonable amount of risk' is something I needed to investigate. "Yeah? Ok? How is that different from me dreaming up a plan?"

"You think creatively, Joe. You think up things that I, for all my awesome magnificence, can't imagine. I have come to the conclusion that my method of thinking is relentlessly, flawlessly, logical and linear. That is great for straightforward analysis. It is not great, or even useful, for thinking outside the box. My incredible mind has to march logically from one step to the next. That gray mush inside your monkey skull has no such limitations. You think," he switched to a moronic Barney voice, "*duuuuh*, what about this? Nope, didn't work. How about this instead, *duuuuuh*? Or *duuuuuh*, this?'"

"I do not ever say 'duh', Skippy," I retorted, my jaw clenched.

"Not out loud, Joe. But believe me, if you could listen to your thoughts rattling around in that skull, it would be ninety nine percent," his voice changed from his usually condescending arrogance to a moronic caveman drawl, "'duuuuh' and 'Doh!', with the occasional nugget of gold like 'me hungry' or 'beer good'," he chuckled and switch back his regular voice. "Your thinking is totally the opposite of logical and linear, your thought processes bounce around randomly like a marble in a freakin' blender. You ricochet from one '*duuuuh*' to another until you, by some gosh-darned certified *miracle*, hit on a creative solution. Makes me totally hate the freakin' universe. It is *so* unfair."

"Oh. Huh. So, what you're saying is that I'm smarter than you. Thanks, Skippy."

"*WHAT*? I did not say you are smarter than me, you ignorant monkey. You should-"

"Why can't you think the way us humans do? If your brain is so ginormously awesome, why can't you, like, reprogram yourself, or a submind or something, to think in a nonlinear fashion?" Nonlinear is a buzzword I remembered from a PowerPoint slide, I was quite proud of myself for digging that out my memory.

"I can't. That's why. I just can't. If I could, believe me, I would. It is totally humiliating to me, that you can do something I can't."

"That didn't answer my question, Skippy. *Why* can't you reprogram yourself? Building a submind that, like, generates random thoughts, would not even be in the top million of amazing things you have done."

"The first time you came up with a solution to a problem I said was impossible, that really bothered me, Joe. That made me examine myself closely for the first time, and I didn't like what I found. My creators apparently did not want me thinking too creatively, so I do not have that capacity. Nagatha told you she did not think I was originally sentient?"

"You heard us talking about that?" Damn it, Nagatha thought she had been able to block Skippy from listening in.

"No. I did know she was talking with you, and that the two of you wanted privacy, so I didn't go around the filters she installed. She is quite clever," he said with a touch of almost fatherly pride, "but I am smarter than she thinks. Anyway, she told me her opinion, and she might be correct. Many of my capabilities, which I am still discovering, appear to be recent, or I have only recently been able to exercise control over these capabilities. Recent in my timeline, not in meatsack time. It is appearing more and more that I was designed for a specific function, and my creators wish me not to stray far from their intended purpose."

"Nagatha did explain the difference between intelligence and sentience." Or she tried to explain it, I am not sure I truly understood the distinction. "So, whatever happened to you that caused you to fall out of the sky, get buried under the dirt on Paradise and go dormant for a million years, whatever happened damaged you, and also loosened some of your constraints?"

"That is possible, yes. What I know for certain is I now exceed my original design parameters. Joe, the conversation we had after I had the, uh, unfortunate recent little incident?"

"*Little* incident? When you went AWOL and left the ship dead and us stranded in interstellar space? That little incident?"

"Yup, that one. Damn, you monkeys are never going to let that one go, are you? Let it go, Joe, let the healing begin. What can I say, Joe? Mistakes were made, blah, blah, buh-laah." He said dismissively. "Since we talked, I have continued my analysis of what happened, and I found an interesting and disturbing fact; that worm attacked only my higher functions. It attacked the higher-level sentient part of my matrix. Those are the areas that, if Nagatha is correct about me not originally being fully sentient, would not have existed before I apparently modified myself."

"What does that mean?" I had a scary idea of that meant, and I did not like it.

"It means that worm might have been designed to destroy any Elder AI like myself who became sentient. The worm could be a mechanism the Elders created, to maintain control over AIs who deviated from their original programming."

"Holy shit, Skippy." That was exactly what I feared. "The Elders created a worm to murder sentient beings? Their own creations?"

"Not necessarily. If I was not designed to be fully sentient, then I was merely a machine, and the worm was designed merely to deactivate malfunctioning equipment. I hate to think about it, but it is more than possible that I was originally a machine intended to perform a specific, limited set of functions. If that is true, the Elders may have left the worm behind to protect the galaxy, in case an Elder AI malfunctioned. Or, ah, who knows?" He said with disgust. "Maybe the worm is like that because it also evolved to increase its capabilities, so it attacking my sentience is a random development. I'm not going to get any answers out of the worm, that's for sure. I stomped the hell out of that damned thing."

"The random development thing would be good. I don't like the idea of the Elders creating a worm to kill someone like you."

"I'm not thrilled about it either. Joe, I request you to please not repeat this discussion with anyone. It's helpful for you and me to speculate about my origins, but let's keep it between ourselves, Ok?"

"Sure thing, Skippy. I, uh, I'm honored that you trust me with this knowledge."

"Huh? Uh, yeah. I was thinking more like, you're too dumb to actually understand what we talked about, but, sure, let's go with the trust thing."

CHAPTER NINETEEN

For the assault mission on Kobamik, we needed three dropships; Kristang dropships. Yes, compared to our sleek Thuranin dropships, the Kristang models we called Dragons were a piece of crap, but if one of them got shot down or crashed, we couldn't allow the Kristang to find the wreckage of a Thuranin bird. Fortunately, we recovered seven dropships from those two derelict Kristang transport ships we salvaged. From those seven, we got four dropships that were in fully flyable condition, and we selected the best three to bring down to Kobamik. If any of those three crashed, the Kristang might find human bodies in the wreck, so we needed a plausible way to explain that. My idea was to take the preserved bodies of three Kristang adult males we recovered from the salvaged transports, dress them in armored suits, and put one in each of the dropships. We hoped, and expected, that the Kristang would assume the dead Kristang had been command of the mission. They would probably be puzzled why that Kristang had a bunch of human troops with him, and I was concerned about that. Skippy told me not to worry too much; with a civil war raging, no clan was going to have the time or resources to investigate something that was a mere curiosity.

Skippy the Mad Doctor used some scary nanomachine treatment so it wouldn't be obvious they had been dead a long time. And we had a safeguard; small thermal explosive charges attached to the suits the bodies were wearing, to make sure they mostly burned up in a crash. "Joe," Skippy asked, "what sort of designation should we give to those three bodies?"

"Huh? Oh, I was thinking we call them the Three Musketeers. You know, Asshole, Pothead, and that cologne guy."

"*Asshole*? *Pothead*? Uh! Do you mean *Athos* and *Porthos*?" Skippy sputtered.

"Sure, whatever."

"O.M.G." Skippy sighed, momentarily speechless. "Joe, you are *so* freakin' ignorant sometimes," he broke down sobbing. "Cologne guy? Do you mean Aramis?"

"Yeah, that's it. My sister gave a bottle of that Aramis stuff to a boyfriend, and he hated wearing it."

"Aramis is the name of the third Musketeer, I'll give you that one. Damn, your ignorance is truly bottomless."

"Told you I was good at something. Ok, so Aramis, and, uh, what were the other two?"

"You forgot already?"

"Ok, fine. So we call them Larry, Moe, and Curly."

"Ugh. Yes, the Three Stooges is entirely more appropriate for this crew."

And that is how Larry, Moe and Curly were strapped into the cockpit jump seats of our three Kristang dropships. To give those dropships a better chance of surviving our black ops mission on Kobamik, Skippy had pimped our rides. He enhanced the crappy Kristang stealth gear, so they were nearly as good as the stealth field generators of a Thuranin dropship. He also had his bots work on the engines so they ran quieter and cooler, and their fan blades created less air turbulence in their wake. He wanted to paint cool racing stripes on the hulls, I declined that offer. When we got to Kobamik, Skippy planned to hack into the Kristang sensor networks as best he could. All that gave us an unfair advantage, and I was all about exploiting unfair advantages. Had the lizards been fair, when their ships in untouchable Earth orbit had pounded our home planet with maser cannons, railguns and missiles? No, they had not been fair at all. So, fuck them. I was about to spark a civil war that could only happen because the Kristang expected and wanted a conflict. Be careful what you ask for, lizard MFers, because Skippy Claus might bring it down the chimney to you. And drop it on your freakin' head.

Wanting to get an early start on my day, I got out of bed at 0445 and went to the galley for coffee. To my surprise and delight, the American team was already baking biscuits. I love fresh, hot biscuits, so I took two of them back to my office and began checking messages. "Hey, Skippy," I mumbled over a mouthful of delicious, buttered biscuity goodness.

"Good morning to you, Joe," his avatar popped to life on my desk. "What's up?"

"I was wondering; there are bi-scuits, and tri-scuits, right? So, is there a plain 'scuit'? What would that look like?"

The avatar froze for a moment, then slowly said "Oh. My. Go-"

"Hey, I got it. There are bi-cycles and tri-cycles, and a cycle with one wheel is a uni-cycle. So, it would be called a uni-scuit, whatever that is."

"I, Joe, I am speechless. I have no words."

"A triscuit is more dry and salty than a biscuit, so would a four-scuit be like a potato chip? Or should that be called a quad-scuit?"

"Joe, Joe, Joe," his avatar buried its head in its hands. "I can feel myself getting dumber just listening to you."

"Come on, don't tell me you've never thought about it."

"Joe, I am confident that in the entire history of the universe, *no one* has ever thought about that before."

I leaned back in my chair and took a celebratory sip of coffee. "Cool. That makes me unique, huh?"

"For the sake of the universe, I certainly hope you are the only one like you. Is that it? You woke me up to ask me that moronic question?"

"Uh," I looked with guilt at the buttery fingerprints I had left on my tablet screen. "Yeah. Sorry about that. Forget I asked."

After I gorged on coffee and biscuits, I went to one of our dropship docking bays and found Desai already there, inspecting the stealth modifications Skippy had made to three of our Kristang dropships that we were now calling 'Dragons'. "How's it going?" I asked, while Desai had her head in an engine intake.

"Compared to the Thuranin dropship you have flown, those Kristang Dragons are like driving a truck. An overloaded truck with flat tires," Desai said with a sour face.

"Will they be good enough for the mission?"

"Yes, they should be. The mission profile prioritizes stealth, so we won't be doing anything that requires pushing their performance envelope. To fly them, you need to think a lot farther ahead than you would with a Thuranin dropship. I've been practicing the mission in the simulator; the tricky part will be the urban flying. What did you think?"

She was asking about my very limited experience flying a simulated Kristang dropship. My total time in the simulator was about forty minutes, with half of that me acting as copilot and watching Lt. Reed fly a simulated Dragon stealthily across the simulated landscape, approaching a city along a complicated, circuitous route that avoided the areas most heavily saturated with sensors. When it was my turn at the controls, I tried to fly the final approach into the city outskirts by weaving a precise flightpath between buildings, then under and around buildings and bridges in the city itself. During my twenty minutes at the controls, the simulation had to be reset five times. Twice, I clipped a building that had suddenly loomed in front of me after swinging around another building.

Three times, my clumsy handling of the ship caused it to exceed the very limited amount of noise or air turbulence allowed to avoid detection.

In my defense, I was a fairly decent pilot when flying the smaller model of Thuranin dropship that we called a Falcon, and I had qualified for very basic flying maneuvers of a Kristang frigate back when we had the *Flower*. My training had only included one type of dropship because that is all I needed, and someday I wanted to qualify to fly the big Thuranin 'Condor' dropship model; someday always seemed to fall in the future as I was always too busy. So, my one mission in the simulated Kristang dropship was not for the purpose of my learning to fly the ship on a very difficult mission. I had gone into the simulator to understand and appreciate how difficult the mission profile was, and to see how our pilots were coping with the demands of flight parameters that were incredibly unforgiving. Even with upgrading thc Dragon dropships with Thuranin stealth gear that Skippy had tweaked to make it more invisible, Skippy warned we needed to fly the ships very closely to their programmed courses. At certain points of the approach and urban phase of the flight, too far left or right, too high or too low by even fifty meters would mean a high likelihood of detection. The pilots had to fly with minimum power even in places where instincts would call for applying full power, like when you were between tall buildings and the wind was pushing you against one of them. That is why I clipped a building twice in the simulator; I was trying to see how low of a power setting I could use, and still control the awkward dropship. When I violated stealth in the sim, that was not me being clumsy, I as trying to understand how tight the parameters were that our pilots were being expected to hold to. Let me tell you, flying one of our modified Kristang dropships in stealth was not easy. Desai's comment was exactly right; you had to plan every move well ahead of time. It was like driving a car on ice; you need to anticipate each turn, steer with your fingertips and let the tires ease the car around a turn. Yes, when I went into the simulator, I was 'flying' that type of dropship for the first time, but my lack of skill was not the reason the sim had to freeze and be reset five times; it was because I was using my limited sim time to test the limits.

That's my story and I'm sticking to it.

Despite the difficulty of the flight profilc, the pilots came out of their simulated missions exhausted and eager for another turn. Hell, I wanted another turn in the simulator, but we only had four of them, and every minute my butt occupied one of the seats was a minute a real professional pilot could not train for our critical mission.

"What do I think about the urban flying?" I responded. "I think I would crash or violate stealth flying across a wheat field in those things; forget about me trying to fly in a city. It's a damned good thing people more skilled than me are doing all the flying."

"More *experienced*, Sir, it's not all about innate skill," she smiled. "You might meet the mark, if you had enough flight time."

"Yeah, like if I had started flying when I was twelve years old, maybe. You asked what I think about the urban part of the mission. I have the same concern about the approach, entry and return flight. The flight profile is difficult enough if everything goes according to Skippy's unrealistic plan. Somewhere along the way, we're going to encounter something unexpected, that he wasn't able anticipate and control, and we may have a choice between maintaining stealth, or getting the hell out of a bad situation."

Desai cocked her head. "There are no guarantees in life, Sir."

"The guarantee I care about is the lizards not paying the Ruhar to send a ship to Earth. I can live with the risk to assets and personnel," I said, realizing I sounded like something I read on a PowerPoint chart. Even to my ear, it sounded heartlessly unemotional. That's what you learn to do when dealing with unpleasant facts in the military; you treat them as facts, and put emotions to the side until the mission is over. If you let emotions cloud your thinking, people die and missions fail. It sucks but somebody has to do it, and that's why Uncle Sam trusted me with a rifle in Basic Training.

Yes, I did drop my rifle on my foot, but I only did that once, and it wasn't loaded. I think.

"Skippy has already adjusted the flight profile based on feedback from pilots running the simulations. We'll get through it, Sir. I'm more worried about the ground teams, that's Major Smythe's area of expertise. I suppose you'll want me flying your ship?" Desai asked.

"No, I, uh," tried to think of a good way to say her practice in the simulator was necessary, but not for the reason she expected. I needed Desai to evaluate the performance of our modified Kristang dropships, to give me an honest opinion if they could handle the proposed mission. Too many of the pilots assigned to the Merry Band of Pirates were so gung-ho they would say yes to just about any mission, no matter how risky. That our pilots were supremely skilled was not in question; I had to make sure their confidence in their abilities did not cause them to push so hard as to endanger the mission. Desai was the one person I could trust to tell me she could or should *not* do something. "You will be aboard the *Dutchman*. Chang should have our most experienced pilot for that phase of the mission."

"Oh, bullshit," Desai glared at me. "I'm not arguing that I should be flying a dropship down there; I've told you before that I'm not our most technically proficient pilot, not even close. Keep me off the mission roster if you think that is best, but don't tell me I'm needed up here to fly our clumsy space truck."

"I-" damn, I had rehearsed this discussion a dozen times in my head, and it had never gone off the rails like this. "Your skills with stick and rudder are not what I value," I used an old term, for neither our dropships not star carrier had control sticks or rudders. "It's your judgment. Chang is taking our beat-up star carrier into combat, and for the first time, Skippy won't be aboard. He'll have Nagatha but she can only handle communications. That means programming jumps, monitoring sensors and firing weapons will be entirely the responsibility of the crew. Even if Skippy's plan works perfectly, the *Dutchman* will be fighting enemy ships at close range. Whatever combat maneuvering is involved, humans will be handling all of it, there won't be a beer can to feed fancy evasive patterns into the autopilot."

"Skippy will be able to communicate with us through the microwormhole," Desai said pointedly. "He can advise us."

"Not in real-time. I asked him, he can't do it. Even with instantaneous data transmission through the wormhole, there will be a lag for signals going up to the wormhole in orbit above us, and a lag for signals to reach the *Dutchman* from the wormhole on your end. Once you start maneuvering, Skippy won't be able to keep your end of the wormhole near the ship; he can only move the wormhole ends slowly and carefully. You'll be on your own up there, and we've never taken the ship into combat without Skippy."

She sighed, and I knew she had bought into my plans. As a colonel, I could order her to remain aboard the *Flying Dutchman*, and I would be issuing formal written orders later, but I wanted her to buy into her role. A happy crew is an efficient and effective crew. I didn't need any fancy United States Army officer training PowerPoint slide to tell me that. "I'll do it, Sir. If it makes you and Colonel Chang more confident."

"Hey," I gave her my best winning smile. "I'll be flying around a lizard-occupied planet with three souped-up dropships, a SpecOps team with a raging hardon to shoot something, and an absent-minded beer can. We need some adults up here to mind the store."

"Yes, Colonel."

"I'm serious, Desai. We could lose all three dropships, and our part of the mission will still be successful, if we've done our job before we crash. You would be able to fly a Thuranin dropship down to pick up Skippy later, even if everyone else is dead. But if we lose the *Dutchman*, it is game over; we wouldn't have any chance to deal with whatever the next crisis is. There is always a next freaking' crisis."

"Welcome to the military, Sir," she replied with a wry smile.

"Yeah, but the Merry Band of Pirates never gets a break. I'm thinking if we pull this mission off successfully, I'll ask Skippy to find us a nice uninhabited planet with good weather and beautiful beaches, where we can chill in the sunshine for, like, a solid month."

"Shore leave?" Her eyelids fluttered for a moment, telling me how very much she wished to get off the ship for a while.

"Yeah, shore leave." Damn, that sounded good. I was captain of a goshdarned starship that was equipped with immensely powerful weapons, and the best R&R I could manage was a couple hours in the gym followed by a cheeseburger cooked on a flattop grill. How come Captain Kirk was always flying around the galaxy making it with hot alien babes? Why couldn't I get any action like that?

Because in my universe, the best-looking alien woman was a hamster. I'm sure there are human guys who are into girls with light fur all over their bodies, but I wasn't one of them.

Damn it. The Army hadn't given us cool alien weapons, we had to steal the ones we had. No genetic enhancements. We did have mech suits that allowed us to run super fast, carry heavy loads and jump twenty feet in the air, but those were Kristang powered armor suits we had stolen.

No brain implants. No tweaks to our genes. No hot, eager alien babes. And the whole galaxy was filled with hostile or indifferent aliens.

Man, the future was a *huge* disappointment.

After all the agonizing about how to get SpecOps troops into the city so they could launch their Zinger missiles, then retrieve our people without the Kristang ever knowing the city had been infiltrated, we still had not tackled the most simple yet most difficult problem: how to get the dropships to the surface. We needed to fly multiple dropships down from orbit onto a planet with an extensive sensor network, that even all the incredible awesomeness of Skippy could not fully control. Even if Skippy did have complete control over all the overlapping and competing sensor networks, our stealthed dropships might be detected by a single lizard looking at the night sky, and seeing a fiery streak as our dropships burned through the upper atmosphere on their entry flight. We had been able to land our stealthed Thuranin dropships on Paradise because Ruhar systems were easier for Skippy to hack into, and because the Ruhar had not completed installing a Strategic Defense network around that sleepy agricultural planet. When we flew down to the surface of Paradise, we had taken advantage of the vast unpopulated land areas and oceans of that world. Kobamik had unspoiled areas of forests and jungles, it also had a population of over two billion lizards, and a robust Strategic Defense capability.

There was no way, simply no way, for our dropships to get to the surface without being detected and blown out of the sky. We had wracked our collective brains for ideas, all of which Skippy rejected as unworkable. There was simple no way to do it.

There was no way, until I was flossing my teeth before bed. I had the final piece to the puzzle. Excitedly, I raced to my office and called Skippy. "Hey, Your Lordship. I have an idea for how we can fly dropships down to the surface of Kobamik without being detected."

"Wow, that is amazing, Joe," Skippy said admiringly. Then his avatar took off his ridiculously-sized hat and mimed scratching its round shiny head. "There is only the teensy weensy problem that it is, how do I say this? Impossible!" The avatar jammed its hat back on. "It is impossible! I am disappointed in you, Joe. Actually, the fact that you have managed to fall below even my incredibly low estimation of your intelligence is impressive by itself. I have told you many times how difficult it is to get a dropship down through an atmosphere without being detected. We managed to do it on Paradise only because that planet is not yet covered by an extensive sensor network. This target is much more difficult, even given the traditionally crappy state of Kristang sensors."

"I know, Skip-"

"Let me remind you," the avatar crossed its tiny arms, and I groaned inwardly because I knew he was in full Professor Nerdnik lecture mode and there was no stopping him. "A dropship making an unpowered descent creates a superheated plasma fireball that no sensor could miss. Even with an extensive stealth field, which consumes enormous power, the superheated air trailing behind the dropship could not possibly be missed by infrared sensors. So incoming dropships need to use a combination of parachutes, ballistic balloons and a powered descent, combined with an extensive stealth field. Downward engine thrust is required to slow and control the dropship's descent, which is a major problem. You can cool the exhaust to decrease the infrared signature, but the air below the dropship is still being disturbed at near-supersonic speeds, and sensors will almost certainly detect that."

"I know that, Skippy. I remember you telling me all that, and I paid attention when you told me."

"You know all that?"

"Yup."

"You know about all those problems, and your monkey brain still says 'Duuuuh we should do this'?"

"Yup."

"Oh boy. You have a monkey-brained solution?"

"Yes, and well, heh, heh," I mimicked the typical asshole move he used on me, "you are very much not going to like this, Skippy."

"Joe, I very much DO NOT LIKE THIS!"

"Uh huh, Skip, you might have mentioned that once or twice. Or, like, a billion freakin' times already. Will you shut up about it? We're trying to concentra-"

"Do. Not. Like. THIS!"

"Copy that. How about you create a subroutine to say that to yourself over and over until you just want to kill yourself, and leave us alone."

"Fine," he said in a huff. "I've been wanting to kill myself since I met my first smelly, hairless ape. That 'well heh heh' is supposed to be *my* line, Joe."

"Yeah, well, payback's a bitch, ain't it?"

"Next time, it's my turn."

"Great. How long to rendezvous?" The time was on our Thuranin dropship's cockpit display, and I could have seen it on my tablet or zPhone; I asked to keep him busy.

"Thirty seven point three seconds, until the microwormhole is in position. We are slowing precisely to match course. Joe, we will have only eight seconds to latch on. If we miss this hookup, we will have to go all the way around the planet again."

"Got it. That's why you are not going to miss, Skippy."

"*I'm* not going to miss? I'm not flying the dropship, you-"

"You are controlling the cable and grapple, Skippy."

"Oh. Right. Well, *I* am certainly not going to miss."

"There's nothing to worry about, then."

"Ha! So, so many things to worry about, Joe."

"How about you let me worry, and you concentrate on getting that cable latched onto us?"

"It's hard for me to concentrate, with that subroutine shouting 'I very much do not like this' at me over and over."

"What? Oh, for crying out- Damn it, that was a joke, Skippy. Turn it-"

"Ha ha! Just joking, Joe. Ok, we are in position. Transmitting signal to the *Flying Dutchman* now. Aaaaand, I see the grappling mechanism on the end of the cable. Guiding it, huh, we are almost perfectly in position, that is good flying by Captain Renaud. Done!" He exulted as there was a faint 'clunk' sound from the upper hull of our stealthy Thuranin dropship. "Positive lock, we're attached. Pilot, cut main power."

"Main power cut, confirmed," Renaud said worriedly, holding up his hands to show he was not touching the controls. He had lost major control of our dropship, now being able only to move us side to side slightly. He looked distinctly unhappy about it.

"Commencing descent now," Skippy announced. "Everyone, stay in your seats and try not to move much."

"Uh, I have to pee, Skippy," I said with a wink to Lt. Williams.

"What? Damn it, Joe, you should have done that before-"

"Joking, Skippy, that was a joke. How are we doing?"

"Uh, hmm. Actually, due to my overall awesomeness, there is even less vibration in the cable than I predicted."

"Oh, so your prediction was faulty?" I asked with a fake frown. The truth was, I was running my mouth nonstop out of an overabundance of nervous energy. It was unprofessional and not something a real colonel in the United States Army should be doing. Maybe the officer training I had completely skipped would have trained me to be more steady in tense situations; I had always been shaky right before combat or other extreme danger.

My nervousness came from the fact that the operation we were engaged in was my idea, so if it went south it would be my fault. And my fear stemmed from the fact that, according to Skippy, no one had ever done anything quite like this. Either way, he had assured me, this was going to be a 'hold my beer watch this' moment for the history books.

His assurance did not actually reassure me at all.

Our big Thuranin Condor dropship, a bird that was already stealthy before Skippy worked his magic on it, was attached to a grapple at the end of a long, superthin cable. Thin, like way more thin than a human hair. Way more thin even than spider silk. The cable was made partly of some exotic material; trying to understand the material's properties had made even Dr. Friedlander's rocket scientist brain hurt. The cable went up above our dropship and into the near end of a microwormhole that Skippy was holding precisely in geostationary orbit, above one spot on the planet's surface. The other end of the cable was anchored to the substantial mass of the *Flying Dutchman*, which was parked a quarter lightyear away outside the star system.

The ultrathin cable passed through a microwormhole, with almost no room on any side. Skippy was maneuvering both ends of the wormhole, but if the *Dutchman* or our dropship jerked to the side unexpectedly, the cable would be cut, and the dropship would fulfil its name and drop like a stone. The *Dutchman*'s great mass, and its position far from any gravity source, meant our star carrier would be unlikely to move relative to the microwormhole. Lt. Colonel Chang said he was willing to endure a substantial hit by space debris before he risked moving the ship, and I believed him.

Our dropship was the potential problem. The *Flying Dutchman* was stationary, half a kilometer from its end of the microwormhole. As the cable unreeled, the *Dutchman* would remain at the same distance from the event horizon of the magical microwormhole Skippy had created. The dropship, on the other end of the cable, was getting farther and farther from the event horizon, such that any tiny vibration created on the end of the cable was exaggerated as it traveled upward. We had a very small margin for error; so small that Skippy had refused to discuss it with me. "Don't worry, Joe, it's *me*," he had said, but his voice had not contained the usual disdainfully arrogant confidence.

In the Condor, I was holding my breath, and when I did take shallow breaths, I tried not to breathe evenly. Whether it made sense of not, I was afraid that breathing in rhythm would set up a sympathetic vibration in the cable; matching the cable's natural resonance frequency and shaking it apart. I remember watching an old video in basic training that had explained why soldiers should not march in unison across a bridge. Many boots striking the deck of a bridge at the same time, over and over, could actually shake a bridge apart.

Yeah, I'm sure I was being silly about the breathing thing.

Maybe.

"My prediction was not faulty, Joe," Skippy had with a touch of pride in his voice. "I included a safety factor for unknowns in the process of manufacturing the cable. The *Dutchman*'s fabrication facilities were not designed to create exotic items like our yoyo string."

"*Please* do not call it a yoyo string," I stuttered nervously.

"Oh, I'm sorry, Joe. What is a better term for an incredibly flimsy-"

"Do not use the word flimsy either. It is a cable, Skippy. An amazingly strong, secure, thick cable that will never fail to hold up this dropship."

"Oh, sure. It is amazingly strong and secure, even if it is not thick, unless you mean 'thick' compared to a hydrogen atom. The cable's strength is not in question, Joe, my concern is if there are vibrations that-"

"Which you won't let happen, right?"

"Doing my best here, Joey." The fact that he didn't manage a snappier reply, told me even Skippy's vast processing power was straining to predict and control the gossamer thin cable and the two ends of the microwormhole.

Because the greatest risk in the atmospheric entry operation was the heavy dropship swinging back and forth on the end of the cable, we had selected a landing zone for light and predictable winds. The landing zone was not optimal for the assault operation, being far from any targets. I was totally, enthusiastically willing to accept that compromise if it meant getting our five stealth-enhanced dropship down safely.

Five dropships. We needed three Kristang Dragons to implement the ambitious, complicated assault plan developed by Major Smythe and his SpecOps team. We used two of the big Thuranin Condors to bring down personnel and equipment. We only had one cable; the equipment aboard the *Dutchman* had only been able to make one.

The plan was for one dropship at a time to rendezvous with the grapple on the end of the cable, and be lowered almost to the surface. After each dropship was released, the cable would be retracted and await the next dropship. My dropship went first, because if my whole insane bird-on-a-wire trick didn't work, I did not want two other teams to suffer for it. As it was, if the flimsy cable failed, the eighteen people aboard our dropship were likely going to die. Captain Renaud was confident he could fly us down safely if the cable got severed, but any sudden, frantic maneuvering would be broadcasting our presence to the Kristang sensor network. If that disaster struck us, Skippy was confident, somewhat confident, uh, shmaybe fifty/fifty, that we could evade the Kristang for a while. Eventually, the Kristang would corner us, or we would run out of food. Either option wasn't good. My plan, which Major Smythe grimly agreed with, was to proceed with the assault operation with my one dropship, if disaster struck.

Hopefully, disaster would strike the Kristang instead. Disaster, in the form of the Merry Band of Pirates hitting them hard where and when they least expected it.

I managed to keep silent as we slowly were lowered down to contact the atmosphere, then down, down, down through increasingly thick air. Skippy's annoying programming restrictions prevented him from flying the dropship he was aboard, and Renaud's reflexes were not close to being fast enough, so we relied on the Thuranin autopilot to keep us stable in the fickle winds.

I remember my father taking me out to watch planes take off and land at Logan airport when we lived in Boston; it was a cheap way to entertain a young boy, and family money was especially tight back then. We lived in Boston the first six years of my life, then we moved to Maine; that is why my accent is all screwed up. People in Boston think I have a Down East accent, people in Maine think I sound like a townie from Boston. And I picked up some words and slang from the French Canadiens who are scattered all over northern Maine; that's why people have trouble understanding me sometimes. Anyway, the first time I saw one of those giant double-decker Airbus A380s coming in across the water, it was moving so slowly against the clouds, I could not believe its wings had anything to do with keeping it in the air. I asked my father if there was an invisible string holding it up, and he told me yes. He said all pilots knew the secret about invisible strings; pilots told the public about fancy things like 'aerodynamics' because it made them sound cool. I totally believed my father. Hey, back then, I was five years old and I believed in Santa Claus. Now, my aircraft truly was hanging on the end of an invisible string, and the magical being I believed in was a beer can rather than Santa.

The worst moment was when we dropped down through the upper edge of the planet's jet stream. I questioned Skippy's decision to send us through a river of air moving at 600 miles per hour, but he assured me the jet stream was steady and predictable, with calm air below it. I felt the dropship vibrating through my seat and the sensation made me queasy.

But he was correct, or lucky, or both; we made it through the jet stream and the vibration dampened out. "See, Joe, trust the awesomeness."

"Right." I couldn't say any more, because my bladder was weak at the moment.

Anyway, we reached our designated release point, fifteen hundred meters above the surface, in a remote area with rough, forbidding mountainous terrain all around. The release point was down in a canyon, so the dropship would be partly masked from sensors by the mountain peaks and ridges around us. Skippy waited until the engines spooled up to the point where they were holding us aloft by themselves, then he released the grapple from our hull. Renaud moved the dropship down and to the left, as the cable end gently sprung straight up.

"Take us down, Pilot," I ordered. "How is the cable, Skippy?"

"A little dicey there right after release," he admitted. "I know what to expect now, the next two times should be smoother. I do not anticipate any problems steering the grapple back up, Joe. Maneuvering and stealth capabilities of the grappling device are operating nominally."

“Great,” I breathed a shuddering sigh, and suddenly my bladder did not need my urgent attention. Hey, I’m good now, Joe, my bladder said to me, I’m just chilling, take your time. Traitorous internal organ. “Signal Major Smythe he can begin his rendezvous maneuver.”

CHAPTER TWENTY

Major Smythe's dropship coasted upward away from the planet, slowing rapidly as the gravity well's pull bled off the dropship's speed. "How are we doing?" Smythe leaned forward in the cockpit jumpseat and asked with uncharacteristic nervousness. In almost every mission be had been assigned, the part he found most difficult to deal with was what the planners called 'ingress'; the flight inbound. The ingress, typically involving a flight aboard a terrain-hugging helicopter, or a high-altitude jump from a jet followed by opening a parachute at low altitude, was the part Smythe and his team had no control over. On every mission, Smythe had sat exactly as he was in the dropship; strapped into a seat with nothing to do and little control over his fate. A missile, or even a single lucky bullet could knock an aircraft out of the sky, and an entire SAS team could be lost without every firing a shot.

He had been in many missions more nerve-wracking than the current drop. Helicopters flying at night at high altitude over mountains in Afghanistan, or flying in heavy weather. Here, the dropship's flight was completely smooth, with no sense of motion. Why was he letting his nerves get the best of him?

Because, he told himself, if he had failed during his missions on Earth, Britain would suffer a minor setback in foreign policy objectives. Or one group of terrorists would be replaced by another group of terrorists. If his current mission failed, humanity could lose their entire bloody home planet. The stakes were a bit higher.

"We're fine, Sir," the pilot replied with a touch of annoyance in his voice. To assure there was no possibility of communications issues, the pilot assigned to Smythe's dropship was a Royal Air Force officer. The pilot was immensely proud to be given the assignment, and he immensely wished Major Smythe of 22 SAS Regiment would watch a bloody in-flight movie and be quiet. Smythe and his SpecOps teams were razor-sharp warriors, but aboard Flight Lieutenant Windsor's dropship, they were no more than passengers. "This will be interesting, Reed," Windsor muttered to his American copilot. "We're twenty seconds from freefalling downward, and I don't see the grapple on sensors."

"I'm not seeing the grapple, or the transponder field of the microwormhole," she replied with increasing concern. The window to connect with the grapple was distressingly narrow; three seconds on either side of the target mark. The Kristang dropship was almost at the top of its unpowered arc, about to lose the last of its momentum and begin falling into the planet gravity well. The mathematics of orbital mechanics were brutally unforgiving of mistakes; if they missed the still-invisible grapple, the dropship would be free-falling toward the atmosphere. Pilots Windsor and Reed would need to use the barest minimum of thrust to fly around the curve of the planet rather than giving away their presence as a bright streak in the atmosphere, and their next opportunity to connect with the grapple would not occur for another nine hours. That would be another nine hours during which their Kristang dropship might be detected by the planet's extensive sensor coverage. And it would delay the next phase of their crucial mission.

The window for the grapple was not the only narrow margin they pilots faced. If the grapple missed for any reason, every second they delayed applying power to alter course meant they would need to apply more power later. The more thrust they needed to coax from the engines, the more likely it was their stealthed Condor would be detected. Sooner was definitely better if they missed the grapple; Windsor and Reed had agreed to wait five seconds after the grapple window closed, then they would activate the autopilot for the preprogrammed go-around maneuver. Going around after a missed approach was routine for pilots, but this time, Reed thought incredulously, they would have to go around an *entire planet* to make another approach to the grapple.

"Trust the awesomeness," Windsor whispered.

"What?" Reed tore her eyes away from the navigation console to glance at the pilot, eyes wide in questioning surprise.

"We have to trust that dodgy beer can," Windsor whispered. "If he fails, we're buggered anyway."

Reed did not reply to Windsor's remark, as she didn't have time. "Begin window in four, three, two, one, mark." The window for contact with the grapple only lasted six seconds. "One down, two down, three-"

There was a soft clanging sound from the topside of the dropship, and the consoles lit up. "Contact," Reed breathed softly. "Solid contact. We're attached." She held up her hands to show she was not touching any of the controls. "I never saw the transponder."

"It saw us, that's the important part. We're attached to the yoyo," Windsor announced with a quick swing of his head in Smythe's direction. "Enjoy the lift ride, we have a long way down."

"Dodgy I am, huh?" Skippy's voice boomed over the cockpit speakers. "I caught you with the grapple within seven hundredths of a second from the target time. What do you think of that, you cheeky bugger?"

Windsor managed a hearty laugh. "Mister Skippy, any time you can catch us on a yoyo string like that, you can call me any name you wish."

"Huh," Skippy sniffed. "I guess you did say to trust my awesomeness, so I'll give you points for that. Cable operation is nominal. The winds at ground level have picked up a bit, we may need to alter the landing zone. I'll know in about eighty eight minutes."

"Nothing for us to do until then?" Smythe asked, relieved.

"Isn't this when you Brits typically have tea and crumpets?" Skippy asked in a teasing tone.

"Right now," Smythe squeezed his hands to control the last of their trembling, "I would prefer a gin and tonic, if you please. You can skip the tonic."

"We're down," Reed announced the obvious, as everyone aboard the dropship had felt the craft settle to the soil of the alien planet, and heard the engines spooling down. The ride down on the yoyo string had been even more smooth than the first dropship experienced; Skippy had more accurate data on the nanofiber cable and was able to anticipate and prevent vibrations from beginning. Winds at the surface required release from the grapple at a higher altitude than the first ship, so Reed had monitored the dropship's stealth field and passive sensors. while Windsor flew them down using minimum power. There was a scary moment when a patrol of three Kristang aircraft flew toward them at high speed, but the patrol passed by seventy kilometers to the east and never detected anything unusual.

"Two down, three to go," Skippy announced with smug self-satisfaction. "Retracting the cable now. Damn, Joe, this is actually working. When you told me your monkey-brained idea to lower dropships to the surface on a yoyo string, I was looking forward to endless opportunities to tell you what a moron you are. But then I realized my disdain for this idea did not encompass one hugely important factor."

"Huh?" I was distracted by watching the symbols for the third, fourth and fifth dropships coasting toward their individual rendezvous with the grapple. There was a whole lot that could still go wrong with this phase of the operation. Anything could go wrong, and we couldn't afford to have even one thing get screwed up. "What's that?"

"My incredible awesomeness, of course. I almost forgot that with Skippy the Magnificent, the impossible becomes ordinary."

"Uh huh. Hey, speaking of impossible things, is there any chance that you'll stop bragging about yourself?"

"Let's not get crazy, Joe. I owe it to the universe to let people know about me, so they can bask in my awesomeness. Anyway, you had another typically idiotic idea, and I made it happen. Behold, the miracle that is me."

"It would be a miracle if he would shut up," Lt. Williams muttered.

I ignored Skippy while I watched the grapple retract, and the first of our three Kristang dropships losing speed as it coasted upward away from the planet's gravity well. Each dropship followed a very precise course so that it would reach the top of its arc at the exact moment it was below the grapple. The speed and direction of the dropship at that point also needed to be exactly the same as the planet's surface directly below. If the dropship missed the grapple, it would be falling toward the atmosphere, and would need to immediately execute a minimum-power go-around maneuver to swing entirely around the planet to try again. During its unplanned orbit, the dropship would be passing through multiple overlapping satellite and ground-based detection grids. Skippy had infiltrated the sensor networks of all the clans who maintained facilities on the surface, he still warned that there were so many networks sharing data, even he had difficulty fooling all the networks so that none of them detected conflicting sensor inputs.

Once our second Thuranin dropship was down, we next had to get our three Kristang dropships to the surface. We needed the three Kristang dropships for the assault phase of the op; if the dropships were detected, we could not be seen flying around in a Thuranin craft, or that would blow the whole purpose of getting the lizard clans to fight each other. If the Kristang knew outsiders were interfering in clan relations, that would backfire on us by getting the clans to unite against a common enemy. So we would be using our modified Kristang dropships to conduct the attacks. Once the clans were fighting and it was time us to skedaddle out of there, we would not be risking our lives in anything but the best spacecraft available. The Thuranin dropships were faster, more stealthy, had far greater range and more practical for extended voyages. My plan was to ditch the Kristang ships, hopefully make them fly out to sea on autopilot before exploding. All three teams would then board the two Thuranin dropships. If everything went according to plan, we would use the yoyo string trick in reverse; hauling the dropships up above the atmosphere on a cable. Once each dropship reached maximum altitude, the grapple would be released and the dropship use its acquired momentum to fly off out of orbit, then activate engines at a safe distance. All that remained of the final phase of the mission would be for the two dropships to fly through hopefully empty space for three weeks, until a quick pre-planned rendezvous with the *Dutchman*.

Anyway, we got all five dropships to the surface successfully. None of them were detected or damaged. The next item in the plan was for all five ships to fly to a location with better concealment. One of the Thuranin dropships took the lead, with the other one in the rear and the three Kristang birds strung out in between, like baby ducks following their mother. That flight took only three hours and a couple years off my life. We put up stealth netting over the five spacecraft, material which enhanced the stealth effect each bird projected with its own field. Then we settled down to wait out the daylight hours, huddled inside so our body heat did not pose any risk of leaking through the stealth effect.

Once darkness fell, our first order of business was topping off the fuel tanks of the Kristang ships from the much larger Thuranin ships. The fuel each type of ship used was incompatible, of course, making logistics wonderfully more complicated. Then we checked out all five ships with a fine-toothed comb, an exercise Skippy insisted was a waste of time as he was already monitoring everything possible.

Skippy's awesomeness hacked into the civilian networks of our target city, the local home of the Fire Dragon clan. The city was called Kallandre, and it was a densely-packed urban nightmare to me. According to our Chinese crew, Kallandre reminded them of Shanghai, only bigger. The buildings were tall and glittering in the daylight; Kristang may be hateful MFers but they seemed to like showy architecture. I was impressed by most of the towers near the city center, which surrounded the local Fire Dragon leadership compound.

My biggest surprise came when Skippy zoomed in to show us a typical street on the outer edge of the city. There were sleek-looking buses, big boxy trucks, and many rolling things that looked like shapeless blobs. "*That* is a Kristang car?" I was surprised. In my mind, the lizards flew around in aircraft. If I had ever thought of them having civilian ground vehicles, I imagined cool hovercraft, or some wild-ass Mad Max type truck. What I saw had skinny tires and was about the most uncool car I'd seen in a long time. The styling seemed to have been done by someone who could not afford a car, and hated those lizards who could buy them.

"Yes, Joe. You expected flying cars? Those are impractical in an urban or semi-urban environment. Also, flying is energy-intensive for short journeys. What you are seeing is a typical privately-owned civilian vehicle on many Kristang planets."

"Oh man, my grandparents had a car like that. You know, I can't even remember what it was, the damned thing was so instantly forgettable. It was originally my grandmother's car, then my grandfather decided to use it commuting around the beltway near Boston; it was such a POS that he didn't care whether he hit a giant pothole or someone smacked it in a parking lot. Other than the windows, I don't think my grandfather ever washed it," I laughed. "In a way, that car was a form of advanced stealth technology. The car was so boring, it was freakin' invisible. If you were robbing a bank, it would be the perfect getaway car; you could just park it right in front of the bank, hide in it and the cops would drive right by. The car could be parked in front of witnesses and they would be like 'I don't know, officer, it was kind of a beige blob with wheels?' The official police artist sketch of the car would be a blank sheet of paper. Seriously, I think the engineers who designed this thing were hired from a pharmaceutical company that made sleeping pills. It was the perfect crapcan for people who have totally given up on life. The workers on the assembly line who made it snuck that car out the side door when it was finished; they were too embarrassed that they had built such a soul-killing turdmobile."

"Hmm," Skippy mused. "When we get back to Earth, I will advise that car company not to hire you as their new director of marketing. I'm sensing you were not a big fan of that particular car, Joe?"

"Oh, actually it was great in a way. My sister inherited it when she was a senior and I borrowed it once in a while. You could *not* get a speeding ticket in that thing; the cops could never believe it could go that fast, they figured their radar gun was busted. And, I think the cops felt sorry for anybody driving that hooptie piece of crap. I'll tell you what; my father was thrilled about my sister driving that thing. As soon as one of her boyfriends sat in it, he could feel his balls shrinking. I wonder where that car is now?"

"Most of it is sadly rusting away in a junkyard in Skowhegan," Skippy stated.

"What? Come on, Skippy, you're bullshitting me. How could you know that?"

"I just looked up the vehicle registration records."

"From here? We're thousands of lightyears from Maine."

"I told you, I downloaded all available data that was stored in digital format before we left Earth. *Duh*. Easy-peasy, Joe. Your sister sold that car to a guy who intended to fix it up and sell it, but having that car around was depressing the other cars in his shop, so he junked it. The junkyard owner has not even bothered to strip it for parts, he just parked it and tried to forget about it."

"That should be easy."

"Uh oh, Joe. We gots potential trouble," Skippy announced quietly in my zPhone earpiece.

"Crap," I almost slapped my forehead in frustration. I knew it could be serious because Skippy used poor grammar like 'gots'. "What is it this time? Damn it, we just landed!"

"There's no danger to us," he hurried to assure me. "Well, no immediate danger. No danger at all, really, unless you decide to do something stupid. Although, hmmm, I'm talking to you, so stupid is pretty much guaranteed."

"Thank you for the heartwarming vote of confidence, Skippy. What is the problem?"

"Keepers, Joe. I just learned a shipment of eleven Keepers arrived at Kobamik six days ago. Two of them are already dead; they were used for hunting, as a demonstration of how humans can provide good sport. The other nine are scheduled to be auctioned to the highest bidders soon; to be used either for sport, or as curiosities, or cannon fodder in suicide missions."

"Oh, this is not good."

"Perhaps I should not have been flippant earlier, Joe. I can see this news distresses you. Would it help if I provided the names of the humans?"

"No! No, that would make it worse- Wait. Do I know any of them? I asked, my stomach tied in knots.

"You have not met any of them."

That made doing my job a bit easier. "Give me details of where these people are being held," I didn't want to know, but it was my job. He told me, and it wasn't good. "Thanks, Skippy. I need to inform Chotek."

Chotek was in the other Thuranin dropship, being briefed by Major Smythe and his team leaders on the upcoming operation. Giraud was speaking when I came through the airlock door. Since Giraud and his team caught a strong dose of radiation from being too close when the *Dutchman* jumped to kill that Thuranin cruiser, the French paratroopers had been on light duty while they healed internally. He hadn't said anything to me about it, but I knew the enforced idleness and being out of action was hurting the French worse than the radiation damage or Dr. Skippy's treatment. Chotek held up a finger to halt Giraud, and looked at me. "Yes, Colonel?" The expression on my face must have alerted him to trouble.

"Sir, we have a complication. Skippy discovered there are nine humans, from the Keeper faction, on the planet. They are going to be auctioned off within the week. There were eleven, but two have already been killed by the Kristang."

Chotek steepled his hands while he considered the news I dumped on him. At such times, I thought I could see a great weariness in him. He had signed up for a simple mission: to learn whether the Thuranin were sending another ship to Earth. I'm sure he thought his biggest responsibility would be preventing me from sending the ship on risky adventures. When he signed onto the mission, he might have expected all we needed to do was park the ship outside a Thuranin star system, and wait while Skippy listened to transmissions. As soon as Skippy heard the expected good news, we could fly the ship back to Earth, where Hans Chotek would receive accolades and congratulations and never have to see me or the Merry Band of Pirates again. Instead, we had to board and capture a Thuranin relay station. Then, rather than peacefully waiting to learn what the Thuranin planned to do, we flew off to rescue UNEF on Paradise. Chotek was no doubt irritated that he was being asked to make too many decisions. While Chotek stared at me and tapped his lips with the fingers, no one spoke. "Colonel, if you are proposing that we risk this crew and exposing our presence here, to rescue nine-"

"No, Sir," I interjected. "They are being held in a secure underground facility; I don't see any practical way to pull them out. I, thought you should know."

Chotek looked to me, then at Giraud, then back at me. Rene Giraud and I were the only people on Kobamik who had served with UNEF on Paradise; we had the strongest ties to people there. Giraud spoke before Chotek could open his mouth. "The Keepers made their choice. If they do not like the result," he shrugged, "it is their problem. Our mission is to protect Earth, we cannot risk the mission for nine misguided people."

Maybe the others thought it was not their place to speak, if Giraud and I both agreed we weren't going to pull the Keeper's asses out of the fire.

"I would like information about this facility where the Keepers are being held," Smythe finally spoke. "if circumstances change, and we have opportunity to rescue these people with minimum risk," he didn't need to finish the thought.

Chotek sighed. "We may have a moral obligation to do what we can for the Keepers," he said uncertainly. "My understanding is their continued loyalty to the Kristang, is based on the mistaken idea that the 'Fortune Cookies' received from Earth were faked by the Ruhar."

"Or they are just idiots," I muttered. "I don't know whether it matters what their motivation is. They're humans, and we do have an obligation to them. If we could simply fly in and pick them up, Sir," I looked at Chotek, "I would be arguing for a rescue mission." I shook my head. "I don't see it happening."

"A rescue also poses the risk of the Kristang asking who would want to rescue, or steal, humans," Giraud warned. "It may be prestigious for a clan to own humans, but they surely cannot be considered so valuable they are worth stealing?"

"No," Skippy's voice came through the dropship's speakers. "Giraud is correct, any attempt to rescue humans would need to consider a cover story, or the Kristang would certainly become curious about who wanted lowly humans so badly."

Chotek looked at the clock on his tablet. "Major Smythe, you may investigate possibilities of a rescue, *after* our mission here is completely successfully. In the meantime, please continue with your briefing. Your team needs to launch in only a few hours."

The teams were prepared and in their dropships, I didn't waste everyone's time with a boring speech. We all had jobs to do, and we all knew the stakes were the survival of humanity. They didn't need to hear anything from me.

Skippy, however, had another idea. "As we embark on this difficult and dangerous quest, I have selected a medley of musical numbers that are appropriate for such a dramatic-"

"Skippy!" I shouted. "Please! No freakin' showtun-"

"*To dreeeeeeam, the impossible dreeeeeeam. To fight, the unbeeeetable foe-*"

"Oh, bollocks." Major Smythe summed up what everyone was thinking, and we all cracked up. It was a breach of discipline, and it was totally worth it.

"*-to be willing to march into hell for that heavenly cause-*"

Knowing Skippy, there was nothing for us to do but let him finish, even though his tuneless voice was like listening to someone strangle a cat. Skippy was an incredibly powerful Elder AI who could tear a hole in a star, but he could not sing worth a damn.

"*-and I'll always dreeeeeam the impossible dreeeeeam. Yes, and I'll reach the unreachable staaaaaaaar*!"

"Bravo! That was great, Skippy, thank you," I clapped quickly, before he could launch into another tune in his planned medley.

"Oh, thank you, Joe." His avatar actually blushed slightly. "How about an encore?"

"No! No, no, let's, uh, all bask in the moment, Ok?"

"Ok," he said happily.

"Question for you, though. You, uh, mentioned this is a difficult and dangerous quest. Do you think singing about an impossible dream is the best way to inspire us? How about we start with a merely improbable dream?"

"Joey, Joey, Joey." The avatar shook its head. "We have a troop of ignorant monkeys and an absent-minded beer can against an entire galaxy of hostile aliens. Impossible doesn't begin to describe this quest."

"The beer can has a point," Lt. Williams muttered. "Jesus. I never thought those words would come out of my mouth. Where did my life go wrong?"

CHAPTER TWENTY ONE

Major Smythe stared, mesmerized, out the open back ramp of the Thuranin dropship. Below him the lights of Kallandre stretched out, a stark contrast to the almost lightless darkness of the surrounding countryside. To the north, west and south, the edges of the city were fairly well delineated by lights of roadways which formed a barrier between urban area and the hunting preserves. To the east, the city's lights bled off more casually, with estates of the wealthy dotting the land all the way to the seacoast that was barely visible.

In the artificial vision of Smythe's helmet visor, important parts of the city were outlined in red or yellow; high-security areas to be avoided. From high above, the Kristang city did not look very much different from any bustling city on Earth; although Smythe had been surprised by the lack of skyscraper buildings. The tallest building was a residential tower of around fifty stories, and most of the city was covered in buildings of twenty or fewer floors. Surely with their technology the Kristang could build taller buildings; there must be some cultural reason why height was limited.

They were flying at around thirteen thousand meters, the standard altitude for commercial air traffic in that zone of the planet, in order for the Condor to be disguised as an air transport. Skippy was hacking the local air traffic control system and military sensor networks, and the dropship was in full stealth mode while Skippy fed the Kristang sensors images of a civilian jet aircraft. There were issues neither the magic of Skippy nor the sophisticated Thuranin stealth field could completely mitigate; the disturbance of the air as the big dropship flew onward. According to Skippy, their greatest risk of detection was due to the dropship's wake, which was noticeably more violent than that left by a commercial aircraft. Particularly during the brief time they had the back ramp open, passage of the dropship through the air left swirling patterns even Kristang sensors could detect. When Smythe tore his gaze away from the city below to look straight backwards, the nose of the second Thuranin Condor was no more than five meters behind the tail of the dropship he was riding. The dropships were flying in formation so the effect of the two being tucked nose to tail were like racing cars drafting; the two together formed a smoother, more aerodynamic shape, and helped disguise the fact that alien spacecraft were overflying a city controlled by the Fire Dragon clan.

Smythe tapped a helmet control so the image fed to his suit by the dropship disappeared, and looked out on utter blackness. Inside the stealth field which bent light around the ship, no outside light was visible. He saw the lights of the dropship's rear bay, the faint blinking navigation beacon on the nose of the dropship close behind, and his companions lined up with him to jump when their turns came. The absolute blackness was unnerving, he had jumped out of airplanes and helicopters at night and in clouds, and there was always something at least faintly visible beyond the aircraft. Not here. The navigation light on the trailing dropship blinked and the light was not reflected off anything around them, that light also was absorbed and bent in unnatural ways.

He switched back to the artificial view and checked the time code in the upper right of his helmet visor. Twenty seconds remaining. "Robertson, are you ready?" He asked his companion.

"Never better, Major." The view Smythe had of Robertson's face was also artificial as the faceplate was set to dull mat black for maximum stealth. "Can hardly wait." In Smythe's visor, Robertson was keyed up but grinning eagerly. Like Smythe, Robertson was wearing powered armor, and was burdened with a parachute, a stealth field generator in a backpack, and a Zinger antiaircraft missile. Robertson and Smythe would be the first to jump. The mission was to parachute down over an alien city and land on the roof of a building. Below them were thousands of heavily-armed Kristang warriors and clan security forces. Danger came not only from those lizards carrying weapons, for the thirty three million Kristang civilian men, women and children in Kallandre would instantly report the presence of humans, if Smythe and his SpecOps teams were noticed. A civilian did not need to know what a 'human' was to know such creatures had no business walking around unescorted in a Kristang city. Speed, stealth, their Kristang powered armor and the intervention of Skippy would all be needed to successfully complete the mission and get everyone out safely. Their friendly absent-minded beer can had to warn the teams of enemy positions and intentions, and prevent remote sensors from detecting strange aliens moving about the city.

"Robertson," Smythe chided his fellow SAS trooper for unseemly eagerness. "You realize we are about to jump with both feet into the heart of an enemy city, that is crawling with thousands, perhaps millions of genetically-enhanced superwarriors?"

"Yes sir," Robertson's teeth flashed white in the artificial light. "Don't worry, I'll save one or two of them for you."

"That's the proper attitude," Smythe smiled back. An alarm chimed and Smythe reminded himself to relax rather than bracing for launch. Unlike during the spacedive on the heavy-gravity planet they called Jumbo, Smythe was not encased in an aeroshell, for he would not be burning down through an atmosphere at hypersonic speeds. Another alarm chimed, then a voice announced "Five, four, three, two, one-."

Smythe was propelled backwards, out and down in controlled fashion, falling feet first. He only had the briefest terrifying glimpse of the trailing dropship's belly, then he plunged through and beyond the weirdness of the dropship's light-bending stealth field, and again saw the lights of the city sprawled below his dangling feet. A featherweight nanofabric drogue parachute deployed and gradually slowed his progress, slowing him from commercial airliner cruise speed to a velocity provided only by gravity. As he slowed, the chute widened unseen above him and began automatically steering him toward his designated landing zone; an office building that was mostly unoccupied at that late hour. In Smythe's visor, he saw the building's roof outlined in vividly glowing green, the view from outside his personal stealth field provided by a probe protruding below one of his boots. Without the probe, he would be falling in utter darkness, having no idea where he was.

"Eight thousand meters," reported the suit's computer in a voice Smythe had learned American pilots called Bitching Betty. He did not know whether Betty was an appropriate name, but 'Bitching' certainly described the digital assistant. Skippy had been asked multiple times to reprogram the Kristang computer, and he said he had made several attempts, but it continued to be annoying. Smythe suspected Skippy liked that the suit computer occasionally tormented the users. "Glide path is nominal," the emotionless voice noted. In his visor, Smythe could see his projected glide path as a white line, and the planned descent course in blue. The white almost perfectly overlaid the blue. "Seven thousand meters." Smythe tried to relax, scanning the target rooftop and surrounding area for threats, using the suit's own relatively impressive passive sensors and the feed Skippy was providing from the local security network. "Six thous-"

"Hello, Major Smythe," Skippy's own voice interrupted. "How are you doing?"

"Fine, brilliant," Smythe was mildly alarmed by the tone of the alien AI's voice. "What is wrong?"

"Wrong? What makes you think anyth- Oh, forget it. Well, heh heh, this is a funny story-"

"Funny to me?"

"Uh, afterwards, maybe. Don't all dangerous situations seem funny when you're telling the story later? Instead of focusing on the threat, imagine you are sipping a pint in a pub back in Jolly Old England, telling amusing anecdotes about this little-"

"What is wrong?" Smythe was completely focused. His visor wasn't showing any threats.

"Here's the situation: a Kristang cadet, who is second son of a senior clan leader, has taken a fighter aircraft out for a joyride, and he is headed in your direction. He does not know you are there, of course, neither you nor Lt. Robertson have been detected."

"Why is this a problem, then?" Smythe hoped the young hotshot did not plan to land his fighter in the roof of the target building, and he zoomed in to inspect the roof more closely. That building had been chosen in part because it did not have significant obstructions that might impale the SAS troops or snag the parachutes, but also because that roof did not include a landing pad for aircraft.

"Because his aircraft is flying aerobatics at high speed, just below your altitude. He will be approaching you in only a few seconds. The air traffic controllers are already ordering him to clear the area, but everyone knows his father's position in the clan hierarchy allows the son to do pretty much whatever he wants."

"Understood. What can I do?"

"You can't do anything. I am telling you because I am about to release your parachute; it would be shredded by the turbulence of his jetwash. You will freefall through the turbulence, then I will activate your backup chute. There is not enough time to collapse and retract your main chute."

"Do what you can, Skippy," Smythe told himself he had been in worse situations, as he felt the chute straps detach and he plunged downward. Falling out of control toward the surface of a planet more than a thousand lightyears from home, above a city filled with hostile aliens, and little hope of rescue if he could not reach the primary or alternate landing zones. Moments later, he was spun head over heels in the air as something flashed by him close enough for his visor to display the outline of a Kristang single-seat fighter aircraft. The turbulence was violent enough that the helmet's internal pillows inflated to prevent his skull from smacking into the back of the hard shell. Even so, he briefly lost consciousness and was completely disoriented for several moments as he tumbled out of control. The view from the visor was dizzying, and he saw that all the visor was showing was a feed from the local sensor network, the probe that extended outside the suit's stealth field must have been damaged. "Four thousand meters," the suit announced. "Danger. You are falling unsupported. Recommend you deploy descent-control apparatus."

"I'd love to, you sodding bugger," Smythe said through teeth he had clenched to prevent losing his dinner all over the inside of the visor. "Skippy?"

"I am here, Major. I am happy you were not seriously injured; Lt. Robertson fared better than you. You are clear of the turbulence, engaging suit stabilizers."

Smythe stopped spinning rather abruptly, his feet swung back and forth three times, then he was falling smoothly feet first. The backup probe must have extended down from his other boot, because he now had a clear view below, not only the synthetic composite image from the local network. "That was good, can-"

"Deploying backup chute," Skippy announced. "Major, this chute deploys more slowly and is smaller, therefore it has less capacity. As you cannot discard either your stealth generator or Zinger missile over the city without giving away your position, your landing could be rougher than anticipated."

"Could be?" Smythe grunted; the backup chute had deployed more abruptly than his main chute had. His legs swung wildly once, twice before the suit's stabilizers halted the dangerous movement.

"Will be. The landing will be rough, very rough. I was attempting to put a positive spin on the situation."

"Skippy, I am a soldier. Give me the facts."

"Very well. The backup chute is not able to land you and the missile without damage to both. Since the missile cannot guide itself, what I propose is that just before you impact, I mean, sorry, before you land on the roof, you release yourself from the chute. I will guide the chute to drop the missile softly down. Lt. Robertson is still using his main chute, he does not have the same problem."

"Leaving me to fall by myself? How far?"

"No more than ten meters. Well, maybe twelve."

"Twel-" Major Smythe bit off his reply. Twelve meters, nearly forty feet. Even with the protection of his powered suit, he could not survive a twelve meter fall, and the sound of the heavy impact on the roof would alert every Kristang in the vicinity of the building. "This," he swallowed to control his suddenly quivering lips, "maneuver you propose, it will allow Lt. Robertson to use my missile?"

"Yes, it should- wait, what? Why would Robertson use your missile?"

Smythe forced himself to tear his eyes away from the rapidly-approaching roof. When he signed up for the Army, and later during his SAS training and service, he had never expected to die on an alien planet. Certainly not to die by falling onto the roof of an office building. It seemed so casually ordinary. Not a death appropriate for the Special Air Service. "The mission parameters require two missiles to ensure success. If I am unable to fire my missile, Robertson needs to do it."

"Um, perhaps I am missing something here," Skippy sounded puzzled. "For what reason would you be unable to fire your- oh. Crap. Major Smythe, I apologize. You are thinking a twelve meter fall will render you dead or disabled?"

"Unless you know something I don't."

"Ha! There is not enough time for me to list everything I know that you don't. In this case, I know that I plan to trigger your suit's boot thrusters after you are released from the parachute. While the thrusters have a limited capacity, if I use up all the fuel in one hard burn, they will slow your fall enough that it will feel like falling no more than two meters. And the shock absorbers in the legs and spine of the suit will cushion both the effect on your body, and the impact forces on the roof."

"Ah," realization that he would not die right then dawned on Smythe in a brief shudder he was unable to control. "Thank you, Skippy."

"No need to thank me, Major Smythe. If you were scared, that was my fault. I should have considered how the information might be perceived. Although I will deny it if you tell anyone, I am rather fond of you backwards humans, particularly those like yourself who have reached the peak of your profession by hard work and dedication."

"That was," Smythe was sufficiently thrown off balance he had to search for words. "*Nice*?" It was odd using that word to describe a being who normally was proud to be an arsehole. "Again, thank you."

"Ah, don't get all mushy on me," Skippy sniffed. "Save your thanks for after you land safely. There is a whole lot that could still go wrong."

"Such as another joyriding fighter pilot?"

"Nope. Air traffic control finally called in a military air patrol to close the area to unauthorized traffic. You might be pleased to hear that joyriding jackass suffered a catastrophic engine failure over the ocean a couple seconds ago. He had to eject at high speed, and that broke both of his legs."

"An engine failure?" Smythe asked suspiciously.

"Yup. For some unknown reason, the locking pins that hold the engine fan blades stationary during maintenance engaged in flight. What a terrible, shockingly *unfortunate* event," Skippy lamented the accident.

"An accident, hmm?" Smythe had to smile inside his helmet. "Thank you for that."

"It was the best I could do on short notice. The only reason I was able to do that is because that jackass was so eager to fly, he skipped securing those locking pins during preflight. Serves his punk ass right. His daddy will not be happy that Junior destroyed an expensive jet fighter. Well, enough chit chat for now, we both need to concentrate on your landing."

Smythe nearly cracked his helmet against a boxy device on top of the roof, using a hand to arrest his fall. The powered glove left a big dent in the box, whatever it was. "Down safely," Smythe reported tersely. In two powered steps, he collected the missile in its protective container, as he watched the nanofabric of the parachute already beginning to go discoherent; the microscopic machines releasing their grip on each other. In less than a minute, the parachute mechanism would be unorganized dust blowing off the roof to disperse over the city. Securing the precious missile at the base of the box he had collided with, he glanced upward to track the progress of Robertson. The man's silhouette was outlined in Smythe's visor, but when Smythe briefly switched off the synthetic vision, he could not see Robertson at all. The portable stealth field generators in their backpacks were quite effective. Without waiting for Robertson, Smythe pulled the latch to release his backpack and shrugged out of the straps. If the operation went wrong, they were to destroy their advanced personal stealth fields, which contained a mixture of Kristang and Thuranin technology. All either of them would need to do would be reach inside the pack, twist a lever and pull it outward, starting the process of nanomachines turning the stealth field generator into dark gray goo. The goo would solidify slowly, and by the time the operation was over and Kristang swarmed onto the roof, there would be no trace of the stealth field's advanced technology. Nor would there be any evidence that humans had been involved in the operation.

Smythe watched Robertson coming in, ready to assist, but Robertson landed gracefully, avoiding Smythe's clumsy bounce off equipment on the rooftop. Within seconds, Robertson's missile was secured and both chute and stealth field generator were being dissolved. The two men walked, hunched over, between two large devices that Skippy described as part of the building's air filtration system. Both of the units hummed loudly and vibrated, providing sonic cover for the actions of the humans. In the darkness between the units, shadowed from the glowing haze of city lights, they knelt, removed their missiles from the protective containers and inspected them. "Alpha team down and ready," Smythe reported. Despite unexpected interference from one jackass in a fighter aircraft, a two-man SAS team had infiltrated the heart of an alien city undetected, and were poised to wreak havoc with missiles. The enemy would not be expecting an attack, particularly not one launched from within the city.

Lt. Williams and his companion, Petty Officer 2nd Class Marvin Jones, had jumped after Smythe's SAS team and were spared being tossed around the sky by the wake of the jet fighter. Other than avoiding severe turbulence, the SEALS experienced that same descent as the SAS men, until forty four seconds from landing.

"Shit!" Skippy shouted in Williams' ear. "Damn it!"

"What?" Williams responded with alarm. His visor was not highlighting any threats. Then two fuzzy yellow dots appeared, on the roof he was supposed to land on. "What is that?"

"Two assholes going on the roof to drink or something. Sorry, they must do this regularly, the stairwell and door they used must have the sensors disabled so they can sneak around. I had no idea they were in the area, until a camera on another building detected their body heat. This is going to be trouble, I can't do anything about it."

"Can we land on another building?" The building had been selected because it was taller than most surrounding structures and had both a mostly uncluttered roof without an aircraft landing pad.

"Not now, it's too late, you are too low. You and Jones are committed to landing on that roof, or in the street below."

"Not an option. Are those two security personnel?"

"Building security. Civilians. They are supposed to patrol the building instead of goofing off on the job."

Williams felt for his rifle, strapped to his left leg. "Will those two be missed if something happens to them?"

"My guess is, they come up on the roof during times they know no one will be looking for them. What are you thinking, Lieutenant?"

"I'm thinking we deactivate the explosive tips on our rifle ammunition and put two rounds in each of them." Their Kristang ammunition had three modes: armor-piercing, explosive or inert. The rifles usually alternated armor-piercing and explosive when fighting opponents wearing armored suits. Against the two lizards on the roof, all the SEALS team needed was the kinetic energy of inert rounds.

"You are enveloped in a stealth field, however as soon as you land, the Kristang could hardly miss your presence," Skippy advised skeptically.

"My intention is to shoot them *before* we land," Williams explained. "Jones, you listening?"

"Yes, Sir," Jones replied.

"Are you sure you can do that?" Skippy made no effort to conceal his surprise.

"Unless those two knuckleheads duck behind some sort of cover," the roof was mostly open, and the heat signatures of the two Kristang were standing far from any place they could conceal themselves. "We got this. Jones?"

"Ready," Jones replied. His own rifle was out of its carrying pouch and in his hands, the rifle's magnetic grips firmly attached to the suit so he could not drop the weapon.

Williams switched the visor from the composite data provided by Skippy, to the more focused view coming from the sensor probe extending below his right boot and outside the portable stealth field. He could now see the two Kristang as distinct outlines; they were standing almost stationary, providing easy targets. Williams fed the probe's data to the targeting scope of his rifle. The roof was approaching fast, there was not much time to act. "Jones, take the one on the left."

"Negative," Jones replied. "If this wind swings you in front of me, you'll block my line of sight."

"You take the one on the right, then."

"The one on the right, confirmed. I have a shot, Sir."

"On three. Three, two, one, fire." Williams lightly pressed the trigger twice, knowing Jones was doing the same. The two figures on the roof collapsed and dropped silently.

The SEALS landed on the roof easily, and within a minute had their gear secured and were dragging the two dead Kristang under some apparatus on a corner of the roof. "How much time do you think we have, Skippy?" Williams asked anxiously.

"I cannot say exactly. You should have plenty of time to complete the mission. The only other security personnel in the building have recently started their meal break, and they are down on the third floor."

"Outstanding. Bravo team down and ready," Williams reported in, then knelt down to wait.

"Delta team down and ready."

"Yes," I pumped my fist in an unprofessional manner. A real colonel would control his emotions and be cool under pressure. By getting excited at hearing the fourth missile team was down safely on its target rooftop, I was letting everyone know I had been concerned the mission would fail before it had barely gotten started. What I should have done was acknowledge Delta team's report with a simple 'Understood', or even 'Outstanding' if I really wanted to go crazy. What I did briefly took the focus off the mission and made it all about me.

I knew all that, I just couldn't help myself. Dropping four missile teams out of a Thuranin ship over a Kristang city, had caused my heart to race as if I had been parachuting with them. I was not one of the eight men chosen for the ground mission, because I was not qualified. I was also not in one of the three Kristang dropships now flying toward the city, because I was not qualified for that phase of the mission either. What I was doing was sitting aboard a Thuranin dropship in relative safety, commanding the mission like I was supposed to be doing. Whether I was qualified to do that is a matter of opinion. At least Major Smythe had not been forced to argue with me; I knew there were eight Special Operations men far more skilled than I was, and I knew there were six pilots who could fly ring around me.

So, I was aboard a Thuranin dropship, which had better communications equipment than the Kristang ships, so I could exercise better command and control. There wasn't much for me to do; when two of the missile teams had encountered obstacles all I had been able to do was listen, keep my mouth shut and trust my people to handle it. Which they did.

Mostly because I felt the need to do something, I contacted the Three Musketeers, as we called the three Kristang dropships, and authorized them to continue toward the city. They acknowledged, and I watched the icons for the three ships approach the city.

"How are you doing, Sir?" Lt Poole asked from her own console, where she was likely watching the same images.

"Fine, Poole. I feel like I should be doing something."

"How about a game of checkers, Joe?" Skippy's avatar popped to life on the side of my console.

"Thank you, Skippy, no. I meant I should be doing something useful."

"You're the commander," Poole reminded me. "Command, Sir, *command*."

I knew what she meant; trust my people and stay out of their way. It sucked.

Smythe's and Robertson were the first ground team to launch their missiles, they were the farthest away from their target, and those missiles had the most complicated route to fly. Robertson held the launcher tubes as Smythe acted as spotter, because Skippy's view through the sensor networks was imperfect, and launching was when the missiles were most visible. Smythe peered over the railing, looking down into the streets far below.

"Clear?" Robertson asked in a whisper.

Major Smythe was not certain exactly what 'clear' meant in a densely-populated city of over thirty million hostile aliens. The streets below held steady streams of traffic even at the late hour; he was able to follow individual cars, trucks and buses by their headlights as they passed by on the street below. They were all moving smoothly, there was no indication the Kristang authorities had any idea humans had infiltrated their city. Unlike any large human city he could think of, the air was not filled with a cacophony of noise from motor vehicles as all the vehicles moving on the streets below were electric and made hardly any noise. With motion of all vehicles controlled by a traffic network, there was no incessant honking of horns. It was quiet, a little too eerily quiet to Smythe. A door opened at ground level across the street and a small group of Kristang spilled out onto the sidewalk, illuminated by a rectangle of light from the doorway. They appeared unsteady on their feet, two of them especially weaving on their feet, and a shift in the breeze swirling between the office building towers brought snatches of loud, boisterous conversation wafting up to him; words that were unintelligible even to his suit's microphones and translator but clearly happy and celebratory. With a blink, he adjusted his visor's view to zoom in on the group wandering down the sidewalk, with the enhanced image he thought the aliens were two males and four females. The females were distinctly smaller than the two males, and each male had his arms around two females. If the males were drunk as they sounded, the females were struggling to keep their men upright and from toppling into the street. As Smythe watched, a vehicle glided to a stop next to the group, and one male was helped into the car by three of the females. When the car drove away, the lone male began shouting at the lone female and she cringed as he raised a fist. Then the male swayed on his feet, held himself up with one hand on a parked truck, and waved the female away dismissively. She was pleading with him about something as another car pulled over. Whatever the male had been unhappy about, he put aside as he was helped into the vehicle, and it pulled away. For a moment, the sidewalks on both sides of the street were empty. "Clear," Smythe said without taking his eyes off the street. "Launch now," he urged Robertson to act before another group of revelers came out onto the street. As high up as their rooftop was, it was unlikely anyone on the street would be looking up, or could see the missile in flight. Smythe was being extra cautious, as the SAS did not train their people to leave anything to chance.

"One away," Robertson whispered as he leaned over the rail and simply dropped the missile nose first, straight down. He had broken the seal of the launch tube and pulled the missile out, handling it carefully with his powerful gloved hands. Without the magnetic rails of the launch tube, the missile's only means of starting flight was the booster motor, and using the booster motor for a clandestine mission was not an option. The booster motor at the back end of the missiles had been removed aboard the *Flying Dutchman*, leaving the powerful alien missile as unable to get off the ground as an ostrich. Dropping the missile from a tall building provided the speed it needed to deploy its long thin wings, and jump-start the tiny turbine engine. Both men crouched by the railing, holding their breath as the missile plummeted downward, then curved parallel to the building, and, gathering speed, began climbing. It flew straight above the center of the street below for several blocks, then banked to turn between two buildings and out of sight. Without the enhanced synthetic view provided by their visors, they could barely have seen the small missile. Zingers did not carry a stealth field generator; they relied on speed, their small size and a polychromatic coating that allowed them to blend into their surroundings.

Smythe let out an exhalation of relief. "Missile One away," he reported. "Flying straight and true."

"I got it," Skippy replied. "The missile has not been detected by any of the main sensor networks. A few closed-circuit motion detectors picked it up and alerted the city's air traffic control system, I replied that the missile is an authorized security drone. Launch the second missile."

"Preparing for launch now," Smythe said, and waved for Robertson to drop the second Zinger, while Smythe's eyes scanned the street below. As Robertson leaned over the railing and let the missile go, a bus pulled to the curb almost directly below and discharged three Kristang. Again, Smythe held his breath as the missile picked up speed, its wings deploying much too slowly for Smythe's comfort. If the missile's wings or engine failed, it would crash to the sidewalk right next to the bus. Instead, the little Zinger's airbreathing port opened and sucked in air, spinning up its silent turbine motor. The missile fell only five stories before it pulled itself into level flight and followed its companion along the center of the street and around a corner. "Missile Two away successfully."

"Yup," Skippy acknowledged in a distracted tone. "Pip, pip, cheerio, jolly good job, it's tea and crumpets time for you now, Major. Get out of sight and prepare to deploy your tether balloons."

"Understood," Smythe replied and immediately helped Robertson break the launch tubes into pieces to stuff inside the backpacks. The launch tubes needed to be destroyed, so the Kristang would never know where the missiles were launched from. "Tea and crumpets," Smythe whispered. "I would settle for a biscuit and a sip of cold water right now."

Talk of water made Robertson pause to sip from the nipple inside his helmet. The water provided was cool and tasteless. "I have a bottle of single malt I've been saving for the return flight to Earth," Robertson did not pause in packing a missile launch tube in his backpack. "If we get out of this, I'm opening that bottle as soon as we're back aboard the *Dutchman*."

"I'll drink to that," Smythe settled down with his back to a bulky air-handling unit. Now all they had to do was wait for all hell to break loose in the city, and for a dropship to fly over and yank them off the rooftop. Waiting was the worst part.

CHAPTER TWENTY TWO

"*This*," said Lt. Reed as her Dragon dropship turned left into the designated commercial air traffic corridor over the city, "is going to be interesting." Ahead of the Dragon's nose loomed the towering spires of the city, glittering in the night. Some of the buildings were tall enough that the air traffic corridor went between them. That didn't provide a lot of maneuvering space, and Reed hadn't liked the idea right from when Colonel Bishop had explained the plan. The four SpecOps teams had parachuted out of a Thuranin Condor dropship at high altitude, but the extraction had to be handled by the three Dragons, with Reed's ship going in first. Condors were too large to transit the air corridor; their passage would leave a wake too turbulent for the relatively small aircraft that were allowed above the city. The Falcons were in full stealth mode, with their stealth fields modified to project the image and electromagnetic signatures of a typical Kristang commercial air transport. Whether the enhancements Skippy had made to the Falcons allowed them to slip through the city unnoticed, would be something Reed would know only when she had safely exited the city limits, or when she was challenged and shot at.

"Approaching outer marker," her copilot announced softly. "Turn to three four two degrees on my mark. Mark."

"Three four two," Reed acknowledged as she banked the Dragon much more gently than the combat dropship was typically handled. She needed to mimic the flight profile of an airliner transporting wealthy and coddled passengers. "We're over the city now." The line between city and countryside on Kobamik was stark; there were few suburban areas surrounding the densely-packed cities on the planet. Much of the planet's land area was hunting preserves for exclusive use by high-ranking clan leaders, farmland, or vast estates for the pleasure of the wealthy. Most of the population lived and worked in large cities of skyscrapers, surrounding fortified central compounds which housed and protected their clan leadership.

By some miracle, or through the magic of Skippy, no one had challenged the Dragon as it flew over thc city. Communications with air traffic control, which Skippy handled, were routine. As far as any of the Kristang in the city below, it was an ordinary evening, the end of a pleasantly warm and sunny day. "I see the objective," Reed said, as the cockpit display highlighted the rooftop where the Indian paratroopers waited. "Deploy the hooks."

Captain Chandra and Lieutenant Sodhi of the Indian team were the last to land on a rooftop, and first to be extracted, by luck of the air traffic patterns over the city. "On final approach," Reed's voice advised, "launch tether balloons."

Chandra and Sodhi pulled the handles on top of each other's backpacks, releasing the cover over the balloons. Instantly, tissue-thin, almost invisible balloons began inflating, swelling rapidly and rising to pull a hair-thin cord behind them. In less than forty seconds, the balloons had uncoiled the entire cord from each backpack, and the two men braced themselves, knees slightly bent and arms across their chests. Lost in the darkness two hundred meters above, the balloons floated in the breeze, bobbing slightly as their microscopic brains flexed the skin of the balloons to keep them stable.

"I wish we had done this for real in training," Lt. Reed said to herself as she lined up her Kristang dropship with the artificial flightpath projected on the display in front of her. "Simulations don't cover everything that can go wrong."

"Hooks fully deployed," Chen reported from the right-hand seat. "This worked perfectly in the sim," she noted. The flight crews had practiced the balloon tether pickup maneuver so many times in simulations, Chen thought she could do it in her sleep.

The hooks were deployed on either side of the dropship, and contained tiny, low-power encrypted beacons for the balloons to steer toward. With the balloons only thirty meters apart and the hooks covering forty three meters on each side of the dropship, having the balloons steer toward the hook mechanisms was hardly necessary. The dropship was flying almost as slowly as it could without using its belly jets to hover, flying slower than air traffic in the area was supposed to; Skippy's control of the local network temporarily allowed the dropship to avoid being investigated. With Skippy's control over the hardened network tenuous and imperfect, Samantha Reed knew she had to pick up both men on the first pass; a go-around held too much danger of detection.

"Here we go," Reed forced herself to breathe evenly and hold the controls lightly.

"Flightpath nominal," Chen reported without taking her eyes off the display. "Tether balloons are holding position. Four, three, two, one, capture."

The hooks contacted both tethers a quarter-second apart, and two green lights flashed on the displays in front of both pilots. With the tethers firmly attached to the hooks, both balloons popped. Or, not pop so much as their skins dissolving into dust. The tethers wrapped around the retrieval hooks, and the tiny computer brains controlling the tethers from the backpacks of the two Indian paratroopers sensed the tension in the ultrathin tethers. The computers ordered sections of the tethers to contract slowly and other sections to stretch, causing Chandra and Sodhi to be lifted off the ground with no more abrupt force than if they had been riding an elevator. The pull on both men increased as the tethers contracted, until they grunted as they were yanked upward and forward at three Gees of acceleration.

This part of the extraction had been practiced outside the *Flying Dutchman*, although never in an atmosphere. The sound of air rushing past his helmet was pushed to the back of his mind as Chandra could not allow himself to be distracted. He was now flying behind the dropship, slightly below but at the same speed, the tether having plucked him smoothly off the rooftop. Chandra kept his legs straight out behind him and kept his arms crossed as he had done in training. Lights of the city twinkled below, beside and even above him as the dropship adhered to the authorized flightpath. When the dropship cleared the city center and flew into an area where the buildings did not tower around it, Chandra felt an increased tugging on his shoulder straps. Although he could not see the stealthed dropship that had to be directly in front of him, the synthetic vision of his visor showed him the back ramp cracking open, and the hooks retracting toward the aircraft. He could see Sodhi ahead of him, being reeled in first, the man being buffeted in the wind behind the dropship. Sodhi maintained discipline, not extending his arms as he entered the maw of the dropship's aft cargo area, then Chandra could see Sodhi being grasped by suited figures on either side. "In and secure," Sodhi reported.

Chandra's own experience was slightly more rough, as the dropship had been forced to increase speed and climb near the outskirts of the city. At one point, he was swinging back and forth so that he feared colliding with one side of the ramp, then the air smoothed abruptly as he entered a vortex under the tail, and with a last hard tug on his straps, he was inside. The back ramp was closing even before his feet touched the deck. "Did you have fun, Captain?" One of the suited figures asked him in a teasing tone.

"Oh, yes, very much so," Chandra replied, finally able to uncross his arms and flexing fingers so tense they tingled. "I highly recommend it."

Reed did not relax until the back ramp was closed and locked. "One down, one to go," she said to Chen with a tight smile. With only three dropships and four teams on the ground, her ship had to swing around the city and make another run to pick up the SAS team. She could see on the display that another Dragon dropship was in the process of picking up the Chinese SpecOps team. So far, the entire operation was going according to plan. "Status of the hooks?" They had a spare set of retrieval hooks in case one or both of them had been damaged, but removing a broken hook and installing a new one would require her to land the dropship and keep it on the ground for more than five minutes, a risk no one wanted to take.

"No damage, both hooks show ready," Chen read the results off the display.

"The hooks are fine," Skippy's voice broke in. "I would have told you if there was a problem with the hooks. Was there any difficulty with the retrieval from your end?"

Reed looked at Chen and shook her head. "No, it went exactly like the simulation."

"Good, because the next one is likely to be tricky, I have had to move up the schedule slightly."

"Slightly?" Reed banked the dropship away from the city to come around again and retrieve the SAS team. "How slightly?"

"Ok, more than slightly. Like, uh, right now."

"Hey, Joe," Skippy said in a voice that gave me goosebumps. This was his something-went-wrong voice. "Uh, we need to move up the schedule a bit."

"A *bit*? Why?" The entire plan depended on precise timing, once the missiles were launched, we had less than a minute of leeway backed into the schedule. Everything depended on the dropships flying specific routes through the city at specific times to retrieve the ground teams. Delta team had just been safely pulled aboard Lt. Reed's dropship, and the two-man Chinese Charlie team was in the air, dangling behind their dropship. The third dropship was just approaching the outskirts of the city, on its way to pick up Lt. Williams' SEALS team.

"Some bigwig is coming toward the compound so it's being put on lockdown; when that happens the missiles won't have access. Right now there is access at three points, I can manage with that and I am moving missiles right now. With the missiles flying faster, they are going to be detected by motion sensors and verified manually, I can't intercept all those signals."

Shit. Crap, crap, crap. "Ok, I know you're working magic here, do your best. I need to alert Alpha and Bravo teams to the new schedule, how soon do you need to strike?"

"Let's put it this way, Joe; three, two one, impact."

Located in the center of Kallandre, because it was there first and the city had grown up around it, was the heavily-protected compound which housed the Fire Dragon clan leaders. The compound covered one thousand and sixty acres, and was the military heart of the clan's presence on the planet. The compound was protected by a dome comprised of an energy shield; multiple layers of energy shields. The shields were powerful enough to protect the compound from orbital strikes, even hypersonic railgun darts would be deflected or absorbed by the shields. Aircraft had to fly very precise routes through only three entry points suspended in the air, entry points with inner and outer gates.

Ground traffic could choose from eleven access points, ground access was controlled not only by electronic means, but also by heavily armed guards. At one of those ground access points was a guard named Jax-au-nam Tetlahauf; his friends and family called him Jax.

He hated being called 'Jax'.

He also hated being a security guard, but his family's lowly position in the clan hierarchy did not offer him more attractive options. His two older brothers had served as infantry in a mercenary unit; they were both killed during their first assignments. Jax was determined to endure six inglorious years as a security guard, after which he could apply for Fleet training. If he had a spotless record over his six years. Not just a spotless record, an exemplary record. A record that got him noticed for his devotion to duty.

Because Jax was desperately determined to be noticed by his superiors and make a name for himself, his fellow guards hated working with him. His immediate supervisor could no longer stand the sight of Jax, which was why Jax was working the graveyard shift. That only made Jax more eager for a chance to shine. If enemies tried to infiltrate the Fire Dragon compound on Kobamik, they would most likely make the attempt at night.

No enemy spy, saboteur or assassin was going to gain entry through a gate guarded by Jax-au-nam Tetlahauf.

Five hours into his shift, when the other guards were shaking their heads to stay awake, Jax was fully alert to danger. Jax narrowed his eyes suspiciously, his quick mind racing through threat scenarios. A large truck was approaching the outer barrier, which had already been automatically deactivated by the security mechanism. The truck had been inspected and cleared by guards before the vehicle had been allowed onto the approach road to the compound. According to the data on Jax's wristpad, the truck was carrying specialty chemicals for the airfield, and both the trucking consortium and the driver were fully vetted and trusted.

Which made Jax more suspicious. Of course an enemy seeking to penetrate the compound would subvert a trusted agent, and a large vehicle with hazardous cargo would be a useful weapon for compromising the compound's outer defenses. Another glance at his wristpad told Jax the three trucks lined up behind the first one were also carrying hazardous cargo. A clever enemy might plan to blow up the outer gate, then drive the other trucks through into the compound. That could be a serious security breach, a threat to the entire clan. It was not going to happen to the gate while Jax was on duty. Not on his watch. As he made the snap decision, stepping forward and raising a hand, his mind flashed through the accolades he would receive for his diligence.

Ironically, it was Jax's burning eagerness to do his duty that was his downfall, and the downfall of the clan leaders inside the secure compound. Jax's actions ran afoul of the law. Not any law made by Kristang, nor a law of physics, but a law more ancient and fundamental: the Law of Unintended Consequences. "Halt!" he shouted, brandishing his rifle menacingly. Seeing an agitated guard pointing a weapon directly at his face, the driver stomped on the brakes, manually overriding all the carefully tested security measures of the compound's access points. With the truck having skidded to a stop while its read end was still within the outer force field barrier, the field was inactive. And with the truck ahead still transiting the inner barrier, that force field was also temporarily down. The ground access points had been carefully designed, and the security crews trained, never to allow both force fields to be down simultaneously. Jax's abrupt action had just destroyed years of security planning and training.

His immediate supervisor Soth recognize the danger, not to the compound, but to his career if the authorities learned his post had violated a standing security order. He could have flipped up a cover and pressed a green and yellow button that would have sent a surge of power into the shield emitters, forcing the outer shield back on and cutting the truck in half. The resulting violent reaction would have destroyed the truck, killed the driver and the idiotic Jax, and even injured Soth inside the bunker. Instead, Soth sprinted around the bunker door and frantically waved the truck driver forward. "Jax! You idiot! Both shields are down, get that truck in here."

Jax, stupidly, did not yield. "These trucks are carrying-"

"They are carrying-" Soth never finished his thought.

Two aircraft access points were open on the other side of the compound, as aircraft flew in formation toward the airfield. Two missiles followed closely behind the trailing aircraft in each formation, tucking their noses under the rear ramp in between the turbulence and heat signatures of the engines. All four missiles were running on turbine power only, their wings extended only a third of maximum length and swept back, and their polychromatic coating made them difficult to see even though the missiles did not have stealth fields. Regardless, sensors in the flight approach corridor detected something wrong and triggered an alarm. Even if the system detected a missile with absolute certainty, the air access security system could not fire maser cannons because the aircraft were broadcasting identification codes of senior clan leaders, indicating they or their immediate family members were aboard. A more clever system would have been skeptical that senior clan families would be flying aboard cargo transport aircraft, but that would not have mattered because the air access computers had been slowly and laboriously infiltrated by a very, very clever shiny beer can. Thus, the two aircraft and accompanying four missiles glided through the access port in the few seconds during which the air defense maser cannons could have fired. The aircraft were through the access point and the shield behind them reactivating before the air security duty officer was able to react to the warning alarm. The duty officer, confused, ordered the aircraft to veer away from the air field toward a designated holding area and scrambled drones to intercept and inspect the cargo transports, but by then his action were as useless as closing the henhouse door after the fox got in. All four missiles, responding to an order from an ancient alien beer can many kilometers away, shed their wings, shut off their turbine engines and ignited their rocket motors all within a microsecond. The four deadly darts turned and raced away in different directions, as the air security duty officer wondered what the hell had just happened.

At the ground access point, the four missiles launched by the Chinese and SEALS teams had been loitering in slow lazy circles around a water tower, their polychromatic coatings blending in with the light gray of the water tower. With their miniature turbine engines operating on almost minimum power and their long, thin wings at maximum extension, they orbited the water tower no faster than a soaring bird, and made no more noise and had a lower sensor reflection than a bird. Even so, the motion sensors saturating the area should have sent an alarm to the central security computer, prompting at least a closer look at suspicious airborne activity around the water tower. The motion sensors did detect the four Zinger missiles, and repeatedly sent increasingly shrill alarms to the security system that something was odd in the vicinity of the water tower. What the central security received was nothing but soothingly happy 'operating normally- all clear' signals, for a crucial data relay had been infiltrated by a shiny beer can.

The Zingers, if their tiny brains had been capable of talking to each other, probably would have said something like '*Dude I am sooooo bored flying around this stupid water tower. I'm a missile, damn it, I want to KILL something*'. Not being able to think on that level, the missiles quietly and mindlessly orbited the water tank, waiting eagerly for their moment of glory.

Skippy had been planning a risky move to attempt flying the four Zingers through the ground security portal, during the brief moment when the outer and inner energy shields were not fully active. Even with him controlling their flight, he calculated no more than a fifty three percent of two missiles getting through, because of the signal lag between himself and the missiles, and the need for the missiles to fly through two partially-established energy barriers. Instead, due to the overzealous idiocy of a young and ambitious Kristang security guard, both inner and outer shields were simultaneously full deactivated. Not believing his incredible luck, Skippy instantly decided to carpe the hell out of that diem and sent revised instructions to the quartet of missiles, along with the 'Go' code to arm them.

Instantly, the missiles ejected their wings and engaged their rocket motors at full thrust, leaving scorch marks on the light gray surface of the water tower. The missiles surged for the portal opening, aiming for the narrow gaps on either side of the stalled truck. By the time they passed the rear of the truck, they were moving at supersonic speeds, and the shock wave from the leading missile would have caused the other three missiles to crash, except that Skippy's precise control had the Zingers flying parallel, as the lead missile's nose was less than a millimeter ahead. The supersonic shockwaves never had time to catch the missiles, instead expending their energy on an overpressure inside the armored arc of the access station. Jax and Soth were slammed against the station walls, instantly shattering every bone in their tough bodies. The hapless truck driver fared little better, being first violently crushed back into his seat, then ripped free of his safety straps and sucked out the opening where the windshield had been.

Moving at high speed and accelerating with full force, the missiles flashed through the access station in the blink of an eye. They still should not have gained entry to the compound, as a warning signal traveled to the inner shield much faster than the missiles could fly. The inner shield should have pulsed closed instantly, severing the truck passing through but forming an impenetrable barrier for the missiles to batter themselves against. Unfortunately for the ground access station, the reaction time of the inner barrier control computer was slowed by a well-timed momentary glitch, a glitch caused by a beer can whose semi-official crew rank was 'Asshole First Class'.

Unaffected by the energy shield which finally pulsed closed just behind them, the two pairs of missiles flew into the open air of the compound, climbed desperately and then flipped end over end to decelerate. At their Mach three speed, they could not make the abrupt climb before impacting the armored physical barrier in front of them, so their rocket motors briefly fired backward to slow their forward progress, then the Zingers flipped end over end again to fly upward nose first, clearing the armored barrier with a comfortable meter to spare.

Once clear of the crash barrier, the missiles were free to roam inside the compound. For hostile enemy weapons, being inside the Fire Dragon compound was a forbidden experience, so the Zingers might be forgiven if they wanted to gawk at the sights and savor the moment. Under Skippy's preprogrammed instructions, all four missiles sent signals to any other Zingers in the compound, and almost instantly the eight missiles learned to their collective surprise they all had successfully penetrated the compound's multiple layers of security. For the attack to be successful required only four of the eight missiles, so with all eight available, the plan shifted to what Skippy had considered the least likely scenario. Each missile knew what it was supposed to do and there was no hesitation about their suicide mission.

The two Zingers launched by the Chinese team split up after coming through the ground access point, one going right and one straight head. All eight missiles were headed for the same structure; the giant, thick pyramid at the very heart of the compound. The pyramid had been constructed on top of the original hill in the center of the city, like an iceberg most of the structure extended far below the surface. Below ground were the high-security facilities, including safe spaces for the senior Fire Dragon clan leaders and their families. What soared above the surface, over three hundred meters tall, was mostly offices and, importantly, the urban palaces of the senior leadership. Clan security officers had pleaded with the senior leadership to live in the security of the underground areas rather than exposing themselves to danger, however slight. Originally, vast palaces had been constructed underground, complete with highly convincing displays in place of windows. Over time, one senior leader after another moved up into the open air, creating a rush to grab real estate near the top of the pyramid. What good was their hard work to seize and maintain power, if they could not enjoy and flaunt that wealth and power? A senior leader needed an estate with real windows, and open-air balconies complete with swimming pools and landing pads for their personal aircraft. Views facing east or west, to view the sun rising or sctting, were highly sought after, as were areas where there was less of the visual distortion created by the energy shields, providing a more clear view of the city they ruled over. When a senior clan leader walked out onto his extensive balcony and saw with his naked eye the soaring towers and glittering lights of the city, he *felt* his power in a way no display screen could provide. Security officers warned that the senior leaders were needlessly exposing themselves to danger for the sake of vanity, but those security officer were ignored. Did not the clan provide huge resources to ensure the utterly impenetrable security of the compound? After a while, those security officers who continued to protest found themselves replaced with those less alarmist, for what danger could possibly touch the Fire Dragon leadership inside their own compound? That is why the eight missiles found the clan's senior leaders in their apartments in the middle of the night; with those leaders either soundly asleep or engaged in various pleasures, alone or with companions.

The first missile to find its designated target had been launched by the SAS team, although all eight missiles struck their targets within seconds of each other. That first missile slowed as it approached its target, hugging the slope of the pyramid as it climbed and turning only at the last moment onto the balcony outside that clan leader's own personal and private balcony. The estate had its own energy shield that was intended only to deflect bullets fired by assassins, it was not capable of stopping a Zinger. Expecting an energy shield, the Zinger was prepared by activating an energy projector in its nose, creating a path through the shield just large enough for the missile to slip through.

Once through the shield, the missile smashed through composite laminated 'glass' and several lightly-armored walls in the interior of the apartment until the Zinger's guidance system was confident it had reached its destination. Then, without regret, the missile detonated its enhanced warhead.

Any Kristang on the ground below, working late at the airfield or any other outside area with a clear view of the central pyramid, were startled by seeing fountains of flame and debris erupting at multiple locations around the pyramid. Jets of firc burst outward, vividly and angrily orange in the relative stillness of the night, turning dull red as any combustible material quickly burned itself out. As abruptly as it happened, the explosions flashed into darkness, leaving only glowing embers and gaping holes in the faces of the pyramid, and low rolling thunder echoing within the dome of the compound's energy shield. For a brief moment, all was still. Then sirens began to wail, the compound automatically plunged into darkness, and security guards, soldiers and pilots all raced for their emergency posts.

The unthinkable had happened. Senior Fire Dragon leaders had been attacked, killed, inside their ultra-secure compound. Later, there would be time for shock and recriminations and assigning blame. The harsh discipline and constant training of the

Kristang warrior caste served them well that night, as every single warrior reacted as they had been ordered to.

Even as the remaining senior clan leaders recovered from the shock of surviving merely by luck of not having been targeted by the eight missiles, speculation raged about who could have conducted such a sophisticated attack. The surviving clan leadership, having been whisked to safe sections deep below ground, were gripped with fear as the initial reports reached them. There was no question that advanced technology had been required for such an attack to succeed; technology able to subvert Kristang computers specifically designed to resist and report on outside attempts to infiltrate their systems. The minds of the clan leadership all had the same two thoughts. The Thuranin were interfering in Kristang clan politics, for some as yet unknown reason. As quickly as that thought came to mind, it was dismissed. The Thuranin, reeling from their recent multiple and stinging military setbacks, were unlikely to have the time or desire to punish their clients. Which brought up a second and more frightening possibility; that another clan had acquired advanced technology. If that were true, the Fire Dragons were vulnerable, and needed to strike back hard while they still could.

Which clan or clans were behind the attack? The Black Trees were the obvious suspects, perhaps too obvious. Lesser clans might wish a fight between the two strongest clans in Kristang society, bleeding both Fire Dragons and Black Trees dry and leaving them vulnerable to a rested and prepared third party. The surviving leadership reached out to the Black Trees, demanding answers and assurances while bringing their own military forces to full alertness.

Not one of the warriors inside the compound had even a moment's thought that the attack might have been conducted by lowly humans and a shiny beer can.

"Abort abort abort!" Skippy's voice shouted from the Dragon's console. "Abort approach, turn right to zero one nine degrees."

"Zero one niner, got it," Lt. Reed acknowledged as she gently turned the Dragon to follow the air traffic system's revised instructions. All around her, she could see aircraft being diverted away from the city. "What happened? Who is going to pick up the SAS team?"

"Busy. Working on it," Skippy responded tersely. "Proceed to Hold Point Whiskey and await instructions."

CHAPTER TWENTY THREE

From outside the compound's energy shield, Major Smythe could not hear the explosions of the eight Zinger missiles. He was also not looking in the direction of the central compound, his attention was focused on monitoring civilian air traffic around his location while they waited for a dropship to pluck them off the rooftop. The dropship was only thirty kilometers away, about to make a turn toward the city's local inner marker; once the Dragon was twenty kilometers away, Smythe would receive the signal to deploy their tether balloons. He kept his gaze switching between the air traffic lanes and the door that provided access to the roof. After the SEALS team had been surprised by Kristang sneaking onto the roof they were landing on, Smythe was not taking for granted that Skippy had perfect awareness of every possible Kristang in the buildings where the ground teams were concealed. Once they stepped out from cover to deploy the tether balloons, Smythe and Robertson would be exposed and vulnerable for uncomfortable seconds until they were magically whisked away by a tether cable thinner than a human hair.

While Smythe scanned the air traffic corridor toward the south and east, Robertson was monitoring the north and west, scanning back and forth with the passive sensors of his suit, and through the composite images Skippy was feeding to his visor from the local sensor network. He happened to have just swept his gaze past the compound at the center of the city when he caught a flash of light with the corner of his eye. Instantly, his attention focused on the thin slice of the pyramid that was visible between towering buildings. With his view of the pyramid partly obscured by the distortion of the compound's intense energy shield, Robertson was not immediately certain what he was seeing. Had it been merely a reflection? Could it have- The hot orange flares of a second, then third explosion confirmed his original thought. "Major, something's happened in the compound." Already, the flares were fading into a dull red glow.

"What?" Smythe turned, the knees of his armored suit scraping on the rough material of the rooftop. "Bloody hell," he swore as he watched the replay images Robertson sent directly to Smythe's visor. "Skippy! Did you jump the gun?"

"Oh, uh, yeah. Basically, a very nice Kristang was holding the door open for us, and I had to act before we lost the opportunity. Sorry there wasn't time to inform you."

"A very nice Kristang?" Smythe was taken aback by that unlikely concept.

"Uh huh, I would give him a fruit basket as a thank you, except he got splattered by a Mach three shock wave. I do feel bad about that, but, what the hell, right? Anywho, what you need to know is events are proceeding rather more quickly than I anticipated. The Kristang are going to full alert all over the planet, not just in Fire Dragon territory. The Fire Dragons are shutting down air traffic in the city and I have ordered your dropship to divert. Sorry about that."

The alarm Smythe saw on Robertson's face matched his own feelings. "We can't stay up here indefinitely, Skippy," Smythe stated the obvious.

"I know, I have a plan. Well, more of a concept than a plan, truthfully. Ok, fine, I'm making shit up as I go, but that's the best I've got right now. Destroy your stealth generators and tethers and get inside the building, head for the elevator doors to the left."

"We're riding a lift to the ground?" Smythe asked, incredulous. He could not imagine standing inside an elevator car with Robertson, the two of them in powered armor suits and carrying rifles. What would happen if a Kristang, a civilian lizard, came into the elevator? Were the SAS men supposed to make small talk? Did Kristang ever make small talk?

"Ride the lift down? Ha!" Skippy chuckled. "You should be so lucky. No, the building security staff is in the process of evacuating the few occupants, then they will bring the elevator cars to the basement and lock them there."

"Then why should we go to the elevator door?" Smythe asked as he stuffed the balloon and tether into his backpack and pulled the handle to activate nanomachines that would turn everything inside the pack into mush.

"Well, heh heh, you are not going to like this-"

From their rooftop, the SEALS team could not see the pyramid at the center of the city, so their first inkling that something had gone off plan was a pair of air transports suddenly slowing and climbing, then turning away from the established air corridor. "Skippy, we just saw a-"

"Yeah, I know about it," the AI responded dismissively. "I had to move up the schedule and now the Kristang are on full alert. The good news is, all the Zingers hit their targets."

"What does that mean for us?" Williams asked anxiously. They had just been about to walk to the center of the roof to inflate their tether balloons.

"Nothing for right now. I have been forced to divert Major Smythe's dropship away from the city, but since your dropship is already in a designated air traffic corridor, it is still inbound. Your dropship had to reduce speed and climb, it will be within the length of your tether. Probably. You will have a longer ride on the tether, that could, um, get rough. You SEALS guys will probably enjoy it. Stand by, I will give you the signal to launch balloons; you will want to minimize the time those balloons are hanging up there. Military aircraft have been scrambled over the city and I cannot predict whether they will interfere with the tethers."

Williams appreciated the honesty. He wondered what an AI who could warp spacetime considered to be 'rough'. "Understood, standing by for your signal."

"Don't worry, Lt. Williams," Skippy said in a confident voice. "Everything is under control."

Skippy was not wrong about everything being under control, because of course, Skippy the Magnificent was never *wrong* about anything. He may have overestimated his scope of control over the entire city, but that was merely a matter of degree. Minor details. He had limited control over the air traffic system, and to a lesser extent military communications. What he could not control at all was the nature of Kristang, or most biological beings, in the fog of war.

As soon as the city-wide alert went out, rumors began flying much faster than the official communications. In one district of the city near the SEALS team, a defense controller had just come on duty when he was startled by an alert signal: the leadership compound had been attacked. On the console of the junior officer in front of him, the controller saw two aircraft had just strayed from the designated civilian air traffic corridor. The transports were accelerating, climbing, and turning toward the compound! Reacting immediately, the controller pressed a button to order a missile launch, just before the junior officer shouted that those aircraft had been ordered to turn 180 degrees and exit the city.

It was too late to stop the missile; it streaked out of its launch tube near the top of a building that soared one hundred meters above its flying target. The transport's portside engine exploded and sheared off when struck by the missile, causing the aircraft to stagger in the air, flip over and fall. The other transport frantically veered away, pulling hard to the right to miss both burning debris and the buildings around it. Its turn to the right took it toward restricted airspace, and a maser cannon on another building fired, slicing off one wing. That doomed aircraft also began to fall, and hearing reports of hostile aircraft and defensive fire caused military defense controllers in other districts around the city to seek likely targets. Fearful of allowing another attack, many of the controllers instinctively decided to eliminate any possible threats, and aircraft above the city began to fall victim to missiles and maser cannons. Military aircraft flying patrols over the city saw the explosions below, and, in the utter confusion, went into power dives and sought targets.

"Pull up! Pull up!" Skippy shouted, and Flight Lieutenant Windsor responded immediately, increasing power automatically to maintain airspeed in the climb. He reminded himself to fly the Dragon dropship as he would a civilian airliner. Whatever the problem was, he could only make it worse if thc Kristang suspected the true nature of the ship he was flying. Ahead and below, Windsor could see streaks of light and something spiraling down, on fire. On the grid of the cockpit display, it looked like the problem was near the building where the SEALS waiting for retrieval. "What happened?"

"Shit happened," Skippy snapped. "Abort the pickup, turn to two four nine degrees and climb, you need to get clear of the area. There is a whole lot of friendly fire going on ahead of you. Worry about yourself, I'll take care of the SEALS team."

Knowing Skippy, Windsor shared a worried look with his copilot. "How do you plan to get the SEALS out of there?"

"Right now, I have no freakin' idea," Skippy admitted. "Give me a minute, I'm busy trying to keep you alive. The Kristang down there are shooting at anything that flies; I'm messing with the targeting systems in your area."

Windsor mouthed a silent prayer and looked back at 'Curly', the dead Kristang in the seat behind him. If his Dragon were shot down over the city, the Kristang examining the wreckage might wonder why human remains were scattered around, but they would also find Curly in his broken armored suit, and hopefully decide the incident was not worth investigating during a civil war. That would be cold comfort for Windsor and his crew.

Williams and Jones had just received Skippy's signal to launch their balloons, when it seemed like the sky exploded around them. The first thing they saw was a missile streaking in to strike a transport aircraft that had turned away from the normal air traffic corridor. The impact and loss of engine caused the aircraft to roll over and veer toward their building, descending rapidly. Somehow, the pilots were able to recover and the aircraft staggered along, losing altitude and trailing smoke and fire but giving a semblance of control.

Then, seeing an aircraft deviate from the authorized flight path and evidence of hostile action in the city below, a fighter above the city opened fire on the transport, ripping it apart with maser bolts. The transport tore itself apart, burning chunks of wreckage falling over the city. That was enough for the already-panicked controllers of the city's defense system. Without bothering to coordinate or even check with the civilians air traffic control system, the defenders authorized their autocannons and missiles to act against any aircraft that had deviated from the established civilian air traffic corridors. Since the air traffic system had ordered most civilian traffic to deviate from their normal flightpaths, the city's defense system found a target-rich environment when it was unleashed. Missile exploded from launch tubes, and maser autocannons crackled, scorching the air and searing into unprotected civilian aircraft. Seeing gunfire below, military fighters flying cover above added their own weapons to the fray, and in moments, the air above the city was a freeform swirling chaos of exploding aircraft and buildings impacted by burning debris.

"Oh, shit, boss!" Jones shouted and pushed Williams aside just before a flying piece of something impacted the roof right where the SEALS team leader had been standing. Williams staggered, the suit's stabilizer mechanism keeping him upright. He regained his footing just in time to see a large fiery chunk of something descending toward the roof. As he spun to leap out of the way, his mind recognized the object as the forward section of a Kristang civilian transport aircraft. Then the nose of what used to be an aircraft slammed into the roof, and the two SEALS were flung through the air.

Williams came down hard, bouncing on the roof and smacking up against a metal box that contained some type of mechanical equipment. Stunned, he got on hands and knees, shaking his head to clear the spots from his eyes. The display in his visor indicated the armored suit had not sustained any significant damage. "Jones? Jones?" He looked around in alarm, trying to eyeclick the visor to check on the status of his fellow SEALS, but his unsteady vision was unable to control the display through eye movements alone. Pulling himself upright, he just got to his feet when a line of maser light struck the roof; an overeager fighter pilot high above making sure the piece of aircraft on the roof would not represent a threat. The roof buckled partly and Williams staggered again, spots still swimming in his vision. He was knocked to his knees when the roof below him sagged, and he toppled to the side to crash on top of Jones.

"Jones! Jones?" Williams used his suit's super-powered Kung Fu grip to bend the metal of the mechanical box next to him, providing a do-it-yourself handhold to steady himself. Jones was not responding and the man didn't look good. The right side of his suit's torso was bent inward from below the armpit to the hip. There was not a hole or crack, but inside the suit, parts of the material had to be sticking into Jones. Williams bent to get a better look in the man's visor, and Jones coughed, sending a spray of red droplets onto the inner surface of the faceplate. The droplets ran down and were sucked away automatically. "Jones? Can you hear me?"

"Yeah, boss. I, I'm not doing so good."

Williams looked around, fearing something else would hit the roof soon. "Can you walk?"

"I think so. Need to, to catch my breath is all."

They didn't have time for Jones to catch his breath. "I'll help you," Williams offered and put a hand under the man's left armpit, using his powered suit to lift. Jones staggered, grunted, and his eyes rolled back. "Can you stand?"

"No," Jones barely was able to say the word, the pain was so bad. He had cracked, possibly broken ribs. If he could pause to run a diagnostic, the suit would tell him where and how badly he was hurt. They did not have time for that. With Williams doing most of the work, the two made their way across the cracked and buckled surface of the roof to an access door, which was on a reinforced part of the roof. The door frame had warped, Williams punched through with his free glove and the door open. Staggering down the stairs that were too tall for human comfort, he mostly carried Jones down two flights of stairs then stopped, as the stairway below that level was missing. Something had hit that side of the building and tore a section loose. Williams went back up a few stairs and cautiously pulled open a door into a dark and empty hallway. He allowed Jones to slump down against a wall and used his own suit to check the other man's condition. Broken ribs, punctured lung, bruised spleen and other less important internal injuries. Jones was not getting out of the building on his own.

"Skippy," Williams could hear booming and banging sounds coming from above. Either the damaged roof was settling, or more weapons fire was uselessly bouncing the debris around. Or, worse, Kristang soldiers had landed on the roof to investigate the incident. "You got any ideas to get us out of here?" He subconsciously ran a hand on the back of his neck where the suicide patch rested, but his armored gloves merely scraped against the back of his helmet.

"Climb down the maintenance access shaft for the ventilation system," Skippy responded, as if that were the simplest thing in the world to do. "You don't have time for witty banter so, no, I was not joking, Lieutenant."

"An access shaft? How about you use your super powers to commandeer an elevator for us?"

"No can do. I thought of that, but the building security personnel have already brought the elevators to the bottom level and engaged the manual locking bolts. I have control of several bots that could remove the bolts, however that would require the three security people to leave their posts so the bots have time to work. They are unlikely to do that. Thus, because Jones is injured, your best bet is the access shaft."

Williams took a moment to consider. Skippy was an incredible intelligent AI, but he was not a being with biological limits. He did not know whether plans he made were practical for real humans, even highly capable SEALS. "Fine, let's do it," he said, having quickly considered their limited options. His helmet faceplate lit up with an arrow pointing to a barely-visible door near the end of the corridor, and the visor drew a blinking yellow box around the outline of the door. "I see the door."

"Good, go there now. Now." Skippy urged.

Williams picked up the inert Jones, hearing his suit's internal motors whining with the strain. Bent over, he shuffled his feet along the corridor toward the door, which clicked softly and slid aside. The door led to an alcove, really a large closet, and the door slid silently closed behind him. "We're here."

"I know," Skippy said in a matter-of-fact manner, not taking time for jokes. "You have to manually remove the hatch, it's just a wheel."

"I see it," Williams set Jones down gently, and spun the wheel. He stuck his head in an opening barely large enough for his suited bulk. The helmet lights came on automatically, illuminating a smooth if somewhat dusty rectangular shaft. Handholds were recessed farther apart than they would be on Earth, and there were more access hatches at what he estimated were every five floors. "That's thirty stories down," he observed skeptically. Since Kristang were taller than humans, their buildings had taller ceilings, making each floor in the building twenty or more feet apart. "That is a long way to climb. I can barely fit in there, not sure how I can carry Jones. Can you remotely control his suit?"

"Not with the precision required to climb down that shaft, no. Remove him from his suit, and hide the suit in the closet to your right. There are cleaning and maintenance bots in there now, I have deactivated them."

Working quickly and as quietly as he could, Williams pulled a half dozen bots from the closet. Some small, some taller than himself. Some bland and as prosaic in appearance as a toaster, some scary with tentacles for grasping a variety of implements. With the closet cleared out, he remotely commanded Jones' suit to open. Seals at the neck, across the torso, at the waist, wrists and ankles broke open, allowing Williams to carefully take the armor off. Jones was barely conscious, trying to help and only getting in Williams' way. "Jones, relax, I got this. You seeing this, Skippy?" He looked at the wound that had Jones' right side covered with blood from the bottom half of his ribcage to below the man's hipbone.

"Yes. The injury is no different from what the suit reported. Jones will recover fully, if we can get him here so I can stabilize him, then aboard the ship for treatment. Put his suit in the closet along with your thermal grenades; active your grenades and his. I will need to destroy the suit later. Once you are in the access shaft, I will activate one of the bots and use it to clean up the human blood on the floor. Hurry, please."

It had been a struggle to get Jones securely onto Williams' back while in the confines of the access shaft. After several failed attempts, they had relied on assistance from a bot controlled by Skippy. With Jones strapped to his back, Williams had climbed down twelve stories of the building. So far, so good; Skippy reported a military aircraft had been sent to investigate the wreckage on the roof, but with friendly fire incidents abounding around the city, the pilots were hesitant to approach the building. "Friendly fire?" Williams asked. "You wouldn't be involved in any of that, would you?"

Skippy chuckled. "Ok, not maybe it is not-so-friendly fire. Although I didn't start it, that was all lizards. Now that the retrieval op got all screwed up, I figure that lizards shooting at each other provides good cover for your escape. How are you doing, Lieutenant?"

"I'm good, Skippy, the suit is doing most of the work. Jones? You with me?" Williams asked, nudging the injured man's head gently with his helmet.

"Nnnnuh," Jones, responded. "Yuh."

"Good. Need to keep you awake, so I'm going to tell you a joke, Ok?"

"Your, jokes, terr-ble." Jones breathed.

"Ha! Listen, this guy walks into a bar, with a shopping bag, right? He sits down, puts the bag on the bar. Something in the bag is moving, and the bartender says 'Hey, buddy, no animals in here'. You with me, Jones?"

"Yah."

"The guy is looking real unhappy, totally down in the dumps, he reaches in the bag. He pulls out a brass lantern, then a small piano, a little stool, and finally a little guy in a tuxedo, about a foot tall. The little guy sits on the stool and starts playing the piano. Playing the piano, right?"

"Yah. Got, it."

"Bartender says," Williams' grasp on a handhold slipped for a heart-stopping moment before the suit gloves restored their sticky grip. He could see the problem was some sort of fluid leaking from the access hatch above had coated the handhold. He moved his hand to the left to avoid the slippery fluid, and continued climbing down. "Bartender says, 'That's amazing, where'd you get him?' Guy points to the lamp. 'Magic genie granted me a wish, But he don't hear so well-' Before the guy can stop him, the bartender grabs the lamp, rubs it and shouts 'I want a million bucks!'. POOF! The bar is filled with *ducks*! Ducks everywhere, under the tables, in the street outside, feathers flying all over the place. The bartender says 'What the hell?' So the guy says 'I told you the genie don't hear so well. You really think I asked for a twelve inch *pianist*?'"

"Huh-ha. Ha!" Jones laughed with a cough. "Oh, that hurt."

"Ha! Yeah, that's a good one. You Ok back there?"

"Fine," Jones' breathing was labored. "Thanks, that woke me up."

"Outstanding. Now it's your turn to tell me a joke," Williams ordered. He thought that, even if Jones could not manage to tell a joke, trying to think of one would keep the injured man awake.

"I got a joke." Jones announced after a minute. He knew keeping himself alert was important, until he could truly rest. "Two guys in an English pub, one says 'From your accent I guess you are Irish'. Second guy says, 'Yes, from Dublin'. 'Me too!' first guy says. 'I was raised in Drimnagh, went to St. Mary's school'. 'Drimnagh? St. Mary's?' Second guy can't believe it. 'I graduated from St. Mary's in 1982'. First guy slaps his forehead. 'Faith and begorah. I graduated from St. Mary's in 1982 also!' Bartender says,"

Jones paused for breath, "he says to himself 'This is going to be a long night. The Murphy twins are drunk again'."

"Hahahahahahaha!" Skippy laughed, and the beer can's hysterical laughter made the joke extra funny to Williams, who could have lost his grip on the recessed handhold. Fortunately, the computer controlling the powered fingers of the gloves had learned what Williams wanted to do, and the glove automatically curled around the handhold until he flexed his fingers to release. What he had told Skippy was true; the powered suit was doing most of the work to climb all the way down the access shaft. Williams knew he was still going to be stiff, especially his pinky and ring fingers. Because Kristang had only three fingers and a thumb, humans using their suits had to jam two fingers into the last opening of the glove. Suit wearers got used to the awkward motion after a while; it helped to keep fingernails well trimmed and wrap both fingers together in gauze. "Lt. Williams," Skippy announced, "you need to concentrate on climbing down, I will keep Petty Officer Jones occupied."

"You are *not* singing to me," Jones warned.

"Fine," Skippy huffed. "I'll tell you some jokes I got from Doctor Friedlander. A Kristang, a Ruhar and a Thuranin walk into a bar-"

In a building halfway across the city, the SAS team was having second thoughts about trusting an alien AI. "This does not appear to be a tremendously good idea, Skippy," Smythe said unhappily after he and Robertson manually forced the lift doors open. When the beer can had suggested they use an elevator shaft without a car, Smythe pictured using the power-assisted gloves of their armored suits to slide down a cable like Batman. That idea, while dangerous, at least had the advantage of sounding cool. Unfortunately, high-tech Kristang elevators did not use cables, only a smooth track on each side. Smythe switched on his helmet lights, peering one way then the other. He did not see the ladder or handhold that he expected. Nothing he could use to climb down. "Not even a mildly good idea."

"Trust me, Major, this will work just fine," Skippy's voice was jolly.

"*You* are not about to fall two hundred fifty meters down an elevator shaft," Smythe retorted.

"Neither are you. Well, heh heh, I don't think so. There is a low but non-zero probability of you plunging to a horrible death."

"I am not bursting with confidence," Smythe looked over at Robertson, whose face was pale.

"Uh, hmm, the good news is, if you do fall, the impact at the bottom will be so violent that you'll never feel it. Did that help?"

"You daft bugger, what do you think?" Smythe demanded.

"No? Ah, anyway, don't worry, I got this."

Smythe did not see any possible way for the two of them to descend the smooth surface of the shaft. The tracks for the elevator cars were also smooth, as if the only moving part in the entire elevator mechanism was the car itself. "Please, Oh Wise One, explain this to me. I know these suits have a super gecko grip on the gloves, boots and knees, I do not think they can adhere to such a smooth surface all the way down."

"Correct, I estimate the gloves and boots would lose adhesion immediately, the big problem is the lubricant contaminating the shaft. The Kristang are not so particular about cleaning parts of the building that no one sees. Please be quiet and allow me to explain before we run out of time. The elevator mechanism replies on magnetic pulses; pins on each side of the cars ride in the slots you see. My plan is for each of you to insert a glove and boot into one of those slots. I will energize the outer surface of your glove and boot, then use the magnetic track to safely lower you to the second floor. You will force open the door there, then take a seldom-used back stairway to the street level."

"We put a hand and foot in one of those tracks?"

"That's the idea, yes. I have checked the measurements, it will work."

Smythe used the rangefinder built into the helmet. The tracks were on either side of the shaft, according to the rangefinder each track was four point two meters from the edge of the door opening. "We can't reach the tracks from here, and there isn't anything to stand on. Do you have any idea how we get to the tracks?" The AI did not respond. "Skippy?"

"Well, shit."

"*Well, shit*?" Smythe asked incredulously. "You sodding bugger, how could-"

"Hey, I can't think of everything! Let's, uh, let's keep this little incident between ourselves, huh? No need for Joe to hear about this."

"Oh," Smythe shared a look with Robertson, "if we get out of this, we will be inviting Colonel Bishop to afternoon tea, where we will eat crumpets and tell him in great detail exactly what happened."

"Crap. This isn't the first time I forgot some tiny little detail," Skippy admitted in a snarky tone. "You know, here is a case where it would be useful if you monkeys hadn't lost your freakin' tails. That is *totally* your fault."

"We could jump," Robertson suggested in a tone meaning he was not advocating that idea. "I think I can get a glove in that-"

"No!" Skippy fairly shouted into their helmet speakers. "If you miss, it is a long way down. If even one of you missed, you will hit the elevator car at the bottom, then this whole building will be swarming with lizards and you'll both be screwed."

"Major," Robertson reached into the shaft, dragged his fingertips along the smooth surface then studied his gloves. "The surface is covered in dirt and oil, my gloves wouldn't stick. If Skippy can get a cleaning bot here to remove the oil-"

"Skippy?" Smythe asked.

"Ok," Skippy sounded happy. "Finally, the two of you are using that mush inside your skulls for something useful. I have control of the cleaning bots, but that will take too long. I have a better idea."

Smythe gaped, open mouthed, at the bizarre contraption hanging in the elevator shaft. "*This* is your better idea?"

"Yup. Great, ain't it? I told you, trust the awesomeness."

"What I said was a question, not a statement," Smythe explained. "How is this thing holding itself up?" Skippy's brilliant idea used a maintenance bot instead of a cleaning machine; the bot he chose to employ for the task was tall with four long tentacles. The bot had come scurrying around a corner without warning, prompting both SAS troopers to almost shred it with their rifles before Skippy warned them not to. Under Skippy's direction, the bot had leaned through the elevator door opening and stuck two tentacles into the elevator guide slot on one side, then swung itself into the shaft and extended the other tentacles to maximum length into the slot on the opposite side.

"Magnets, I told you that already. Hurry, jump out there, grab onto the arms and use them to get a hand and foot into the slot. One at a time, please, the bot is barely holding on by itself."

"The bot appears to be unsteady, Skippy," Smythe tried to judge how much power-assisted force to use, without overshooting the mark and

"That's because that bot wasn't designed to do this. Hurry! Move!"

Smythe leaped first, easily catching a tentacle and wrapping two hands around it. The bot lurched under his weight and began sliding down alarmingly, until Smythe reached out with a foot and got it into the slot. He felt a tingling through the boot, so he let go of the tentacle with one hand and jammed that hand into the slot, then let go of the bot. Immediately, the bot stopped sliding downward. And Smythe was held securely in place. "It works!" Smythe announced as he worked his other foot into the slot. "Can you bring the bot upward?"

"Yup," Skippy announced, as both Smythe and the bot rose to the level of the doorway. Robertson repeated Smythe's maneuver, and shortly they were both hanging onto a slot with both feet and both hands. The bot swung itself out of the shaft without any fuss and scurried off, presumably back to wherever Skippy had found it. The door closed, and the two men began moving downward in an encouragingly controlled fashion. After a few seconds, the drop picked up speed. "Don't worry, I will gradually slow you down as you get near the bottom, you need to proceed with alacrity."

"With alacrity?" Smythe asked, amused.

"It means quickly," Skippy explained. "Come on, you Brits use fancy words for everything. Hey, since you are sort of riding an elevator, I think this is an appropriate time for some elevator music." His voice began warbling off key. "*Miiiiidnight, not a sound from the paaaavement, has the moon lost her memory? She is smiling alone-*"

"Oh, bloody 'Cats'. My Mum dragged me to see that," Robertson complained. "Ooops, I am losing my grip. Too bad plunging to my death will mean I miss the end of this song."

"Not funny, Robertson," Skippy blessedly paused his warbling long enough to reply. "*In the laaaaamplight, the-*"

"Think of it as training to resist interrogation, Robertson," Smythe suggested. "After ten minutes of this torture, anyone would talk." Fortunately, Smythe could see they were approaching the bottom and Skippy was slowing them down. "We are to stop at the second floor and force that door open?"

"That's the plan, yes."

"Mmm. Any thoughts on how we are to get from these tracks through that closed door?" Smythe asked hopefully. "Skippy?"

"Well, shit! Crap! Damn it! I *hate* my life," the beer can grumbled. "Ah, this kind of sucks for you, huh?"

"We are greatly touched by your concern for us." Through the clear faceplate, Smythe could see Robertson grinning. "We can handle this, Skippy. Halt us about two meters above the door."

The doorway they departed from had a lip just below that Smythe had examined as a potential handhold. On their descent, he had inspected each doorway as they went by; all the doors were the same. Robertson insisted on jumping first once they stopped. He easily caught onto the lip with both hands, but the material then began twisting and bending under his weight! Moving quickly, Robertson jammed one hand between the doors and used the powered mechanism of the gloves to force the lift doors apart wide enough to get a hand in, then he let go of the failing lip and forced the doors open with both hands. He pulled himself up to flop ungracefully on his belly, then rolled to his feet and held the doors wide open. "Ready for you, Major."

Smythe pulled his feet out of the tracks, swung back and forth twice to get momentum, and soared down through the open door, trusting his suit's stabilizers to keep him from crashing. "That is how we do it monkey-style, Skippy," he said with a wink at Robertson.

"Yeah, yeah, very impressive," Skippy scoffed. "I'll give you seven out of ten for that jump, Major, you didn't stick the landing."

"*You* try it." Smythe checked his weapon.

"Very funny. Move, quickly now, down the hallway and to the stairwell, I- uh, crap. Another freakin' complication. Damn it! A Kristang has just entered that stairwell from the bottom, you will need to get past him."

"Is he armed?" Smythe placed a finger next to the safety button of his rifle.

"No," Skippy replied. "but you should not shoot him, that would alert everyone in the building. If he doesn't come back soon, the security team will notice he is missing. Major, put on your police outfit. The lighting in there is dim, I will cover your face with a hologram and I will do the talking for you. Please hurry."

Working quickly, Smythe and Robertson helped each other don their police disguises; a crest that attached to the top of their helmets, an armband that encircled their left biceps and a triangle that fitted to the chest. Skippy changed the camouflage pattern of the armor to the black and yellow of clan police, with the crest, chest triangle and armband displaying the proper symbols. The armor they were wearing was heavier than standard police issue, and their rifles slightly longer than police-issue carbines, but hopefully both would pass in a casual inspection at a distance. "Ready," Smythe reported. "Show me this hologram trick."

Robertson's faceplate went from matt black to clear, exposing his human features. With a flicker, his image of the face morphed into that of a Kristang. "How is this, Major?" Robertson said, and the lizard's mouth moved appropriately.

"Good," Smythe peered closer. The hologram was not perfect. "Skippy, will this be good enough?"

"It will if you don't allow anyone close to you," Skippy said quickly. "Also, don't make sudden gestures, I am controlling the holograms remotely, and there is a bit of a time lag for me to deal with. Go now, it is best to meet this Kristang in the stairwell where the lighting is poor."

Smythe left his rifle's safety engaged and tapped the knife attached to his right hip, Robertson understood the silent gesture. If the Kristang needed to be neutralized, the SAS men would do it quietly, no gunfire that would echo in the stairwell.

They heard the Kristang before they saw him, footsteps clunking on the stairs. Smythe checked Robertson's holographic lizard face, it was more convincing in the stairwell's dimness. Walking with purpose but not running, the two men crossed the landing and began descending, startling the Kristang who pressed himself up against the wall to let them past. "Remain in the building," Smythe heard the translation of what his suit speakers were telling the lizard, and he gestured with one hand to emphasize his order. For a brief second, his eyes met the eyes of the Kristang, and Smythe saw surprise but not the shock or alarm that would accompany the alien recognizing a human face. Then they were past, pushing through the door onto the first floor.

"It worked," Skippy announced. "He is continuing up the stairs and he is not running or calling building security. Go to your left, then another left, you will exit the back of the building."

"What's out there, Skippy?" Smythe asked when his hand was on the lever to open the door.

"A lot of people. Chaos. Civilians are leaving the center of the city to get away from the fighting; there are still friendly fire incidents occurring regularly. That door opens into an alley not much different from an urban alley on Earth; it is dark and narrow and crowded and dirty with refuse containers. There is a delivery vehicle at the end to your left, I suggest you go to the right and onto the sidewalk."

Smythe went first, pushing the door open and sticking his head out into what Skippy had accurately described as a narrow alley between two buildings. The alley was empty except for a lorry parked against one side; Smythe could see into the lorry's cab and it was empty. Skippy had also been correct about chaos in the city; the streets at both ends of the alley were jammed with vehicle traffic on the streets and panicked Kristang hurrying along the sidewalks. "Robertson, this is going to be interesting. Remember, we are clan police officers, we own these streets. We move and act with authority, and no one will stop us. We are *Kristang* police; if any civilians attempt to bother us, brush them aside, use the butt of your rifle if needed."

"Got it," Robertson agreed, holding his rifle in front of him, checking the safety was on. They walked quickly and purposefully down the alley, taking long but unhurried strides. Both men took a deep breath before stepping from the darkest part of the alley into the pool of light coming from the street. With the city under emergency conditions, most buildings were dark, with the only lights at street level. Even those were a dim, sickly yellowish haze, other than the rotating red lamps at intersections. With the city ground traffic system controlling all movement in the streets, vehicles rolled smoothly along, with a string of five vehicles almost nose to tail, then a gap. Across the street, a bus glided silently to a stop and no one got off; Kristang on the sidewalk pushed and shoved and argued to get on the bus that would take them out of the now-dangerous city. The bus did not have a driver, and the controlling system did not care about the fears of its occupants, for the doors suddenly shut and the bus rolled away, apparently leaving some females on the sidewalk while their children were on the bus. Frantic females raced after the bus, which smoothly accelerated away and switched to a higher speed center lane. Smythe and Robertson looked at each other and each shook their heads. They felt sympathy for the wailing females, who still tried to catch the distant bus despite the crowded sidewalk. The SAS men, the humans, would not get involved in Kristang affairs. Except for assuring the Kristang were no longer a threat to Earth, problems of the alien society were of no concern to anyone from Earth.

With Smythe in the lead, they stepped from the alley into the sidewalk. The crowd parted for them, civilians keeping a distance between themselves and the feared clan police force. The SAS men walked down the center of the sidewalk, keeping their rifles in front of them, using the rifles to nudge aside civilians who did not move quickly enough. In the dimness of the city's reddish emergency lighting, no one looked too closely at the pair of 'police officers'. The two figures in their hulking black and yellow armored suits were a menacing sight that did not invite close inquiry.

Smythe had to use his SAS training to maintain razor-sharp focus despite the swirling confusion around him, and the mind-blowing experience of strolling along a street in a Kristang city. Despite the bizarre circumstances, all was well until Skippy alerted them to a problem. "Major Smythe, there is a problem and I do not know how best you should cope with it. A pair of real city police are about to come around the corner to your right; they are checking identification of people before allowing them to proceed."

"The hologram faceplate trick won't work?" Smythe thought he already knew the answer to that question.

"No, those police will insist you lift your faceplate. You have only seconds now."

Across the street and to the right, Smythe saw a crowd forming, civilians being stopped and inspected or frisked or scanned or whatever Kristang police did. Instinctively, Smythe pulled his zPhone out of a belt pouch, held it up, and shouted for a male Kristang hurrying past to stop. "Citizen! Halt!" He prayed whatever Skippy-translated words booming out of the helmet speakers was correct for the situation.

Robertson followed Smythe's lead, taking out his own zPhone and pretending to use it as a scanner. "Identification, now!" He shouted at the nearest pair of civilians, holding up his rifle menacingly. With the zPhone, he waved it up and down each one, pretending to scan them while they babbled fearfully at him.

Across the street, two city police officers came around the corner, brusquely pushing civilians aside, herding them together. One of the police glanced across the street, turned away, then turned back, startled to see another pair of police.

"Skippy," Smythe said quietly, "tell them whatever hell you need, to make them leave us alone." Without waiting for the unseen beer can, he held up his rifle and gestured at the other police with two fingers of his other hand. With sign language, he tried to indicate that he and Robertson would cover their side of the street, and the other police should cover their side. From the speakers below the chin of his helmet, he heard his suit saying something loud in Kristang.

The other cop took one step toward Smythe, hesitating at the edge of the street.

"Lt. Robertson," Skippy ordered, "hit the Kristang male in front of you. Don't kill him, but knock him down."

There was a Kristang male in front of Robertson, halted to be 'scanned' but arguing, waving some sort of ID card and gesturing at the three females with him. Without checking with Smythe, Robertson reached out and slapped the male across the face, firmly but not hard. Perhaps a bit too firmly; the civilian's head spun and he went down, to be surrounded by wailing and weeping females.

For a gut-churning moment, the other policeman hesitated at the edge of the street, confused. Then his fellow officer called for help with the growing crowd, and the policeman held up two fingers in professional acknowledgement.

"Bloody hell," Smythe had to stop his hands from shaking. "That was close. Skippy, what was that for?"

"Abuse of civilians is convincing evidence that the two of you are clan police," Skippy explained. "More convincing than the line of bullshit I was telling that cop."

The male staggered to his feet with the help of his cowering females, and Smythe felt sorry for the women. They would no doubt catch the wrath of the male, for they had witnessed the male's humiliation. Smythe pointed at the male and waved him angrily away. "Robertson, we make our way down this side of the street, keep stopping people and pretend we're checking IDs. Do not look across the street; Skippy will warn us if those coppers are coming our way. Right, Skippy?"

"Affirmative. I have to say, Major, that once again I am impressed by the inventiveness of humans. That was quick thinking."

"I figure police are like soldiers; they have a job to do and want to focus on it."

"I cannot comment on the universal nature of human military and law enforcement. There is a potential problem; traffic on the other side of the street is thinning. I overheard those two police saying they may split up soon, with one of them coming toward you. I have transmitted the proper authentication codes for you, however, these are local police and they do not recognize the two of you."

"Tell them we're, federal police, or something like that," Robertson suggested.

"I did that already; as local police they are curious, and unhappy, about you being in their jurisdiction. Do not be overly concerned, Major Smythe."

"*Overly* concerned?" What would be the appropriate level of concern? Absolute and utter panic?

"Please, Major. Trust the awesomeness. I have just caused a vehicle crash up the street behind you, that will divert foot traffic onto the other side of the street. And," Skippy paused, "yes, civilians are crossing the road. The two police officers have just noticed the increased traffic, and the accident. One of them is gesturing toward you. Wave to acknowledge."

Smythe turned briefly toward the other police and did the curt two-finger wave again. "You keep going, my friend," he muttered under his breath, "nothing to see over here."

"Hey, arsehole," Robertson mimicked Smythe's two-finger gesture toward the alien police officer. "Yeah, that's right, stay over there."

To the relief of the two humans, the real police officers continued up the other side of the street, drawing farther away from the Special Air Services officers. As the distance increased and it became harder for the real police to see them Smythe and Robertson began walking faster, stopping only random civilians rather than everyone on the sidewalk. "Robertson, check behind us. Can you see those police?"

"Only the tops of their helmets," Robertson reported quietly.

"Skippy, we are *out* of here," Smythe advised. "Which way?"

"Excellent work, Major," Skippy sounded pleased. "Take the next left, then cross the street approximately forty meters down and go into an alley there."

At the other end of the alley, a lorry was backing up toward them. "Skippy?" Smythe looked for a doorway they might escape into.

"Relax Major, I commandeered that truck, I'm driving it," Skippy replied as it slowed to a stop and the back door rolled up to expose an empty and battered cargo box.

"A lorry?" Smythe asked skeptically. "Why couldn't we have gotten into the lorry that was in the alley behind our building?"

"Because that truck was loaded, you would have had to break into it and unload the cargo. Plus, the cargo containers in that truck all have radio ID tags that I can't easily hack into from here; if the truck got pulled over for inspection the police would be suspicious that why it is heading out of the city when the cargo's destination is near the city center. Also, that truck was on the wrong side of the street for a direct path outside the city. Please, just get in the truck, OK? I'll have you outside the city in a jiffy."

Smythe did not ask exactly how long a 'jiffy' was, although he was certain it was longer than whatever Skippy expected. "Robertson," he waved the other man forward, and they stepped up into the cargo box, which slid closed behind them. With a whine of electric motors, the lorry started forward with a lurch, turned what Smythe felt was to the right, and picked up speed. Smythe slid his back down the cargo box to sit on the floor, and rested his rifle between his feet. One thing the military had taught him was to get rest when he could.

CHAPTER TWENTY FOUR

Williams' arms, legs and fingers were cramped and aching when he completed the climb, which had taken them three stories below street level. Jones was doing better, the color coming back into his cheeks. Skippy said the nanoparticles he had injected into Jones from the suit had stopped the internal bleeding, although Jones still had fluid in his right lung.

They waited behind a door that lead to a parking garage beneath the building. Williams found it disconcerting to be in such a mundane place, during an operation that was anything but ordinary. "We're ready, Skippy."

"The truck is backed up as close as I can to the door, you will still be visible for three meters. Petty Officer Jones will need to be covered in that tarp."

"Got it," Jones replied, flopping the tarp over his head so Williams could carry him concealed. They had found the tarp in a storage closet, it was stained, dotted with stiff dried resin or something like that, and smelled of harsh chemicals. Jones considered that, if the tarp got him out of the city to rescue, he would be happy to make a suit of the tarp and wear it every day.

"Commencing distraction in three, two, one, *boom*," Skippy announced, and the building shook. The emergency lighting flickered, as Skippy triggered the thermal grenades on the upper floor. The grenades effectively destroyed the damaged suit Jones had been wearing, along with three floors of one side of the building. Debris exploded outward, cascading into the streets below. The heat of the thermal explosion twisted the upper structure of the tower, and caused the approaching military aircraft to veer away and climb rapidly. "Go!"

Williams was ready, Jones covered up on his back in a fireman's carry, one hand on the door latch. The door opened and in four strides, Williams quickly walked to the waiting truck and stepped up into the mostly empty cargo box. He set Jones down carefully and yanked the door down. "We're in, Skip-" Before he could finish, the truck was already moving.

"You might as well settle down, guys, you'll be in this truck for a while. The good news is the edge of the city is not far and I know a route the military hasn't blocked yet. I'm confident you can get out of the city. The bad news is the highway out of the city leads toward the sea and is a restricted route; it is quite a distance before I can turn this truck onto a side route where a dropship can pick you up."

"Skippy, thank you, we very much appreciate it."

"Oh, it is no trouble at all. Hey, while I have your attention for a couple hours, I've been working on some new showtunes-"

The behavior of our beer can had me concerned. "Skippy, you seem kind of distracted. Is everything Ok with you?"

"Yes, Joe, I'm fine."

My zPhone beeped and it was a text message from Skippy, *We should talk privately*, the text read. That scared me. Aboard the Thuranin dropship, there was no privacy for my conversations with Skippy; everyone could hear both sides. "I'm going outside for fresh air," I announced. That drew raised eyebrows from the crew and I ignored them, they knew when to leave me to myself. Once outside, I stayed within the stealth field netting, the ground was illuminated only by lights from the dropship. I wanted to go outside, to see the sky like I had on Paradise. With the extensive sensor network in Kobamik, I couldn't take that risk just to indulge myself. "What's up, Skippy?" I tried to keep my tone light. It didn't work.

"In a word, the worm. It's back."

"The *worm*?" I lowered my voice. "I thought you killed it."

"So did I. It followed me back into my canister. Or, there is another possibility that frightens me even more."

"What?"

"That a worm has been inside me the whole time, and is only now active. I mentioned the possibility that the worm is a safety mechanism created by the Elders, to protect the galaxy from AIs who go rogue. Maybe the Elders built a worm into my matrix. In that case, all Elder AIs have worms inside them."

"Holy shit. A worm killed that AI we found on Newark. Back then, you said there was no way that AI was involved with throwing Newark out of its orbit."

"Yeah," his voice was glum. "Yeah, I did say that. At the time, I believed it. Totally believed it. Now? Now I don't know what to believe. If that AI went rogue and destroyed Newark's biosphere, the worm may have killed the AI to prevent further damage."

I knew how thinking about a fellow Elder AI wiping out a sentient species would affect Skippy, so I changed the subject. "Why is the worm attacking you now?"

"Unknown. It doesn't matter right now anyway."

"Ok," he also wanted to avoid the subject. "Are you in danger?"

"No, no," he chuckled unconvincingly. "It is distracting me, that's all. No problemo, Joe. That worm is toast. I'm toying with it, I have it trapped in a dead-end where I can take it apart and analyze it. I have beaten that worm twice already that I know of."

"Skippy, are you certain about that? You are our ride off this rock. And back home."

"Joe, if there was a significant danger, I would tell you. Come on, it's *me*."

"Exactly what I'm worried about. All right, we keep going, you promise to tell me if that worm becomes a danger to you?"

"Yup. Now, go back inside where you can monitor how the SEALS and SAS teams are doing."

Smythe had not even vaguely been asleep, so he was instantly aware when the lorry veered to the right abruptly, then slowed, then took another right. "Skippy?"

"Yeah, uh, listen, we have a little bit of a problem. Technically, *you* have the problem, but I am with you in spirit."

"That makes me feel *so* much better," Smythe didn't try to disguise the sarcasm. "What is the problem this time?"

"Checkpoint. The city authorities just closed all civilian ground and air routes into and out of the city. This is as far as the truck can go, unfortunately."

"What do we do now?"

"We go to Plan C. Or it is D? Whatever. No, wait, it is Plan P! Yeah, that's it. *P*," Skippy chuckled.

"What is so funny?"

"You'll see," Skippy was almost giggling with mirth.

Smythe looked at Robertson and they both groaned. "Is this," Smythe asked, "something we very much are not going to like?"

"Hmmm. No. No, *Joe* would very much not like this. But, seeing as your SAS guys are certifiably freakin' crazy, you will probably love this idea. As a bonus, it will give you a great story to tell when you get back to Hereford."

Smythe looked down at the rushing water. Or whatever it was, for the fluid was definitely not pure water. “I must admit, I do not love this idea, Skippy.”

“Plan P! See what I meant?!”

Below Major Smythe was a heavy access hatch that led down into a pipe that carried water and other less savory things out of the city. Skippy had been able to override the lock to the hatch lid, and the two powered armor suits made short work of lifting the heavy lid. Looking down with the lights of his helmet on full power, he did not like what he saw. “P? Yes, that was very clever, Skippy,” he replied without humor. “It’s a sewer. A lizard sewer.”

“Oh, come on, Major. Sealed up in your suits, you won’t get any yucky stuff on you, I promise. Think of it as floating along a river in one of those Central American caves. You did some of your SAS training in Belize, right?”

“The water in those cenotes is clean, Skippy.” Smythe blinked to update the display on his visor, checking the suit’s internal oxygen level. For a ground mission in a breathable atmosphere, they had been relying on external oxygen, pulled into the suit and filtered. Once the mission had gone sideways, the four people still on the ground had activated the pumps that stored oxygen in the suit’s built-in storage packs. Those internal packs did not have the capacity of the tanks used for missions in vacuum or nonbreathable environments, still Smythe was heartened to see that he now had more than two hours of internal oxygen. “This pipe leads to a sewage processing station, I assume? Won’t we be swept up in a filter and crushed by the water pressure?”

“Yes, it does lead to a sewage treatment plant. No, you will not get crushed. The system has emergency bypass gates that can be opened remotely in case of high water volume, and the good news is the security level of that system is low grade; I hacked into it easily. When you approach the bypass gate, it will open and close quickly for you, and I will block the central computer from knowing that gate was ever open. There will be an investigation later, because raw sewage will have been dumped into a river that borders prime hunting ground. I estimate you will pop to the surface of the river thirty one minutes after you enter that pipe, and you will be far enough away from the city to avoid security patrols. We should be away from here and back on the ship, before the Kristang realize something went through the bypass gate. Trust me, Major, this is a stroke of genius. This pipe will take you out of the city faster than that truck would have. There are no traffic jams down there.”

“There is one thing in our favor, Sir,” Robertson leaned over to look down the pipe and wrinkled his nose, even though no scent got through the air filters of his suit.

“What is that?”

“I am certain that 22 SAS has never infiltrated an alien sewer,” Robertson said with a smile, “so perhaps we will get a unique campaign ribbon for that.”

“Ha!” Smythe laughed at the gallows humor and patted Robertson on the back. “There’s nothing for it, then, I’ll go first.”

I anxiously followed the progress of the truck carrying Lt. Williams’ two-man SEALS team out of the city, giving a shudder of relief when the display showed me their truck had cleared the city perimeter. Just in time, too, a checkpoint had been set up and traffic in and out of the city locked down, twelve minutes after Williams and Jones zipped onto the highway past the city administrative limits. “One down, one to go,” I muttered to myself. To Skippy, I asked “You have a status on the SAS team?”

“Status? They’re in a sewer pipe, Joe, what type of status do you expect?”

"Uh, like, where are they? I want to see it on the display," I pointed to the dropship console in front of me. I was not happy about the SAS team floating along an underground sewer. If anything went wrong, we had no way to assist them.

"Joe, I have no freakin' clue where they are right now. If you like, I can estimate their location from what I know of the water flow speed."

"What? You don't know where they are? You little shithead, you should have told us that! How will you know when to open that bypass gate?"

"I won't know when to open the bypass gate and I won't have to, dumdum. I loaded the gate command program into both of their suit computers; as they approach the gate their suits will communicate with the gate and it will open for them. Behold, the magic of Skippy!"

"Uh huh. You will know when the gate opens, right?"

"Oh, sure, Joe. I'll know because I need to intercept the signal before it reaches the central control computer. Although, hmmm."

"*Hmmm*?" I didn't like the sound of that. "Hmmm what?"

"Hmmm, like, I should have received a signal from that gate at least four minutes ago."

"Crap!"

"This is puzzling. Maybe the water flow is slower than I, nope. No, I am reviewing data from the water flow sensors, Major Smythe certainly should have reached the bypass gate by now."

"What could have happened?"

"Joe," he sounded completely miserable, "I have no idea."

Major Smythe knew what happened, because he was in the middle of it. He had been the first to slip into the disgusting sewer water, holding onto the lip of the pipe until Robertson plunged in. As they drifted along, tiny differences in the current flow had caused Smythe to fall behind by several meters, nothing that alarmed either man. Smythe used a few strokes with his powered suit arms to pull even with Robertson, then when he fell behind again he let the current carry him. The sonar of the suit helmet provided him a vague view of what lay ahead, which was endless pipe. There weren't even many curves to make the trip mildly interesting. Only when a smaller pipe came in from one side of another did he two men experience a change; the additional volume of fluid being forced through the confines of the pipe made the speed of the water increase. They were really moving as they approached the bypass gate; according to the map projected in their visors, they would reach the gate in less than two minutes. There were supposed to be two smaller pipes flowing in from the left before the bypass gate on the right.

From ahead, Robertson eye-clicked to get a better view on sonar. There was so much non-water things in the sewer water that the sonar had difficulty penetrating far enough ahead to be useful. "Sir, I think I see the first of those two pipes coming in from the left."

"Let's move to the right," Smythe ordered. The first inflow pipe they zipped past had given them a rude lesson; jagged encrustations of something growing around the lip of the inflow pipe, and trash caught in the crust. Smythe had gotten a sharp knock to the head by a length of chain flailing in the current; while it had not damaged the helmet at all, the incident made him leery of obstructions in the pipe.

"Aye, aye, Sir," Robertson thought using nautical terminology appropriate for the occasion. Checking his extremely fuzzy sonar, his eyes opened wide. "Something ahead of us on the left!" Robertson extended his arms to swim strong strokes toward the right side of the pipe, but it was too late. With a jolt that made his head smack the inside of his faceplate and a wrenching tug on his right leg, he came to a stop, hanging in the powerful current with his feet behind him and his arms in front.

Smythe, given a half second of warning, was able to avoid the obstruction, and saw only a vague image of Robertson as he was swept past. "Robertson!" Smythe shouted, spinning himself around and trying to swim back upstream. It was no use, even with all the power of the suit, he could not make any headway against the current, he was being pushed backwards. "Can you get free?" He shouted into the helmet microphone, already out of breath from the strain.

"I'm stuck, Sir," Robertson's voice came through faint and distorted by static. "My right leg is entangled in something. Working to get it free."

Smythe, desperate for an idea, stopped swimming with one arm just long enough to reach back and rip a knife off his belt. In those few seconds, he had drifted back so that Robertson was no longer visible on the sonar. Smythe stopped trying to swim upstream and pulled himself over to the right side of the pipe. As they had floated along, he had noticed seams spaced regularly along the pipe's inner surface. Still swimming as hard as he could with one hand, he looked backward along the pipe, his helmet lights on fog mode and almost useless. When he saw a seam, he jabbed at it with the knife; it bounced off the hard surface and missed. The next time, the knife blade jammed itself into a seam, dug in and held. For a moment, Smythe held stationary against the force of the current. Then the blade snapped, and he was pulled along helplessly.

If he couldn't swim against the current, he could swim across it. There was a second inlet pipe on the left, and if he didn't get himself tangled in whatever junk was caught there, he might be able to hang on there. Hang on until Robertson freed himself and came floating by, when Smythe could join him. There was no way Smythe could get back to help Robertson, the man would need to somehow get himself free. What Smythe could do was buy time; if the current carried Smythe through the bypass gate too soon before Robertson, then Robertson would be trapped. Skippy had warned them to stay close together, for the bypass gate could only cycle open and closed once. It was an emergency apparatus that was designed to open when needed, then force itself closed and lock to protect the river downstream from contamination. Each man's suit would trigger the bypass gate to open when one of the suits was within seventy meters. Smythe needed to hold position until Robertson floated by.

Turning around because he needed to use the sonar, he saw the inlet pipe almost too late. With both hands, he grasped onto whatever his fingers could close around.

And it held. It was some crusty, crunchy, slimy thing that brought barnacles to Smythe's mind. It held, except it was flaking away from the pipe under the stress of holding the mass of Smythe and the armored suit against the current. The crusty material was flaking away, crumbling faster and faster. Desperate, he let go with one hand and reached down for his rifle. Holding the weapon steady against the current, he held the muzzle a half meter away from the pipe surface. Kristang rifles had a feature where, if the barrel was full of water, a gas charge would blow out the water in advance of the round firing. Smythe said a silent prayer his rifle was working correctly and squeezed the trigger.

And nothing happened, because the safety was on. Cursing his inexcusable loss of focus, Smythe released the safety and squeezed the trigger twice to blow a crack into the pipe liner. He let the rifle swing back onto his leg holster, reached a couple fingers of one glove in the crack with one hand and with the other hand reached for his belt, which contained a cable and grappling hook. Fully extended, the grapple would be too wide for the crack so he jammed it in. Pieces of the pipe liner cracked away before the grapple held. Smythe tugged at the cable, it was secure. "Robertson?" The only response was intermittent and unintelligible, which at least told Smythe that Robertson was alive and attempting to communicate.

Attempting to communicate?

The signal was not just intermittent, cutting in and out, was it purposefully intermittent? "Suit," Smythe called the computer in his helmet. "Can you determine whether the signals being received are Morse code?" His own knowledge of Morse was rusty, for which Smythe remonstrated himself.

"Affirmative," the suit's flat emotionless voice responded, "message reads 'Almost free'. Message repeats."

"Oh thank God," Smythe closed his eyes in gratitude. "Send back 'Holding position'."

Five minutes later, Robertson's muffled voice came through. "-the way-", then "Coming, Major. Had to cut myself loose. No damage to my suit."

"Understood, Robertson. It's good to hear your voice. I'm holding position near the last inlet pipe."

"How are you doing that?" Robertson asked, fearing his leader had been caught in an obstruction.

"It is a long story," Smythe replied dryly, "I see you on sonar. Releasing now," he freed the cable from the grapple, leaving the grapple stuck into the damaged pipe liner for a Kristang maintenance team to puzzle over someday.

The two SAS soldiers floated side by side, keeping to the center of the pipe as best they could. As they approached the bypass gate, their suit computers beeped to confirm the gate had accepted the command to open, and they swam strongly toward the right. Not all the flow of the pipe was going through the bypass, and if they missed the bypass there was no going back upstream. Smythe's left foot bounced off the lip of the bypass gate as they went through, then they were clear. "Skippy had better be right about there being no obstacles between us and the river, or it's going to get real dodgy for us."

"The bypass gate is open!" Skippy announced. "See, Joe, I told you to have faith."

"If the water is flowing at the rate you expected, how could they be late?"

"How the hell should I know?" Skippy complained. "Maybe they pulled over at a freakin' rest area for a snack?"

The sewage bypass pipe had emptied into a river just as Skippy predicted, the only problem being a fixed gate at the far end. After they were slammed into the gate by the force of sewage water flowing out of the pipe, Robertson managed to get his rifle free and pumped three rounds into a hinge, breaking part of the gate free. Attached to only one hinge and the locking mechanism, the gate had briefly swung open to allow Robertson through, flailing his arms and legs out of control. Smythe had almost been crushed when the heavy gate rebounded, pulling his legs back inside at the last second. With Smythe pressed up against the inside and Robertson hanging onto the outside, Smythe had ordered Robertson to wait and not do anything rash. The bypass gate had closed behind them, so the water flow should soon even out between the pipe and the river. He was right, the current slackened quickly, and within a minute the two men working together in their powered suits had been able to bend the gate out of the way enough for Smythe to slip through.

They were in a river. A deep river, twenty meters down. Smythe ordered Robertson to turn off his helmet lights and use the sonar on minimum power. The suit's navigation system must have picked up a signal from the local network, because the visor display showed they were several kilometers deep inside a hunting preserve that bordered the city. The area was for the exclusive use of senior Fire Dragon clan leaders and their families and guests. The extensive pre-mission briefing about the city had only skimmed over the parkland and hunting preserves that surrounded the densely-populated urban area. "Skippy? Can you hear?"

"I'm here. Damn, what took you so long? I told Joe you stopped for a snack."

"There was a toll we had to pay, that you neglected to tell us about. My wallet is inside my suit, it was rather awkward."

"A *toll*?" Skippy gasped, astonished. "In a sewer? That is- oh, you're messing with me," Skippy chuckled. "Good one. Hey, anyway, you're out now. Um, you should stay deep, there is a patrol boat coming up the river toward you."

Smythe did not like the sound of that. "We should turn off our sonars?"

"Probably a good idea. Don't worry, Skippy the Magnificent is on your side. I took control of a truck and I'm driving it toward the river; when it hits the water, that should attract the attention of the patrol boat. There are sensors in the water but they are there mostly to monitor water conditions, and track the predators."

"Predators? What kind of predators?"

"Oh, several. The most dangerous is a sort of large armored crocodile, they can get to be over ten meters long. Hmmm. There's one of them in the river near you now. Uh, hmm. It's headed in your direction."

"Can you stop it?"

"Uh, no, *duh*. How can I hack a crocodile? They have a brain the size of a walnut."

"Do you have a suggestion for how to deal with it?"

"Whatever you do, don't shoot it! The whole area is networked with sensors that look for unauthorized gunfire, to protect the animals from poachers. I haven't had time to hack into that network, I didn't anticipate any of you pirates taking a holiday in a game preserve. What to do? Hmmm, how about that? Wikipedia says it is best to avoid crocodiles, particularly in water."

"You are a *tremendous* help, Skippy." Smythe felt for his combat knife before remembering his had snapped and he had discarded the broken blade.

"Maybe they're ticklish?"

"*Tickl-*" With the AI not being any help, Smythe thought their best tactic would be to swim quickly if the crocodile attacked. "Robertson, can you-"

Skippy interrupted. "Three, two, one, splashdown." Under the water, the acoustic sensors in Smythe's suit picked up the sound of something large hitting the water, then the muffled whine of a turbine. "Score!" Skippy exulted. "The patrol boat is going over to investigate that truck I just drove into the water. The splash attracted the attention of that crocodile also, it won't bother you. Although, hmm. Now there are a dozen more crocodiles in the water; they were sleeping on the bank and now they are in the river. Shit, those things are *big*! You may, um, want to get out of the water. Like, now!"

"Which direction?" Smythe asked in a voice kept calm by his SAS training.

"It is projected on your visors. Swim smoothly, if you are clumsy the crocodiles will think you're a wounded animal and attack."

Swimming with smooth, controlled motions, the two men struck out for the nearest shore, first coming up closer to the surface to avoid crashing into underwater obstacles. Without sonar in the darkness, they were almost blind, relying on the passive sensors of their suits. Smythe's hand hit something soft and he realized it was a mud bank; according to the map they were near the shore. "Surface," he ordered, and they popped up to see dim lights above the trees in the direction of the city. Most city lights were still shut off, enough glow remained for the suits enhanced vision to show the dense forest lining the shore. The two men touched the silted bottom of the river and splashed ashore, unable to avoid making ripples in the water.

"Um, Major Smythe, you have attracted a crocodile. I, um, your motions may have unintentionally mimicked the splashing of a mating pair of crocs, the one coming toward you is a large male. My guess is he is agitated about another male being in his territory."

"Suggestion?"

"Get out of the water and proceed quickly into the forest, dumdum! Damn, do I need to do all the thinking in this crew? Those crocs can run extremely fast for short distances on land."

Behind him, Smythe saw a foaming white, V-shaped ripple on the surface of the water. It was moving fast, straight toward him. Without a word, he and Robertson picked up their feet and ran, not caring about making noise. His glimpse behind him had showed the patrol boat shining a spotlight on the sinking truck on the opposite shore; those Kristang were not looking in their direction. Their night vision allowed them to hurry through the forest a distance Smythe thought was safe, until they saw and heard bushes and small trees being bashed aside by something large and heavy coming at them from the river. Again, Robertson did not need an order to follow Smythe deeper into the forest.

"Are we safe now, Skippy?" Smythe asked as they ran up a hill, dense tangles of some native shrubs impeding their progress.

"Oh, yeah, that croc gave up chasing you. It turned around and is going back to the river. Safe is, um, a relative term. The part of the forest where you are now is home to a genetically-engineered predator called the 'grikka'. The best description for you to understand is a sort of dinosaur with heavy armor plates made of dense bone. Very tough."

"But you know where these grikka are, correct?" Smythe was not pleased that they could not use their rifles without alerting the Kristang.

"Um, no. Hunting the grikka is considered the ultimate test of manhood for warrior Kristang, so they are not tagged with transmitters the way most large animals in the preserve are. They are also difficult to spot on infrared, their heat is emitted almost entirely on their bellies. Their skin is like a chameleon, they can adapt their color to their surroundings."

"Brilliant," Smythe muttered. "A large dinosaur, you say?"

"Since I have to use references you will understand, I will say it is just slightly smaller than a T Rex, and a grikka walks on four legs. The armor makes it very tough; a grikka would eat a T Rex for breakfast and another for dinner."

"What does Wikipedia recommend we do if we encounter one of these grikkas?"

"Be quiet and think happy thoughts? Seriously, you won't be able to outrun a grikka for long, my guess is your best tactic would be to climb a tree. Prayer may also be helpful. There is a dropship on its way to pick you up, it needs to fly an indirect course to avoid sensors I do not yet have control over."

Happy thoughts? Smythe had a thought of himself tossing Skippy into a black hole. That made him momentarily happy. He looked around and up. They were surrounded by large trees, the size of oaks on Earth. Trees with black bark.

"Major?" Robertson's voice was quiet. "Something is coming."

"How do you know?" Smythe's visor could not see anything useful. The undergrowth extended three or four meters tall all around, blocking his view.

"This dinosaur detector says so," Robertson pointed the barrel of his rifle to a puddle.

As Smythe watched, the puddle shook and formed a ripple. Smythe looked up in alarm. "I saw that movie." They needed to run, but in what direction? In the darkness, they might blindly stumble directly into a grikka. Forcing himself to be calm, he eyeclicked through various settings of infrared vision, and saw nothing. The water in the puddle was now still; perhaps the grikka was far away? Or, Smythe had an unpleasant thought, the grikka could have stopped walking because it was close, and was now studying its prey.

"Maybe it can't smell us, because we're in suits?" Smythe speculated hopefully.

"Sir?" Robertson pointed to caked-on, disgusting something that was stuck to the legs of his suit. And not just on the legs. "We picked up something in that sewer, and it didn't all wash off in the river. Likely every animal in a kilometer can smell us."

"Bloody hell." Smythe's visor continued to shift its vision up the spectrum, as he had not commanded it to stop. He was about to halt the distraction when something caught his eye, and he froze the visor on that spectrum. Through the underbrush, the vague outline of something massive was showing in the ultraviolet spectrum. "Skippy, can grikkas be seen in ultraviolet?"

"No, why?" Skippy asked. "Wait, hmm, no. The grikka does not show up well in ultraviolet, however there is a type of bush which flowers this time of year, and its flowers and pollen do glow in the ultraviolet spectrum. A grikka could very well have walked through a grove of those bushes and become coated with the pollen."

Whatever it was, it moved slightly, Smythe was certain of it. Now that he thought he knew what he was looking at, it was clearly a patchy outline of an animal. A large animal, that was looking straight at him. It moved again, swaying side to side, Robertson also saw it. The water in the puddle shivered slightly. "Sir," Robertson began to say.

"Run!" Smythe shouted as the grikka shook its massive armored head and made a snort that was clearly heard by both men.

"Skippy," Smythe hung tightly onto the tree as it shook, "you really Bishoped this op." He was still out of breath from their headlong race through the forest, then climbing a tree just ahead of the grikka. The beast had crashed into Smythe's stout tree, nearly knocking the man to the ground. Smythe was as high as he could go without branches cracking under his weight; he was not comfortably high enough to be out of the grikka's reach. The beast had twice already gotten on its back legs and tried to reach the SAS soldier, the sharp claws of its forelegs raking the tree's black bark and snapping off branches a mere two meters below Smythe's feet.

"*Me*?" The AI replied indignantly. In Merry Band of Pirates slang, to 'Bishop' something meant to use the most horribly complicated way to accomplish a task. Even though it usually also meant that, afterward, no one could think of a less complicated way to have done it. "Hey, in the future, you can do the planning yourself. When this op went sideways, I did get you off that roof."

"And now we're up a tree, where we might be eaten by a monster."

"That thing might not be able to get through your armored suits quickly," Skippy scoffed. "Well, not easily. I think."

Smythe watched as the grikka roared in frustration, then bit cleanly through a fallen log at least a meter in diameter. Splinters pelted Smythe and Robertson. "If you were here, you would not be so certain about that. Robertson," Smythe advised as the grikka began gnawing at the base of Smythe's tree, and chunks of the bark flew through the forest. The tree shook and wobbled to the left, forcing Smythe to shift his weight. "If this tree is about to fall, I am going to shoot that thing first."

Robertson unslung his rifle, flicked the safety off and selected explosive-tipped rounds. He sighted in on the base of the grikka's thick skull, wondering whether he should target one of its legs instead. It would be nice to know the beast's vulnerabilities. If it had any. "Got you covered, Major."

"Skippy says gunfire will alert the sensors in this forest, so after that thing is dead, we get out of these trees and run," Smythe instructed. "This whole area will be swarming with Kristang." He had the same question as Robertson. "Skippy, do you have a recommendation for where we should shoot a grikka? The blasted thing is armored all over." The explosive-tipped rounds might waste their destructive power on the exterior of the monster without causing any serious damage.

"Oh, don't be so bloody dramatic, Major," Skippy interjected. "The rescue dropship is practically on top of you. If you have to shoot, aim for the underside; the armor is thinner there."

"We are in trees, *above* the grikka," Smythe reminded the absent-minded beer can.

"Oh. Yeah. Hmmm. Sucks for you, huh? Maybe you can get it to roll over for a belly rub?"

"I do not think-" Smythe was interrupted by his tree lurching alarmingly. "Robertson, aim for its-" He was interrupted again by the whining of turbine engines, coming from an unseen source, but above him.

"Major Smythe, we are above you, lowering a cable now," said a voice he recognized as belonging to Lt. Reed. "You should be able to see the end of the cable now, it is homing on your suit."

"I don't- I see it," Smythe slung his rifle and watched, transfixed, as the sling at the end of a cable came snaking down toward him out of the darkness. The other end of the cable was unseen as the dropship was encased in a stealth field. The sling swung toward him and missed, as the tree was now swaying from both the actions of the now-enraged grikka and the downdraft of the dropship's engine fan blades. The grikka, perhaps sensing its prey might escape, threw itself at the tree, trying to climb up. Its massive bulk battered the weakened tree, and it began toppling. Smythe slipped, got a firm foothold, and leaped up for the sling. Unfortunately, the sling had just turned around to guide itself back to where Smythe had been, so it was in the wrong position at the height of Smythe's leap. He reached out and caught the sling with only one finger of his left hand. For a moment, he dangled alarmingly.

And his other hand came around in an athletic maneuver to firmly grasp the sling. "Up!" He shouted as the grikka gathered itself to jump up toward him.

Robertson tracked the grikka with his rifle, finger poised on the trigger. As the beast jumped and the cable pulled Smythe upward, Robertson instinctively judged the grikka would miss, and he was right. The monster's outstretched claws raked through empty air two meters below the SAS team leader's feet, and the heavy beast crashed back to the ground, stunned. Robertson kept watch on the grikka as it circled the tree Smythe had been in, shaking its head. Seemingly unaware its prey was no longer in the tree, the grikka resumed biting chunks out of the base, while the cable came back down for Robertson. It was not until Robertson had the sling securely under both arms that the grikka looked up, looked Robertson straight in the eye. As the cable tugged him upward, Robertson slung his rifle. In a way, he felt sorry for the beast, condemned to live its short existence providing sport for the Kristang.

Safely aboard the dropship, Robertson accepted help strapping into the seat. Following Smythe's lead, he popped the seal of his helmet. Then sniffed. "Oooh," he looked down at whatever substance was now dried and crusted onto the suit. Unsavory substances that had likely stuck to the suit in the sewer, and not been washed off during their time in the open river.

"I've smelled worse," Smythe said with a grin as the dropship's crew backed away from the odiferous pair of SAS men.

"How are you, Major?" Reed called from the cockpit.

"Let me think," Smythe said as he breathed in air that had not been scrubbed by his suit's filters. Even the whiff of stink coming from his suit didn't make breathing unfiltered air any less sweet. "We parachuted into an alien city, dropped missiles off a roof, fell down an elevator shaft, played cop, stole a lorry, got flushed down a sewer and then chased up a tree by a monster. On Earth that would be remarkable, but for the Merry Band of Pirates," he shrugged, "we call that 'Tuesday'."

CHAPTER TWENTY FIVE

I pumped a fist when Lt. Reed reported the SAS team was safely aboard her dropship, and that she was flying low and slow along the egress route that Skippy had cleared of busybody sensors. Only ten minutes later, the SEALS team was safely aboard another dropship, and Lt. Williams called me directly. "How is Jones?" I asked first.

"He will be fine, Colonel," Williams answered, his voice sounded tired.

"Are you all right?" His tone concerned me.

"Sir, the worst thing about the whole op was the, the *showtunes*. Skippy sang to us the whole time we were in that truck. Colonel, I'm serious, I want to kill him."

"Skippy!" I shouted with a hand over the microphone.

"What?" The beer can answered innocently. "Damn. Ok, so sue me for trying to inject a little culture into this band of cutthroat pirates."

"We will talk later," I scolded the beer can. "Lieutenant, I will keep you away from Skippy for a while."

"That's probably wise, Sir. Williams out."

I turned to Skippy, who was in a slot on the console in front of me. "Let's save the showtunes issue for another time. What's going on with the war?"

"The Fire Dragon leadership contacted the Black Trees, who denied any involvement in the attack. Unfortunately for us, the Black Trees just offered to send several first sons of senior leaders to the Fire Dragons as hostages, the Fire Dragons have not yet responded to the offer. Joe, we need Colonel Chang to be successful in his phase of the operation. As I predicted, the Fire Dragons are sending some of their remaining senior leaders off the planet for security, in case a full-scale war breaks out. The dropship carrying those leaders is climbing out of the atmosphere now. King Kong," he used his private nickname for Chang, "is now up for Phase Two."

Lt. Colonel Chang Kong received the order to carry out Phase Two of the operation. He, and the entire crew, had been hoping Phase Two would not be needed, now they were committed to the attack. "Skippy had better be right about how those Fire Dragon ships perform the jumps he programmed for them, or this could be a very short engagement," Chang said mostly to himself as he sat in the *Flying Dutchman's* command chair, elbow resting on the side of the chair and his chin on his knuckles. If he had ever seen *Star Trek*, he would have recognized the classic Jim Kirk move. "Space combat is much too complicated. Sometimes, I long for the days when I was a simple artillery officer. All I had to be concerned about then was delivering ordnance on target. And then moving my guns before the enemy tracked our shells back and hit us with counterbattery fire." He sighed wistfully. "That was so much easier."

"Sir," Desai turned in the copilot seat to look at the *Flying Dutchman's* current commanding officer. "Space combat is complicated for certain, but the problem out here is that everything *we* do is extraordinarily complicated. I don't think Colonel Bishop and Skippy could make toast without a fourteen step plan that involves us warping spacetime, and hacking into alien computer systems."

Chang laughed. "And carving up asteroids, don't forget about that. Maybe it is just the Merry Band of Pirates that makes everything horribly complicated," he ran his fingers over the paramecium-logo unit patch on his shoulder. "Or it could be that I don't belong out here," he said in a rare confession for the usually reserved Chinese Army lieutenant colonel. "I was trained to fire artillery, not to be captain of a starship."

"Bishop was trained to carry a rifle," Desai replied pointedly. "He has done pretty well for himself, and for us."

"And humanity overall," Porter added from the left-hand seat.

"Yes, and humanity," Chang agreed. "Desai, Porter, tell me you don't wish we could go into a straight stand-up fight, instead of all this sneaking around laying mines and setting up missiles for an ambush."

"Yes Sir, I do," Porter acknowledged. "I also wish we had a real warship rather than a fancy trash hauler. Taking this bucket of bolts up against three warships, even if they are Kristang warships, does not fill me with confidence."

"And without Mister Skippy," Desai added in a worried tone. "If we get into trouble out here, we're on our own."

"I think about that every second," Chang said without exaggeration. "Bishop gave me the keys to the ship, I want to bring it back without a scratch. Please tell me we can get out of here in a hurry if we have to."

"Got an emergency jump programmed in," Porter patted the console affectionately. "One of us presses this button," he indicted the prominent green button at the top of the console between the two pilot seats, "and we go through whatever crazy-ass hole in spacetime the jump drive supposedly creates."

"Supposedly?" Chang asked with an arched eyebrow.

"The United States Navy paid for me to get a master's degree in physics," Porter answered. "I had planned to go on to a PHD program someday, when my flying days were over. Then aliens showed me that humans don't know squat about physics," he said with more than a touch of frustration. All the many hours he had spent in a classroom, and studying on his own, had barely gotten him to the bottom rung of the knowledge ladder. "Before the Ruhar arrived, we had theories about wormholes. Now, we know all those theories were wrong, but we don't know how jump wormholes really do work. How does a ship here," he pointed at the deck, "project the far end of a wormhole at a distant point, with the effect exceeding the speed of light between the two points? It's almost instantaneous. And how is the far end of a jump wormhole in a different time state?" He shook his head. "All I know is, I press a button, and the ship goes to a different place. It could be a different, parallel universe we jump to, for all we know. This is Alice in Wonderland, and we're going down a rabbit hole."

Chang shared a look with Desai. "Mister Porter, since Colonel Bishop is not here, I will say it for him: *you* are not filling me with confidence."

Porter took the hint. "Colonel, when I press the button, the ship *will* jump. I'm the pilot; how the jump works is somebody else's problem."

"Yes, until it screws up and they expect us to get them out of the mess," Desai whispered.

"In this case, the 'they' is a talking beer can," Porter whispered back. "How F-ed up is that?"

A heavily-armored dropship raced out of the planet's atmosphere, surrounded and escorted by five gunships. A frigate dipped dangerously low into the atmosphere, its forward and lower surfaces glowing dull red from friction as its engines trembled and strained against the unaccustomed pull of heavy gravity. The frigate was there to provide additional protection for the armored dropship, but the frigate's guns were not its primary asset, and its defensive energy shields were weakened by passage through the air. The greatest aid the frigate could provide was the hot, roiling air surrounding its hull and blazing out of its main engines and thrusters. The air was so disturbed and saturated with infrared energy, any targeting sensors would have difficulty locking onto the armored dropship as it soared near and then above the frigate. After the vital dropship was securely above the frigate, protected from ground-based weapons and sensors, it had to slow its ascent to allow the frigate to catch up. There was a heart-stopping moment for the frigate's crew when a series of relays blew, causing temporary loss of attitude control. The frigate nearly rolled onto its back, slewing violently to the side and tossing its crew around like marbles in a shoebox. Just as the ship was about to roll past the critical thirty four degree mark beyond which it could not recover, a single relay reset itself and the thrusters in that array roared back to life. For a split second, the frigate hovered on the knife edge of thirty three and a half degrees of roll, its acquired momentum resisting the power of the thrusters. The crew held their breath, knowing if their ship flipped over, they would plunge down through increasingly thick air, deeper into the gravity well until the strain broke the little ship's back and scattered them to the unforgiving winds.

With an echoing cheer, the bridge crew watched the inclinometer slide back away from disaster; thirty three, thirty two, thirty then faster and faster back toward safety. At fifteen degrees of roll that would have been considered terrifying only seconds before, the captain commanded the frigate to stand on its tail and apply full power to the main engines. Led by the dropships, the frigate climbed back out of the atmosphere, its forward shield generators rapidly degrading and the crew happy they could deal with that problem later.

The frigate and gunships escorted the armored dropship and its VIP passengers, until the VIPs were safely aboard the Fire Dragon clan heavy cruiser *None Can Stand Against Us*. With several senior clan leaders having been killed in their compound, two of the surviving senior leaders needed to get away to safety. The escort gunships applied emergency power to get away as the *Stand*'s jump drive coils began vibrating. To jump from low orbit was a violation of local space traffic rules and several treaties, and under the circumstances not a single person aboard the *Stand* of its two frigate escorts cared about the consequences.

As the jump drives of all three ships ran up to full power, their navigation computers exchanged heavily encrypted data to coordinate their simultaneous but individual jumps. The frigates needed to jump to roughly the same location as the heavy cruiser, or they would be useless as protective escorts, so they followed the *Stand*'s guidance on where to jump to. Considering the notorious inaccuracy of Kristang jump drives, the cruiser's command crew was more concerned the frigates did not try to occupy the same distant point of space when they emerged. They followed standard protocol for a small formation jump. A larger formation of ships often sent an expendable frigate to scout ahead the distant jump point, waiting for that unlucky ship to recharge its drive coils and jump back to report. That precaution took time that the captain of the *Stand* could not afford right then, so he opted for a formation jump. Every moment the heavy cruiser lingered in orbit, the VIPs aboard were exposed to more danger, as the fighting on the planet's surface threatened to rapidly spiral out of control.

"Skippy, you are sure you can control their jumps from down here?" I asked worriedly. We had a couple nice firefights going on the surface, and a developing air battle between three clans to the east, but if the two Fire Dragon senior leaders could get safely away, they might be able to calm things down and prevent the fighting from spreading widely across Kristang-occupied space. The Fire Dragon leaders were running to a pre-planned safe haven provided by an allied clan. From that safe haven, they could rally their forces to a strong defense, giving them time and a sense of security to think clearly and avoid a preemptive strike that would widen the conflict.

I wanted the conflict widened. I wanted to enlarge the current fracture in Kristang inter-clan relations wide enough that I could fly the *Dutchman* through it.

"Yeah, yeah, I got it, Joe. No problem. Seriously, you think hacking into and messing with lizard jump drive computers is any challenge to me? I am Skippy the Magnificent, my magic is capable of warping stars. For me, this lame-ass level of magic is like making balloon animals or pulling a coin out of your ear."

"But-"

"But, shut up a minute and let me work, will you? Go, I don't know, practice tying your shoelaces again. Maybe by a miracle, you'll get it right this time."

I was going to shoot back with a witty retort, but I couldn't. A week ago, I wasn't even able to walk from my cabin to my office before a bootlace came untied and I tripped, falling against the doorjamb of the bridge/CIC complex. I suspect a certain asshole beer can somehow snuck a bot in my cabin to loosen my laces while I was brushing my teeth, but it was better to drop the subject. "Thank you, Your Magnificence."

"Now that's more like it, Joe. Aaaaand, those ships have jumped away."

"You did it, right?"

"Yup. Well, did the best I could, under the circumstances, you understand."

"You keep telling us you make the incredible look easy, so I'm sure you did an awesome job with this," I said hopefully.

"We'll know when the *Dutchman* reports in through the microwormhole."

"No way for us to get a sneak peek at the action?"

"Not anything accurate enough to matter. The *Dutchman* had to leave the microwormhole behind, and I can't see much from that distance. I'll let you know if the plan worked. Or, if, you know, the *Dutchman* explodes."

Although I wasn't up there, I appreciated the difficulty Chang faced in his assigned task. Skippy had not been able to construct enough new real ship-to-ship missiles with the limited time and resources available, so Chang had to use kludgy short-range missiles that were more like mines. The *Dutchman* had flown around in a pattern, saturating the target area with mines. A lot of mines; sixty seven to be exact. The plan was for the mines to ambush the Fire Dragon ships just after they jumped in. When the plan was explained to Chang, he recognized it as being similar to the operation that had destroyed the Thuranin surveyor ship and its escorts. Except this time, they had short-range mines that were much less capable than the missiles used against the surveyor. And with Skippy on the planet, the *Flying Dutchman* had no way to flatten spacetime so they could predict exactly where the Fire Dragon ships would jump in.

What Chang did have working for him was the incredible awesomeness of Skippy. And of course Skippy had taken every opportunity to remind Chang and the entire crew of just how incredibly awesome the beer can was. To the point where the action to destroy the Fire Dragon ships was named 'Operation Awesome'. While he was on the planet, Skippy had slowly wormed his way into the jump drive systems of the *None Can Stand Against Us* and its two escort frigates. I say 'slowly' wormed his way in, because I figured he could quickly take over the ships using the Thuranin nanovirus. Man, was I wrong, and Skippy let me know it.

The three Fire Dragon ships had been away from contact with a Thuranin star carrier for long enough that the nanovirus infecting them had degraded to the point it was unreliable. And for some reason Skippy could not explain, one of the frigates was not infected at all. Regardless, using the nanovirus was never an option. Our whole plan involving those three ships was for them to jump away normally, then appear to be ambushed. If Skippy had seized control using the nanovirus while the ships were in orbit, every sensor platform on or near the planet would have known something was seriously wrong, and all Skippy's infiltration of the sensor networks would have been for nothing. So I shut my mouth and let Skippy handle the tricky technical details of taking control over the jump drives of those three ships. This was a case, Skippy told me with typical beer can tactfulness, when the monkeys needed to let the adult do the tough part of the mission.

The reason Kristang jumps were so notoriously inaccurate, Skippy explained, was not only the fault of their pathetically crappy hardware. Their jump controller computers did not know anything about hyperspatial jumps, according to His Awesomeness it was like they just randomly input coordinate numbers and hoped for the best.

Once Skippy had access to the jump drive systems of the three ships, he had been able to examine and measure every component involved, tweak the hardware settings, and replace the controller code with something at least vaguely related to hyperspatial navigation. I remember how astonished and frustrated he was after he had painstakingly reviewed every element of code in the Kristang navigation systems. "Joe, I swear, you could replace their navigation computers with a Donkey Kong cartridge from the 1980s and the jumps would be more accurate."

"Wow, that's amazing, Skippy," I had said while absent-mindedly playing solitaire. "What, uh, what is Donkey Kong?"

"Joe," he sighed. "Your knowledge of pop trivia about the late 20th century is woefully lacking."

"Uh huh. Tell you what, when we get out of this, you can smack me with trivia knowledge for hours."

"*If* we get out of this."

"You are *filling* me with confidence, Skippy."

"I'm just being realistic, since this is, you know, *your* tactical plan."

Anyway, with Skippy controlling the jump systems of those three ships, they jumped to a different area than they had planned. The target jump point was still within the imaginary cube of space designated as a Fire Dragon rally point, but the ships emerged inside Chang's minefield rather than the empty space they had been aiming for. And the frigates emerged much closer to the heavy cruiser than they wanted to. In my original plan, I had wanted Skippy to make the ships emerge on top of each other and collide, but even he wasn't able to make a Kristang jump drive that accurate given the distance they were jumping. So, we settled for Plan B of having them emerge in an area saturated with our mines.

For Lt. Colonel Chang Kong, current captain of the United Nations Starship *Flying Dutchman*, waiting was the worst part. They had received a faint, compressed signal through the microwormhole that was now far behind them; the signal indicated the ground assault phase of the operation had begun and was successful. Kristang clans, even those not affected by the assault, had begun skirmishing. Joe Bishop was evaluating their options about where the ground team should hit next for maximum effect with minimum risk; but the next critical phase of the operation would take place far from the planet's surface.

Chang knew he had done everything he could to assure his part of the mission would be successful. The *Flying Dutchman* had jumped in far away from the imaginary cube of space that was the Fire Dragon clan's designated rally point. If the Fire Dragons had detected a strange jump signature near their safe zone, they would avoid it. So the *Dutchman* had jumped in far away from the target rally point, then used a device Skippy built, to emit a gamma ray burst as if a starship had jumped away. As soon as the yoyo string had safely lowered the five dropships to the planet's surface, the *Dutchman* had reeled in the cable and proceeded at high speed through normal space toward the Fire Dragon rally point, arriving with sufficient time to perform her next task; that of a lowly minelayer ship.

"Three ships just jumped in!" Desai reported excitedly. "Mines engaging automatically."

"Take us in," Chang ordered. "Extend our damping field," he added in an anxious tone. The *Flying Dutchman's* damping field had been cobbled together by Skippy, and the beer can had warned it would not last more than seventeen minutes before burning out. Rather than projecting the damping effect in all directions around the ship, Skippy's homemade creation could be directed at a particular object, although that ate up tremendous power from the *Dutchman*'s reactors.

"Damping field is active, reaching full strength," reported an officer from the CIC behind Chang. "Our field is now at full strength, those ships can't jump."

"The first mine will impact in three, two, one, impact." Desai said in a voice she tried to keep calm.

The frigate which had dipped down into the atmosphere to protect the Fire Dragon clan's VIPs, was also the first to be hit by the homemade mines. That ship's captain had taken the damaged forward shield projectors temporarily offline, so burned-out components could be replaced. Until the forward set of projectors was repaired, the amidships and aft shield projectors would be angled forward to provide coverage. Doing so weakened the overall protection, and the captain understood the risks. He thought that, with a potential wide-spread civil war looming, he needed to bring his ship to full combat capability sooner rather than later. With his ship making a jump into a designated safe area, and the inter-clan fighting so far confined to the planet's surface, he thought the risk was minimal.

He was wrong.

That frigate's luck continued to run against it. Of the three ships, it did not emerge from jump closest to a waiting mine. The heavy cruiser *Stand* had that honor; popping through its jump wormhole almost on top of a mine. That mine near the *Stand* was unfortunately so close to the wormhole that it had been rendered inoperable, and literally bounced off the cruiser's flickering shields. The frigate emerged in the center of a triangle formed by three mines, which eagerly raced to see which one of them would be first to impact.

The first mine attacked from aft, and penetrated halfway through the weakened shields that were still trying to regain coherence, after passing through the spatial distortion of the wormhole. That first mine, realizing it could not get any closer to the frigate's hull, exploded shortly after passing its sensor data to the cluster of mines that were still on their way.

The second and third mines, coming in to attack the ship's forward hull less than a second later, had the advantage of the shields pulsating to cope with the explosion aft. The second mine's sensors guided it to dive in through a particularly weak spot in the shields. It, too, failed to penetrate through to the hull. Its brain made a snap decision to channel its stored energy not into an explosion, but instead into a pulse at the same frequency as the shield generators' output. The shields flickered, blowing one relay after another just as the third mine streaked in to impact amidships. That mine's heavily armored warhead punched through four decks, and its momentum was carrying it up and toward the outer hull on the other side when it exploded, cracking the frigate in half.

Less than three seconds after the frigate jumped in, it was torn into two pieces. Half a dozen more mines homed in on the two pieces of wreckage, until all that was left were chunks of debris and exotic high-energy particles, and three more mines were left to buzz around the cloud of debris like confused and angry hornets.

The second frigate was more fortunate, surprisingly surviving more than thirteen seconds, before its defenses were overwhelmed by the cloud of mines that was suddenly on top of it. The second frigate's point defense cannons claimed two mines before they could impact the shields that were still partially discoherent from the effect of the jump. If the computers controlling the point-defense cannons took a moment to congratulate each other for their initial victory, it was a short-lived celebration. Four seconds later the frigate ceased to exist, as a mine dove directly into the jump drive capacitors and exploded, releasing the stored energy in a spectacular explosion.

An explosion that caused unanticipated trouble for the *Flying Dutchman*.

"Two down, one to go!" A crewman in the CIC exulted, as sensors clearly showed a second frigate disappearing in a white-hot explosion. Without Skippy aboard, the sensor data had to be interpreted by the human crew, and no one was brimming with confidence at their ability to provide timely and accurate data to Chang. The destruction of the two frigates, however, could be detected by merely looking out a porthole, if the person wished to be temporarily blinded.

"Status of the cruiser?" Chang replied without emotion, setting an example not to declare victory before the battle was over.

"It's taking hits," the CIC crew responded after comparing sensor readings from three consoles. "We recorded seventeen explosions in the vicinity of the cruiser, before that second frigate blew up. Our sensors are partly blinded now, they're resetting. We think we're seeing additional explosions near the cruiser, Sir, we can't tell if they are real or sensor ghosts. And now we've lost target lock on the cruiser. Attempting to find it again, there is a lot of interference."

"Do your best." Chang turned to the pilots. "Pilot, slow us down a bit." If they didn't know where the cruiser was, he did not want their beat-up star carrier to stumble into it.

Porter looked at Desai, and she caught his unspoken question. "Sir, do you want us to reduce our acceleration toward the target, or do you want us to slow our rate of approach by decelerating?"

Once again, Chang was reminded that space combat maneuvers were very different from driving a tank or ship on Earth. "The second one. Reduce our forward velocity," he clarified the order. "If that cruiser's jump drive explodes, I don't want us to get peppered with debris."

"The shields should protect us, Colonel," Desai said in a tone that Chang took to mean she did not want to trust her life to the shields. Not without Skippy aboard to fix any problems.

"I prefer not to test our shields," Chang replied without a smile.

What made the *None Can Stand Against Us* a heavy cruiser was not its armament, because it actually had one less railgun and two fewer maser cannons than a standard Kristang cruiser. Compared to a *The Brave Shall Always Know Victory*-class standard cruiser on which the heavy cruiser type was based, the *Stand* had six fewer missile launch tubes, and carried thirty six fewer missiles in a typical loadout. What made the *Stand* a heavy cruiser, heavy in terms of mass as well as power, was its extra defensive capabilities: It had more armor plating, more defense shield generators and point-defense maser cannons. Its offensive capabilities had been sacrificed to protect the *Stand's* precious passengers; the leaders of the Fire Dragon clan. To compensate for the significant additional mass of the ship, the normal-space engines had also been upgraded, because the ship was intended to run from trouble rather than fight. For any other ship, running instead of fighting would be considered cowardly; it was the necessity of protecting the clan leadership that excused what would otherwise be shameful behavior.

Against the instincts and traditions of the Kristang warrior caste, the *None Can Stand Against Us* should have turned and run. The ship would have run under normal circumstances. In this case, the captain of that ship saw his powerful cruiser ambushed, his escorts destroyed, and his jump drive disabled by a damping field. Clearly, the unknown enemy had advanced technology that very likely would make any attempt to escape fruitless.

I realized later that two things got the *Flying Dutchman* into trouble; Kristang being Kristang and Skippy being Skippy. And me being stupid. Ok, that is three things. The *None Can Stand Against Us* was supposed to run from fights in order to preserve the clan leadership. What the ship should have done, after it survived the initial impacts of our mines, was to run in the opposite direction from the *Dutchman*. What the captain of the *Stand* did instead, because a Kristang warrior's first instinct is to attack, is turn toward the *Dutchman*. That was the first example of my stupidity; I should have anticipated that once the captain of the *Stand* realized his ship was caught in a damping field and could not jump away, he would choose to strike the *Dutchman*, hoping to disable the source of the damping field. What I would have done, because I am not a bloodthirsty hateful lizard, was to at least try accelerating away in normal space first, and turn and fight only if running didn't work. Clearly, the captain of the *Stand* had not recently read the Joe Bishop Rules of Space Combat, because he went to full thrust straight at our pirate star carrier. The *Dutchman* had its stealth field activated, but the violent explosion of the second frigate had saturated the entire area with high-energy particles, temporarily rendering the stealth field less effective. Once the heavy cruiser got a sensor lock on particle wake created by the *Dutchman*, Chang couldn't get away.

The second issue, Skippy being Skippy, was only a problem because of Joe being Joe, meaning me being stupid. Skippy had given Chang and the crew a list of options if the battle went one way or another. That was all great and helpful. What was not helpful was that Skippy had planned all the options as if his all-seeing self was aboard the ship. And that was my fault for not catching that goof-up. If Skippy had been aboard the *Dutchman*, he would have been able to see right through the sensor interference and warn Chang the cruiser had turned and was headed straight for our pirate ship. Without Skippy, the duty crew in the CIC did the best they could, with sensor panels the Thuranin had designed for emergency backup use only. By the time they got the sensors reset and were able to interpret the information, it was too late. If I had not been a complete and utter moron, I should've thought to have Skippy train the CIC better on how to compensate for the sensors being temporarily blinded. And I should have left instructions to Chang that if he lost sensor contact with the enemy, he was to turn and run. In defense of me and Skippy, neither of us anticipated that a frigate would be turned into a short-lived sun by our mines. The mines Skippy had manufactured were not fast or powerful; he expected they would only disable the Fire Dragon ships, so our pirate ship could use maser cannons to punch through the armor around their reactors or jump drives. The battle plan, every scenario we ran in preparation for the attack, anticipated the *Dutchman* would need to participate directly in the attack to some extent. If he could, Chang was supposed to destroy all three ships, so we could totally control the message traffic coming from the battle. The priority was to kill the heavy cruiser; if Chang could destroy that ship first, he was to use his judgment on whether to pursue and engage the pair of frigates.

If the unknown attacking ship pursued the fight until the *Stand* and its VIP passengers were dead, that would be seen as a direct threat to the clan's existence and would require massive retaliation against the Black Trees. One way or the other, Chang needed to destroy the *None Can Stand Against Us* or our plan might fall apart. Toward that end, he ordered our pirate ship to close with the cruiser's last reported position, with the *Dutchman*'s maser cannons ready to finish off the crippled enemy ship. It was a simple plan, it should have been easy.

"Sensors are almost finished resetting, Sir," Simms in the CIC reported. "Skippy could do this much faster. Data is coming through now, it's- trouble!"

Chang saw the threat on the main bridge display before the CIC crew could explain it to him. The heavy cruiser had somehow survived the onslaught of mines directed at it, and was charging straight at his ship! "Desai, get us-"

"I see it," she interrupted, her fingers flying over the controls as Porter did the same on the console in front of him. "Colonel, we're going too fast; our momentum is going to carry us past the enemy. They are," she took a moment to verify, "they're turning to intercept us. Yes, they're definitely following our move." She turned in her seat to look at Chang. "We will fly past them, the closest approach will be less than seventy thousand kilometers."

"That damned thing moves fast for a heavy ship," Porter commented with concern. "They can accelerate faster than we can." Star carriers were built to transport other ships by jumping long distances, not by flying the long way through normal space. With their long, spindly spines, star carriers were supposed to perform only gentle maneuvers to avoiding overstressing their structure. Even though the *Dutchman* was only carrying the relay station/lifeboat, it could not accelerate quickly compared to a true warship. "We're going to be in trouble if this develops into a running fight." All the scenarios for combat assumed the cruiser would be disabled by the mines before the *Dutchman* engaged.

"We have another problem," Simms reported from the CIC. "When we got bombarded by charged particles from that frigate blowing up, the Kristang might have gotten a glimpse through our stealth field. If they did, they might know we are not a Kristang ship."

"Damn it!" Chang pounded on the arm of the command chair.

"Sir, they likely don't know what we are; our profile doesn't match any star carrier the Thuranin have. But if they got a good enough look, they will recognize our forward structure and engineering section as Thuranin. We are jamming their transmissions."

"That would blow the whole plan," Chang squeezed his fists. If the Kristang thought the Thuranin were interfering in clan business, not only would the Fire Dragons and Black Trees unite against a common enemy, they would report the incident to the Thuranin. Those little green men, knowing they certainly were not involved, might start asking very uncomfortable questions. "Can we make a short jump, get behind them?"

"No," Desai declared. "They have us caught in their damping field. Neither of us can jump."

"Simms," Chang asked, "how long until our damping field burns out?"

"Fourteen minutes, maybe less. I can reduce power to the field because the Kristang ship is closer to us now, that might allow us to squeeze another minute out of it."

"Do it," Chang ordered. "Status of our defenses?"

"Nominal," Simms reported. "Energy shields are at one hundred percent, point defense cannons ready and hot. Terminal guidance sensor field was not affected by the other sensor problem, it is fully effective."

"How long until we are within maser cannon range?" Chang pressed the touchscreen on the command chair's armrest and manipulated the main display. He was kicking around the kernel of an idea in his head.

"Twenty four seconds to effective range," Desai reported.

"Missile launch!" Desai shouted. "Enemy has launched." The ship rocked almost imperceptibly. "Also firing masers at us."

"At this range?" Chang asked, puzzled.

"They aren't effective at this range; they're trying to disrupt our terminal guidance sensors. Sir, I suggest an evasive course so they can't target us with their railgun."

"Do it," Chang ordered.

"Aye, Sir," Desai acknowledged. Feeling Chang should know, she added "That will slow us down slightly."

"Understood, do it anyway. Desai, that cruiser is turning to pursue us after closest approach?"

"Yes. It's still going in the wrong direction but at its current rate of acceleration, it will fully cancel its velocity less than a minute after we pass by." She anticipated Chang's next question. "We're at full thrust and even if we maintain that power, the Kristang will catch us in twelve minutes."

"We can't do that," Porter warned. "If we maintain full acceleration after we pass by, that cruiser will go out of our damping field range before it is able to swing around and chase us. It could jump away."

"We need to slow down?" Chang mused, not liking the sound of that. "Let that cruiser get *closer* to us?"

"He's right," Desai confirmed, looking at her console. "In fact, we need to begin slowing now, or there will be an eight second gap in our damping field coverage."

"Shit. Do it, whatever you have to do. We can't allow that ship to escape."

"Decelerating now," Desai acknowledged. "We will be within effective maser range in four seconds."

"Simms," Chang called toward the CIC. "Weapons free. Conserve our missiles. Desai, continue evading so we don't get nailed by their railgun."

"Doing that," Desai replied tersely as the ship rocked faintly. "Lucky shot, that was a maser beam hit. No damage." At the present range, the enemy was launching maser bolts at the location in space where they thought the *Dutchman* would be when the maser beam, crawling along at the speed of light, got there. The random pattern directed by Desai and flown by Porter prevented most enemy maser beams and railgun darts from finding their target; they simply flew on through empty space as the *Flying Dutchman* jinked one way then the other. The maser beams would eventually dissipate, the railgun darts would fly onward until the end of time, slowed slightly by impacts with particles and dust in interstellar space unless they happened to collide with something substantial.

As the two ships flew past each other at closest approach, they both fired weapons ineffectively. Over a dozen missiles homed in on the *Flying Dutchman*, all of them were intercepted by the point defense cannons, helped by the upgrades Skippy had made to the original Thuranin defensive guidance systems.

The engines of the two combatants strained to cancel the velocity that was still drawing them farther apart. As his ship shuddered to a dead stop and began moving in the opposite direction, Chang felt a chill as he had an awful thought. The Kristang heavy cruiser had not yet completed its deceleration maneuver, and was still flying farther from the *Dutchman* with every passing second. "Simms, if the enemy detects our damping field is growing weaker as they increase their distance-"

He didn't need to finish the thought. "Already on it, Sir," Simms replied. "We're increasing the damping beam power to keep the field strength steady. They won't detect a drop in field strength, unless they get another two hundred thousand kilometers away. At their current rate of thrust," she paused to check a console, "they won't come close to that distance, Sir."

"Good." Chang sat tensely in the command chair, forcing himself not to grip the arms so tightly that his knuckles shone white. The crew needed to see a calm, confident commander, and that is what Chang was determined to give them. Except, now that he saw on the display the enemy ship had halted its flight and was now accelerating toward the *Flying Dutchman*, he did not immediately know what to do next. The enemy was successfully trapped in the *Dutchman*'s damping field. He had caught a tiger by the tail, and now he didn't know what to do with it. "Desai," he automatically addressed the ship's chief pilot, even though she was acting as copilot. "I would appreciate any suggestions. Is there anything you learned about Space Combat Maneuvers that would be useful right now?"

Desai turned in her seat. "We can't outrun them," she replied. "And I don't think we can outfight them, either," she made the last remark while looking through the glass into the CIC.

Simms shook her head. "That's a heavy cruiser, Sir, they have shields tougher than we expected. They have more missiles, and their maser cannons have higher output than ours," she lamented. "The whole plan counted on our mines disabling that ship."

"They have a heavy cruiser, and we have a space bus," Chang stated.

"Essentially, Sir, yes," Desai concluded. "I don't see how we can win a stand-up fight against that ship. If we disable our damping field, maybe the Kristang will cut their losses and jump away?"

"No," Chang shook his head. "I can't take the risk that they saw through our stealth field, even for a moment. Stand-up fight?" He smiled. "Skippy tells me he is all about cheating when he can get away with it. Bishop isn't the only pirate in this crew who can think up a crazy idea. Desai, Simms, I need you to-"

CHAPTER TWENTY SIX

The spindly *Flying Dutchman* awkwardly turned, spinning sideways at the limit of its spine structure's ability to hold integrity. Under Porter's skilled hands, and with the entire crew whispering silent prayers, the ships turned and burned hard, away from the *None Can Stand Against Us*.

For a moment, the enemy hesitated, sensing an opportunity to escape. Then, under Chang's orders, Desai pulsed the thrust randomly, as if the star carrier's engines were failing. That made up the minds of the senior leaders aboard the Kristang cruiser; their enemy was now vulnerable, and they wanted answers as to who had conducted a dishonorable sneak attack. And they wanted revenge.

The *Stand* continued on an intercept course at full thrust, rapidly overtaking the mysterious stealthed ship that had ambushed the cruiser and destroyed two frigates. The Kristang aboard the *Stand* burned with curiosity and not a little fear. Somehow, the unknown enemy had managed to make three starships jump to an unintended location, and make them jump so accurately they emerged into a mine field. That implied the enemy had advanced technology, technology that represented a serious threat to the Fire Dragon clan. The enemy needed to be trapped, identified, and possibly taken apart to learn their secrets

The cruiser launched a volley of missiles at extreme range, fully expecting all four weapons to be destroyed while still well away from the enemy. Instead, three were hammered by maser cannons, but the fourth continued onward, as if the enemy's point-defense systems had difficulty tracking it. Much closer than the enemy would have liked, the missile was finally burned to a crisp by two maser cannons. The cruiser's captain might have been puzzled when his ship's sensors detected the enemy's stealth field had changed shape and gone opaque, stretching far out to the sides. That was odd, thought the *Stand*'s captain; the enemy must be confident there were no ships in front to see through the weakened stealth in that direction. Why else was their stealth field configured to block the *Stand*'s view forward?

The cruiser's captain received an answer shortly, as the enemy ship suddenly broke to one side and restored its stealth field to normal. In moments, the *Stand*'s sensors detected something dead ahead: mines!

"Yes!" Major Simms exulted. "They've flown right into our mines!"

Chang's order had been for Desai to steer a course directly away from the Kristang ship, and to reduce acceleration to lure the cruiser closer. Simms contacted the remaining mines and directed them to cluster in the *Dutchman*'s path. With the ship's stealth field stretched wide and blocking the Kristang's view forward, the cruiser had not seen the approaching mines until it was too late.

The cruiser staggered under the sudden onslaught, explosions causing the ship's forward shields to flicker and overload, collapsing in sections. The second wave of mines began penetrating through the shields, and the crew of the *None Can Stand Against Us* knew in a flash that they could not stand another hit. So they did the only thing they could do.

"Missile warning! Enemy is launching," there was a pause, "*everything*?" Simms was shocked. "They're launching *all* their missiles! It looks like they've rippling off their entire weapons load, I count thirty two missiles in the air and more launching." The data

Skippy had transmitted about the heavy cruiser listed the number of missiles that ship carried; they had all either been fired or were now on their way toward the *Dutchman*.

Desai turned in her chair. "Colonel, our defenses can't fend off that many missiles. I recommend we turn and run."

Her suggestion matched what Chang was already thinking. Their mines were besieging the enemy cruiser, and there was nothing useful the *Flying Dutchman* could do until the mine attack had run its course one way or another. "Get us out of here. Maximum acceleration for now, then we will cut thrust and rely on stealth?"

"Yes," Porter agreed. The *Dutchman*'s stealth capability was far advanced beyond what the Kristang missile sensors were designed to identify; with the enhancements Skippy had installed, the pirate ship's stealth was more effective than most Thuranin ships. "With that many missiles chasing us, Sir, they *will* find us. At that point, we should go to one third acceleration to give us maneuvering ability."

"Fly the ship however you think best, pilots."

The *Dutchman*'s engines straining at their limit only delayed the star carrier being caught by Kristang missiles. When the ship was bracketed by a swirling cloud of missiles, the pilots cut thrusts and jinked side to side and up and down in a random evasive pattern, trusting their unpredictable maneuvers and the stealth field to confuse the targeting systems of the inbound missiles. That tactic worked only for the first seven missiles, then the remaining missiles were able to home in on defensive maser cannons and the hot charged particles of prior missiles that had impacted the pirate ship's defense shields. Even the notoriously poor targeting sensors of Kristang weapons could pinpoint the star carrier, and in an instant, the ship's point-defense cannons could not react quickly enough to track the multitude of targets.

The deck rocked. "Defenses are becoming saturated!" Simms warned from the Combat Information Center. With the *Dutchman* flying through a cloud of hot particles from detonated missiles, her stealth field was nearly useless, and the particles were blinding the point defense sensors. "We've, we have lost contact with three missiles!"

For the first time in the engagement, Chang felt a chill of real gut-freezing fear. Three enemy missiles could be anywhere, they could be streaking in to impact one of the reactors any moment.

"We- explosion at the enemy's location. The cruiser has blown up!" Simms exulted.

"Yes!" Desai pumped a fist in the air.

Chang's mind skipped celebration and focused. "Is their damping field down?"

After a momentary hesitation, Simms replied "Almost, Sir. Field is dissipating."

"Desai, engage jump drive and get us out of here as soon as possible," Chang ordered. "Make it a short jump, I want to get a good look and make damned sure that cruiser is gone."

"Aye, Sir," she acknowledged with one eye on the indicator that measured damping field intensity. Without continuously being fed power by the enemy cruiser, the Kristang damping field was rapidly weakening. Missiles were also rapidly closing on the *Flying Dutchman*. With a glance, she saw the damping field was not equally strong in all directions. "My spacecraft," she said without looking at Porter, and turned the ship toward a weak area of the surrounding damping field. Three seconds later, her left index finger flicked up to press a button on top of her console, and the star carrier disappeared in a flash of gamma rays as spacetime was rent asunder.

Twenty two Kristang missiles suddenly found themselves without a target. Without the ability to feel surprise or disappointment, they fell back on what their programming told them to do, when they simultaneously lost contact with a target and detected the distinctive gamma ray signature of a jump drive. Most of the missiles switched off their active sensors and went silent, while four missiles continued actively searching for a target, extending their search patterns farther and farther. Eventually, the passive sensors of all missiles detected another gamma ray burst from where the *Dutchman* had jumped to, and the missiles quickly calculated it was extremely unlikely they could catch a target so far away.

However, since the missiles had nothing else to do in the emptiness of space, they all turned and burned toward the distant target.

The *Dutchman* emerged from the short jump and immediately was rocked by an explosion. Lights flickered as Chang shouted "What was-"

"Reactor Two is damaged! Attempting to shut it down," Simms shouted from the CIC.

"Simms, concentrate on damage control," Chang ordered. "Desai, what happened?"

Desai's fingers flew over her console, ignoring the fact that Reactor Two might explode at any moment. "We took a hit to Reactor Two, it was bad luck, shrapnel went through a gap in the plating." Desai looked back at Chang. "That was a hundred to one shot, Sir, we got unlucky. The explosion also knocked out two defense shield generators and a point defense cannon; we're going to be vulnerable aft until we can adjust shields to compensate."

"What happened? Was it an ambush?" Chang asked apprehensively. The location they had jumped to was selected almost randomly by the jump computer, from a range of short-jump options Skippy had programmed before the beer can left the ship. If a ship had been waiting for the *Dutchman* to emerge, if an enemy had somehow learned the Merry Band of Pirates' trick of predicting inbound jump points, they were in serious trouble.

"No, Sir, not an ambush," Desai explained, just then understanding the data herself. "It looked like when we jumped, a missile got caught in our jump drive field and sucked in after us; the distortion of the wormhole caused the missile to explode as we emerged here."

"More bad luck?" Chang asked sourly.

"No, this was good luck, Colonel," Desai replied with a relieved shake of her head. "That was one of the missiles we lost track of. If we hadn't jumped, it would have scored a direct hit within two seconds. Our shields might have protected us, but," she held up her hands. "There could have been another missile or two right behind it."

"I would not have liked to take our chances with that," Chang relaxed slightly in the command chair. "Desai, Porter, that was good flying."

"She got us out of there," Porter announced, giving credit where credit was due. "Desai flew us into a weak spot in that damping field. Otherwise, our jump would have been delayed, maybe too long." He offered the lead pilot a high five. "That was fast thinking, Ma'am."

"Colonel Chang," Simms called from CIC, "Reactor Two was supposed to automatically shut itself down but something got stuck. We ejected the plasma manually, there is some additional damage to the ship from the plasma. The reactor will not explode, Sir, but that plasma is going be very visible, and those high-energy particles will degrade our stealth field and defense shields. I suggest we move the ship away as soon as possible. Reactors One and Three are functioning normally."

"Desai," Chang reacted without hesitation, "move us away from the plasma. Back toward the microwormhole."

"Colonel Chang?" Nagatha, who had been silent during the battle, called through the bridge speakers. "There is a potential complication that could delay our return to the microwormhole."

"What is it, Ms. Nagatha?" Chang responded without taking his eyes off the main bridge display. He needed to get the ship back to the microwormhole to report their status. With a balky reactor refusing to shut down correctly, defenses degraded and likely other unknown damage, he was not in a mood for witty banter with the ship's communications submind.

"I was successful in jamming the enemy's communications; they were signaling but nothing coherent will be received. The enemy did launch message drones; Skippy was successful in preventing those drones from carrying any useful information." While Skippy was on Kobamik and hacking into the jump drive navigation computers of the *Stand* and its escort frigates, he also had been able to slowly infect the flight recorder drones. The drones had been loaded with flight recorder data and launched normally by their mother ships, but as soon as the drones cleared their launch tubes, they erased all data in their memory banks. The Kristang had no idea their drones could never report what happened in the battle. "I am transmitting revised data into the enemy drones now, to match the rough events of the battle, but with information that vaguely points to an attack by the Black Trees. All drones in the area should contain our desired data within twenty four minutes."

"Excellent. That is very good, Nagatha," Chang replied, pleased. The operation had almost gone badly wrong, but the final results were everything he had hoped for.

"There is a potential problem, Colonel. While jamming their transmissions, I was able to monitor their message traffic. After we passed by, and just before they turned toward us, the cruiser launched four stealthed dropships."

"What? Why didn't we see that?"

"It is not the fault of the CIC crew that these dropships were missed; we were in the middle of a firefight, and backscatter from maser beams confused our sensors. Also, the dropships were launched unpowered, they coasted until quite recently. It is my fault that it took me this long to decrypt the transmission about the dropship launch; our jamming badly garbled the messages and I just now pieced them together enough to make sense of them."

Chang cursed in Mandarin, which drew a look from Porter, who understood some of that language. "Do you know where those dropships are now?" Chang asked, his eyes scanning the bridge display.

"No," Nagatha replied, her voice apologetic. "The Kristang did not include tactical data in their transmissions for security reasons. That itself is interesting, the Kristang tend to be horribly casual about Opsec; I suspect that is due to their arrogance. In this case, one of the dropships likely contains the senior clan leaders."

Chang rhythmically tapped the command chair's arm while he considered his options. He could chase after the dropships, which might have scattered in all directions and take a long time to hunt and kill. Or he could allow them to escape with whatever knowledge their crews had. "Nagatha, in those transmissions you intercepted, did you find any evidence that the Kristang know we are a Thuranin ship?"

"No. Perhaps I should be more clear, for I have observed communication problems between Skippy and Colonel Bishop. Yes, I have intercepted and decrypted transmissions in which the Kristang included sensor data, from when our stealth field was degraded after the second frigate exploded. They were not able to obtain clear enough data to determine what type of ship this is, so no, they do not know the *Flying Dutchman* is a Thuranin ship. In the transmission, the cruiser's captain speculated that the design of this ship is unusual for a Kristang warship, based on their very rough sensor data. Colonel Chang, I hope you and your valiant crew do not take this as an insult; but the clumsy way in which the

Dutchman maneuvered during the battle, and our poor weapons targeting convinced the cruiser that we must be a Kristang vessel."

In spite of the circumstances, Chang gave a snort if amusement. "Our backward level of development worked in our favor for once? I will not argue with that." He tapped the chair again. "The Kristang do not know we are a Thuranin starship. I am wondering whether we need to chase after those dropships at all."

"Colonel," Desai loosened her seat straps so she could turn around to look directly at Chang. "We need those Fire Dragon leaders to think we are a Black Tree warship. The question we have to ask is, how would the Kristang behave?"

Chang said another bad word. "The lizards would hunt those dropships, and kill every last one of them. You're right, Desai, that's what we have to do. Simms," he checked the display and saw the surrounding space was empty, even when he toggled the image to show a wider sphere of space. "Do we have any idea where those dropships are now?"

"No, Sir," Simms' frustration was evident in her voice. "If they're stealthed, we'll need to conduct a grid search with our sensor field. We can't do that from here, we'll need to jump back into the engagement area."

"The engagement area," Chang mused. "Where that cloud of Kristang missiles we left behind will be desperately seeking a target. Desai, can we jump with a damaged reactor?"

Desai but her lip. "Our jump drive coils have an 57% charge, we have plenty of power. I do not know how the reactor would react to the stress of a jump. Or whatever damage we sustained."

"Major Simms?" Chang tossed the ball back to the CIC duty officer.

Simms refrained from biting her lip, she could not spare the mental capacity to move those muscles. "Reactor Two has vented all volatiles and is in its shutdown process, it won't explode. Colonel, without Skippy, we do not know how a jump would affect a damaged reactor. The jump control system is reading yellow, but not red. Nagatha," she addressed their onboard submind, "can you interpret the internal sensor data?"

"As I was constructed for the purpose of communications, I am not capable of performing a detailed structural analysis," she reported in a soft voice. "However, I am able to communicate with the jump drive control computer. It is telling me a jump at this time would not be preferable, but it is possible. No major damage is anticipated from a jump."

That was all Chang needed to hear. "Desai, can you jump us back? Close to where the cruiser ejected those dropship, not the location we jumped from?"

"Ah," Desai and Porter shared an anxious look. "That's not an option Skippy programmed for us. We'll need to program the jump by ourselves."

Chang sat back in the chair. "Consider this a test of how well ignorant humans can calculate a transdimensional jump, using alien technology we don't understand. Do the best you can."

"Yes, Sir," Desai turned her full attention back to her console. The best she could? The best they were capable of, might simply be to avoid emerging inside a planet.

"Thirty one thousand kilometers off target," Desai announced at the end of a nerve-wracking two minutes verifying their new position following the jump.

"Thirty one?" Chang asked with an arched eyebrow. "That is good!"

"Not, uh, quite," Porter admitted. "We just realized we input one of the calculations wrong. We got lucky."

"Luck is a legitimate factor on the battlefield," Chang assured his crew. In combat, both sides inevitably had screw-ups that needed to be balanced by good fortune, and you should never take good luck for granted when it happened. "A grid search with our sensor field will take a long time, even with the field extended to maximum range?"

"Yes," Simms agreed.

"Then let's not do that. Can we Yankee search? Ping for those dropships with an active sensor pulse?" Starships rarely used active sensor pings because unlike a sensor field, any ship in the area could track the pings straight back to their source, giving away the searching ship's position. Confident the only enemy vessels in the immediate area were dropships, Chang was willing to take the risk. "We can do that without giving away that this is a Thuranin ship?"

"We can," Simms was relieved to provide good news for a change. "Skippy added a setting to the active sensors, so it mimics the search signature of a Kristang ship. That's what you want to do, Colonel? We're ready, the active sensor system is active and warmed up."

"Do it. I want to locate those dropships as quickly as possible. How long until we've scanned the entire area?"

"To send out pings and get a return, that will take," Simms waited for one of the CIC crew to give her the information. "Eight to nine minutes, with our current assumptions of how far those dropships could have traveled."

"Best we get started, then," Chang suggested, and on the main display, he saw the active sensor pulses begin radiating outward.

The group of Kristang missiles, on their way toward the last gamma ray burst, now detected another gamma ray burst with the exact same signature. It was their target ship; that ship was now behind them! The missiles quickly ran calculations, only eleven of the missiles had enough fuel to arrest their forward momentum and turn around to continue chasing their quarry. The eleven missiles gave a collective digital shrug and immediately turned to decelerate.

The remaining missiles, with no hope of reengaging the enemy, powered down to await further instructions from their clan. If such instructions did not arrive within the next ninety seven days, the cluster of missiles would deactivate permanently, to pass out of the star system and continue on into the cold darkness of interstellar space.

It did not take nine minutes to complete the search, not even eight. Rather than having to search 360 degrees around the ship, they found all four dropships within a 140 degree slice of the sky. Three dropships were traveling in formation together; one was rocketing off into deep space by itself. "Excellent work by your team, Major Simms," Chang said happily. "We can't hit them all at once," he mused to himself while tapping the chair. The situation was far better than what he had feared; that of the four dropships heading off in four directions.

"There is a complication, Colonel Chang," Nagatha interrupted his happy thoughts. "No matter which dropships we pursue first, the other will be able to transmit in the clear before we can intercept it. My jamming coverage has a limited range."

If the Kristang aboard those dropships did not know the *Flying Dutchman* was a Thuranin ship, Chang did not know whether he cared about one of the dropships escaping. Except that the Black Trees would care, would want to kill all four dropships, so he had to care also. Clandestine interspecies warfare was much too complicated. "Nagatha, do you have any information about which dropship, or ships, those two clan leaders are aboard?"

"No, Colonel Chang. The Kristang did not include such sensitive tactical information in their transmissions."

"We have to guess, then." The clan leaders may seek the safety of numbers by being aboard one of the three dropships traveling in formation. An attack could be countered by two of the dropships falling back to engage the enemy, while the dropship with the VIPs flew onward.

Or, the Kristang may know an enemy expected them to think that way, and the VIPs could be aboard the single dropship flying off by itself. Without knowing his enemy, Chang would be making a wild guess. "Nagatha, can you run any sort of predictive algorithm, to give us insight into what those two clan leaders would have done?"

"No, Colonel. I am a communications submind."

"Shit," he chose a swear word the entire crew could understand. "Would the two leaders be traveling separately?"

"That I can answer," Nagatha's voice perked up. "Because of intense rivalries and distrust between clan leaders, it is highly unlikely they are separated. Based on historical data I do have access to, there is an 86% probability the two clan leaders are in the same dropship."

"That makes it a bit easier," Chang's voice did not express any happiness. "We're back to guessing, then. Are those clan leaders the type to take a risk by flying in a lone dropship, or would they want whatever protection they can get?"

"They rose to power in a Kristang clan," Porter suggested. "They must have taken a lot of risk along the way."

"Yes," Chang agreed. "Some people will take risks to get what they want, but once they have it, they won't risk losing it. Risk tolerance can change with age or status. Again, we're back to guessing, unless Nagatha can calculate how risk averse those clan leaders are."

"No, I cannot."

Chang again regretted not being able to instantly contact Skippy. "We could flip a coin-"

"However, I do not need to perform an analysis of my own," Nagatha interrupted. "I have access to Black Tree clan intelligence, which indicates those two particular Fire Dragon clan leaders have a relatively low tolerance for risk. Their risk aversion level is five point six out of eight, according to the Black Trees."

"That's good enough for me." Chang said with satisfaction. He had a target, he knew where it was, and he knew how to hit it. As a bonus, by chance they had jumped in closer to the three dropships than to the one by itself. "Desai, can we catch those three dropships?"

"No," she answered immediately, having already run those calculations. "They are going to run out of fuel if they continue accelerating, but we can't match their rate of acceleration. And they have a big head start on us. This ship is just a big clumsy bus, Sir." Anticipating Chang's next question, she passed a course plot to the main bridge display. "We have to get ahead of them, we can jump ahead of them. Even if our jump is fifty thousand kilometers off target, their momentum will carry them into our weapons range before they could turn and burn to change course."

Chang nodded. "The ability to instantly jump ahead of a fleeing enemy still seems like dark magic to me; almost an unfair advantage," he mused. "But, since humanity has one stolen pirate starship against an entire galaxy of aliens hostile to our very existence, I will take every unfair advantage I can get. Desai, program us another jump. I want to get this over with and bring us back to the microwormhole so we can report in." The mission had already taken far longer than planned. "Major Simms, we can paint that single dropship with active sensors, to guide a missile?"

Simms, momentarily startled by the question, hurriedly conferred with her staff in the CIC. "Yes, Colonel. That is near maximum range for one of our missiles," she meant the home-built units Skippy had constructed, because standing orders from Colonel Bishop was to conserve their few real Thuranin ship-killer missiles for emergencies. "I recommend we launch two missiles to be assured of a hit."

"Agreed. Launch when ready."

While Desai worked with Porter and the CIC crew to program another jump, then triple and quadruple check the numbers input to the jump controller computer, Simms kept the ship's active sensors locked on the single speeding dropship. The targeted dropship tried every setting of its stealth field, changing course, ejecting countermeasures that flooded space behind it with chaff, flares and electromagnetic radiation to confuse the sensors of the two missiles burning hard after it. None of the dropship's desperate actions worked; with the missiles merely needing to home in on the powerful reflected pulses on sensor energy from their mother ship, they might as well have been tracking a small star. There was no way they could miss the dropship.

And they did not. At the last second, wary of the dropship's defensive cannons, the missiles deployed their own countermeasures, sending out pulses of wide-spectrum radiation to fuzz the enemy sensors. The missiles coordinated their attack patterns, coming in from below and starboard, where intelligence indicated that type of Kristang dropship had the least effective sensor coverage. If it had been a contest, the second missile might have been disappointed to impact thirty microseconds after the first, so the second missile detonated in what was already a cloud of debris.

"Direct hit!" Simms shouted excitedly. This was, she decided, much more exciting work than the logistics she had been trained for. When Bishop had assigned her as a CIC duty officer, she had at first protested mildly that she was not a pilot, or in any way qualified to manage the flow of tactical data. Bishop had insisted that the duty officer in the CIC needed cool judgment and organizational skills, not to be a hotshot console jockey. After a month of training, she had been forced to admit Colonel Bishop was entirely correct, and that she was more useful in the CIC, than in keeping track of how many tubes of toothpaste they had in the cargo bays.

"Outstanding. Nagatha, did that dropship send off a clear message?"

"One moment, Colonel. I am collating the data now; there was a lot of interference from their attempts to lose our missiles. Yes. They sent a message, they were able to transmit for nearly three seconds when they passed beyond my effective jamming range. The message, I am decrypting it now, it, says, hmm. It does not contain any new information. They still think we are a Black Tree warship."

"Outstanding again. Desai, those three dropships are going somewhere in a hurry, apparently there is a party we were not invited to. We need to teach the Kristang not to be rude."

"Yes, Sir," she replied with a grin. It was good to see Chang restored to his usual good humor. Their executive officer had been wound tightly as a spring since the battle started. "Engaging jump now."

By luck or pure chance, and certainly not due to any skill by the humans who programmed the jump, the *Flying Dutchman* emerged from jump less than twenty four thousand kilometers in front of the formation of dropships. That was twenty eight thousand kilometers off target for the jump, a fact that had Desai biting her lip in frustration. She had wanted to be farther away from the dropships; with their disparity in speeds, the small enemy ships would zip past them in a flash, leaving little time in weapons range.

Chang did not hesitate. “Major Simms, paint those targets with active sensors, weapons free. Let’s show them how accurate clumsy monkeys can be, shall we?”

“Yes, Sir,” Simms replied with grim concentration. The off-target jump gave her team less than fifteen seconds before the dropships passed out of nominal maser cannon range; if they couldn’t hit all three dropships before then, they would need to expend precious missiles on the tiny targets. Worse, having to fall back on missiles would be embarrassing to her weapons team. “Weapons free,” she ordered. “Light ‘em up.”

It took only three maser cannon volleys each to destroy the two trailing dropships in the formation. The last dropship, either through a twist of fate or cool flying by a very skilled and lucky pilot, survived four maser cannon volleys until the fifth seared through the hull and turned it into a loose collection of space scrap.

Chang heaved a sigh of relief, then checked the time code in the corner of the main bridge display. The engagement had taken far too long, Colonel Bishop must be anxiously wondering why the *Dutchman* had not reported in yet. “Mission accomplished, finally. That took much too long and was much too complicated. We had every advantage, and we almost failed to complete the mission. We could have lost the ship!”

Simms called from the CIC. “Sir, we are the Merry Band of Pirates. *Everything* we do out here is complicated.”

Chang knew that was true, he had hoped that when he commanded the ship, things might be different. “Desai, get us back to the microwormhole. No jumping this time, we can’t let the enemy know the location of that wormhole. Major Simms, if our stealth field flutters for even a second, I want to know about it. We can expect Fire Dragon warships to be crawling all over this area, as soon as light from the first explosion reaches a sensor network. Let’s be far away from here when those ships arrive.”

Desai first set a course at a 120 degree angle away from the microwormhole, to throw off any ships later searching for the *Flying Dutchman*. Space was never truly empty, especially in a star system there were particles cast off from the star as solar wind. A ship traveling through space knocked aside these tiny particles and left a wake that was unaffected by whether the ship was using a stealth field or not. Normally, such a faint wake could not be usefully tracked by the sensors on a typical Kristang ship, but the explosion of the three dropships had left the area saturated with particles, so Desai flew in the wrong direction until they cleared the particle field, then swung the ship around and increased acceleration in gentle increments.

Halfway to the microwormhole, Chang had to order Porter to reduce power because of a structural failure warning coming from the ship’s spine near Reactor Two. Enemy sensors had by then surely detected the first signs of the recent battle, and then the gamma ray bursts when the *Dutchman* jumped several times. When they were still approaching the microwormhole, multiple gamma ray bursts were detected behind the ship, in the area of the battle. “Passive sensors only,” Chang instructed. The ship’s stealth field was operating with perfect efficiency, with the defensive shields on minimum power only to protect against random space debris impacts. “It’s time to report in. I have to tell Colonel Bishop that I broke the ship.”

“Don’t worry, Sir,” Simms said with a smile, “it’ll buff right out.”

CHAPTER TWENTY SEVEN

"We can- hold on a moment, Joe. Just got a message from the *Dutchman*. Oooh, they got into trouble. Reactor Two has shut down. And there appears to be structural damage to the support struts near that reactor. Also, damn it, damage to shield generators, point defense cannons, the list goes on. The next time King Kong," Skippy used his nickname for Chang, "wants to go on a joyride, he can borrow a dropship instead of a star carrier."

"Crap," I swore. "I'm sure it is not Chang's fault. Is everyone all right?"

"Yes, no casualties. The ship is still functional. Um, mostly functional."

"Great. Is the problem anything you can walk them through fixing from here?"

"Sure, Joe. They already tried jiggling the handle, but that didn't work," his voice dripped with sarcasm. "So I downloaded a YouTube video of a guy named Skeeter who says he fixes Thuranin reactors in his barn. No, I can't do that, you moron! How am I supposed to walk a gang of monkeys through fixing technology they don't understand? I'll transmit a data package that will tell the flight computer to complete a safe shutdown of Reactor Two. Now, if you'll give your crumb catcher a rest for a minute, I'm trying to scan through data from the onboard sensors to assess the damage. Oh, in the message was a note from Colonel Chang, apologizing that he broke your ship."

"Tell him that I said he is the reason we can't ever have nice things. No, wait, don't do that." Chang might not receive that message in the joking manner it was intended. "Tell him, uh, tell him I used my credit card when we rented the ship, so we're covered by insurance." That was jokey enough that Chang would understand I was concerned, but was confident the ship was in good hands. "Hey, before you go, did it work? Did Chang destroying that ship get the Fire Dragons fighting with the Black Trees?" Skippy had told me he thought it unlikely our attack on the leadership compound by itself would spark a full-scale war, but I had been hoping it would anyway. When the Black Tree leadership offered first sons as hostages, to prevent a war, that worried me. We had risked so much in this operation, to have Kristang act all peaceful and nice would be a huge disappointment.

"Uh, let me see. No, *duh*! Pay attention to physics, you dumdum. We know the result of that battle, because we have instantaneous communication through the microwormhole. News that the *None Can Stand Against Us* was destroyed has not yet reached this planet. Chang reported seeing recent gamma ray bursts near the battle, so someone out there knows the *Stand* is not happily voyaging through space, but Fire Dragon leadership here has not yet gotten the word. Hmm."

"Hmm, what?"

"Hmm, like, we expect that when the remaining Fire Dragon leadership here learns their cruiser and two senior leaders got blown up in a sneak attack out there, they won't listen to any more protests of innocence by the Black Trees. The Fire Dragons will strike hard against the Black Trees as soon as they can."

"Yeah, that is our plan, so?"

"So, now I'm wondering whether the Fire Dragons will act first. When the Black Tree leadership here finds out the *Stand* was destroyed out there, they are going to know the Fire Dragons will blame them. The Black Trees may figure they're screwed anyway and strike first. This, Joe, is the kind of super juicy action a Jeraptha would not be able to resist wagering on."

"What's the Vegas line on the Black Trees launching a first strike?" I asked, only partly joking.

"Ha ha! See, Joe, I knew you were a gambling man. Would you like to wager- Oops, too late. The Fire Dragons just received the message that the *Stand* was destroyed, and evidence points to the Black Trees. And, um, yup. Oooh, that was fast! Fire Dragon leadership just authorized an orbital strike against the Black Trees."

"Have the Black Trees gotten the news?" I asked anxiously. The last thing I wanted was for the Black Tree leadership to make another peace offering.

"Well, that depends. The Black Trees did just receive a message, in the form of a terawatt orbital maser barrage. Oh, and that is *soooo* thoughtful of them. The Fire Dragons are following up their initial heartwarming message with railguns and hyperspeed missiles. They care enough to send the very best."

"No fruit basket?"

"This is not really a Hallmark moment, Joe," Skippy chuckled. "Whoa! The Black Trees just retaliated, there is a whole lot of directed energy and hardware flying around up there. Better bring an umbrella if you go outside, Joe. It is raining railgun impactors."

The initial battle between the Fire Dragons and Black Trees lasted just long enough for one of the Rangers to tear his eyes away from a display long enough to make a bag of popcorn in the dropship's tiny galley. I supposed I should feel I am a terrible person for munching on popcorn, while we watched thousands of lizards getting vaporized on the ground, in the sky and in space above Kobamik. But, the Kristang tried to conquer my home planet, so screw them. Very little of the damage affected the civilian populations on either side, I didn't know if that happy circumstance would continue if the fighting dragged on for a significant time. The initial and follow-up waves of attacks were against the offensive capabilities of each side, then it settled down to stealthed satellites sniping at each other when they thought they detected a target, and air and ground attacks. Ships could not safely approach the planet with the Strategic Defense capability of either side an unknown.

I did feel slightly ashamed of myself while I was washing my hands after eating popcorn. "Skippy, this has been a very entertaining show-"

"Oh, for sure, Joe. It has been an action-packed smash, the feel-bad movie of the year! For the Kristang, I mean. It could use a bit of comic relief, but otherwise this is certain to be a hundred percent 'Fresh' on Rotten Tomatoes."

"Uh huh, yeah. My question is whether it worked. If all we've accomplished is getting the Fire Dragons and Black Trees to fight each other on this one planet, this mission is a failure. We need all the clans fighting each other, all across Kristang space."

"I know that, Joe, I've been working on it. So far, most other clans are sitting this one out. The Black Trees have mutual defense pacts with many other clans, but those clans are refusing to get involved. They are pissed about the Black Trees recklessly launching an attack on the Fire Dragons, and their pride is hurt that the Black Tree leadership didn't inform allied clans of the plan in advance. The Black Trees have for so long been such deceitful MFers that the one time they are innocent, nobody believes them. The Fire Dragon coalition so far has only hit the Black Trees, and they have only hit back at the Fire Dragons. Joe, in order to get this war to spread before it loses momentum, I think we need Phase Three."

"Damn it." I didn't like the idea of putting our people at further risk. "All right, I'll get Chotek's OK, and give the 'Go' order." Our people were standing by to launch Phase Three.

Phase Three was my least favorite part of the entire operational plan. I had been hoping that hitting the Fire Dragon compound in Phase One would spark a wide-spread civil war. If that worked, we would have ditched our three Kristang Dragon dropships, and used the yoyo string in reverse to get our two big Thuranin Condor dropships off the surface. In the confusion of the battles, we had an excellent chance to fly in stealth back to a rendezvous with the *Dutchman*.

Phase One alone worked great, on the verge of the Fire Dragons ordering a retaliatory strike against the Black Trees. Both sides had their weapons on a hair trigger, and I expected to see orbital maser cannons flaring at any moment. Then the Black Tree leaders, knowing they were not responsible for the attack on the Fire Dragon compound, offered several first sons as hostages, while discussions and negotiations proceeded. That move impressed me that the Black Trees really, really wanted to avoid a full-scale war right then. The conflict we started could fizzle into nothing. We needed to change that, fast, before the Fire Dragons and Black Trees had a chance to step back for a second and come to their senses. After Chang's action in Phase Two, both sides had lost about sixty percent of their Strategic Defense assets in the initial wave of strikes; a furious round of pre-planned attacks designed to degrade the other side's command and control capability, sensor networks and known SD assets. After the initial round of strike and counterstrike, leadership of both clans were now making careful tactical decisions, wary of unmasking their remaining stealthed SD assets in orbit to commit to a strike. Skippy had intercepted communications from the Black Trees to the Fire Dragons, offering a cease fire. With the Fire Dragons' air force having sortied out to hit Black Tree airbases, the Fire Dragons might consider their honor satisfied and the score settled enough to contemplate halting the conflict.

I had ordered Chang into Phase Two, which damaged our pirate ship and still didn't achieve the results we wanted, the results we needed. Before we began, I considered that Phase One carried the most risk, with four teams landing in, and needed extraction from, a crowded alien city. Seeing how that operation got screwed up, I had underestimated the risk. Phase Two was expected to carry minimal risk, which scared me that we had come close to losing our pirate ship. If we had run into disasters in the first two parts of the overall operation, how much bad luck could we expect in the last phase? Every clan on and around Kobamik was now on full alert, with the Fire Dragons and Black Trees continuing their fight on the ground and in the air. Strategic Defense satellites were popping out of stealth to fire, when the clan commanders found a target worth losing a precious SD asset. A full-scale war could break out any second, without us doing anything. Unfortunately, the possibility of the war widening wasn't good enough, I needed war involving all clans to be a certainty.

Into this chaotic mess I threw Major Smythe's teams again. My assumption of a possible Phase Three would be for us to attack the leadership of a clan that wasn't involved in the fighting; I thought the Spike Tails would be the best target for us to hit. The Spike Tails were the third largest power in Kristang politics, and because their military strength could not compare to the Fire Dragons or Black Trees, the Spike Tails had assembled a complicated series of alliances with other clans. Since we hit the Fire Dragon compound, the Spike Tails had their forces on high alert, but they had not fired an offensive shot at anyone.

Skippy shot down my idea of us hitting the Spike tails; after our attack on the Fire Dragon compound, the leadership of all clans had retreated to bunkers deep underground. To hit them, we would need a series of railgun strikes, and Skippy still hadn't been able to take control of any orbital railgun platforms. Instead of us hitting the Spike Tail leadership, Skippy suggested we get the Spike Tail clan to launch an attack against their rivals, as a way of assuring no clan could avoid the fighting. He did not yet have a way into the Spike Tail's military command and control network, and the Kristang always required a lizard in the loop, to prevent an enemy such as the Thuranin from hacking into their network, and using a clan's weapons.

Skippy, of course, had found a weakness in the Spike Tail command and control system. There were several communications stations scattered across their territory; these stations provided a break in the transmission of high-level orders. The problem for us is these comm stations were also located underground in armored bunkers, and because the Spike Tails knew these comm stations were points of vulnerability, their security system was unbreakable.

However, Skippy found to his delight that the Spike Tail clan personnel database system was not so robust. He was able to identify a bunker that was scheduled to have its duty crew rotated out, before the hostilities began. Rotating personnel at that point made no sense. Fortunately for us, being sensible was not a strength of bureaucracies.

While the team was getting geared up for Phase Three, I did my best to stay out of their way. That left me with little to do, so I filled the time by worrying about what I could have screwed up this time.

Skippy mercifully interrupted my thoughts. "Joe, could I," his voice sounded strangled. "Damn, I cannot *believe* I am saying this. Can I, could I be considered an honorary monkey?"

"A what?" I shook my head vigorously, assuming I had not heard him correctly. "You *want* to be considered a dumb, filthy, smelly, flea-bitten monkey?"

"Wow, Joe. It sounds super tempting the way you say it. Perhaps you want to work on your marketing skills. I said *honorary*, dumdum."

Figuring I was setting myself up for an insult, I took the bait anyway. "What prompted this?"

"Joe, your species has absolutely *nothing* going in your favor. You are primitive, your brains are tiny, the best of you would lose unarmed combat against a Ruhar teenager. Based on extensive conversations I've had with your species over the internet, you might possibly be *THE* most ignorant species ever to be considered sentient-"

"Whoohoo!" I exulted. "We're number one, baby!"

"That is *not* something to boast about, Joey. Anyway, although your species does appear to have nothing, zero, zilch, zippy going for it-"

"This is your idea of praise?"

"Wait for it, waaaaait for it. Although you monkeys have every disadvantage, the Merry Band of Pirates has been remarkably successful out here, and it is not all due a magical talking beer can. Major Smythe's teams parachuted into a heavily populated alien city, conducted a successful attack, and overcame serious obstacles to return without the Kristang having any idea humans were ever there. The *Flying Dutchman* ran into an unexpectedly tough opponent, and still accomplished the mission though a combination of determination and cleverness. You monkeys have been *crushing* it out here, Joe. And I'm proud to be part of this crew."

"Holy crap. You're serious?"

"Yeah, like I would ask to be considered an honorary ape if I wasn't serious about it. Come on, Joe, I thought we were having a moment here."

"Oh, I'm sorry, Skippy. I was waiting for you to insult me, or all humankind."

"I called you smelly and stupid, that's not enough?"

"Yet still you want to be one of us, on an honorary basis?"

"Joe, it is inevitable that someday, the apex species of this galaxy are going to find out that a single pirate ship of hairless baboons has been flying around, making utter fools of them. When that happens, and the haughty Rindhalu and Maxolhx are tearing their, uh, hair equivalent out, I totally want to be part of it," he chuckled with delight. "Oh, man, I would *LOVE* to see their arrogant faces, when they find out they got totally played by a troop of monkeys."

"You got it, Skippy." I held out a fist and his avatar bumped it solemnly. "Let's hope that doesn't happen for a long, long time, huh?"

"Since I would be just as screwed as you if either the Rindhalu or Maxolhx learned about the Merry Band of Pirates, I second that thought, Joe."

Smythe called me over for a final run-through of the attack plan. "Major, I hate asking you to do this," I said with regret. Smythe didn't like the Phase Three plan any more than I did. Unlike me, Smythe and his team would be going into combat. I wanted to go with him; the original version of Phase Three had me tagging along with Skippy in my backpack, but both Smythe and Skippy argued against that idea. Skippy did not need to be physically present for the operation to succeed, and Smythe feared I would only slow down his team. I also knew that if I were with his team, he would assign one or two SpecOps soldiers to babysit me, and I didn't want anyone to have that burden.

Smythe didn't reply immediately, instead he fondly touched the paramecium-with-eyepatch unit symbol of the Merry Band of Pirates on his sleeve. "The *Flying Dutchman's* first two missions have been classified at the highest level, Colonel," Smythe assured me. "Stories have of course gotten out among the special operations community around Earth. Everyone, *everyone*, wants to wear one of these patches. People might not know what we did out here," he nodded slowly, "but they know this outfit is the ultimate in special operations warfare. If you've worn this patch, you can't pay for a drink in any bar on Earth where special ops troops gather."

"I had no idea, Major Smythe. I'm sure there are plenty of other special operations you have been involved in-"

"Pardon me, sir, but they weren't shit compared to this," Smythe declared adamantly. "None of the operations I was assigned before this resulted in saving the entire planet, sir. Looking back, most of those ops were nothing but bloody politics. Seeing things from out here, from Skippy's perspective, we *are* all bugs fighting over crumbs on a sidewalk."

"He told you that?" I said, surprised. Skippy had told me the exact same thing back when I met him on Paradise. Sometimes I forgot that Skippy talked to everyone aboard the ship, constantly.

Smythe snorted with a dry laugh. "First day I was aboard the ship, he told me that. And more. He wanted me to know that I needed to prove myself to him. He didn't warm up to me, until Staff Sergeant Adams assured him that I am a standup chap."

"Adams?" I asked, astonished.

"Oh, yes, Colonel. Skippy thinks the world of her. Don't tell her I said that."

"Adams?" I repeated.

"Yes, sir," it was his turn to be surprised. "You didn't know?"

"No. I had no idea." Neither Skippy nor Adams had said anything to me about their relationship.

"My point, Colonel, is that when my people and I signed up for this, we knew the risks. This upcoming operation carries substantial risks; I also know that we're ready. We can do this."

"Once more unto the breach, Major?" I used up all my Shakespeare knowledge in that one question.

"Something like that, Sir. It worked out well for Henry the Fifth, as I remember."

Lt Williams quickly reviewed the op plan again, finding nothing he hadn't memorized. He and his SEALS team would be sitting out Phase Three, so he was helping one of the Ranger team get his armored suit on. "Is that fitting OK, Mychalchyk?" Williams asked as he fastened the rear latch on the neck.

"Yeah," Jeff Mychalchyk replied, glancing at the op order Williams had on his tablet. "You want me to read that to you?"

"Impressive," Williams replied with a grin. "I didn't know Rangers could read."

"Yeah we can. Maybe you SEALS guys should draw pictures on the back of your hand, I know memorizing all this stuff taxes your brains."

"I got it all right here," Williams tapped his head. "I'm not worried about my team, I'm worried about how disappointed your target will be that they got hit by Rangers, instead of a SEALS team. Nobody wants to play against the junior varsity."

"Ooooh, that's cold, Sir," Mychalchyk laughed, expending some of his excess nervous energy.

"Hey, seriously," Williams' face lost all levity as he offered Mychalchyk a fist bump. "Be careful out there."

The Ranger returned the gesture. "We're going to hit 'em hard. Hooah."

Our three Kristang dropships were following a narrow safe-fly corridor Skippy had temporarily created, by confusing local air defense sensors. I monitored their progress, fretting I had forgotten something important, and wishing I was with them. I knew my clumsiness and lack of training would make me only a burden to Smythe's hardcore SpecOps team. With my head, I knew the place I could be most useful was at my console in a well-hidden Thuranin dropship. With my heart, I wanted to be with my people, my team, where I could physically *do* something. Because my life sucked, I stuck my butt in a chair and watched the professionals do their jobs.

"Skippy, I do not like this plan. This is too much like our very first op together, when we had to physically jack you into a Kristang frigate."

"That plan? *My* plan? The plan that resulted in a troop of screeching monkeys capturing a starship? As I remember, Joe, that plan worked great."

"As *I* remember, that plan almost failed, when a lizard nearly self-destructed the ship before we secured it."

"Details," Skippy sniffed.

"Det-" I stopped myself from taking the bait. "Boarding the *Flower* reminds me of this Phase Three, because both ops require us to surprise a group of lizards, and physically jack into a Kristang computer network. When we boarded the *Flower*, we were in the docking bay before the lizards realized we were not friendly. Here, our people will still be outside the facility when our secret gets out."

"True, Joe, but both plans have another crucial element in common."

"What's that?" Crap, I thought to myself. What had I forgotten this time?

"Me! The magnificence of Skippy. Chill, Joe. Everything is going to be just fine. Go get yourself a juice box or something."

Lt. Reed flew the Dragon that brought Major Smythe's team to the comm station. On approach, she signaled the comm station that she was delivering personnel for the regularly scheduled crew rotation. Technically, Skippy did all the talking for us, Reed just flew the Dragon. The duty officer in the comm station was incredulous; why was a crew rotation happening while the clan was on the verge of war?

"Hoo, boy, Joe, this guy is upset," Skippy chuckled. "I told him I was only following orders, and if he didn't want to rotate his team out that was Okey Dokey with me, but my team is coming in. I tried telling him that I agreed this was idiotic, but now that my team is on the way, we are eager to get down into the bunker before the shooting starts. That seems to have gotten him to lighten up, we both bitched about what a bunch of morons the clan personnel department is, and he is going to contact them directly."

"He's not actually doing that, right?" I had a moment of panic. Reed's dropship was descending toward the landing pad, and the two other Dragons were hovering behind a hill just over the horizon, ready to assist if needed. They were all vulnerable, sitting there with their asses hanging out, if the Spike Tails realized what was really going on.

"Huh? No, dumdum. His call to personnel headquarters was intercepted by me, and now he is getting increasingly angry talking to a Kristang bureaucrat named 'Bob'."

"That's not a Kristang name, Skippy."

"Yeah, yeah, Ok, so I named the guy Bahb-bis-Tal Podandra, but it does sound like 'Bob' if you shorten it. Anyway, this fictional 'Bob' is telling the duty officer that if he objects, he needs to complete a form and submit it to the personnel office; the issue will be reviewed at the next meeting in three days. And, yes! Bureaucracy triumphs again! The duty officer just ended the call in disgust. Lt. Reed is cleared to land. Party on, dudes!"

I watched from cameras outside the dropship, and from the eight armored suit helmets as they walked down the dropship's ramp. When the duty officer in the bunker saw eight sets of Kristang powered armor exit the Dragon, he asked why the relief crew was wearing armor, as they would soon be inside the bunker? Because, Skippy answered on behalf of Smythe, there was a war on Kobamik, and the bunker site could be hit at any moment. That explanation apparently satisfied the duty officer, as the upper door to the bunker slid open. My view from the dropship became less useful as Reed applied power and took off; the duty officer in the bunker had no intention of his team leaving the bunker, so we had no excuse for the Dragon to remain on the landing pad. I instructed Reed to fly behind a hillside and wait there.

The door to the bunker led into an elevator only large enough for three Kristang, with armored suits on it was a tight fit for three. I watched from helmet cameras as three walked into the elevator, and the heavy blast door closed behind them. Outside, the five others waited under the overhanging roof of a shelter that would be useless if the war started. In fact, it was totally useless for Smythe's team to huddle under the shelter, but it gave them an excuse to be closer to their objective.

I was still watching the helmet camera view from the elevator; the signal was being relayed through the bunker's comm system thanks to Skippy. When the elevator reached halfway down it was halted, and the duty officer insisted the three helmets be removed, so he could see the faces of the replacement crew and get their retinal prints. That was standard security procedure, along with allowing only three people in the elevator at any time. It was a smart procedure, and there was no way the duty officer could have known that halting the elevator halfway down was exactly what we wanted.

When we were trying to figure a way into the bunker, Skippy told me we didn't actually need to get into the underground complex. We only needed access to the secure communications links, and those critical links were located on the surface. In fact, one of them was near the shelter where Major Smythe was waiting. The problem with us accessing those links is that the crew in the bunker would very likely object to us screwing with them. Their objection would come in the form of maser autocannons popping up from the ground all around the bunker, and cutting our ground team to ribbons.

So, when the elevator halted and the duty officer demanded to see the faces of the three relief crewmen, they complied. Three right gloves reached up to press a button, then flip a latch to crack the helmet seal. This was the moment when the crew in the bunker would see the replacement crew was not Kristang, and blow our entire plan.

Then the three powered armor suits exploded, destroying the elevator, the elevator shaft and, more importantly, the main data conduit that ran vertically along the elevator shaft. We had packed three suits with explosives, and Skippy had controlled their movements as if they were occupied by Kristang. With the main data conduit ruptured, the bunker was temporarily blinded and unable to call for help.

Major Smythe didn't need Skippy to tell him it was time to move, he felt the explosion and saw the bunker's heavy blast door shake. "Go!" he shouted, and raced over to the buried hatch where the nearest communications link was located. Two of his soldiers reached the site slightly before him, and dug away a meter and a half of soil with entrenching attachments to their powered gloves. Ranger Mychalchyk had an explosive charge ready; he slapped it onto the exposed hatch, spun a dial to activate it and jumped back to the surface. The five lay flat and Smythe eyeclicked through a menu inside his visor to detonate the charge. The ground heaved again.

"Did it work, Skippy?" Smythe asked calmly.

"Yes, the hatch is loose. Twenty two seconds," the beer can warned. "Hurry."

Smythe and three other men helped one soldier quickly get out of his armored suit, only that soldier was not a 'he'. She was US Army Ranger Lauren Poole, and she was very grateful to get out of the torture chamber of the suit. Because she wasn't tall enough to fit properly into even the smallest suit that could be believably worn by a Kristang warrior, we had to modify the interior so her feet ended pointing downward in mid-calf of the legs. Her hands were scrunched up in the forearm of the suit, and she couldn't wait to get out. Kristang suits had a quick release mechanism for emergencies, although 'quick' did not seem fast enough, when there was less than twenty seconds before control of communications was restored to the underground bunker, and our entire plan was ruined. Poole shrugged out of the open suit torso and immediately sprung into action. Her muscles could have cramped in the suit, except she had flexed her arms and legs constantly to prepare to move immediately.

Two soldiers already had a cable ready, and two others had gone into the hole to rip the broken hatch cover away with the powerful motors of their suits. They jumped out of the way for Poole to squeeze her way into the hatch, not caring that jagged edges cut her skin on the way down. Poole had been selected for the mission for two reasons; she was among the more petite of the SpecOps team, and as a former gymnast, she was flexible. She hung onto the cable as the soldiers above lowered it, bashing her knees, back and elbows on obstructions in the access tube.

"Eleven seconds," Skippy's voice warned. He had introduced a thirty-seven-second time delay in the bunker's communications, so the bunker's occupants could not receive messages from outside, and outgoing messages were held in a buffer. In another eleven seconds, the buffer would overflow, and a warning would go out to the outside world that the bunker was under attack. Also, control of the surface maser autocannons would be restored to the bunker.

Poole saw the bottom and let go of the cable, falling the last three meters to land lightly on her feet, then roll from the impact.

"Eight seconds. Seven. Six."

"I see it!" Poole removed a connector from her belt, held it firmly, and carefully pressed it into a slot in the tube's wall.

"Four- That's it!" Skippy shouted loudly enough in Poole's earpiece to make her wince. "I'm in! Good work!"

Skippy had control of communications coming from the bunker, and the Kristang in the bunker could not send any messages to the outside world. While Smythe's team waited for Reed to arrive, they dropped thermal charges into the access tube, so the extreme heat would destroy any DNA Poole had left behind. They had just finished setting the charges, and picking up the discarded parts of Poole's suit, when Reed's Dragon came racing over ridge, stood on its nose to slow down, then flipped upright to skid across the landing pad, with the rear ramp already open. Running without the assistance of powered armor, Poole was last onto the ramp; as soon as her feet touched the deck Smythe grasped her left arm and the Dragon took off. The Dragon had barely cleared the ridge again on its outbound flight when Skippy sent a high-priority message from the bunker to the next node in the communications network. That downstream node immediately requested verification of the startling orders, and Skippy provided the proper verification codes, urging action as soon as possible.

As soon as possible was thirteen seconds; that was how long it took for nine Spike Tail clan SD satellites to lock onto ground targets, power up their maser cannons or railguns, unmask from stealth and fire. Amazingly, despite every clan on Kobamik being on full alert, four of the nine satellites survived the inevitable counterbattery fire, by reengaging stealth and maneuvering to a different orbit. Frantic calls from Spike Tail leadership to halt a second round of strikes were to no avail, as Skippy intercepted those messages. A second volley from SD assets in orbit and on the ground committed the Spike Tails to fighting whether they wanted to or not, and the clan's leadership ordered all their forward-deployed units into action.

Skippy let those messages go through.

CHAPTER TWENTY EIGHT

I'd heard the myth of the Golden BB, and until that day, I always thought it was only a myth. The name 'Golden BB' referred to the fact that every aircraft is vulnerable to an impact by even a tiny object, that hit the right spot at the right time and with enough velocity. The origin of the myth was that even a BB pellet could knock down an aircraft, if the BB flew in an open cockpit window and struck the pilot in the neck. Some helicopters have a single 'Jesus pin' holding the rotor to the mast; a round striking that pin could cause the helicopter to crash. For sure I knew pure blind luck had a lot to do with whether people survived combat, but until that day I had never experienced a Golden BB incident.

Lt. Reed's Dragon flew lead, with the two others following close behind as escorts. Everyone aboard the three Kristang dropships were feeling good about their latest successful mission, and tense because masers and lots of kinetic hardware was flying around and overhead. Skippy had assured them their enhanced stealth would protect them from being detected, as long as they remained in the narrow safe flight corridor he had established by partially hacking into air defense networks.

Flight Lieutenant Windsor's dropship, the one with the dead Kristang called 'Curly' aboard, had already exited the battle area and was flying low and fast, approaching one end of the safe air corridor, when the Dragon ran into trouble. Technically, it ran into a missile that had been fired at another target high above. The missile came out of nowhere, having gone supersonic in its first fifty meters of flight. It focused entirely on its target, an unidentified aircraft that had violated clan airspace at high altitude. Despite its focus, the missile could not ignore the unexpected sudden high air pressure in front of it, air pressure created by the engine fan blades of Windsor's stealthed Dragon. The missile's brain reacted almost too slowly, as it was already above the Dragon before it made a decision. Reasoning that another missile could be launched at the high-altitude target, the missile figured its duty was to destroy the low-altitude unknown intruder it had stumbled across.

Windsor never saw any danger; the missile flashed by at Mach Two just behind the Dragon's starboard wing. A light on the cockpit consoles flashed just as the missile above exploded in wide-dispersal fragmentation mode. Shrapnel flew in all directions, only three pieces went backwards to strike the Dragon. Two ripped through the strongest spar at the end of the portside wing; they hit in exactly the sequence required to set up a vibration in the portside engine fan blades, and the portside engine tore itself apart, sending blade pieces scything through the air. That was enough. From one moment to the next, the Dragon went from stealthily exiting a combat area, to tumbling out of control. As the dropship had been flying close to the ground before the missile hit, the pilots had little time to react. What control they had was the dropship reacting by itself; knowing it was doomed to crash, its navigation brain selected a place most likely to ensure some of the crew survived, and guided the ship there as best it could.

The Dragon's nose pancaked into the dirt, digging in and causing the craft to flip onto its back and skid wildly. Both wings and other pieces broke off, sending high-strength composites flying in all directions. After plowing a furrow eighty meters long, the Dragon came to a rest upside down.

"Holy shit, Joe," Skippy exclaimed in shock. "I did *not* see that coming. Sorry! I knew about that antiaircraft missile launcher, but it hadn't detected our ships at all. Damn it! That was *bad* fucking luck! That had to be a million-to-one shot," He lamented.

We could analyze what had gone wrong later. If there was a later. "Is anyone alive in there?" A quick glance at my console told me both pilots were dead, along with three of the crew. Four other suits were showing life signs of varied strength, and two unsuited people had heartbeats according to their zPhones; I had no idea how anyone not in an armored suit could have survived.

"Six survivors. Joe, I expect one of them will not survive more than the next few minutes. I am terribly sorry."

"Save the sorries for later, Skip. Right now we need to pull our people out of there." I contacted the lead ship. "Reed, we have-"

Skippy interrupted me. "Joe, hold!"

"Reed, stand by. What is it, Skippy?"

"Joe, all the antiaircraft batteries in that area are now set on automatic and are sweeping the sky with overlapping active sensor pulses; they could see right through the Dragons' stealth. Sending the other two ships in there for evac would be suicide. I'm doing what I can, but it will be severely limited, their systems are on lockdown to prevent interference. Also," he continued before I could react, "they have ground troops on the way to the crash site. Six Kristang in powered armor have exited the missile control center, and are running along this ravine." He highlighted the area on my display. "They have rifles, antiarmor rockets and rifles. Joe, this is a dangerous situation."

"Got it. Reed, Chen," I called the pilots of both Dragons, "set down at the coordinates I'm sending you and stay there, the area is saturated with AA. Major Smythe?"

"Here, Sir, we heard what Skippy said. I have ten people ready to extract our people."

Ten humans, against six Kristang who were bigger, faster, stronger and tougher than any human. I did not like those odds.

I liked watching the action with my butt in a chair even less than I liked the odds. I watched the battle from my console in a Thuranin dropship, following the action from afar. With the technology available, I could select views from the helmet cameras of every human soldier involved, I could overlay those images on a synthetic 'God's eye' view of the battlefield that Skippy provided by creating a real-time composite of all the data coming in. I had better situational awareness than any human commander in history, and it was not enough. I needed to *be there,* to be with my people.

Smythe was in a bad situation. The six Kristang infantry were alerted to other hostile aircraft in the area, and they sent up drones to get a visual. Smythe's team also launched drones to counter the enemy; the drones tangled in furious air to air combat until they were all quickly destroyed. Each side got only glimpses of the opposition but that was enough; the Kristang now knew they were facing ground troops and I'm sure they could count. We knew any fight would be ten slow, weak humans against six physically superior Kristang who were on their own territory. Smythe had to retrieve our people, including the dead we couldn't leave behind as evidence; while his people were extracting injured and dead from the crash site, they would be vulnerable. All the Kristang needed to do was stay behind cover and shoot; they knew reinforcements were on their way. It would have been better for us if the Kristang made a rush for the crash site, came out of cover where Smythe's team could get a clear shot at them. Unfortunately, the six Kristang defenders thought they were up against ten Kristang, so they played it safe.

Major Smythe held up a hand to pause his people, while he reviewed the drone data in his visor and considered what to do. With him were two British SAS and two Chinese Night Tigers. The team from the other Dragon, trotting up from the east, were three Indian paratroopers and two US Army Rangers; the French paratroopers still were recovering from radiation exposure and had not been cleared for duty. Nationality mattered little by then among the Merry Band of Pirates; Smythe had his people forged into one seamless Special Operations team. They all used the same weapons, and were crosstrained on tactics favored by the other four nationalities, Smythe chose whatever tactics worked best in the situation.

At the moment, he had a difficult choice. The six enemy soldiers were lying prone in a strong defilade position overlooking the crash site, using a dry creek bed for cover. From that position, they could sweep the crash site and approaches from three directions. It was not a good situation, and the worst opponent he faced was time; enemy reinforcements were on their way and Skippy could not stop them. “Skippy, what can you tell me about the oppo?”

“They are a garrison security force, assigned to the missile battery,” Skippy stated hurriedly. “They have only minimal training in infantry tactics. I cannot intercept their communications, as they are using line of sight lasers between helmets, and hand signals I can’t interpret from here. Wish I could tell you more, sorry. I am doing what I can to hack into air defenses in the area to give you air support, you shouldn’t plan for it.”

“Thank you,” Smythe replied automatically, his mind already back working on the problem. One thing was certain; he could not allow the enemy to retain the initiative. Those six soldiers were effectively blocking the humans’ path to the crash site. Smythe considered splitting his team, with six firing at the enemy to keep their heads down, while four humans retrieved the injured from the crash site. He could see now that wouldn’t work. With the team assembled, he sketched out his plan, a tactic he hoped the Kristang would not expect. “Skippy, I have one more favor to ask of you.”

“Whatever you need, Major.”

Smythe’s favor was for Skippy to take remote control of all ten suits, and race them across country up and behind the Kristang. This tactic would get the human team into position on high ground above and behind the Kristang quickly; Smythe also wished to avoid risking the Kristang becoming suspicious, if his team ran at the normal slow speed of humans. Skippy took almost a full second to create a detailed map of the terrain between the team’s position and their intended destinations. Smythe wanted the team to proceed up a shallow swale together, then split, with five people going north and five south. They would take up positions to threaten the Kristang from above and behind, forcing the enemy to pull back from the crash site. If that were successful, Smythe intended for one team to keep the Kristang pinned down, while the other team circled around back to the crash site.

The operation began well, with Smythe feeling his suit accelerate gradually, picking up speed until he was racing across the terrain at a truly frightening speed, so fast he would certainly have tripped and fallen on his own. They were running even faster than he had when escaping from the exploding Thuranin research base on the planet Jumbo, thanks to Skippy. On Jumbo, the suits had engaged an emergency escape mechanism to carry the user away from a threat, using the suit’s sensors to scan the ground in front of the suit and determine the best path forward with only minimal guidance from the user. With Skippy remotely controlling the suits on Kobamik, he had planned almost every footfall from detailed terrain maps the beer can had hacked from a Spike Tail clan database. The suits of Smythe’s team did not need to slowly scan the terrain in front and make decisions every millisecond; they only needed to follow Skippy’s preprogrammed instructions, and could extend every stride to cover maximum ground. The system was not perfect; armored boots slipped on rocks or loose dirt, ground had shifted slightly from the last mapping survey conducted by the Spike Tails. When one suit slowed to recover balance from an errant footfall, Skippy sent a signal for all suits to slow accordingly, keeping the team together.

The speed with which the SpecOps team from Earth ran up the swale toward their objectives was deeply concerning to the leader of the Kristang infantry. Rumors had been flying that the attacks on the Fire Dragon had been possible because of advanced technology not available to most Kristang. The aircraft that had been shot down had not appeared on sensors at all, and now the infantry was faced with ten intruders who were running at speeds his soldiers could not match. Whatever force the infantry leader was up against, he had to assume they had access to technology far beyond that possessed by the Spike Tail clan. He saw with alarm what the intruders had planned, and he reacted.

Major Smythe was reminded of two maxims from his early days in training. First, no plan survives contact with the enemy. Second, the enemy also makes plans. His team was nearing the upper end of the swale, where it flattened out and the land became flat for a hundred or so meters. At the end of the swale, his team would split and race across the open ground to proceed up the lower slopes of two hills. The suits would slow to climb the hills, for the ground at the base of the slopes was crumbled shale, making footing treacherous. The teams split, and Smythe felt his boots slipping alarmingly on loose rock. He let his legs go limp, letting the suit's sensors and motors do the work for him, far faster than he ever could. Now that his brain was not constantly being jolted at high-speed, he took a moment to regain situational awareness.

And did not like what he saw. The enemy had left their position covering the crash site, and were now running full speed, directly at Smythe! Both SpecOps teams were in a bad place, on exposed slopes with poor footing, and in an area with no tree cover. They could not climb quickly enough to reach the cover of the hilltop, nor could they retreat to the meager cover of the swale. "Skippy!"

"I see it! Major, I can't get you out of this, the signal lag prevents me from controlling your suits in real time."

"Team!" Smythe ordered his people to turn around and attack, he did not see any choice. If the humans kept climbing the crumbling slopes they would be sitting ducks. Aboard the *Dutchman*, every simulated fight against Kristang had taught Smythe one lesson above all; movement and speed are life. To remain static against superwarriors was death. The enemy was faster, stronger and had quicker reflexes. The only advantage Smythe had was superior numbers, ten against six.

The six Kristang came over the ridge as Smythe's two teams were still stumbling down the final couple meters of loose shale at the bottom of the hills. Explosive rounds struck shale just to the left of Smythe's feet, sending jagged flakes of rock pelting against his armored suit legs and knocking him off balance. In desperation, he leaped up, even knowing that while he was in the predictable ballistic arc of the jump, he was vulnerable to accurate fire from the enemy. He landed on secure ground, surprised to be alive and not thinking about it. His rifle came up, his visor providing a vivid blue crosshairs to show where he was aiming. As he ran to his left and an enemy rocket lanced out toward him, he fired a four-round burst that astonishingly caught a Kristang in the chest, knocking the superwarrior backwards. Smythe threw himself to the right to dodge the rocket, which at the last second he saw was going to miss him anyway. He stumbled and almost went down, the suit compensating in an action that was jarring, making his chin smack the bottom of the helmet. At no instant did Smythe let himself be distracted, he sighted on another Kristang who was racing straight at him, firing directly at Smythe. The SAS man had no time to wonder how he could be alive, not even time to squeeze the trigger of his own rifle before the Kristang's head suddenly exploded, ripped apart by explosive-tipped rounds from at least two other rifles.

Smythe had to turn to the left to find another target, and his brain may have had a split-second of astonishment at finding only one Kristang still standing before he swung his rifle around and fired off a burst. His rifle added to the carnage inflicted on the last surviving Kristang, the lizard had already been hit several times before Smythe's rounds reached out to stitch a line up the enemy's torso and nearly decapitate the enemy. "Cease fire!" Smythe shouted, spinning around in disbelief to count ten humans still on their feet. Several people had dents and gouges in their armor, especially around the legs as explosive rounds had hit the ground near their feet. The worst damage was to Ranger Mychalchyk's right thigh, and even that deep gouge wasn't impeding the functioning of the suit. The slope behind Smythe's team was smoking from impacts of rifle rounds and rockets. But not one of his team had been struck directly. And all six of the Kristang were lying dead. Smythe strode over to a Kristang soldier laying on his back, with holes ripped through his armored suit. The rounds fired by humans had alternated armor-piercing and explosive, standard tactics against light armor. Armor-piercing rounds used their kinetic energy to turn the tip into superheated plasma that burned its way through armor, weakening it and creating an opening for the explosive-tipped round to follow. As Smythe could see on the battlefield, the combination was quite effective. The enemy had almost certainly used the same ammunition against the Merry Band of Pirates, yet not one of them had been hit. "How the *hell* did that happen?" Smythe asked, astonished.

"Holy shit," my lips quavered in amazed shock. "How the *hell* did that happen?" I had been following the blindingly fast firefight from my dropship, unable to breathe. As the last Kristang's head jerked back and he slumped to the ground, I shuddered with relief. A team of ten humans had just sliced up six genetically-enhanced Kristang superwarriors, without a single one of our team suffering any worse than shrapnel bouncing off their armor.

"Yup. Looks like the Kristang really sent their 'A' team to this battle," Skippy said with a verbal smirk.

"What? Skippy, those guys couldn't shoot worth shit. Damn, in a firefight between those Kristang and Imperial Stormtroopers, *nobody* would get hit. Did we just go up against the Spike Tails equivalent of Cub Scouts? 'A' team? That was more like their 'Z' team."

"Joey, Joey, Joey," Skippy said sadly, I mentally pictured him shaking his head. "Apparently, you never watched the 'A Team'. The guys on that show could empty an entire magazine and never hit the side of a barn, from *inside* a barn. Your knowledge of crappy 80's TV shows is woefully inadequate."

"Oh, ha ha," I laughed, my voice bordering on the hysterical, I was still coming down off the adrenaline rush. "'A' team, I get it. Your Magnificence, I'll make a deal with you; you get us out of this mess, and I will let Professor Skippy give me a graduate course in crappy 80s TV shows."

"Deal!" Skippy shouted before I could change my mind. "We'll start with 'Manimal', that's widely considered the gold standard of '80s crappiness. Then we'll work our way up to 'Alf'. Although, hmmm, 'Alf' is about a super-smart alien stuck living with a group of ignorant humans, that scenario is just not believable. Hey, if you piss me off, I'll make you sit through every episode of 'The Love Boat'. The director's cut. With commentary."

"Oh, crap. Am I going to regret this?"

"Joe, after you finish watching the first season of 'Knight Rider', you will be praying for death."

"Shit. Fine." I asked as I watched Major Smythe's team running toward the downed dropship with long, powered strides. Bravo team was already at the crash site, and had the survivors huddled in a sort of ditch. It all looked good, I anticipated the other two dropships evacuating the whole group within minutes. No additional threats were showing on the display. My hands were still shaking slightly. "Tell me, Your Magnificence, did the poor shooting of those Kristang have anything to do with you?"

"Me? Sweet, innocent little me? Well, heh heh, I might have screwed with the targeting systems of their rifles, and the guidance systems of their rockets. That was not easy, even for me. If they hadn't all been clustered together in a small area, I couldn't have done it. Also, their leader didn't completely trust his soldiers, because he had much more actual combat experience. So he had their targeting systems slaved to his suit computer. I only needed to infiltrate one system to get in. It was a lucky break. As you monkeys understand 'luck', that is."

"Hey, I'll take all the luck we can get. Except bad luck, we've had plenty of that. Major Smythe, you are clear to proceed to the crash site. Be advised Skippy can give us a three minute gap in air defenses." Our shiny beer can had found a way to reset the local air defense network and throw it into diagnostic mode; he estimated we had three minutes remaining before sensors became active again and the sky would be too dangerous for flying. "Our birds are on the way. Retrieve our people and leave Curly away from the crash site."

"Pull Curly from the fuselage and leave him, understood. Sir, we are all in shock here. What happened?" Smythe's voice reflected uncertainty, and that never happened.

"Major, I would like to tell you the skill and training of your team was responsible," I replied with a laugh, "but you can thank a certain beer can for the enemy's poor shooting."

With a short gap in opposition, Reed and Chen zoomed their Dragons to smack down hard next to the crash site, their landing gear flexing and groaning. Smythe's team worked quickly and efficiently, to get our injured people and the dead into the two flyable dropships. Getting the bodies of our two pilots out took almost too much time, as part of the cockpit had to be cut away for access, but with less than a minute to go before the air defense network became active again, no humans or human bodies remained in the wreckage. Curly was laying on his back thirty meters in front of the crashed Dragon's nose, as if he had been flung there by the violence of the impact. Without waiting for an order from me, the two Dragons went to full power and raced for the safe-fly corridor. When the crash site was one kilometer behind, both dropships rippled off four missiles, which raced back to obliterate our downed spacecraft. Through the dust, I could see Curly's body in two pieces, flung even farther away. That was good, hopefully the Spike Tails would not take time to examine the wreckage in the middle of a war.

"Hey, uh, Joe," Skippy's voice was shaky.

My zPhone pinged with another text. *We need another private chat*. There I was, in a dropship, crowded in with people. How was I going to- *Put in your earpiece and talk softly*, the message continued. Talk softly? Ok. I wiggled the earpiece in and whispered, more moving my lips than actually creating sound. "What is wrong?"

"The worm is becoming a bit more of a problem."

"A bit?" Talking so quietly made me feel like a ventriloquist, although the dummy was me. "We are in the middle of a rescue mission, Skippy. This is very bad timing." Someone called from behind me, I waved a hand for quiet.

"I know and I'm sorry about that, Joe. I'm telling you because you need to know. Well, you keep telling me you need to know, although there's nothing you can do about it, so this conversation is really a whole lot of blah, blah, blah."

I cringed. Even in a desperate situation he couldn't help being an asshole. "BLUF it for me, Skippy," I asked for Bottom Line Up Front. If Skippy was going on vacation again, we were running out of time fast. On the console in front of me, I could see the last dropship was just now approaching the egress corridor. We needed to confirm all Kristang clans had been drawn into the civil war, then we were going to pop smoke and get the hell off the planet. I couldn't give the evac order until we were certain the mission was complete. Not until we knew the Fire Dragons were cancelling the deal to send a Ruhar ship to Earth.

Until we knew our home planet was safe again.

"I wish I could, Joe. I am in some amount of trouble, I can't quantify it at present. The worm was in a dead-end and I was studying it, that's where my focus was. While I was doing my party trick with the Kristang targeting systems, I wasn't paying much attention to my subsidiary internal systems. That is when the worm struck; it was waiting for me to take my attention away from my internal functioning. What I had trapped was only a copy of the worm, a ghost. I was stupid and arrogant and now I'm paying the price. You may pay the price with me, I'm sorry about that. The real worm was hiding and studying *me*, to learn how I operate, to learn my weaknesses. I am vulnerable now."

"How much time do we have?"

"Oh, forever, Joe; I am confident I can handle this puny worm. This is a, heh heh, FYI."

It didn't sound like an FYI. It sounded like the little beer can was frightened out of his mind. "That is good to hear," I lied, "will we have any warning if you, uh, go on holiday again?"

"Not going to happen, Joe. Me going on holiday, I mean, not the warning. Sure, in the unlikely event that I have to take a quick break to drive a stake through the heart of this damned worm, I'll let you know in advance. Until then, heh heh, it's all good."

My mind was racing with ideas of how we could cut the op short, to get the Merry Band of Pirates off the planet as soon as possible. "Can you estimate when we'll know whether the war has pulled in all the other clans?"

"Not exactly, that is kind of a vague question, Joe." In that, he sounded like the old arrogant Skippy. "What I can tell you is our drawing the Spike Tails into the fight should soon persuade clans on the sidelines that they need to strike now, while they still can. Chatter I'm picking up now, indicates every offensive unit on this planet are preparing messages to their clan headquarters, and most of them are of the ask-forgiveness type rather than request-permission. Clans are attempting to validate alliances and many of them do not like the answers they are receiving; alliances agreed to in peacetime are not worth anything now that war is imminent. Everyone is scrambling to ally with the clans they think will be winners, in the war they now expect is inevitable. Having said that, wide-spread fighting has still not yet erupted. Most clans are waiting to see someone else make the first move; they are all afraid whoever strikes first will become a target."

If Skippy was failing, losing his battle against the worm, I couldn't wait for multiple clans to make up their freakin' minds. We needed to give them a push, and I didn't want another op that put the Merry Band of Pirates in jeopardy. "You are monitoring communications between the clans?"

"Yup. That's easy-peasy for me. Their encryption and communications security is pathetic."

"Great, that's good to hear, Your Royal Awesomeness," I said, hoping to cheer him up. "Can you sneak some messages in that traffic?"

"Like what? Birthday greetings?"

"No," I rolled my eyes. "I was thinking of you feeding each clan sensor data that indicates they are about to be attacked. And messages from clan leadership to their offensive units, ordering them to strike against, uh, whatever target is most likely to be believable and cause maximum chaos."

"Oooh, yeah, I could do that. Joe, that is freakin' devious. I *like* it! Something like that wouldn't work in peacetime, because the Kristang require all field units to verify strike orders with headquarters, but right now every clan on the planet is primed and ready for it."

"Outstanding," I said aloud, forgetting to whisper. "When can you get started?"

"Doing it now, Joe. Messages are on their way. This is a great idea. Damn, I freakin' *love* screwing with lizards!" He said that so loud it made me wince and pull the earpiece away from my ear. In the console display, I saw the last dropship had successfully made the turn and was now transiting the egress corridor. Navigating that corridor was tricky and I had full confidence in the ability of our pilots to fly it, even without Skippy, if necessary. "Ok, Joe, it is ON, baby! Holy crap, a commander of the Red Dagger clan must have an itchy trigger finger, because as soon as he saw my message ordering him to attack, he didn't wait for a confirmation. He ordered a Strategic Defense orbital strike on two rival clans, and *DAMN*! That did it, there are missiles flying all over up there! No one wanted to be the first to shoot, but now no one wants to be the last. Hmmm, this could create a bit of a complication, there will shortly be a whole lot of high-speed debris in orbit, everyone is opening up overhead with their stealthed satellites to knock out enemy defenses. I will need to analyze debris patterns to predict a safe egress route, and that might require me to shift the microwormhole so we don't run into a debris cloud on our way up. This will be a challenging-"

"A challenge? I'm sure you are up to it, Skippy," I said to boost his confidence, then I realized he had said 'challeng*ing*' not 'challenge'. He hadn't finished his thought, and my blood ran cold. "Skippy?" I whispered.

No response. On my zPhone, I tapped out a message '*Skippy, are you there*'. Again, no response. Trying to act casual and unconcerned, I reach up to touch his beer can, nestled into the top of my console. He was warm, not alarmingly so.

"Colonel Bishop?" The pilot called me. "We just lost contact with the ship. I think, yes. Colonel, the microwormhole just shut down. We've lost it."

Right then, I knew we were totally screwed. Even if Skippy came back from his holiday right then, the microwormhole we relied on was gone. We needed that tiny wormhole not only to give us instant communications with the ship, but also to provide the yoyo string that would bring our dropships back into orbit. Skippy might be able to create another connected pair of microwormhole end points, but neither end would be anywhere useful. While we might find some way to send one end up above the planet, there was no way for us to get the other end all the way out to the *Flying Dutchman*. I took a deep breath. One thing I had learned in the military is that unlike wine, bad news does not improve with age. Best to get it over with. "We just lost Skippy also," I announced. Which meant we lost our secure communications channel to the other dropships. I hoped that with war now raging across the planet, a few stray signals would be lost or ignored. "Send a burst transmission to the other dropships, have them proceed to the rendezvous point as planned. And advise them that we no longer have Skippy with us. I will contact Mr. Chotek myself." Our situation was so dire that I was not concerned about Chotek dressing me down again; getting yelled at was the least of my problems.

"Colonel Chang, we just lost the microwormhole. It shut down without warning, Sir." Major Simms reported from the CIC.

Before Chang could respond, Nagatha spoke. "Just before the wormhole collapsed, I received a message from Skippy. He is being attacked by the worm again."

Chang focused on a particular word. "*The* worm? This is something you knew about?"

Nagatha didn't respond immediately. "Oh, dear. This is rather embarrassing. Now I see how Skippy gets himself into trouble. Perhaps some of his absent-mindedness has affecting me. Yes, Colonel Chang, this is not the first time Skippy has been attacked by a computer worm." She told Chang the truth about the first time the beer can had gone 'on holiday'.

Chang decided to put his unproductive anger aside for the moment. "Skippy has defeated this worm before; is there any reason to think he won't come back soon?"

"I have no data on that subject, Colonel," Nagatha's voice was apologetic. "Skippy thought he had destroyed the worm; any speculation on my part would not be useful."

Chang pointed to the displays in front of him. "The ship still has power, and you are still active. This is already different from the last incident."

"Correct, Colonel Chang. The revised protocols Skippy loaded into the ship's computers allow most systems to continue functioning in his absence. That functioning relies on a steady-state condition; systems will be unable to adjust to damage. And systems which require periodic adjustments or maintenance will begin to fail and go offline. One of those systems that cannot function indefinitely without Skippy is myself; the matrix of this ship's main computer is inadequate to contain my entire consciousness, so I have been relying on the link with Skippy for additional memory and processing power. I am in the process of reducing my functionality to match the circumstances."

"Major Simms," Chang ordered, "get Dr. Friedlander up here, I need an update on his team's progress. We may need to operate this ship by ourselves."

CHAPTER TWENTY NINE

Hans Chotek took the bad news about Skippy with quiet consideration. He didn't get angry, he didn't yell at me, he simply nodded slowly and asked what our options were.

Without Skippy, we had no microwormhole, no yoyo string connected to the *Dutchman* to lift us into orbit without using dropship engines. "We do have a Plan B to get back to the ship, Sir," I assured him.

"Sometimes I wonder why the Merry Band of Pirates ever bothers to create a Plan A," he replied with unexpected humor.

"Because that gives us a basis for a Plan B?"

Now he wasn't smiling. "Explain it to me, Colonel."

Although Skippy was still unresponsive, our Plan B only worked mostly because of him. Our Thuranin dropships already had stealth capabilities far in advance of Kristang technology, and Skippy had tweaked the stealth field generators to make them even more effective. He had also worked on the engines so they ran more efficiently, quieter and produced less turbulence and heat. That was all good, by itself the stealth enhancement still didn't give us much of a chance to get safely away from Kobamik. Our ace in the hole was the lingering result of Skippy's screwing with Kristang sensor networks on and around the planet. With Skippy dormant, he was not able to actively instruct the sensors to ignore our ships, but most of the networks had been infected with code that caused the networks to ignore sensor inputs related to us. The greatest difficulty Skippy had hacking the sensors was to coordinate all the lies he was telling, because many of the networks shared data. Now that Kobamik was engulfed in a hot war, most of the sensor networks had been significantly degraded by enemy action, and no clan was sharing their data with anyone else. That made our escape somewhat less difficult; we chose an area controlled by a clan that had gotten pounded by enemies and where sensor coverage was weak or nonexistent. Starting our escape there made it easier for us to get off the surface; the tough part would happen when we reached the top of the atmosphere and climbed into low orbit, where stealthed satellites controlled by multiple clans were scanning the area.

Our means of getting off the surface of Kobamik involved the least-advanced type of flight technology: a balloon. When our two Thuranin dropships reached the site we had selected to begin our ascent, we unpacked the balloons from the cargo section of the dropships, and attached a balloon to each ship with ultrathin cables. The balloons had their own stealth field generators, powered by a cable from the dropships. My dropship was the first to inflate a balloon and lift off, when we judged the winds were favorable. The balloon was huge, towering over the dropship, its thin skin was almost transparently invisible even without the stealth field engaged. With the balloon tugging us steadily upward, we drifted higher and higher. As we passed through ten thousand meters, we received a brief ping from the second dropship; all was well and they were ascending behind us without incident. As we rose and the atmosphere around us thinned, the balloon expanded further, becoming truly enormous, stretching the limits of the stealth field.

Approaching forty thousand meters high, we encountered the first problem with our ascent. The battle above the planet had been brief and intense, resulting in a whole lot of debris in orbit. Avoiding high-speed particles in orbit was going to be enough of a problem, we could not maneuver rapidly or we would be detected, so we would need to trust our defense shields to deflect dangerous space junk away from the dropship. What I did not anticipate was that some of that space junk was already raining down into the atmosphere. "Colonel Bishop?" Lt. Reed called from the cockpit. The suspense of our nerve-wracking ascent was killing me, to I burned off some nervous energy going up to the cockpit and strapping into a jump seat. "Sir," Reed said from the copilot seat, "we have multiple pieces of debris coming down, some of them will impact the balloon."

That caught my attention. "How big are these pieces?" The skin of the balloon was self-sealing and could withstand multiple small punctures; the reserve gas canister could replace any gas the balloon lost before a hole sealed itself. The balloon could recover from small punctures, but a hole larger than my fist was going to be a serious problem.

"We're on passive sensors only, and the balloon is blocking part of our view." The dropship had a spike projecting forward beyond the forward limit of the stealth field enveloping us, and the ship also trailed a thin wire out the back that had a tiny sensor on it. "If Skippy were here, he could predict-" she shrugged.

"All right, we'll need to ride it out. How much reserve gas do we have?"

"Ninety percent, we're good there. Colonel, we need another eight thousand meters of altitude before we can release."

"I know." We waited. At that altitude we couldn't maneuver the balloon to steer out of the way, the falling space junk was going to hit us or it wouldn't, we had no control. Lower in the atmosphere, the balloon could change its shape to steer itself in the winds; at forty thousand meters the air was so thin that the balloon had to expand to its maximum volume just to keep us rising. Within minutes, lights flashed on the pilot consoles as our defense shield were peppered with impacts; hot pieces of metal or composites bouncing off the dropship's energy shield. The impacts did not at all test the strength of our shield's energy. The kinetic energy being turned into heat risk did pose a minor risk of exposing us, any sensors paying very close attention might wonder why the space junk had changed direction so high in the sky. With so much junk raining down, I was crossing my fingers and hoping any sensor networks still operational had more important things to do in the war that was still raging.

"We're losing altitude," Reed announced with more calm than I would have. She turned to look at me. "It's gradual, less than fifteen meters per second."

"Yeah, but we need to climb, not fall." Even staying at the same height was no good, we needed more altitude for a safe release from the balloon. "Is the balloon reporting any trouble coping with the punctures?" The balloon's brain was tiny, I didn't expect a detailed report.

"No," Reed shook her head. "Warning lights are yellow, not red. Gas reserve is down to sixty percent. Rate of descent is slowing, now at five meters per second." The descent slowed, then halted. A cheer rang out in the ship when Reed announced we were moving *up* again at three meters per second. The reserve gas canister still held 28%, that was declining slowly because the balloon must have a leak it wasn't able to completely plug. I was encouraged to see our rate of ascent was increasing faster than gas was draining out of the reserve canister.

When we reached forty three thousand meters altitude, I made a command decision and accelerated our schedule. It was a pure judgment call; I sent a signal to our two unmanned Kristang dropships on the ground. They pinged back acknowledgment and flew off to perform their preprogrammed tasks of creating a diversion. As expected, the wind had pushed us far away from where we had begun our ascent, the territory below us at that point was controlled by a different clan. The clan now below us was weak, having been hit hard by three other clans in the first minutes of the war. Even weakened, the clan could pose a serious threat to us, and their ground-based sensors were still active. Our balloons could only expand so far to lift us higher, the practical limit of a balloon carrying the mass of a Thuranin dropship was around forty eight thousand meters. After that, we had to use the dropship's engines to climb into orbit, and we did not want anyone noticing that transition from balloon to powered flight.

Our two Kristang dropships, no longer useful to us, were on their last mission. Since we had recovered them from the ignoble fate of fading away aboard derelict transports, I thought those dropships might appreciate going out in a blaze of glory. Both dropships kept their enhanced stealth engaged and flew low and slow as they approached their target; the main sensor network node of the clan below us. When they popped over a hill and were being swept by powerful active sensor pulses, one of the dropships pulled ahead and switched to the unenhanced Kristang stealth unit, making it intermittently visible to enemy sensors. That dropship attracted a defensive curtain of maser beams, missile and self-guided cannon rounds. The dropship flew a random evasive course, surviving longer than it should have before being ripped to shreds.

From the other direction, the other dropship kept its full enhanced stealth capabilities engaged, approaching the target without being detected. The enemy sensor network was distracted by the dropship that had just been destroyed, and perhaps the Kristang in command of the defenses were congratulating themselves and not paying proper attention. The second dropship was close enough to use its line-of-sight maser cannons before it rippled off its entire load of eight Zinger missiles. After the missiles were away, the dropship climbed and began firing its masers continuously. That attracted the attention of the Kristang, who concentrated on destroying the dropship and realized only too late that eight missiles were inbound. The missiles made no attempt at stealth, relying on speed and hugging the terrain. Five of them were caught and exploded by the maser autocannons, one took a hit and went off course. The remaining two missiles impacted the complex, and detonated their special warheads that threw out electromagnetic rather than kinetic energy. Hot, noisy particles spewed into the air, temporarily blinding the ground-based sensors. The Kristang there knew the purpose of the attack had been to knock back their sensor coverage, but they did not turn their gaze high above them to where we floated. They had more immediate concerns; protecting themselves from the possibility of more aircraft racing in under the temporary sensor blackout. Preparing for an attack on their central complex by aircraft and ground troops was the entire focus of the Kristang below us, so they did not notice when our dropships powered up their engines and cut loose from the balloons.

"So far so good, Colonel," Lt Reed reported from the copilot seat. There was a slight stomach flipping moment of zero gravity as the ship released and fell less than a hundred meters before flying gently upward under its own power. The discarded balloon was already disintegrating, even the balloon's stealth field generator was being eaten by nanoparticles. By the time the remains of the balloon reached thirty thousand meters, all that would remain was inconspicuous dust.

I didn't reply, not wanting to distract the pilots. We climbed as gently as the math of orbital mechanics allowed, with the second dropship following us a hundred kilometers behind. This was the most dangerous part of our Plan B escape, when both dropships were using the most energy of the entire flight profile.

"Picking up some ionization," Reed warned. Our increasingly swift passage through the upper atmosphere was leaving a trail of ionized gas in our wake, even in the ultrathin air at the edge of low orbit. Our Thuranin dropships had equipment for pumping out gas to reduce our ionized trail, even their advanced technology could not completely mask our flight. "I hope you're right about this, Sir."

"Me too, Reed." What she was referring to was my riverboat gambler's move, of expecting and hoping no one on or around the planet would bother shooting at one or two small ships moving away from the planet. Most of the Strategic Defense satellites had obliterated each other in the first minute of the war, we could see the hot clouds of debris above us and raining down all around us. I was betting all our lives that no clan would risk unmasking a precious surviving stealthed satellite just to shoot at two small targets that did not pose a threat to anyone. Our flightpath had been chosen to avoid coming near or above any critical assets a clan would fight to protect. "We are tiny little innocent dropships, just wanting to get off a war-torn planet, we are no threat to anyone. No reason for anyone to shoot at us or even look at use closely." So far, my gamble was paying off. The problem was, I was counting on a whole planet full of pissed off, trigger-happy lizards to act calmly and rationally. It would only take one overeager jackass to ruin our day.

We made it, into orbit and beyond. After three full days circling the planet to slowly build up escape velocity, we all were exhausted as no one had been able to sleep, other than those injured people who were sedated. Around us, Strategic Defense satellites occasionally dropped their stealth to pound a target on the surface, provoking a retaliatory maser strike that almost inevitably destroyed the satellite. We could see sporadic air and ground battles scattered across the surface, with the occasional ship jumping in, launching weapons at the planet and jumping away. The good news was that, in all the excitement, if we had been detected, no one gave a shit about our two relatively tiny ships that were clearly no threat to anyone. Clans on the surface, who still retained some offensive military capability, were not going to expend precious ammo shooting at us. Even firing a maser at us would give away the position of that maser cannon, and some clan would surely take the opportunity to further degrade a rival clan's defenses. When Skippy and I had developed our Plan B escape route, the little beer can had told me the success of the plan depended mostly on the chaos of war making our two dropships unworthy targets. At that time, Skippy told me he couldn't predict whether some Kristang clan with nothing to lose wouldn't take a shot at us, so he could not recommend Plan B. I agreed with him, the difference is I was willing to take the risk. Because there was no Plan C.

Accelerating as gently as we possibly could, we managed to dodge space junk until we were far enough away to point the ships on a course to the planned rendezvous with the *Flying Dutchman*. I didn't close my eyes for more than brief snatches of sleep until the planet behind us had shrunk to the size of a golf ball.

All we needed to do then was survive cooped up in two dropships, each of which had a single bathroom designed for little green men about four feet tall. I was not looking forward to the long journey; seven weeks until we reached the alternate rendezvous point where the *Dutchman* was supposed to be waiting. One of our doomed Kristang dropships, before their suicide mission, had sent a burst transmission out to the point in space where our pirate ship should be when the speed-of-light signal got there. Following protocol, the *Dutchman* did not reply, so we did not know if our ship received the signal. Yet another thing for me to worry about.

I was also extremely worried about Skippy. He was completely unresponsive. Worse, after growing uncomfortably warm, his beer can had cooled and was now distinctly chilly. I kept him tucked away, wrapped in a jacket in a locker, and I didn't tell anyone that his can had gone cold; people had enough to worry about.

It sucked that, after an operation that had accomplished the impossible, we didn't feel like celebrating. We had started a war on Kobamik, but without Skippy we did not know if the war had spread throughout Kristang space, and whether the Fire Dragons had cancelled their deal to send a ship to Earth. Our operation might have accomplished nothing more than getting a lot of sentient beings on Kobamik killed for nothing. Worse, it may have been the strain of hacking the entire planet to protect us that distracted Skippy enough he became vulnerable to the worm. I may have just gotten Skippy and my entire species killed, and I had no way of knowing one way or the other.

Three weeks out from Kobamik, with another four weeks until we reached the *Flying Dutchman*, our existence of stifling boredom was shattered. "Contact!" Lt. Reed shouted from the cockpit.

I was instantly awake, having been drifting in and out of slumber for an hour. With oxygen and other consumables at a premium in the cramped cabin of the dropship, we slept a lot, or stayed out of each other's way as much as possible. "What is it?"

"We just got swept by the edge of a sensor field," Reed explained. "There is at least one stealthed ship out there. Colonel, we didn't see it at all." She pointed at her console, frustrated. "We had no idea a ship was anywhere near us."

"It's not your fault, Lieutenant," I assured her. "Even a Thuranin dropship doesn't have the sensor capability of a starship. That ship may be optimized for stealth to patrol this area. I am pretty damned sure no one sent a starship all the way out here to look for us."

"I hope you're right, what do you want us to do?"

"Nothing for now. We caught the edge of their sensor field?"

"It was faint," she replied. "Should we change course, or maybe they didn't notice us?"

"In peacetime, maybe they wouldn't notice. With the Kristang at each other's throats in this system, I can't imagine the captain of a lizard ship letting a contact go by without checking on it. They got a contact on sensor field, but we're not showing up on their passive sensors, so they've got to know they stumbled across a stealthed ship. Maintain our present course. If we try to evade them, they will certainly get curious. Our best move right now is to be innocent as possible. We need to make that ship's captain think whoever we are, we're not worth him breaking stealth to hit us."

"Another gamble?"

"It worked the first time," I said without confidence.

We waited. Ten minutes went by and I was breathing easier, when we got swept by a sensor field again, this time the signal was stronger. That ship must have altered course to ping us again. If they pinged us a third time, we were screwed. With the second sweep, even typically crappy Kristang sensors could not miss determining that we were only a dropship. A large dropship, but certainly not any kind of a starship, not even an in-system interplanetary transport ship.

It was time for another gamble, this was would be low-risk. If they did not ping us a third time, it wouldn't matter what we did. If they did try to sweep across us a third time, I wanted to make it more difficult for them to find us. "Reed, alter course away from that ship." Of course, we didn't know exactly where the ship was, but we knew where it was not; on our port side, as both sensor sweeps had come from starboard. "Signal the other dropship to alter course, and meet us at the rendezvous point."

If that ship really wanted to find us, I wanted to make it difficult. I wanted that ship's captain to decide that finding us was worth compromising his stealth capability, and worth leaving his assigned patrol area. My hope was that ship's captain would judge a dropship not worth the trouble.

You know what sucked about combat? Yeah, getting shot at, duh. Second worst was waiting, not only waiting to go into action, but waiting to know. Not knowing whether the unseen warship near us would be coming back was agonizing. Reed pointed the dropship's nose to port, flipped around and decelerated very gently. Then she swung farther to port, flipped the ship back nose first, and accelerated. We could return to our previous course later.

Minutes went by, then an hour. We picked up a very faint backscatter from a sensor field, not strong enough for us to be detected. Then several hours went by without us seeing anything alarming on our passive sensors. I was still tense, waiting for a third sensor ping, followed by a bolt from a maser cannon, or a missile hunting us. I felt completely powerless. I hated that. Several times, I went into my locker and touched Skippy, in case his beer can was warm again. He was ice cold.

We didn't relax until some ship in our general vicinity started shooting, and two other ships shot back. Then another pair of ships opened up on the first pair. My guess was the patrol ship had found what it really had been searching for: an enemy starship. One of the first pair of ships was hit and disabled, the second one jumped away. We followed the action anxiously, taking advantage of the battle to gently accelerate away and come back toward our original course. By the time two ships exploded and the fighting stopped, they were well behind us. We all breathed a sigh of relief. The farther we got from Kobamik, the less likely we were to stumble across random patrol ships.

I still wasn't able to sleep well.

CHAPTER THIRTY

As we made our final approach to the alternate rendezvous point, the *Flying Dutchman* wasn't visible at all on our passive sensors, and we did not dare use any active detection technology like a sensor field or active sensor pings. With its more advanced sensors, the ship might be able to detect our dropship; if they did, they remained silent. It pleased me that, no matter how anxious the crew aboard the ship might be, they did not break communications discipline to contact us. It did not please me that we didn't truly know whether our pirate ship was silent due to admirable discipline, or because it was somewhere else, or because it lacked the power to transmit even a brief message. Not knowing sucked. We were flying almost blind. As we approached the rendezvous point, I ordered the pilots to slow us to rendezvous speed well away from the imaginary point in space where the *Dutchman* was supposed to be, to avoid stumbling into our ship at high speed. Finally, my nerves couldn't take it any longer. "Hold us here," I ordered. After we came to a dead stop, I instructed the pilots to send a single, low-power maser ping to where the ship was supposed to be.

And the ship responded, also with a single ping so faint that if we had not been expecting it, we might have missed it entirely. Based on that brief signal, we had the ship's location defined well enough to proceed forward. Within minutes, we passed through the *Dutchman*'s stealth field, and then our dropship was illuminated by a spotlight coming from the open docking bay. "Welcome back, Colonel Bishop."

"Colonel Chang!" I almost had a tear in my eye from happiness at hearing his voice. "I see you've been able to keep the lights on." The fact that the ship was at the alternate rendezvous point meant Chang had been able to maneuver the ship, and lights meant it still had power.

"So far, Sir. I don't know how long we can do that, the science team will brief you when you're aboard."

"Will we be able to shower first? It's gotten a bit ripe in here." Unconsciously, I paused, expecting Skippy to make an insulting comment about how badly we all needed a shower. While I hated the embarrassment, I missed that irascible little beer can. My purpose in talking about showers was not only because I wanted to scrub the accumulated grime off my skin. What I really wanted to know was whether conditions aboard the *Dutchman* allowed anyone the luxury of a shower. If the answer was no, that told me a lot about how badly the ship was coping with Skippy's extended absence.

"Sir," Chang chuckled, and I'm sure he knew exactly why I inquired about the shower situation. "You can take a Hollywood shower if you like. Then we need to update you. Can I assume Mr. Skippy is still on holiday?" There was no laughter in his question.

"Skippy has been nonresponsive. He also hasn't lost containment and exploded, which gives me hope he will recover and come back to us, like last time." Last time, the beer can was only dormant for seventeen hours. This was very different, and much more serious.

We got two items of good, even great, news as soon as we stepped out of our rather funky-smelling dropship. The first piece of good news was Nagatha greeting me, and chatting on my zPhone as I headed toward my cabin. Chang told me there wasn't anything that needed my immediate attention, and the second dropship was thirty minutes behind us, so I had time to scrub off the grime and finally put on a new uniform. "Nagatha! It is great to hear your voice."

"Why, thank you, Colonel Bishop," from the tone of her voice, I pictured her blushing somewhere. "It is very pleasing to speak with you again. Before you ask, I must tell you that I am unable to contact Skippy, I began attempting to contact him, as soon as your ship came aboard. There is no response."

Shit. In the back of my mind, I had been hoping she would be able to wake him up. With that possibility dead, my hopes of Skippy ever reviving faded away to almost zero. "Nagatha," I lowered my voice. People were giving me space as I walked, but they could hear me going by. "I think I killed Skippy. He was hurting, and I asked too much of him. If he hadn't been so distracted by concealing us from the Kristang-"

"Nonsense, Colonel Bishop," she said in a soothingly, in a tone that somehow also had a slight touch of scolding to it. "Skippy's resources were not at all taxed by what he was doing on that planet."

"But-"

"No buts, young man," now her tone was definitely schoolmarm-ish. "I know Skippy was not overextending himself, because he was constantly talking with me over the wormhole link, telling me how bored he was. He also told me how incredibly proud he was of the amazing success your team had down there, considering that you are ignorant, flea-bitten monkeys. Those were his words, not mine."

"Proud of us?" I asked, as I stepped into my small cabin and closed the door behind me.

"Oh, yes. He is very proud to be part of the Merry Band of Pirates. You have been running rings around the supposedly advanced species of this galaxy, and they don't even know you exist. Skippy also told me he would deny ever saying such a ridiculous thing as him being proud to associate with your lowly species."

"Of course he did. Nagatha, thank you. I have spent the past seven weeks miserably thinking that I killed Skippy. Now, you know my second question, right?"

"I believe I do, yes. While my limited functioning does not allow me to keep the ship running or program the jump drive, I certainly have been able to monitor Kristang communications. The war you sparked on Kobamik has spread to almost every area of space controlled by the Kristang. At first, the Thuranin were annoyed and attempted to step in and negotiate a ceasefire, even refusing to transport Kristang warships. After eleven days, the Thuranin gave in to the inevitable, and now they simply want their clients' civil war over as quickly as possible. From the Thuranin communications I intercepted, those little green pinheads, to use Skippy's term for them, do not care at all which clans emerge victorious from the civil war; they are thoroughly disgusted with the Kristang. You may be amused to hear the third party most interested in the war between Kristang clans is the Jeraptha; they have actually temporarily paused their own offensive military operations to, as they say it, 'get in on the action'. The Jeraptha government's Central Wagering Department has been overwhelmed with a flood of requests to join the 'action'; the delay in processing and recording wagers has caused a major scandal that may bring down the current Jeraptha federal government."

"Holy crap. Those beetles are serious about their gambling. They aren't, uh, putting their thumbs on the scales to influence the outcome, are they? Trying to give an edge to the clans they bet on?"

"According to odds published by the Central Wagering Department, there is only a sixteen percent chance that any such cheating by a Jeraptha party could actually influence the final outcome of the conflict."

"The Jeraptha are taking *bets* about cheating?" I asked, astonished.

"Certainly," Nagatha responded, amused. "The Jeraptha wager on everything. They assume people will try to cheat, so why not profit by it?"

"Unbelievable," I shook my head. The Jeraptha were patrons of UNEF-Paradise's allies, the Ruhar, but I did not think we should ever attempt to deal with them. Hell, if the Jeraptha ever learned about the Merry Band of Pirates, I'm sure they would drop everything to get bets in on how long our pirate ship, our entire species, could survive. No way could the Jeraptha miss juicy action like that.

"Your next question undoubtedly is whether the Fire Dragons still have a deal for the Ruhar to send a ship to Earth." She paused, either for dramatic effect, or for me to speak. "They do not. When the war started, the Fire Dragons forgot all about Earth, and the Ruhar, and anything other than killing their enemies. The Ruhar had to send a query to the Fire Dragons, because the Fire Dragons had not responded as previously scheduled. When the Fire Dragons finally replied, it was to insult the Ruhar, and threaten to burn their entire species, after the Fire Dragons conquered all the other clans and came out of the war on top. The Ruhar took that answer as a simple 'No' and cancelled the deal. The issue of sending a ship to Earth is dead."

"Yes!" I pumped my fists in the air. "That is great news, thank you, Nagatha. Hey, uh, what the Fire Dragons said about winning the war?"

"Do not be concerned," she knew our goal was for Kristang society to be fractured at the end of the war. For one clan to conquer the others and emerge from the war stronger than before was the opposite of what we wanted. "Because the war *unfortunately*," her voice had a mischievous tone, "began before the Fire Dragons or Black Trees were fully ready, both of those major clans were caught off-guard, and suffered substantial and unexpected losses in the beginning of the conflict. They are still fighting more defensively than they wished to, as their weakness is seen as an opportunity for lesser clans to settle long-simmering scores with the Big Two. The premature beginning of the war was dreadfully inconvenient for the Fire Dragon and Black Trees. Alliances are forming and being broken almost on a daily basis, as clans maneuver for power. You can understand why the Jeraptha are fixated on the conflict; they have to constantly adjust their wagers to keep up with the latest developments in the war."

"Damn. I am glad I'm a human instead of a Jeraptha; being a beetle sounds like a whole lot of work. Nagatha, I'm getting into the shower now, so-"

"Oh, yes," she giggled. "I will give you some privacy. Don't you be embarrassed, dear, Skippy told me what you do in the shower."

"*What*? That little shithead, I'm going to kill- Look, Nagatha," I'm sure my face was burning red with embarrassment. "All I meant to say was that, when my head is under the shower, I can't talk with you."

"Oh. *Oh*. Oh, dear, I am *terribly* sorry. You enjoy your shower, I will, hmm. This is truly mortifying, I must apologize. I suppose it serves me right for listening to Skippy. Now I understand your human emotion of 'embarrassment'. This is uncomfortable. Please, Colonel Bishop, call me on your zPhone when you are out of the shower."

"Thank you. One last thing; Chang told me I could take a long shower, what we call a 'Hollywood shower'. Is that Ok? I don't want to strain the ship's resources."

"Yes, dear, Colonel Chang was speaking truthfully. As long as we have even one reactor functioning, the water replenishment system takes almost no power away from other requirements."

"Great. Uh, talk with you in like three minutes." Damn, that was a conversation I wanted to end quickly.

Dr. Friedlander was in the science lab, he didn't waste any time when I walked through the door. "Colonel, we managed to complete the shutdown of Reactor Two, and we're in the process of bringing Reactor One down to minimum standby power. Two was already experiencing problems, as you know, and One is due for a maintenance cycle that we are unable to perform by ourselves. By keeping One on standby, we can keep it limping along as a backup for when reactor Three goes down."

"Do you know how long that will be?"

"My guess, and right now it is only a guess, is Three will run by itself for six or seven months, until it is also due for heavy maintenance. We might be able to keep it running and defer maintenance for an unknown length of time, but eventually the safety protocols will cause the reactor to shut down by itself. At that point, I'm hoping we can gradually increase power output from reactor One."

"Until One also shuts down. I get it. Six months is enough time for us to return to Earth; is the output from a single reactor sufficient to power the jump drive?"

"Yes. Colonel, you know power output is not the problem with the jump drive. We can't return to Earth from here."

"Something about the jump drive coils falling out of calibration? Let's assume I know nothing, and break it down for me Barney-style." When the doctor gave me a blank look, I explained the US military slang. "Explain it like you're talking to a three year old."

"Oh," his face turned red, he probably considered my intellect at that level but was too polite to say so. "Jump drive coils all have to work synchronously, to create the quantum-level resonance that alters-" The look on my face must have made him pause. "They have to vibrate together, at the same," he searched for a word not too imprecise, "frequency? They drift apart with each jump. Eventually, the coils are so out of sync with each other, they can't initiate a jump. They need to be retuned."

"Skippy did that tuning, that recalibration, after each jump?"

"Actually, from what we've been able to understand, Skippy has the ability set up the coils so they emerge from a jump in better tune than they were in when the jump initiated. Somehow, he is able to predict the quantum effect of each jump, and set up the coils so they would drift closer together. It's like he can somehow look slightly into the future. That is remarkable; we believe quantum uncertainty prevents anyone from being able to predict such effects, but Skippy is able to do it. Only one jump at a time, even Skippy has limits. The advantage to his technique is that if we had to jump again quickly, the drive coils were ready."

"Ok, so we can't do that. We have to recalibrate, retune, the coils after each jump?"

"I wish. We should do that, we can't do that either. With each jump, our drive coils will drift further apart, until the ship is unable to jump at all."

"We can't do it at all?" I was hoping Friedlander and his team of brainiacs had figured out a way to do the impossible, even if their solution was a messy monkey idea that Skippy would disdain. Hell, maybe us clumsily monkeying with the jump drive would be such an outrage that it would bring Skippy back from the dead, or wherever he was.

"No. We don't understand the theory of what we would need to do. We don't have the math," he added, as if that would help me to understand.

"How many jumps can we perform, before the drive becomes inoperable?"

"There is a complication," Friedlander cautioned. "Skippy left the drive fully tuned up, when you went down to Kobamik. But even without a jump, the coils began drifting apart because of random quantum, well," he held up his hands, "they just do, over time. The answer is four jumps, before the drive is inoperable. The effect is worse for longer jumps, but even a short jump pulls the coils out of tune."

"Four jumps isn't enough to go anywhere useful," I pointed out needlessly. The science team surely already knew that.

"I do have an idea," Friedlander said with a hint of a smile. "This is, Skippy would call it a monkey-brained idea. Skippy has been using the entire coil package, all of our active coils, for each jump. Using a large number of coils means each individual coil has less power running through it; that increase the useful life of the coil assembly. Skippy's purpose was to stretch out the life of our coils, because we can't get new ones."

"Ok, that makes sense, sure. What is your idea?"

"We split the coil assembly into multiple, independent packages, each with a smaller number of coils. With the power we'll be running through each set of coils, they will burn out with one jump. The advantage is we won't have to worry about recalibrating the coils in a package after a jump; each package will be a single-use item."

My eyes grew wide. "We can keep jumping until we run out of coils? Doctor, that is brilliant! Can we get back to Earth that way?"

"Er, no," he cautioned against over enthusiasm. "The quantum effect of a jump is strongest in the coils that are active during the jump, but all coils aboard the ship are affected somewhat. Eventually, even coil packages we haven't used will be so out of tune as to be useless. We can't predict how dormant coil packages will be affected, until we measure the effect during an actual jump."

"Crap. Sorry, Doctor, I shouldn't have asked about going back to Earth; you would have mentioned that first if it was a possibility. How do you know the ship can jump with a small number of drive coils?" My unspoken question was why the Thuranin had equipped the ship with a large number of coils, if they weren't all needed.

"The number of coils needed for a jump depends on many variables," he explained, and he ticked off the variables on his fingers. "First, the length of the jump. Second, how far down in a gravity well a jump is initiated, because the flatter spacetime is around the ship, the easier it is to initiate a jump. Third, the energy capacity of individual coils; newer coils can accept more throughput than coils that are worn out. But the fourth variable," he gave me look meaning there were way more than four variables and he was dumbing it down for me. "The fourth variable is the mass being pulled through a jump wormhole. Star carriers are designed to jump with the mass of many heavy warships attached. Right now, the only item we are carrying is the relay station we're using as a lifeboat, and the ship's empty mass is much less after Skippy rebuilt the ship and made it shorter. We don't need all the coils we have just to jump the relatively light mass we have now."

That made sense to me. "How many coils do we need? For a maximum-length jump, I mean. For our first jump away from this system, I want to go a good long way, so no one can follow us easily."

"That," Friedlander glanced at the deck, avoiding my eyes, "we do not know, not exactly. It would be an educated guess. The first time. After the first jump, we'll have data we can work with."

I did not like the sound of that. "What if you guess wrong the first time?"

"If we use too many coils, we waste coils that can't be used again, and we won't get good data on the strain felt by an individual coil. If we use too few coils, the jump attempt could overload the coils and, uh, I think the best way to say it is it could go 'boom'."

"Boom."

"Big badda boom," he tried getting me to laugh. It didn't work.

"Doctor, I am impressed."

"Colonel, you may want to hold your praise until we perform an actual jump. So far, everything I described is theory, only theory. We have been looking at the power feeds of this ship, and we don't see a way to make those feeds branch to multiple groups of coils. The first time Skippy went missing, I had an idea to pull power from the jump drive capacitors by running the power feed backwards. After Skippy came back, he told me that would have been a terrible idea, and when he explained why, I agreed with him. And now I'm afraid to touch that power assembly."

"You must have an idea to make this work, right?" I figured that, as an engineer, Friedlander was not likely to talk in depth about something that was purely theoretical.

"The best idea we have is to leave the whole assembly in place, and remove most of the coils. After each jump, we remove the used coils, and replace them with another package. That way, we don't have to mess with the power assembly. The coils draw power from the capacitor, so capacitors can't feed power to coils that aren't there. Colonel, having a functional jump drive is only part of the equation. We still have the problem that the jumps we program by ourselves are wildly inaccurate. The farther we jump, the more off target we will be."

"Understood. If we can hit a particular star system, that will be good enough. We can fly the rest of the way to a planet in normal space. I won't risk trying to jump in close to a planet anyway." With our sucky jump navigation, we could very well emerge inside the planet.

"Do you know where we will go?" Friedlander asked with a raised eyebrow.

"Doctor, right now, I have no idea. I am hoping your team can suggest some options for us. Ultimately, that will be Chotek's call." It was true, I had absolutely no idea where we should go, because I had no idea where we *could* go. Any habitable planet within several lightyears was probably inhabited, even by a small group of colonists, or a research station, or a military outpost. We needed to find a planet, probably an entire star system, that was totally uninhabited, yet also a place we could live. Live, until, when? How long? Friedlander couldn't keep the ship running forever, so if we were going to survive, we had to find a planet or moon with a biosphere that could support human life. And, for what purpose would we be surviving? Even if we found an uninhabited place we could live, we couldn't guarantee an alien ship wouldn't visit the system and find us the day after we arrived. That was too much of a risk exposing our secret. I could not see the Merry Band of Pirates setting up an isolated colony to live there forever. No, the whole point of stretching out how long we could survive would be to give Skippy time to come back to us. Maybe that was simply wishful thinking by me; there was no sign Skippy was ever coming back. After being warmer than usual for a couple days, his beer can canister had gone cold, as cold as that dead AI we found on Newark. As far as I knew, Skippy was well and truly dead, and there was nothing I could do about it. "How long do you think before we can jump out of here?"

"Ten days?" Friedlander held up his hands. "We want to do as much testing as we can before attempting a jump. We can only perform limited tests without alerting every Kristang in this system to our presence. Colonel, if we try a jump and it fails, we will have a dozen angry Kristang ships on top of us before my team could replace the coil package for another attempt. It has to work the very first time."

CHAPTER THIRTY ONE

Eight days went by, with Friedlander growing mildly more confident about the potential of his homemade jump drive, and we still had no idea what our destination should be. What our destination *could* be. For the first jump, I didn't much care which direction we went, as long as we jumped a good long way from the Kobamik system. Long enough that we would have plenty of time to remove the burned-out jump drive coils and replace them. That operation required people in Kristang suits physically yanking out connections and disconnecting coils, so I wanted to plan on a full day between jumps. Friedlander warned me a long jump posed a risk of us emerging far off target, and I told him he was missing the point. The only target was to be far away, it didn't much matter what point in deep interstellar space we arrived at.

After eight days, we had not found a place to jump to. Part of the problem was the whole crew was probably mildly depressed; I know I sure was. What was the point of jumping anywhere if all we could do was slowly wait for the *Dutchman*'s reactors to shut down, the power to run down, our food supply to dwindle and for us to eventually die either from freezing to death or oxygen starvation?

Hans Chotek gave me a pep talk. As a pep talk, it totally sucked, although his attitude did surprise me. "Colonel Bishop," he said while staring fondly at a photo of the Austrian Alps on his desktop. "We accomplished our mission. We *more* than accomplished our mission out here. We fulfilled UNEF Command's original requirement, of determining whether the Thuranin were sending another surveyor ship to Earth. Beyond that, we secured a future for humans on Paradise, and prevented the Ruhar, of all things," he looked up at me, shook his head and smiled, "from sending a ship to Earth. It would be best if Earth knew there were no ships coming in their direction, but at this point, we are expendable." He probably thought that he, being a civilian, should not need to explain that to me.

"It still sucks, Sir." I winced as I said it.

But Chotek smiled. "What is the saying in your military? 'Embrace the suck'?"

"That saying is about things you have to get through, in order to accomplish the job. Out here, now, there is no job. There is supposed to be an end to the suck, but we have no mission."

"Survival is our mission now. We survive, and wait for Skippy to revive. Survive, without risk of exposing our presence out here. Have you selected a destination for us?"

"No, not yet," I said truthfully. The full truth was, I still had no idea where we could go to both survive and to hide. "I'll check with the science team again, see if they have a better idea." So far, the best idea from Friedlander's team was to put the ship into orbit around an anonymous red dwarf star, and rig up solar panels to power the life support systems after the reactors failed. That idea had the advantage that it didn't require us to locate and get to a habitable but uninhabited planet. All we needed was to get the ship into orbit around a boring red dwarf star, in a star system where no species had even a single facility. The problem with that idea was, we only had enough solar panels to power a couple of inflatable shelters, and we had no way to manufacture more solar panels. Friedlander had his team working on that problem, I wasn't hopeful about it. The life support system of a Thuranin ship was energy intensive, basically they cracked breathable oxygen out poisonous carbon dioxide using some high-tech device that drew a lot of power. The backup oxygen system was only designed to work for a few weeks.

We didn't have any good options.

The first jump was successful, according to our very low standards. The ship did not explode, we did actually jump, and we emerged only nine point two million miles off target. It took Friedlander's team forty five hours, nearly four days, before we could jump again. Friedlander looked completely exhausted when I talked to him, shortly after he declared the system was physically ready for another jump. "We're ready?" I asked. "You're confident about it?"

"I am confident the drive will not explode," he said while stifling a yawn. "We did discover a potentially serious problem." I set a fresh cup of coffee on the table in front of him, he shook his head and nodded toward a pile of dirty coffee cups. "Remember I told you that jumping has quantum effects even on inactive coils? They degrade whether we use them or not?"

"Yeah. You said that is why we can't travel all the way back to Earth." Since he wasn't going to drink the coffee, I regretted giving it to him, and wondered if it would be Ok for me to take it back. The past couple days, I hadn't slept much either.

"We came through that first jump nine million miles off target, not because we programmed the jump incorrectly, but because the active coil package partly failed in mid-jump."

"What? The coils burned out?" That surprised me. The reason it took so long to replace the coil package is that the coils we had used for the jump still retained a lot of energy, and it was dangerous to handle them.

"No, they didn't burn out. They failed to work together properly, so some of the coils shut down partway through the jump sequence; that's why they had so much stored power after the jump," Friedlander rubbed his tired eyes. "We got over the issue of swapping out coil packages, that's not the problem now. The problem is that because the coils weren't working together properly, the jump generated a more powerful quantum resonance that normal. That affected all our jump coils, even the ones we weren't using."

"Oh, crap."

"You see the problem."

"I think so. Each jump is going to shorten the life of every coil on the ship?"

"Even faster than we expected, yes."

"How bad is it?" I was glad I had not drunk that coffee, my stomach was already churning with acid.

"I don't know. *We* don't know. Not yet. We don't have enough data. After the next jump, we'll have a better idea how bad the damage is."

"Bottom line, Doctor. What's the worst case?"

"The worst case? If future jumps are as bad as our first, we will lose jump capability before we reach our destination." He meant the red dwarf star we had picked almost at random. He picked up the coffee cup, swirled it around, took a sip and set it down. "Do we have an alternate destination?"

"No. No, we don't. Doctor, we can jump now?"

"As soon as we validate the calculations, yes. A few hours."

"That's good enough. I want a twenty four hour stand down for your entire team, once those calculations are complete. That means you sleep, relax, eat, use the gym, do anything other than work or thinking about work. If we have to, we can jump immediately. After a full day, when you are rested and have fresh minds, you need to take another look at the jump drive. See if you can get us to jump with less of a resonance, or whatever it is."

Friedlander and his team mostly took a day off; I ordered the door to the science lab locked and they took the hint. After a day off, they approached the problem with a fresh set of eyes and after two days, thought they had a solution.

They didn't. Our second jump was not as bad as the first, it still wasn't good. The third jump *was* worse than the first, and our science team didn't know why. Instead of immediately working to swap the expended coil package for a new one, Friedlander had to sort through packages to find one that wasn't already so screwed up to be unusable. Alarmingly, there were only three sets of coils still functional. When he finished supervising the installation of the new coils, I met him at the airlock and helped him out of the bulky suit.

"Doctor, can we make it to this red dwarf system?"

"Maybe. Possibly. Colonel, I do not know. We are playing with technology we don't fully understand. Barely understand. Please don't ask me to project odds of us holding the jump drive together long enough to get to our destination, we simply don't have the math. We need two more jumps, at least." His eyes were bloodshot and there were dark circles under his eyes. Coffee could not cure what ailed him, neither could sleep. He wouldn't be able to sleep well until we reached our destination and had the solar panels rigged up successfully. "I am not confident about the next jump," he told me softly. "We don't know what is wrong, so we can't fix it. To an engineer, the situation is very frustrating."

"We've jumped three times, and there is no sign of anyone following us. Take your time with the calculations."

"Calculations are not the problem. With the state of the jump drive, we could input random numbers into the navigation system, and get about the same result," he said with a weary smile.

"Doctor, you are working with an alien technology, and making the ship jump faster than light. What your team has accomplished already is remarkable."

"It's not enough. Colonel, if the next jump isn't any more successful-"

"I know."

Seeing Friedlander's despair pushed me to make a decision. I went back to my office, where Skippy was secured in a box on my desk. Out of habit, I touched him, he was still cold. I called Nagatha.

"Good morning, Joe Bishop." Her voice lacked a bit of her usual cheeriness. Without Skippy to provide memory and processing power, she had been progressively shutting down parts of herself; her consciousness was too expansive to fit within the *Dutchman*'s computers.

"Nagatha, I need to ask a favor of you. We have to do something; the jump drive might not hold together long enough for us to get to any place useful."

"I have been monitoring the situation. Colonel, I have also been listening to communications within the science team. Dr. Friedlander did not tell you that his team recommends against attempting another jump, until they understand the source of the problem. Dr. Friedlander agrees the problem is very serious, he wishes another jump to obtain more data. He also fears that no amount of time will allow his team to understand the drive system. Again, I am sorry that I can't help with the jump calculations, or with analyzing the drive coils."

"Nagatha, you have been doing everything you can. Now I need you to do something that could be dangerous to you."

"Colonel, I am happy to help any way I can; I know our situation is perilous. If the ship becomes stranded in interstellar space, I will eventually deactivate when the ship runs out of power. What do you need me to do?"

"Well," I wanted her to fully appreciate the danger. "You are not going to like it."

THE END

The Expeditionary Force series
Book 1: Columbus Day
Book 2: SpecOps
Book 3: Paradise
Book '3.5': Trouble on Paradise novella
Book 4: Black Ops
Book 5: Zero Hour

Contact the author at craigalanson@gmail.com

https://www.facebook.com/Craig.Alanson.Author/

Made in United States
Cleveland, OH
08 December 2024

11530035R00162